GOD
&
HARVEY GROSBECK

Books by Gilbert Millstein

THE LATE HARVEY GROSBECK

NEW YORK: TRUE NORTH

NEW YORK *(text)*

SHORT STORIES, SHORT PLAYS
AND SONGS BY NOËL COWARD *(editor)*

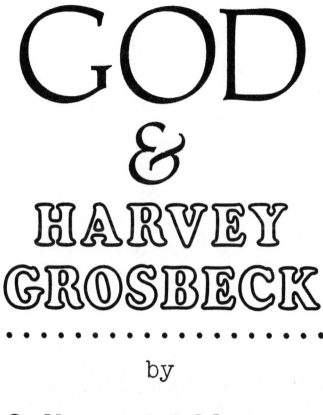

GOD

&

HARVEY GROSBECK

by

Gilbert Millstein

DOUBLEDAY & COMPANY, INC.

GARDEN CITY, NEW YORK

1983

Library of Congress Cataloging in Publication Data

Millstein, Gilbert.
God and Harvey Grosbeck.

I. Title.
PS3563.I4237G6   1983   813'.54

Library of Congress Catalog Card Number 82-46015
ISBN: 0-385-12450-3

Designed by Judith Neuman

For my wife, Barbara

GOD
&
HARVEY
GROSBECK

1
· · · · · · · · · ·

Every three weeks, Grosbeck went to his doctor, less the vale-
tudinarian than an English tripper on a low-fare excursion to the
Delphic Oracle: sweating; half determined to sneer, half to believe;
adding up the expense in his head (the brain so many bits of torn
paper with figures on them that didn't add up); looking intently in
the waiting room at a huge nineteenth-century German lithograph.
This took up most of one wall and it showed half a dozen doctors in
top hats and butcher aprons standing over operating tables, laughing
and pulling green and purple intestines out of bodies, the subjects'
mouths open and screaming in pain (the color was quite good; it en-
hanced the awful tableau) silencing the polite little signs elsewhere
in the waiting room which begged people not to smoke. (THANK
YOU.) But, Jesus Christ, wouldn't you know the Germans would
think up something like that. I tell you, to this day, you can't tell
what the sons of bitches think is funny, the dirty, suety bastards.
Mmmm. And, oh yes, he waited for the Delphic Oracle to disgorge
a portent. For Grosbeck, the three or four other people in the waiting
room looked like nothing so much as the sticklike figures in paintings
done by an artist he knew: they were quiet and mysterious and did
not exist in the space they took up and when Dr. Salomon came out
of his office in his white coat he seemed to scatter them as he crooked
a finger at Grosbeck to come in, come in. They seemed to have been
there forever. There before Grosbeck came, they would be there
when he left. Like the people on the subway during rush hours, they
were not genuine passengers; they had been hired to fill up all the
seats and to exacerbate.

Now, Dr. Salomon was funny. What else could a Swiss be who
had fought in the French Resistance and then got his medical degree
and then drove sports cars in European races and had not done very
well because he was absentminded and skeptical? If he knew how he

had happened to end up in a ground-floor office on lower Fifth Avenue, treating elderly refugees (to say nothing of calling Paris three times a week to tell his brother-in-law what pills to get for his sister who was a neurasthenic in her old age; he was a firm believer in placebos), he did not say. He was a year older than Grosbeck and had wonderful pouches under his eyes and a mouth he kept pursed in the manner of a champagne salesman slanging a chorus girl. He had eyes which said, You are a liar and a thief, but I *will* myself to have a soft spot in my heart for you, even though I Left My Heart in Avignon. He once said casually to Grosbeck (while poking at his patient's prostate) that he drove sports cars with those eyes and that he used them in the maquis, together with a machine pistol and a long knife. He said. Grosbeck found it all so romantic. Dr. Salomon had a way of talking about these things as though he had read them in a book in a foreign language and could not quite translate. He kept a distance from his patients, all the while embracing them, soothing them, adjuring them to be well and not to bother him with silly complaints.

He called Grosbeck "professor," and inquired of him what he had done today to change the world now that he was an editorial writer uptown for the most powerful newspaper in the world. He also called Grosbeck "*mein kind*" or "*mon petit*" or "my boy." His voice was plangent but not so clangorous as that of a cantor on the High Holy Days. His accent in all languages (including Italian) was execrable. Dr. Salomon did not neglect, ever, to ask Grosbeck whether he, Salomon, should go on living. Grosbeck invariably answered, in the spirit of this mummery, this mugience, that Dr. Salomon had missed the point, the point being, would Grosbeck go on living? Dr. Oracle of Delphi said he would, that he had the physique of a weight-lifter. Was he not now carrying the weight of the world on his shoulders? The two of them behaved like low comedians of another day, and Salomon was Grosbeck's cure. He would listen to Grosbeck's chest and back and seem to be eavesdropping. He would draw blood and send it to some dishonest laboratory to measure a phenomenon called "prothrombin time." Grosbeck hadn't the remotest idea what that was but it seemed to satisfy Dr. Salomon. As he drew the blood into a vial and withdrew the needle, Dr. Salomon always got a drop or two on Grosbeck's pants. Well, not always, but often enough to make Grosbeck suffer. "Ah," he would say, "you are bleeding to death, aren't you? I always was clumsy with sharp things." He would grin a little, dab at Grosbeck's stringy arm with a piece of cotton, wet another and permit Grosbeck to rub the blood off his pants, put up the vial of blood in a rack, and tell his patient to go with the God of his persuasion. "I dislike knives," he might confess. (What about in the maquis? Did he put away the knife and use only the machine pistol?)

Grosbeck, blood drawn, his narrow chest and back having said Fine, Fine, for Dr. Salomon, would put his shirt, tie, and jacket back on and ask permission to piss on the way out. Dr. Salomon would say, "Save me some. The woman before you couldn't sissy today. I will see you in another three weeks and in another and in another . . . You will outlive everybody. I will write you up in a paper." Grosbeck would leave the office and neither snow nor rain nor heat nor whatever stayed him from going to the street telephone at the corner to ring up his wife. (Dr. Salomon kept a lock on his telephone, but Grosbeck understood that.) He behaved like a buffoon with his wife, too. "He says I lost weight," he might say. "He says I've got another three weeks, he doesn't want me to miss a visit." Attached to the telephone, he would wag his behind jocosely. "Sure, I lost weight; the checkbook is one check lighter. Kidding aside, should I come home? How about it? I don't have to go to work right away. The world will little note nor long remember . . . but you will and I will . . . and, hell, we'll have breakfast after and *then* I will tell the world what it should know about the World Bank. I can't bring you a flower, it's too early, nothing's open. Yes? No? No. I thought not. How come? What do you mean, none of my business? The very mole on your right cheek is my business . . . every fold in the belly. There's a girl jogging . . . with a dog on a leash . . . Jesus, what an attractive dog . . . Oh, I forgot . . . seminar . . . What goddamned seminar? Sure, you told me, you also told me to be sure to call the minute I left him. All right. All *right*. That girl just went around the corner. Later. I adore you, too . . ." Grosbeck hung up and hailed a cab, high as a kite.

It had been much different some years before. Life had had the effrontery to humiliate Harvey Grosbeck by giving him a heart attack in full view of all the people he worked with on The Newspaper. He had just finished reading two pieces of copy, being then merely an editor, not a thunderer, a maker of opinion. One of them read, "The nation's death toll neared the grim predictions of safety experts as the homeward crunch began in the final day of the long Memorial holiday weekend. Freeway-laced California led the carnage with thirty-seven fatalities, followed by twenty-eight in Indiana. New York was a distant third." And the other read, "There are sharks in the waters that the President's defense bill must navigate between now and final passage. One shark is" Senator someone-or-other. "Another shark is Election Day. Another shark is the filibuster." What did it all mean? He fed the homeward crunch and the grim safety experts to the sharks, thought of the carnage on freeway-laced California, and became ill. It was probably no more than coincidence. He had not fallen, clunk, on the floor, carrying typewriter and copy with him. Nothing that vulgar. Instead, he had felt the banal pain in his left arm and across his pigeon breast, going down to about w-e-e-e-ll, the top of the pot belly, and, of course it had interrupted the jeremiad he was delivering, ad libitum, to some unfortunate reporter with a law degree and a hangover and a fleck of egg salad on his mustache and a terrible longing to prove the outlandish notion that any collection of words he caused to march gravely down the page could tell anyone anything.

There had been an ebb, that fine afternoon, in the unending flow of significance into the City Room of The Newspaper and the reporter had been in full flight talking to Grosbeck, picking his nose in excitement and pulling chunks of badly digested information and philosophies (read in the summaries and extracts from the works of thinkers who had spent a lifetime arriving at the wrong conclusion) out of his addled head. The reporter was saying to Grosbeck, "Harvey, I won't go so far as to say I've got life taped . . ." (Ugh) ". . . but, here's what I think now. I've given it a lot of thought, too. You can't not after you've seen what I have in the past few years." Seen? What in God's name, you callow idiot, can you have seen? Have you seen the waters of Manahatta give up the dead in warm weather? Hudson River and 125th Street, white male; East River and Dover Street, white male; Harlem River and 151st Street, black male; East River and 108th Street, black male; Fulton Street and East River, black male; Hudson River and 100th Street, black male; Hudson River and 55th Street, white female; Fulton Street and East River, unknown. Have you seen the cops poke these packages of margarine with a boat hook and try to pull them in, so that suddenly there is a snout, a hole, where the belly button was and the dead whale spouts gray filth for a few seconds and the ruined flesh tears away as the thing is brought in over the side bound for the icebox, the medical school, Potter's Field? Grosbeck's appetite for Lake District-Balkan melancholy, for the dismembered poor, the forgotten, the distraught, the gangster with the head torn away who had been dumped or had jumped from the splintered wooden dock down the slimy spiles into the dirty drink was boundless. In theory. He had, in truth, never been a police reporter.

But, the reporter was saying, "I've come to the conclusion there is no such thing as black and white, only gray areas. No such thing as just good and evil, no such thing as just two sides to everything. It took me law school and five years of reporting to come to it. Really, Harve, what there is is simply complicated concatenations of motive." The reporter warmed to his warmed-over plagiarisms.

Grosbeck held up a monitory hand. He had alternately bored and terrified other people who talked like that. "What I think you're trying to tell me, Maitland," he said, "is that there is a soothing and charitable explanation for everything. That there are exceptions to every rule, that there are always 'extenuating circumstances,' 'saving graces,' 'understandable lapses,' 'permissible strayings' from the straight and no, no narrow at all; an alluring climate of 'ifs,' 'buts,' 'perhapses,' 'on the other handses,' 'it remains to be seens,' 'only time will tells,' 'endless possibilities,' 'alternatives' (you understand, I hope, that anything can have only one alternative?), or, sometimes, 'viable alternatives.' 'Viable,' right, Maitland?" When he repeated— not used, but repeated—words like that, Grosbeck spluttered. For Grosbeck, the English language had ended on Pearl Harbor Day. He thought of himself as the road-company Académie Française, or Murray and the Oxford English Dictionary, and he pictured himself as a body of very old men sitting around in a small room near to buried in books, papers, and dust, guarding the language with a dirk held in trembling fingers. When the usage of a word changed—and these days it did so with great speed—Grosbeck was driven to the point of moral despair and physical illness. Change entered the musty room with a new locution, snatched away his rubber dagger, and gaily ripped up the language of Anthony Trollope.

"You are saying to me, Maitland," Grosbeck went on, rocking

slightly in his swivel chair, "that sinister and dexter stray hand in
hand, in love, indistinguishable one from the other, bathed in 'compassion' and invigorated by 'insights.'" Grosbeck now found it
difficult to construct a sentence in the company of people who ad-
hered to this mushy kind of jiggery-pokery. Murder and buggery and
destruction had become "aberrations," "tangential" to something or
other, "ancillary," or "corollary," or "subsumed under." People got
"grants" or "funding" to make "feasibility studies" and then, after
"consulting," "coordinating," "communicating" and "getting back
to," held important "conferences," "round tables" and "seminars" in
Bangkok at the Hilton on "per diems" and produced "position
papers" which were burned ritually in Washington. It was a living.
Rotted leavings, all of it. Dirty little cheeseparings of thought. Filth
from under the nails and between the toes of thinkers long dead
and light years away. Deceptions and obfuscations. And all, all
stirred complacently into a horrifying *olla podrida* (there were some
aspects of Italian cooking that were not good for Grosbeck's stomach) and spooned up daily by barbered apes interrupting their infernal chattering and buzzing only long enough to sniff at one another's
behinds and to applaud the smell. Such hatred. Such hatred. And for
what? As well ask the ancient moon, as well ask Cagliostro.

No matter. "Black and white," Grosbeck was saying, "everything
is black and white and why don't we say so? Only two ways about it,
about everything. I'm fed up with the judicious weighing of this or
that or the other thing. Give me . . . I insist . . . give me what I
know to be there . . . two things . . . black and white . . . black and
white . . ." It was after the third "black and white" that Grosbeck
sank decorously, fully conscious, and, for once, quiet; sank and lay on
the floor, dizzy and breathing hard. As he lay there, he thought, I
need a shine and the suit could stand a pressing.

What could be seen there on the floor was a puddle of a man who
had fought the onset of the years with his mouth to the disadvantage
of the rest of the body. The mouth was all muscle, the rest (he
firmly believed) shrunken beneath an enormous head and spiky
white hair, spindly legs and venous hands which pawed in rage at everything and brought down disaster on the hydrocephalic head.
When the mood was upon him, he called himself Quasimodo or the
World's Largest Midget. What else was to be expected of someone,

a Jew, brought up in an Irish neighborhood and reared on the drawings of such idealists as Eakins.

Unexceptionable was, in fact, the word for his looks, and there were both men and women who thought him reasonably good-looking, men and women both who lusted after the body, if not the soul, of this homunculus. (Despite the change in fashion over the years, he had stuck stubbornly to women, denying men their way with polite regret.) Most of the time, Grosbeck disliked himself with an intensity he reserved for the bitterest of enemies and he was so constituted as to regard the merest acquaintance as an enemy. Grosbeck knew as much about himself as he did about everyone else, which was next to nothing.

For the moment, there on the floor, the mouth was open, but saying nothing. Rather, a wheeze came out of it, brought up from somewhere in his innards, and it sounded like a sour bugle and brought people running from everywhere else in the City Room. Grosbeck's picture of what his insides might look like was unscientific in the extreme. If he thought about them at all, he thought about one of those old-time hanging medical charts, printed on oilcloth, with cardboard attachments, which could be folded back to show what was underneath: heart, lungs, spleen, kidneys, sphincters, veins, arteries, capillaries; miles of intestines in red, green, blue, black; yards of knobby bone and skeleton fingers spread wide; the face in ghastly profile, showing an ignoble nose and one fish eye. As to the head. He got that off the phrenologist's chart: the Mountains of Liederkranz, the Valleys of Domrémy, the Quadrant of Passion, the Slice of Contempt, the Dot of Kindness, Amativeness, Philoprogenitiveness, Combativeness, Destructiveness, Alimentiveness, Time, Tune, Comparison, Causality. Thirty-five in all; some gave it as forty-three. Grosbeck was wont to say that he had a hell of a lot of F. J. Gall, and, invariably, nobody knew what he was talking about except some nut here and there who also read palms.

Soon, Grosbeck was surrounded by people, Maitland shouting, "Get the doctor, get the doctor!" (The Newspaper had a model industrial medical department and was equipped to perform such minor operations as the excision of independent thought, but not appendectomies.)

"Get an ambulance, get an ambulance!" a woman shouted. She had a voice deeper than that of Maitland and wrote indignant articles on feminist topics. She dressed like the hostess at an Alice Foote MacDougall tearoom of the twenties, all beads and batik, and she was taken seriously. She was a secret horseplayer, a fine wife and mother, and believed in herself. Dozens of reporters, rewrite men, editors, secretaries, copyboys, mechanics, and other spear carriers just passing through stood over Grosbeck, buzzing and buzzing, looking at one another and wringing their hands. Nobody touched him, since most had read only the outdated Red Cross manual, which counseled leaving the victim alone until the doctor got there. One man, who had read a later set of instructions, moved as though to punch Grosbeck in the chest and breathe into his mouth, but then drew back, since the last time he had attempted that the beneficiary of his ministrations had died there and then. Besides, Grosbeck was still conscious and blinking.

Thought came to him in his pain and dizziness and nausea like a mirrored diploid revolving in a ballroom. He remembered how, some years before, he had watched an epileptic copyreader, who, having registered some kind of objection to the facts of a story, had suddenly rolled up his eyes until only the whites showed and had then fallen on his back, kicking the floor furiously with the backs of his feet while his tongue pushed itself six inches out of his head (it was gray) and he made the noises of the spheres at the top of his lungs. At one point, the copyreader had kicked off his shoes and his pants had crept up his shins and Grosbeck had noticed that he was wearing socks with elastic tops. Grosbeck would never have worn anything like that, even though he was finding it more and more difficult to get what he wanted. Grosbeck followed the dictates of his father (how easy to praise or blame one's forebears for everything) who was among the last of *his* generation to give up the detachable collar and who had worn socks with garters to hold them up. So, of course, had Grosbeck. All his life, it seemed, even as an infant at his mother's breast. Getting them these days was an adventure for Grosbeck and he went about it resolutely, a hunter in an untracked jungle.

One day, after having tried half a dozen stores in which the salesmen either looked at him curiously or turned away with a shake of the head and a smile to wait on other customers, he had gone into a Fifth Avenue department store just across the street from St. Patrick's Cathedral, figuring that the nearer to church he was, the closer to God. He had reconnoitered the aisles. He was keyed up but cool.

Grosbeck gave the perfumes, the jewelry, the scarves, pantyhose, face creams and other greases, gloves, and leather desk pads a wide berth. Off in the distance, he could see, through the rising vapors, the elevators, the doors of which never opened, but he knew he would not need them in any case. Before their doors, he saw a herd of mostly female elephants—a chancy, dangerous lot—waiting and swaying on their big, red-painted feet (strange how they all wore high-heeled shoes), trumpeting indignantly at one another and swinging their trunks in irritation. Every so often, a small male, chewing on a bundle of straw, would detach himself nervously from the herd, swallow, and then, trunk down, trot quickly across the store to a side-street entrance and disappear into one of the cross-town runs. Grosbeck's nose was legend among hunters and it was not long before he smelled, upwind, the scent of the men's furnishings counter, a tiny outpost in this women's place.

Seconds later, he was standing, legs spread wide, before an aristo-cratic, beautiful old woman with white hair, pince-nez glasses on a black-grosgrain ribbon, and a print dress, clearly marking her the Goddess of Men's Furnishings. Perhaps, he thought . . . Well, why not. In for a penny, in for a pound. At last, at last. . . . If not here, then where?

"Pardon me," he said.

"May I help you?" she asked with a ravishing smile and just the glint of gold in the space between incisors and canines. She put a hand up to her hair and patted it, the eternal coquette for all of her goddessness. (She had, as befitted her station, eschewed the bouffant and kept her white hair clipped relatively short. She looked, this deity, like a founder of the Girl Guides, now retired, and living in genteel poverty on a hundred-acre estate in Greenwich, Connecticut. Grosbeck had once actually been in Greenwich, having overcome an understandable reluctance to leave his *queréncia*, New York City.)

"Why, yes," said the White Hunter. "I would like . . ." He hesi-tated.

"Yes?" she urged him.

"Do you have, by any chance, men's socks?" Best approach this thing tangentially.

"Of course," she said, her hand (one of half a dozen) sweeping gracefully above the glass display cases. Grosbeck was almost persuaded that he had reached Angkor Wat.

"What I'm looking for," he said, "is, I guess, not all that common these days."

"Try us, sir," she responded.

"All right, then," Grosbeck said, throwing back his shoulders and drawing himself up to his full height, which was in the neighborhood of five feet six inches, give or take an inch or so lost in the passage of the years. Damn all.

"What I'm looking for is men's socks." Then, it all came out in a rush. "I'm looking for them in black or navy blue, long-stemmed Egyptian cotton lisle, made in England, ribbed, and guaranteed not to stay up by themselves. And the garters to hold them up."

A sense of loss pervaded him for an instant. He said, almost stammering, "I realize you don't see much of that anymore . . . I have extremely tender calves," he said. "They're out to pasture now," he continued, "but if you could see them you'd understand."

The goddess tittered and the splendid jewelry on her limbs jingled and jangled. "Oh, sir," she said, entering fully into the spirit of the thing, "don't you ever hesitate for a minute to show me. We see all kinds of things here." The tone was one of teasing noblesse oblige, the accent Larchmont Lockjaw, not exactly what Grosbeck had expected to encounter in goddesses. He was somewhat taken aback, but pressed on. He flushed darkly and took his courage in both hands, or, rather his left pants leg. He raised it just enough to show the top of the sock he was wearing and the garter just below the knee. The leg was hairy, but, God be thanked, there were no varicose veins yet.

There was a hole at the back of the sock and the elastic of the garters was so badly stretched that it was almost useless now. But Grosbeck, a desperate man, would stop at nothing. He had thrown his last counters on the green baize. Devil take it, there was nothing more to lose. The goddess leaned over the display case and regarded Grosbeck, one leg in the air. With some difficulty. Coolly, she looked at the leg and then stepped back. Grosbeck put the leg down. He felt the advent of rebuff. But, no. "Certainly, sir," she said. Her voice was like the belling of the gray cathedral across the street on Easter Sunday. Drops of moisture broke out on Grosbeck's furrowed

brow and on his upper lip and he pulled out a handkerchief and patted himself dry.

"We do, indeed, carry socks of that description," she said. "My,
yes. And the garters. One-inch-wide elastic for those apt to chafe
behind the knees; an inch and a half for those who feel the need of
substantial support. *And,* one clasp or two." She stopped, the certainty radiating outward from her, a kind of self-possession which,
Grosbeck realized, must come from years of riding to hounds.

"We have always carried socks and garters of that kind." She
paused. "We always will." Another pause, this one nigh infini-
tesimal. "For gentlemen like you."

"Thank you," Grosbeck said. His voice cracked with strain and relief. He swallowed. "I'd like eighteen pairs, half black, half navy
blue, and three pairs of the inch-and-a-half garters. I don't chafe."
The transaction was almost completed, the rest mere detail: the
cashbook with eight duplicates, the taking of socks and garters—
precious beyond compare—from dusty boxes hidden under the
counter, the examination of paper labels and exclamations of
"That's *it*"; the wrapping in tissue paper and interment in boxes; the
solemn handing over to Grosbeck; the extraction of cash from Grosbeck's right pants pocket. (He had stopped carrying a wallet ever
since hanging his coat up in the office one day and finding his wallet
gone an hour later. He had never used credit cards. He believed
them to be the Antichrist.) There was the slightest touching of fingers as the exchange of money and merchandise was made, the
faintest of smiles from the goddess, a murmured *vale:* "Don't forget
your receipt, sir." There was an irrepressible look of triumph in Grosbeck's eyes. He gave her the tiniest of formal bows from the waist,
the sketchy outlines of a salute.

Ah, but all that was so far in the distant past. Grosbeck had not
had time to wear out even one pair of the garters or to grow a hole in
any of the socks when he had his heart attack. More, he had not yet
torn the last of the identifying labels off the remaining half dozen
pairs when something, someone had pinched his coronary artery
vengefully and given him what the doctors call an "infarction." Infarction. To Grosbeck, the word connoted breaking wind, and, *garçon
méchant* that he was, it meant that people with heart disease were
flatulent, walked slowly (with a cane?) and lived in constant fear of
farting themselves dead. Infarction is for the *goyim,* Grosbeck

believed, having read that the head of the Heart Institute in some sun-dappled (as it was described) resort city in Florida, a respected and beloved, etc., etc., etc.; a superb tennis player and golfer (for his age, which was in the middle fifties), had dropped dead while jogging to the country club. Such a surge of joy as Grosbeck had felt, to think of that deeply tanned *schlemiel* in his tailored running suit, pedometer in one hand, stop watch in the other, Havana cigars in his locker, staggering, falling and dying without a word (for a change) in the clubhouse driveway. Jews get heart attacks.

There would be no more exhortations from *him* to buy Israel bonds; no more deep plunges in the pool, at the end of which the white teeth came to the surface, followed seconds later by the grinning face, the black hair with its sexy streaks of gray, the washboard-muscled middle and the golden swimming trunks no bigger than a burlesque *shiksa*'s rhinestone-studded G-string. Good husband and father, from stuffed derma thou came; to stuffed derma thou shalt return. No more in the halls of Hadassah (the blinding sun and the dying, clacking, dusty palms outside) shalt thou hymn the praises of Zion from a safe distance of six thousand miles. No more shalt thou, businessman pillar of the community, build inferior, ugly houses with foundations that sink in sand and walls that crack at a raised voice and patios made of crappy imitations of Spanish tile. No more shalt thou bribe the county board of assessors. No more shalt thou *kvell* over thy brassy wife and assy daughters (while getting an expensive taste of something else on the side). You, and they, covered yourselves over every day for the sun with potions and lotions that made your greedy faces look like old briefcases made of the finest leather. (Do not omit the genuwine brass fittings.) Nevermore, jogger and raiser of money for hearts, Jews and other causes, not so much ecumenical (although you didn't neglect to pick up a few bucks for the *goyim*) as profitable, involving as the causes did a number of naturally swarthy New York Italians with no visible means of support and the ability to speak volumes while saying very little. Mamzarim and Mafiosi, to come right out with it.

It was not strange that such lucubrations should have occupied Grosbeck's mind during those minutes he lay on the floor. Have not the learned ones told us all about that? How a man's life unreels before him like one of those murky art films, the discussions about which take longer than it did to make the picture? M. Auteur with a

blooming hole in the heart. That is what the victim does—lucubrates
—until the doctor comes, or the police, or what Grosbeck named
"the parafakes," ignorant attendants with vapid, well-meaning
smiles and clumsy hands, speaking some kind of pidgin and having a
very sketchy idea of what they were about.

A short time before the company doctor arrived, Grosbeck had got
to thinking that, on balance, he had been better off the time he was
attacked by two men on Mulberry Street during the San Gennaro
festival. He had lost teeth and some ribs had been cracked, but, at
least, he had gone unconscious right away. (The thugs were thorough, meticulous workmen, those two, and Grosbeck had believed,
ever since, that he had been set upon because he had made indiscreet
observations about an important drug peddler who lived in his apartment building and who had decided that he should be punished
lightly. On Mulberry Street, he had not been witness to all the tedious minutiae involved in getting a body to a hospital with the
breath still going.)

The Newspaper doctor showed up late, of course. There was a
reason, as there always is. The company doctor was a good-looking
man with a good-looking wife. The good-looking wife had failed to
return home several nights in recent weeks, and, just now, although
Grosbeck could not know it, she had telephoned the doctor in the
tower office he occupied at The Newspaper. The doctor's wife had
telephoned to say she wouldn't be home. No, not just that night.
Any night. No, not ever. Did he remember that rather attractive,
dark-haired girl they had met at the Monet opening? He did, didn't
he? Well, they'd met for tea, quite by accident, in one of the department stores. Didn't the doctor know the stores had restaurants in
which one could get a light bite while shopping? No drinks. No, no
drinks. But, later, they'd found a bar on First Avenue in the Fifties
and had had margaritas. And frozen daiquiris. Strawberry. Yes, strawberry. Too many, in fact, and too expensive. I know, I know, you
shouldn't mix things like that and that's how it began . . . She'd
barely had enough left for cab fare. Or *not* enough. So . . . well, anyway, the girl had suggested they both drop over to her apartment.
She does some sort of consulting work. Don't ask me! How should I
know exactly what. It *looked* important. Charts and graphs all over
the place. Quite nice furniture, too. She has good taste. What? Japanese prints (Hiroshige, she told me) and some porcelain and a lot of

little things. No, she didn't have a strobe-light system, she's not that kind. Well, one thing led to another . . . How many bromides does she know, Dr. Parmenter wondered, ticking them off, and why hadn't he kept a list of them so that he would be ready for this, just as he was for his patients at The Newspaper?

Who needs to be married to a persistent bore? *I* do, Dr. Parmenter said to himself, grief washing over him without warning. She . . . oh, is there really any necessity to go into detail? But, Ned, I'm not coming back. It's simple, really, it is. Remember, we don't have any children, for one thing, and there isn't a lot I want, so don't get scared. I don't place as high a value on material things as you do, Ned. Where had she got that from? Some combination of women's magazines and Jane Austen? The doctor kept women's magazines in the waiting room of his office at The Newspaper, and he had read several reviews of a biography of Jane Austen, so he knew what she was thinking about. I've got a job lined up. It's not that hard for someone like me to get paid for doing good works in somebody's office. What? Fund-raising. There's plenty of that around, I don't have to tell you. No, I do *not* intend to live with her. I'm not ready for that, yet. Each of us has her own life. I'll find a small place somewhere. All right, I've been looking and I've already put down a deposit on something. All I want is my clothes and the jewelry. Please. Please! There's no need to get clinical. You're not dealing with one of your clinic specimens in front of a group of students. Never. I *said* never! And hung up.

By the time he got to Grosbeck, the doctor believed himself to be as sick as his patient. He had, had he not, just had a wife cut out of him, cut out of him without leaving any visible mark? Some plastic surgeon, that woman. All that had happened to Grosbeck was a heart attack. In the doctor's head, however, he experienced an untoward excitement. The subconscious in his pants told him that, once again, the world might be his oyster. He looked at his nails, nicely rounded and polished, as he made his way through the office crowd to Grosbeck's side. "Can you hear me?" he asked Grosbeck. Is the Pope a Catholic, Grosbeck thought, wincing a little for effect. The doctor's hands moved carefully in his bag, as though he were delivering a baby, and they emerged with a stethoscope and a needle. His hands moved swiftly on Grosbeck, opening buttons, laying the horn of the stethoscope on the chest, inclining backward on his knees to look at the patient, preparing the needle and injecting the sedative. He smiled fatuously at Grosbeck. "We're going to be all right, Mr. Parlatore." Parlatore? He didn't even know Grosbeck's name, although both of them had worked for the paper for a long time.

"We're going to get you to a hospital and into bed. Intensive care. Don't let that alarm you. These days, we put people in intensive care for hangnails. Ha ha. You're covered, of course. The Newspaper takes care of all that. Cradle to grave. Ooops, I beg your pardon. Slipped, didn't we? You won't even have to sign anything. Do you have your card with you?" Grosbeck nodded. "All righty, then, let's be off." He frowned and turned around. "That ambulance here?" Nobody knew. The question was answered for him when three men in short white jackets buttoned to the throat came across the floor like chimpanzees in a vaudeville act. Obviously, they didn't work for The Newspaper since none of the jobs on the paper prescribed costumes of that sort. They were of three different nationalities. None of them really understood any of the others and all three were laden with objects of mercy they may or may not have known how to use. They leaped and turned and went "Hup, hup" and bent down over Grosbeck and bent the stretcher into several different shapes before they got it right.

They got Grosbeck out of there and down the elevator on the stretcher with his tie pulled away, his jacket under his head, his pants open (exposing his striped boxer shorts) and his shoes next to his head. He was grateful that the shoes did not smell. The ambulance ride to the hospital, which lay in the lee of the Brooklyn Bridge, was extraordinary. The streets of New York City do not lend themselves to speed, contrary to the practice of the people who drive on them, because of the holes in the asphalt, which are never repaired, or, if through some slip in the system, they are, are filled with material so insubstantial that a day's traffic is enough to make them deeper than ever. Repairs are made only following marches on City Hall. None of the marchers has ever been known to comment on the graceful classical lines of the building, selfish creatures that they are. The potholes and their conscientious neglect are neither accident nor mistake. They are an integral part of the economic system, which operates both cunningly and with a kind of spectacular stupidity. There has to be an endless supply of holes to be filled so that contractors can be paid too much for more thousands of tons of as-

phalt and so that the dignity of labor will be upheld. How else
would all those deserving city workers be kept at work? What sight is
there more noble than a city worker in his rough clothing, leaning on
a crowbar and scratching, looking blankly off into some undefined
distance, forever out to lunch?

Grosbeck could see nothing of this in his jolting, soiled-white
chamber of an ambulance, nothing save the centerfold of a porno-
graphic magazine which one of the attendants had shoved thoughtfully through a slat in the roof of the infernal machine. Grosbeck
looked at the pictures indifferently. There was barely enough room
in the ambulance for the stretcher. The rest of the space was littered
with efficient-looking equipment. There were, as well, old shoes and
newspapers, tire irons which jangled like the leg shackles on a con-
vict going to the gallows, burned-out automobile batteries, and the
driver's laundry. Grosbeck might as well have been in a trapper's
cabin in the Yukon, a piece of moose waiting to be roasted.

All the way downtown, the driver leaned on the siren, announcing
Armageddon. Nobody paid any attention, Grosbeck knew. The City
had become accustomed to all kinds of sirens—sirens which belched,
blathered, peeped, crowed, sighed like blast furnaces, or went off in
rising and falling intervals, not sure of what warning, what end they
were signaling; as though each siren were being cranked by a
different salesman pushing his own particular brand of hell. The jolting was annoying, but it took Grosbeck's mind out of itself. When it
wrenched his back, the pain in his left arm diminished. When his
leg fell off the stretcher on a left turn and his big toe rammed painfully into the side of the ambulance, the blow reduced his nausea.
The inside of the ambulance was not airtight and filled quickly with
gasoline fumes. The driver bounced up and down in his seat, keeping
the siren going, yelling in triumph and banging the steering wheel
with a fist every time he made traffic bunch up at an intersection as
he went through a red light legally. "One for our side," he said. He
might have been the driver of a fire truck on his way to pick up a six-
pack of beer for the battalion chief.

Don't *think* things like that, Grosbeck; think, you *must* think, of
these humble civil servants going about their duties with the best
will in the world, striving only to do good both for your body and
the body politic. The ambulance in which Grosbeck was transported
belonged to the City of New York. There were two other kinds—

those which belonged to what were called "nonprofit" or "voluntary" hospitals, institutions which routinely turned away patients who, either unconscious or in agony, were in no position to prove that they had ten thousand dollars with them, a fan of credit cards, or enough medical insurance to pay for a new wing of the hospital; and ambulances which belonged to private livery services, services which also provided huge cars to take people to airports, restaurants, and whorehouses, and, following that, to homes in the suburbs.

A lively competition for patients had sprung up between the City and voluntary hospitals for patients, since there was much money to be made, and the drivers and attendants of these had come to be known as "bodysnatchers," after the ghouls who once furnished medical schools with cadavers for dissection and the glorious ends of knowledge. They raced their machines recklessly to the scenes of accident and illness and not infrequently collided within a few feet of a prospect or ran over him. The vehicles, crumpled and smoking, had to be towed away—this meant business for towing companies and jobs for their employees—while someone called a third or fourth ambulance, which frequently arrived not only to succor the original victim, but the broken and bleeding drivers and attendants. Grosbeck had come to think of them as Burke and Hare, the Edinburgh entrepreneurs, who, when cemeteries failed to yield up enough specimens of the right sort for the lecturers, murdered to get fresh meat. Grosbeck remembered the bit of doggerel:

> Up the close and doun' the stair,
> But an' ben wi' Burke & Hare.
> Burke's the butcher, Hare the thief;
> Knox the bully boy that buys the beef.

Loud as the siren was and uncertain the channels to be navigated, neither the driver nor one of the attendants in the back with Grosbeck stopped talking. "Angotti," the driver yelled, turning back to look at this attendant. (No need to look ahead. Who gets in the way of an ambulance?) "Hey, Angotti, the old guy look like he needs oxygen?" The driver was a big, red-haired Irishman with a pimply face.

Angotti was a fallen-away Italian Roman Catholic from Brooklyn, who was working as an ambulance attendant and cabdriver only because he had been caught three times stealing automobiles. His employers had decided he was inept beyond redemption. For the time being, this was a living. Like all southern Italians, he was small and swarthy. Seen one, you've seen 'em all. "How do *I* know?" he yelled up front. He looked down at Grosbeck. "Hey, how's the breathing coming along, Pop?" he asked. He breathed gorgonzola and beer into Grosbeck's face. Grosbeck nodded as vigorously as he could, offered the simulacrum of well-being. He half expected Angotti to push a runcible spoon with a piece of pepperoni on it into his open mouth.

"Says he doesn't need it, Boyle. Says he's having a ball." Grosbeck rolled on another turn. "Listen, you want I should strap him down?"

"No," said the driver. "What if the whole damned stretcher goes over with him? Then, you won't be able to get at the straps. Don't do anything unless he passes out." The second attendant, who sat at Grosbeck's head, was a Paraguayan who spoke no English—a cliché with mahogany Indian features which never moved. He lacked only a rusty black English derby with a parakeet feather in it.

"Boyle," Angotti said, "I don't know about the oxygen. The thing hasn't been working right. You were off the other day when we picked up that unconscious woman. Put the mask over her the right way. The thing even hissed and the tank was full, but she died. D.O.A. They tell me there was *something* wrong. I don't know what. You'd never know, looking at the dial. And I don't know if it's been fixed. Anybody say anything to you?"

"Not word one," Boyle screamed above the siren. "Don't worry. We ain't gonna be too much longer. What I'm worried about is that unloading dock at Emergency. Yesterday, I rolled in with something —male or female, I can't remember—and there was a lousy garbage truck. The guys were out having coffee. Took twenty minutes to get back. The back was open and it smelled . . . *And,* they had the keys with them. Some people . . ."

For a little while, he drove looking straight ahead, concentrating on the siren. Then, he looked back again. "Angotti, how's the hackie business? You getting much? The kind of passengers we get here, there's not much action."

"You kidding," Angotti screamed back. "You didn't read the other night, another guy got shot up like holes in cheese the other night in the Bronx. They ripped the lock box right out of the floor."

He shut up for a minute. He grinned. "Boyle," he said, "Boyle, you know what?" He was close to bashfulness for a second and then decided to speak his mind.

"What, Angotti, you got something . . . ?"

"Well," Angotti said, running a hand through his black hair. "Wait a minute," he said, looking down at Grosbeck. "This guy's trying to say something." Pause. "No, it was nothing." He looked over at the Paraguayan. "Yo, Pancho," he said. No answer. "Yo, you, Speedy Gonzalez, keep an eye on the old man, will you? Don't you know you're my favorite Aztec?" A dignified declination of the derby.

"Boyle," Angotti said, "I got a plan for the funeral of that driver. None of your ordinary junk, see? Now, get this. First off, the funeral is held over in the garage on the West Side. I don't know if we can get away with it, but I think we can. The great thing is it's never been done before and if anything'll bring those television cameras out, this is it. There's a funeral procession to the garage . . . all cabs . . . and not fleet cabs, either . . . just the private-owned ones with the radio. I hate the fucking fleet owners."

"Why's that?" Boyle asked, looking interested, but not at the traffic ahead of him.

"They suck your blood out," Angotti said. "I don't drive for no fleet unless I have to . . . and I don't. I got this friend owns his own cab and I take his night shift. But, listen . . . you listening?"

"There anything else to do?" Boyle asked.

Grosbeck asked himself the same question. He also asked himself when these two boatmen on the Styx would get him to the hospital, any hospital. And would he, in addition to being laid out with a heart attack, be deafened by the siren?

Angotti spun out his dream. "Get this," he said. "We got a class procession first, right? All the cabs in good condition, the brakes work, the springs aren't busted, the ashtrays clean, carpets on the floor, new meters, the windshield wipers work, the fenders aren't bent or the backup lights broke, they all got new tires and they all came out of the car wash and a wax job just for the occasion. All the drivers got new caps, new windbreakers, shoes in one piece, no toothpick in the mouth and they all keep their mouths shut on the way."

"Sure," said Boyle. "Oh, sure. That'll be the day."

"I mean it," Angotti said. "That's the way I see it. Follow me. In the garage, the body is laid out at the repair pit, on the platform, and we put the rack up in the air. Get it? What's the word? A symbol. He's above it all now, this stiff. And, no embalming. Instead, the

Puerto Rican mechanic gives him a lube job and you can hear him cursing San Juan Crista Maria when the gun doesn't go in right or it's overloaded. The grease spurts out all over the guy's face and the mechanic wipes it away with a rag. A *clean* rag and it leaves a nice shine on the stiff's face. The eyes are closed with half-dollar tips out of the changemaker. You know something else, Boyle?"

"What?"

"I got a theory. My theory is if this guy didn't get shot, he would have gone out getting laid in the back of the cab somewhere over near the old asphalt plant on the East River Drive with the meter running all the time. It's only a couple of blocks from a good neighborhood, remember. So, she says to him, 'How's this for the fare?' and he looks at her through the rear-view mirror and the last thing in life he says is, 'You got anything smaller?' and he gets a heart attack that oughta teach him which it does."

"Funneee," Boyle said.

"Anyway," Angotti went on, "we're all around the bier, they lower the rack for the ceremony. They got all the hundreds of broken umbrellas he's picked up in his time, the lefthanded gloves, the empty cigarette packs, scum bags, and pennies and they're piled around the side of the coffin. The coffin's open and in his left hand he's got the whisk broom he used to clean the floor. In the right, there's a new trip sheet. It's got one entry on it. Guess what? 'Heaven,' and a note in the next column, 'Flat Rate.' The Big Garage in the Sky. Maybe we oughta include his thermos with the cold coffee and his lunch in the paper bag with the grease stain."

Grosbeck found himself fascinated. He was present at the birth of literature, he was convinced, possibly of poetry, from an *idiot savant* who did not know what he was doing, who couldn't spell the word "literature" and who wasn't, in any event, addressing himself to Grosbeck.

Angotti kept talking faster than the ambulance moved, his voice more excited than the tongue of any siren. The voice took on a sorrowful note. "This guy was with us all the way from fifteen-and-five through the seventy-five-cent drop and ten cents a seventh of a mile and nothing's too good for him. He's got on a whole suit and tie and it's *clean.* He's perfect. I got to thinking, maybe we ought to let him wear the pants and flannel underwear top he had on when it happened, but no. You know how drivers are. It's the *image*, what would the public think?"

"Screw the public," Boyle said, edging his way between a bus and a truck. The bus driver looked at Boyle with a dirty eye. The truck-driver spat at the side of the ambulance.

"So," Angotti said, "it's a whole suit, the one he used to wear when him and the old lady went out for Chinks. That couldn't have been more'n once a week. The dispatcher reads the service. It's a short one. It has to be, because we're all pretty close to shift change and the guys want to get home. Also, they don't retire his medallion. His wife inherits it and she takes it home and sells it for three grand more'n he paid and everybody's happy. We leave the undertaker's hearse to pick him up and get him out to the cemetery. Just the wife, immediate family. The rest of us have got to go. What it adds up to, I don't have to tell you, is, 'He died for us all,' and that's what that dope on the six o'clock news says. And that's about it."

"Jesus Christ on the Cross," Boyle said, impressed finally. "Not a bad idea."

As a piece of *commedia dell' arte*, the performance left nothing to be desired, unless it was the unfortunate circumstance that Grosbeck had had to attend it with a heart attack. Also, whenever the impulse to laugh came over him on the way downtown, the ambulance struck a pothole and his teeth clacked instead, making him sound like a large wooden box full of brass doorknobs falling. Boyle and Angotti confirmed him in his hopeless love of New York City; the ride through the streets confirmed him in his hopeless hatred of its works. He barely had time to construct a metaphor between the wreckage of his heart, the insult to a body which, if not perfect, was comfortable enough to suit him, and the destruction of the city he had grown up in. It was a modest enough metaphor. Other men have made monstrous ones, confusing themselves with God and getting away with it.

These little vapors of thought vanished in the emergency room of the hospital. He was hauled off the wheeled stretcher in which he had been deposited in a hallway and dropped onto another. Rattle, rattle went the wooden box of doorknobs. He was wheeled rapidly into another space, elevated roughly, and flung, with voluptuous grace, up and onto a bed by two vaudevillians who seemed to regard him as the top mounter in a pyramid act. The first thing done to him was the administering of some kind of drug which made his ears ring and his eyes start out of his head. The needle was so large that for a moment he thought he was in an animal shelter and would be put up for adoption when he got better.

"Don't pay any attention to anything you feel," he was adjured by the veterinarian. "It's standard."

"Standard," mumbled Grosbeck.

"Goes away in thirty seconds."

"Thirty seconds."

"If I were you, I'd say as little as possible for a while."

"Little. Possible."

"Once that feeling goes away, I'm going to ask you a few questions. I've got to."

"Got to." Echolalia.

Another young man, wearing a stethoscope, pushed his way past the veterinarian who stood poised with his horse needle pointing at the ceiling, burning to stick it into Grosbeck again. "That'll be it, I think," said the doctor to the veterinarian. "I think we can talk now," he said. He looked down at the name scrawled on a piece of tape pasted to the foot of the bed. "Mr. Grosbeck," he asked, "do you feel nauseous?"

Grosbeck tried to lift his head—a pointer on the scent of something. He could not. His neck appeared to have been bolted down with a bent steel bar. "Am I what?" he asked the intern, or resident, or attendant, or fake. "I wish there were some way of telling one of you from another. Same stethoscopes, same damned white coats. I know the length of the coat marks one of you from another, but I can't remember—not since I had my tonsils out. Long time ago. Am I talking too much? I've got a point to make. Bear with me. You don't have much choice, anyway, do you?"

"Mr. Grosbeck, all I asked was, 'Are you nauseous?' "

"Nauseous. Yes. The old days. One doctor—in his office—one nurse—next to him. Ether over the nose, the choking, the waking up, the 'How's that feel, son? They're out. And now, how would you like some ice cream? All the ice cream you can eat?' " For once, the startling resonance and volume of Grosbeck's voice had been reduced to the whisper of a beggar with a handful of pencils. "Bastards. They know you can't eat much."

"Mr. Grosbeck, please don't exert yourself," the doctor said. "You seem to have had a moderately serious infarction—we'll know more when we run a couple of more EKGs—electrocardiograms. We're doing everything we can to make you comfortable and get you better, but we do have to have the answers to a few questions. Now, once again, are you—were you—nauseous?"

Grosbeck felt as much anger as was possible. "Did I understand you to ask me whether I'm *nauseous?*" he asked.

"Yes," said the doctor.

"No," Grosbeck said. "No, I am not *nauseous.* I am *nauseated.* Do you follow me?" Since he was unable to lift his head, Grosbeck rolled it from side to side in the vain hope that this would convey the uttermost contempt.

"I'm not sure what you mean, Mr. Grosbeck," said the doctor. He looked over his shoulder for help, but the veterinarian had gone away and the only two other cases left in the emergency room were a broken leg and a case of delirium tremens.

"Do you know why I am nauseated, Doctor?" Grosbeck asked.

"That's what I'm trying to find out, sir," the doctor said.

Grosbeck's voice took on strength. Fuck infarctions. "Well, Doctor," he said, "I am *nauseated* because *you* are quite obviously *nauseous* and you make me *nauseated.* I don't want to dwell on it . . ."

"Please don't, Mr. Grosbeck. This is an emergency."

"I'll dwell on anything as long as I goddamned well please," Grosbeck went on. "*You* induce sickness in others with English of that kind and I fear for your competence. I sure as hell wouldn't like to have you operating on me . . ."

Two orderlies showed up. "Get him out of here," the doctor told them. "I don't much care what you do with him . . . oh, get him upstairs to ICU. They're expecting him." He was tempted to hit Grosbeck with the stethoscope but this man was just the kind of bastard who'd hit back with a million bucks' worth of malpractice suit.

Grosbeck was wheeled off, the doctor following, Grosbeck mouthing abuse at the fluorescent lights in the ceiling.

While waiting for the elevator, the doctor reflected that he had seen a good deal, but that this was surely his first case of hysterical pedantry and he did the only thing of which he was capable. He gave Grosbeck another large injection of sedative, knowing (or believing) that it could not hurt him. The elevator arrived and Grosbeck, eyes closed, mouth still open, was wheeled into it. As usual, the floor of the elevator was about an inch above the level of the corridor and Grosbeck's teeth clacked once more as his tumbril was pushed into it. He did not know this. He was unconscious.

Grosbeck, the flower of civilization as we know it, the quintessence of thousands of years of cultivation, a man in socks which required garters to hold them up and a copy of a Trollope novel in his jacket pocket (a paperback duplicate; he kept the edition bound in red buckram at home on the bookshelves), was finally deposited in a bed in the intensive-care room of the hospital and connected up to half a dozen television screens behind his head. They were for the doctors, not for him. Lights blinked on and off or ran playfully across the screens, left to right. Was it possible that they had Jewish machines with the waves of light running from right to left? Or Chinese machines going up and down? He had been dressed, as are all hospital patients, in one of those short green gowns in which it is possible to strangle while exposing oneself. The machines clicked and clacked, low and apologetic. Nurses carrying trays with bottles and pills on them, each labeled so that the possibility of a mistake was only seven in ten, moved silently about the room. They smiled or looked grave. Their cheeks were made of some kind of colored substance through which ran tiny wires; a switch upon being thrown in some other part of the building lent animation to the cheeks, produced whispered words for doctors and cute-stern injunctions to patients, which told them nothing, as intended.

In the bed at Grosbeck's left lay a *buba* of ninety-one, whose refusal to die had exasperated the entire staff of the intensive-care unit. She had enraged people further by insisting that she was eighty-eight. She wore a *sheitl*, or wig, in the Orthodox Jewish manner. It was forever askew, down over her eyes or ears, as she moved restlessly in bed, and she flirted. Flirted! Grosbeck knew he should have marveled at the gallantry of the indomitable old lady, but he agreed with the staff. That was before his trip up Sinai to help Moses down with the tablets and he was not yet ready for compassion. The old lady was a nuisance to him just then, and he was certain her family felt the same way. Its unpleasant, assertive members came into intensive care to see her giving the impression they were on their way out. Her malady was to have lived far too long, but at least she had enough left of her marbles to flirt and be continent. At Grosbeck's right, the situation was different. A man lay in that bed, cancerous and torporous, about eighty-five pounds of man with mouth open and nothing more to say. *Finito.* There were no windows in the room. Intensive care includes a mite of claustrophobia, a dollop of fluorescent lighting without shadows. And yet, in their beds, with the raised pillows, the three sick people looked like equally matched rowers waiting for the starter's gun to go off so they could scull furiously down the Schuylkill River and up to the top floor of City Hall in Philadelphia.

Grosbeck remembered that if one stood on the steps of the Philadelphia Art Museum (the Greek Garage, as it was known) and looked at Alexander Stirling Calder's statue of William Penn on top of the City Hall, Penn seemed to be voiding through eternity, the reason being that he was carrying a rolled-up proclamation of some sort in his hand. The angle was just right and the unfortunate sculptor had not foreseen that he was fashioning a practical joke which visitors would photograph and show their friends.

Dr. Salomon stood at Grosbeck's side and the patient reluctantly put aside all such reverie. "What have you done to yourself, you foolish man?"

"Nothing," said Grosbeck. "It's all a mistake."

"Something you ate, no doubt?"

"I don't know," said Grosbeck. "I don't feel too bad now. After an ambulance ride like that, you either get better or go away. Where do you find those people?"

Dr. Salomon nodded sympathetically. "We will know more in thirty-six hours," he said. "About you, that is, not the ambulance crew. Of them, we will never learn anything. Your wife is coming to see you. Nobody else and not for long. After a couple of days or until I take you out of here, your loving children, the precious ornaments of a life well spent [Dr. Salomon looked dubiously at Grosbeck] may see you, each of them, for no more than twenty minutes, one at a time. You told me, I believe, that they are all in Katmandu, meditating one month, running drugs the next?"

"No, I didn't," Grosbeck said. "I told you one of them had taken a trip there and come back. All I said was I picked him up in the airport lounge and we had a few drinks. He insisted on the best brandy they had. He was well brought up."

"Oh," said Dr. Salomon. He talked of the matter at hand. "You have unquestionably had a heart attack, and the cardiograms will confirm me in thirty-six hours. Everything we know tells me you were ready for it. Overdue. Smoking, drinking, eating too much, pinching the behinds of women other than your wife, arguing . . ." He waggled a finger at Grosbeck. "Is there no end to the making of *mishigas* in people like you? Are you never satisfied? What did you have for dinner last night?"

"You find out," Grosbeck said pettishly. "All you've got to do is open me up and you'll know."

The doctor clucked. His face brightened. He took another tack. "I assure you," he said. "You will not die like those other two. Not your kind. But what *was* it? Summer sausage, Italian bread, perhaps a Brie running like water, eight ounces of cheap vodka? You've told me how you drink. Everything in a hurry. Always something else to do right away. Schedules, schedules. Then, perhaps, a tiny piece of the hashish you find so satisfying and so voguish? A run at your wife? Was it your wife? Were you even home?"

Nobody had told Dr. Salomon yet that Grosbeck had been stricken while defending an outmoded philosophical system, and Grosbeck preferred to listen rather than explain. "Or," Dr. Salomon went on, "did you run across an intersection too fast this morning on the way to work and then get into a fight at the office?"

Well, it hadn't exactly been a fight; more like polite discourse. Grosbeck polite? For him, polite.

"Ah, youth, youth," the doctor sighed. Grosbeck lifted a papal hand and made religious motions at the doctor. "Why," he asked, "should this day have been different from all other days?"

Dr. Salomon responded with a laugh and answered, "*Boruch atoy pre hagofen,*" blessing the wine. He patted Grosbeck's arm. "I'll tell you a joke," he said, "and then I've got to go. It will give you something to think about. There are these two old Jewish men sitting on a bench in the park, and one says to the other, 'Sol,' he says, 'you know what your trouble is? You're pretentious.' The other one looks back at him and answers, 'Pretentious? *Moi?*'"

Grosbeck sniffed, put out.

The doctor relented. "All right," he said, pulling a letter out of his pocket, "I've got something more in your line. I got this this morning. It says that the Euthanasia Educational Council has changed its name. Henceforth," he said, reading the letter once more to be sure he had it right, "henceforth, its name will be Concern for the Dying. Yes."

Finally, finally, Grosbeck laughed, pulling wires and disarranging the things to which he had been attached. "That's enough," Dr. Salomon said, pleased with himself, pleased with Grosbeck, moving Grosbeck around and stilling him. "You are better. You *will* be better. I have said so. You will conquer the world, that world of yours uptown which you profess to hate so much, but you will also drink, smoke, eat, and, ah, do everything else in moderation from this time forward. No, you will *not* smoke. Why do people in your business tell those lies about us? Or get it wrong? Do I steal from the government or neglect to pay my taxes?"

"I don't know your accountant," Grosbeck said. "I can't say. I do, when I can get away with it, which isn't too often. They don't take money away from you the way they do with people on a salary. They are removing me from your class. They are making me your serf or they would if the company weren't paying for most of this."

"My malpractice insurance alone . . ." said the doctor.

"All deductible," Grosbeck reminded him. "That's a pretty expensive-looking suit you've got on. I don't like the style, the cut, but who ever heard of a doctor—and a European doctor, at that—who knew how to dress? You look like an *alter kocker* going dancing."

"And you," the doctor told Grosbeck, "look like an *alter* who *went* dancing and got out of wind. Wait, wait. I am going to turn you over to the resident. He's an Indian—from India. He has the whitest teeth and he will smile and smile at you and talk about *kamavachara*. I learned that from him. He gave me this booklet." Dr. Salomon pulled it out of a different pocket from the one into which he had stuck the letter about euthanasia.

"*Kamavachara*," he read, "is the six pleasure heavens, or lower heavens, presided over by Sakra (Indra) where the souls of good men who have not attained nirvana are rewarded until their merit expires, after which they are reborn on earth. Believe me, if there is one thing Dr. Mukerji is good at, it's transporting patients to *kamava-*

chara. That will be good for you. You will join all those rich boys and girls with dirty feet and saffron robes and finger cymbals on Times Square. You will have a begging bowl and tracts and acne. You will be reborn and I will give you money on my way to the theatre."

Dr. Salomon stopped. Like all cynical men, he was sentimental. "On second thought, no," he said. "Not Mukerji. I will leave the others to him. They don't have far to go. For you, something else. You have a long way to go. For you, there will be nirvana here on earth."

"Thanks," Grosbeck said, "from the bottom of my . . . my . . . heart."

"*De nada,*" the doctor said in his atrocious accent. "I will see you later. Remember, your wife will be here soon. She won't cry or carry on. I didn't have to tell her. She has a great deal of common sense. But you, you are a fool. You are lucky in her. You will be here for a few weeks and then I will send you home to be with her for a few more and then you will go back to work. And then, for the rest of your long life, you will come to see me once every three weeks so that I can tell you your heart still beats. You will lose weight on a salt-free diet and you will not smoke, and"—he hurried on to the question Grosbeck obviously was about to ask—"you will be able to sleep with your wife or anyone else after about eight weeks. But carefully, at first. I don't recommend someone else right away. Someone else is apt to be too exciting for someone in your condition. And, remember. You have had a heart attack and you will never be the same. You will be good, but never the same. Think of it this way. What, after all, is the heart? It is a muscle, it was torn, it will repair itself, but it will never be perfect again.

"What difference will that make? Almost none. And you will have an advantage. Instead of that one big artery doing all the work for the poor heart, there will be many others through which the blood will push to help take up the burden so that the coronary will not have to do it all. Ah, Grosbeck, you are so fortunate. Had you been younger, you might have died instantly. Young bodies are not so well prepared. It is well known in the statistics. I have a book I would like you to read. While you are in the hospital. It is called, *Thank God for My Heart Attack.*"

"Forget it," Grosbeck said. "The title alone is enough . . . I don't go in for self-improvement. Not that way." He grimaced. "Let me ask you a question, Dr. Salomon. How long ago was that book published?"

"I don't know," the doctor said. "Some years back. I bought a lot of copies—remainders they call them?—for very little money, to give my heart patients, so I suppose it was quite a while ago."

"I thought so," Grosbeck said. "How do you know this guy is still alive?" He was triumphant, the doctor crestfallen.

"I didn't ask," Dr. Salomon said stiffly. "And, furthermore, it doesn't make any difference. The principle is the same."

"Sure it is," Grosbeck said. "I bet this guy lasted long enough to see this thing in print and then keeled over."

"I'm sure I don't know," the doctor answered, "and that is beside the point. I have a copy outside in my bag. The nurse will give it to you."

"I'll throw it on the floor," Grosbeck said.

"I will charge you extra for bad behavior," the doctor said.

"Go ahead," Grosbeck said. "Sue me, too, for deficiency in acquiescence in your nostrums. Go practice your secondhand psychology on someone else."

The doctor bowed extravagantly. "You are incorrigible and a baby," he said. "I think I will have you looked after by a pediatrician. He will give you shots for distemper and blurred vision." He patted Grosbeck's right hand.

"No," he said, leaving. "I will do no such thing. I need you as much as you do me. You will come to my office regularly when you are out of here and tell me what is happening. Please omit the canards about the medical profession. I want to know everything else. You will be the newspaper I don't have time to read. Between the medical journals and the drug-company literature I don't seem to have an extra minute. You will be a welcome interlude."

He looked at his watch. "Already, I am late and there are people who have the bad taste to have convulsions or neglect to die on schedule. Late, late. Everything gets later and later. Within a year, I shall be running twenty-four hours behind and find myself treating the patients of other doctors who are running even later than I am." He whispered to a nurse on his way out the door of intensive care. She nodded and closed the door against Dr. Salomon. The only sounds in the room after that were the sounds of machines and the snorting of the patients on either side of Grosbeck. He was bored and scared, but he felt no pain at all now, and regarded himself as one of those patients in a movie—something terribly wrong, of course, but not a mark on him, the beard beginning to grow a little, but, outside of that, nothing untoward.

Madeline Grosbeck was let into intensive care with the deference and hush accorded a witness at an indoor hanging. At the moment, the prisoner was being fed a pill, and, in order to get at his mouth, the nurse had to push aside the tube up his nose. Grosbeck tried to lift his head, talk, and gesture. Madeline showing up at his bedside in a hospital was nothing new. She had had to go through pretty much the same thing when he got beat up in Little Italy. At Madeline's appearance, the *buba* said, suspiciously, "Hoo ha," and the man dying of cancer fixed her with a long stare and then shut his eyes. Better he should die without getting any ideas. The chances were she was full of, to use the current cant, suspected cancer-causing agents, anyway. Had a feminist been picking away at the poor old man's brain, it ("it," of course, not "she" or "he") would have denominated him as "sexist."

"Madeline," said Grosbeck.

"Harvey," said Madeline. Too many old movies, Grosbeck thought critically.

"Your office found me uptown on the East Side," Madeline said. "I don't know how. I was in the middle of a walking tour. I had a class going through one of those Ernest Flagg model tenements . . ."

"For the deserving poor," Grosbeck managed to say. "I know."

"Suddenly, I saw Tully, that reporter friend of yours, come running up the stairs to the balcony. You know those outside balconies Flagg designed for the inner courtyard." Grosbeck groaned silently. Did she have the blueprints in that trunk of a handbag she carried? Madeline put a hand over her mouth and blushed, then took it away and placed it on Harvey's cheek, bent over him and kissed him.

"Harvey, oh, Harvey. What happened?"

"Not a hell of a lot," he said. With all the impedimenta in and around him, it sounded like, "Bell hit the pot," but she understood. He did not think it necessary to try to tell her about ". . . black and white . . ."

"My poor darling," she went on and a tear rolled off her chin, without, however, disturbing her *maquillage*, which might as well have been made of porcelain. The words were pure old movie, but Grosbeck did not resent that. For him, Madeline had always been, would always be, the most beautiful woman in the world. "Sweetheart," she said.

"Lover," he answered. For her to have talked any other way and for him to have answered any other way would have been unthinkable. Both of them had been brought up badly. Still, it was better than what one heard today out of the mouths of lovers. Besides, he had been in and out of the lives and beds of enough other women to know that this was the tiniest of faults. He went along with it, even got to enjoy it as their marriage grew older.

He had, by God, learned also to put up with her habit of watching television. The thought was apropos. Sure enough, Grosbeck noticed acutely that, upset as she was, Madeline's eyes wandered every so often from his face to the screens behind him that measured how well or ill he was, how he stood, lifewise, at the moment. For Madeline, it never mattered what was on the set, as long as picture succeeded picture and noise was coming out. What did she expect to see on these screens? Gary Cooper? The taking of the Khyber Pass? Hedy Lamarr sitting in a silken tent nibbling on caviar? A commercial for the Red Cross depicting famine in the Sahel with the measly natives passing out on the bodies of their measly camels? Look, there were plenty of times in their marriage when *he* didn't smell like eighty bucks an ounce. True, he didn't smash things. He didn't believe in physical destruction, but he was expert at emptying a room to the embarrassment and fury of his wife.

One night, at a party, he got hold of some wispy man who had had the bad luck to speak of women as a "minority." Grosbeck went at him with the efficiency of a butcher cutting up chops. "Minority," he said, pulling at his drink, getting some of it on his chin, wiping the chin and then putting the glass down on a table meant to be covered with coasters for drinks. "There are more women than there are men. You know that, don't you? So, what makes them a minority?"

"I think you know what I mean," the man said.

"No, I don't," Grosbeck said, putting on his dumb act. "All I know is there are more of them than there are of us. If, of course, you include yourself as one of us."

"What I meant," the man said, "is the way they're *treated* . . . They might as well *be* a minority."

"Don't give me that," Grosbeck said. "There're more of them than there are of us, they're voracious, they're . . ." He reached down for his glass and drank. "I've got to tell you," he told the man, "they're hungry. Hungrier than you know. And they're no better than we are. Want the same things, the same money, got the same ambitions, want to do everything we do, and so on. Nothing against that. High time they got them all. But, don't let me hear you talking about women as a *minority*." Grosbeck could be tendentious beyond belief and he was a master of the obvious. "One other thing I think I ought to tell you," he went on. "Babies. They're the only ones can have babies. Minority or no minority. Maybe you're one of them. You go have a baby and be a minority."

The performance was breathtaking. A space had cleared around Grosbeck and the man and when he had done saying the last thing, the man disappeared. Grosbeck was left with his drink, and, on a mantelpiece, a plate of cold miniature frankfurters with colored toothpicks in them. The host's cat, a big male whose claws had not been removed and whose balls had been left intact, bit his ankle and ran too.

Madeline was taller than Grosbeck and put together like anything but a museum curator who gave walking tours describing old buildings in New York City. To Grosbeck, she was Ada Clare, the Queen of Bohemia, sitting in Charlie Pfaff's cafe under the street on Broadway above Bleecker Street, ragging Walt Whitman (the pederast) and running off (only to run back) with that famous piano player and composer, what's-his-name—Louis Moreau Gottschalk, the toast of two continents, etc., etc., etc., and he, Grosbeck, poetaster, littérateur, sometime journalist, etc., etc., etc., had finally had her for his very own. Ada Clare had wasted away in drink and died of tuberculosis, but Madeline had flourished and they had got married. She used alcohol in any form, mostly to cook with, and she had preserved her looks and Grosbeck's body with great care ever since they had met in someone's house and he, between marriages, had asked her to go out with him. He had told her precisely where to meet him and at what time, at what restaurant, what theatre they would be going to.

She had, characteristically, stationed herself in the lobby of another restaurant across town and Grosbeck, recalling that she had mentioned it favorably, had put two and two together, gotten a cab to that restaurant, and, fifteen minutes before curtain time, had found her. Never in her life thereafter would she concede that Grosbeck had asked her to meet him at the other restaurant, not even when he pointed out that his restaurant was only three doors away from the theatre. He loved her for that, too. Yet, how had she failed that he should have a heart attack? What had she overlooked? No one would ever know what lapse in taste caused Grosbeck to have a heart attack while saying, ". . . black and white . . . black and white . . ." Unless it were wrong thinking, which is not measurable. There were plenty of nuts who would swear it was flawed thinking, but what did they know? Madeline's face was bony and her features Middle Eastern or Mediterranean and she kept her hair black. Her legs were still spectacular and her teeth all her own. She resembled a mosaic from Byzantium, a figure on a wall at Pompeii. She was a good-looking broad. Grosbeck reminded her frequently that her marriage to him might have been her most egregious lapse in common sense.

"Small talk, give me small talk, Madeline," Grosbeck said. "Everywhere else, I get big talk, and, as the doctor told you, we have only a short time together."

"What are you saying? Harvey?" Madeline asked.

"Madeline, don't have a *fit*. They're not about to measure me for a winding sheet. Salomon told you, didn't he, that for the first few days or so I was not to be taxed? Physically. The other kind of taxes go right on. That's a joke. Tell me a joke, Madeline. Salomon did, why can't you?"

"I don't know any jokes, Harvey," said Madeline.

"Yes, you do," Grosbeck said. "All those people you work with, they're jokes. That's what you're always telling me, isn't it? What about that curator of yours who sent the American art to Wiesbaden when it was supposed to go to Westchester? The drunken one, the one with the guardsman's mustache who still wears those ratty dinner jackets to openings and drops food."

He was beginning to rise to heights of malicious imagining. "Come on," he went on, "the one who lives in a garbage can and comes to work in a hired limo."

Madeline said nothing. There was, at the moment, nothing to say to that. Bryan Custer *did* drink too much, he did look soiled and disarrayed, but he also *did* have a good heart. Madeline would never be able to convince Grosbeck of that. "That's no heart," he would say to Madeline. "That's a gallstone that went the wrong way."

Grosbeck had not been reassured by what he felt to be Dr. Salomon's cavalier attitude. He thought it very possible that he would die. Once before, upon regaining consciousness in a hospital, he had been certain that he *had* died. So, while it cannot be said that he was prepared to go, he did have some idea of what it would be like and he didn't want to leave. There was so much to be done. What, for example? Never mind. He wasn't in the mood to face the God of Israel (if that One happened to be his) to explain himself and make excuses and to be told, "*Yo soy el Camino, y la Verdad; nadie viene al Padre, sino por Mi.*"

"My God," Grosbeck said at the knee of God.

"*¿Si, mi hijo?*" asked God.

"Nobody ever told me you were a Puerto Rican."

"*Si, mi hijo.*"

"You mean like in the joke?"

"Here is no joke." God took out one of those things which look like a curry comb and which are called Afro picks and ran it through His abundant circle of hair two feet above His head. There were pompons attached to the rhinestone frame and they bobbled as the pick was pulled through the tangled thicket of black hair. Then, God pulled down the chest zipper on His dashiki and showed Himself. "It is hot," He said in English.

"My God," Grosbeck exclaimed. "You're a woman."

"*Si, mi hijo,*" God answered with a beatific smile. "*Una mujera.* We got *rights.* You just be damned glad, man, We ain't a fag and a Fuzzy-Wuzzy too. Yours is long gone, man. I rose—I'll stick with English—from one of those Pentecostal churches, the ones they put in storefronts and old synagogues on the Lower East Side. Get *down,* man. Put aside the things of your childhood. They made *Me* Numero Uno."

He ran a dirty thumb and forefinger around an earring He had on. It was made of some base metal and was turning green and it had infected the Holy Right Ear slightly, pulling the Ear out from the Head and making God look lopsided. "I should have known," Grosbeck said. "You got any following outside New York?"

"She-ee-e-ut," God said with scorn.

"I guess you do have me," Grosbeck said, "otherwise we wouldn't be talking."

God nodded. *"Mira,"* He said, pointing at Grosbeck. *"Mira.* You bet you little kike ass I got you." He laughed. *"Vaya con Dios, mi hijo."* He pulled Grosbeck to his feet and gave him the small tour.

God's Heaven was like the subway station in Times Square, littered with empty pink-and-gray vials of amyl nitrate ("Get *down*, suckah"), old newspapers, pieces of hot-dog roll stained with black dirt and yellow mustard, cops disguised as junkies. The cops could be told from the real junkies only by the fact that they were on their feet. The real articles tucked themselves away near the overflowing wastebaskets, nodding, showing only the whites of their eyes. The place was alive with teen-age whores of every color, bolder than brass, watched narrowly by their pimps. There was something for every taste: man whores in men's clothing and women's clothing; woman whores of every age, color and description. Plump and thin, tall and short. There w̩re, for those who cared to seek them out, blind whores and whores with terrible growths on their necks or other parts of their bodies; and whores who spent the night, when not actually working, pulling hairs out of their rouged cheeks with a pair of tweezers, wincing at every pull. Some of them had stood tweezing in one place for so long they had little ends of hair piled up to their knees. Here and there, like atmospheric details in a medieval painting, Grosbeck could see what at first he thought were shafts of Divine light. They were only the long blades of knives with the glint of yellow electric light on them.

There were many booths in Heaven, selling dolls made of chemical wool, toys that fell apart on being taken out of the box, cameras that didn't take pictures, little metal statues, either of the Statue of Liberty or of Commodore Cornelius Vanderbilt. It was impossible to identify them. There were picture postcards of Heaven and banners proclaiming its Kingdom—in the most vulgar of colors—produced in Japan—and posters commemorating the other God who had been hustled out of town on a commuter train (an hour late leaving Grand Central because of a fire in the tunnel) and was now presiding both over a Reform synagogue and a Presbyterian church, so ecumenical was that One now, so clean-shaven, so badly dressed, so orotund of address and up-to-date on His social-science references, so empty-headed, so nothing at all.

In an odd way, Grosbeck preferred the Puerto Rican lady God. She, or He, or It smelled like a *bodega,* Her two front teeth were missing, and, when He smiled, which He did often, She seemed to be getting ready to mug the Blessed who had just arrived in His Domain. Nothing of the sort. Instead, She said kindly to Grosbeck, "*Dígame, mi hijo,* you hongry?" At least, He made an attempt to speak the language. Grosbeck said he was. God led him up the stairs and pushed him gently toward Eighth Avenue. They stopped at a small restaurant with the sign on it, COMIDAS CRIOLLAS, and other arcane words. "*Nah, kindele,*" God said in Grosbeck's language. "*Fress,* already. I speak your language good. You want a little taste after, look aron'. We got anything you got in mind. Sniff it, drop it, shoot it, fuck it, we *got* it, *mi hijo.* Nobody gonna stick you. You in *Heaven,* man. You hear? Heaven. Ain't no Hell no more. They passed a *law* on that, *mi hijo.* Went all the way to the Supreme *Court.* Litygaytion like you head could come off. Nothin' but Heaven now. You dig?"

"Dig," intoned Grosbeck.

"What was that you said, Harvey?" Madeline asked.

"I said I *dig,*" Grosbeck answered with a faint grin.

"What are you laughing at?" Madeline asked. "Dig what?"

"Ain't laughin' ay-tall," Grosbeck said. "Dig everything."

"Are you all right?" Madeline asked.

"Never better," Grosbeck said, "but you owe me a joke."

"What is everything?" Madeline asked.

"I'll tell you some other time," Grosbeck said. "It would tire me too much to try to explain now and you know I'm not to be agitated. What about that joke? Only one. Two would be too rich for my blood right now. Salomon said so. Come to think of it, maybe you shouldn't bother. He's already told me one. You want to hear it?" Madeline said she didn't, that Salomon was right. One was enough.

One of the nurses came over. Her cap was on crooked, but she was a good sort. She came from Gary, Indiana, and she consorted with the resident, Dr. Mukerji, in a broom closet, whenever either of them had the time, which was often, as the patients knew. There was some kind of correlation between their absence and the condition of the patients in intensive care. Nobody had compiled any figures, but it was common knowledge that the more intense things got (hence the name intensive care) between Dr. Mukerji and Nurse Rawson, the more patients were inclined to give up and die. The resident and the nurse were much given to saying to bereaved relatives, "Sorry, I really am," and that seemed to satisfy everyone, except, possibly, the dead. Nobody could satisfy them, anyway, nobody on earth. Only *Dios*, in Heaven. *He* cared. *She* was sorry, He really was. Everybody came to His pad got *comidas criollas*, no matter what kind of diet they'd been on.

Rawson playfully tweaked the big toe of Grosbeck's left foot. "We've had it for today, Mr. Grosbeck," and, the lilt still in her voice, swung about gracefully to address herself to Madeline. "We mustn't tire him out, must we, Miss Farkas? We'll just save that for your wedding night, won't we? That bad, bad boy."

"Farkas?" asked Madeline. "Didn't they tell you I'm Mrs. Grosbeck?"

"I beg your pardon, I'm sure," said the nurse. "Those people out there, they're so *careless.* Back home in Indiana—ha ha—I knew *everybody.* Here, half the time, you can't tell whether it's the doctor or the undertaker coming. I don't mean that. But, you know what I mean. So many people. In the beds and out of them." She helped Madeline on with her jacket.

"You know something? Your husband, he's a nice-looking man for his age . . ."

"What did I hear you say, Rawson?" Grosbeck asked. "What's your goddamned age got mine hasn't, except no wrinkles in the ass?"

"Oh, Mr. Grosbeck, you weren't supposed to be listening. You're supposed to be resting." She turned back to Madeline. "Most of what we get in here . . . He's a gentleman, isn't he? I can always tell. Those legs. I bet he was something on a tennis court."

"My husband doesn't play any longer, Miss Rawson," Madeline said. "He swallowed a ball once while trying to return a volley and it settled just below his knee. It traveled downward. They had to operate. If you look closely, you can find the scar just above the ankle."

Miss Rawson continued. Nothing Madeline said was going to divert her. "Just the right amount of hair on those legs. You won't mind my saying that's exciting—more exciting now that it's gray. And the chest. A real aristocrat. You can see the ribs right through. He's a little soft now, but he isn't a kid anymore, is he? My, he must have been something when he was young."

"I wish I could say the same for you," Grosbeck said to the nurse.

"Miss Rawson," Madeline said, "really . . ."

"I wouldn't mind having something like that," said Rawson. "If I were a little older, of course. You're a lucky woman, Mrs. Grosbeck. That Mukerji. Dr. Mukerji, Mrs. Grosbeck. Have you met him?" Madeline shook her head. "Not what I would have picked out if I had my choice," the nurse said. "But when you live as far away from here as I do and you work the hours I do, you take what's around. Beggars can't be choosers. Half the time I can't understand what he's saying, but I always tell myself, Does that make any difference in a broom closet? He *does* have his points." Rawson giggled. "He could be a little cleaner, I'll have to admit, but . . . why am I telling you all this, Mrs. Grosbeck?"

Madeline said she couldn't understand why.

"What I think it is, Mrs. Grosbeck," Rawson went on, "is we establish a sort of intimacy with our more seriously ill patients and that sort of extends itself to their relatives and . . ."

"Where did you read that?" Madeline asked the nurse.

Rawson looked hurt. "Why," she said, "that's just the way I feel. We did take a course in *attitudes*, that's part of the way they do things these days, but what I did, I carried it a step further—farther? I'm a better nurse for it. I pride myself I'm as close to my patients as I can get until they leave. One way or another. Pride myself on it. That's why I became a nurse. I wanted to do something for people. And their dear ones."

"I'll bet," Madeline said. She experienced a curious twinge, looking at this creature, so young, so ardent, so . . . "Remember," she said, "he's had a heart attack. Mukerji hasn't."

"Oh, Mrs. Grosbeck, don't say things like that. Don't even *think* them. I would never . . . It wouldn't be professional. It wouldn't be *right*."

"No," said Madeline, "but it might be fun, eh?"

"Well, if you must know, Mrs. Grosbeck—and I won't hold anything back—he *is* kind of cute. I've never gone out with an older man, even the doctors. I bet he can go when he wants to," she said, looking at Grosbeck. "Am I right, Mrs. Grosbeck? Just between us?"

"Just between us," Madeline said, "I think you had better cut this out."

"Mrs. Grosbeck, you *didn't* take me seriously," Rawson said. "You know me better than that."

"No, I don't, I don't at all. I've just met you. And he's been in this bed for only three hours and already you're thinking about . . ." She cried a little.

"Mrs. Grosbeck," said Rawson, putting an arm about Madeline's shoulders, "don't you cry, now. You mustn't worry. He *will* be all right. Dr. Salomon told me so. And, besides, I can tell. I've been in intensive care long enough to know. Sometimes I'm wrong, but not this time. I shouldn't be saying all this, I'm not supposed to, but you take my word for it. We'll get him out of here if we have to *kill* him. Pardon me. You understand the spirit I said that in. I wouldn't say it if I didn't know. And he did say he wanted you to tell him a joke. You could say I told it for the three of us, couldn't you?"

Madeline looked at Nurse Rawson and nodded. "Yes," she said, "you could. You've been very kind and I thank you. It *is* a kind of compliment to be told your husband is still attractive. Is there anything he's going to need?"

"Not a thing. Anything he could possibly want we have here." She checked herself. "Not everything . . . know what I mean?"

"Yes," Madeline said, "know what you mean."

"Word of honor," the nurse said. "God bless you, Mrs. Grosbeck." She edged Madeline out the door of intensive care. "Myself, I don't pray much out loud, but it does go on in my head. It isn't easy in my profession, but it does me a world of good. I'm not much for giving advice, but it's still the best medicine there is. I keep the radio low at night when I go to bed, and, if I'm alone, I just listen to revival music or some highbrow preacher talk and I hear and I don't hear and there is God going around in my head and telling me things are going to be all right and I go to sleep. I can't tell you what the electric bills are like between the radio and the lights. I leave the lights on all night. What's that old song say, 'I'm afraid to go home in the dark.' But it all makes me feel better."

"Thank you so much, Miss Rawson," Madeline said quickly before the door was shut on her face. "Harvey and I can't thank you enough . . . I think . . ."

Grosbeck was in intensive care for four days, a time in which he believed himself to be reflecting on his life, but, in actuality, a time in which he was kept doped up so thoroughly that everything about him had a roseate glow. Rawson came and went and so did a number of other functionaries. All of them did something to him, in accordance with the rituals prescribed by the medical profession. Mostly, they looked at him, rubbed their chins and then their hands and said, "Aha." Every time Grosbeck tried to talk to one of them, the functionary would fix the oxygen mask more firmly over his nose and mouth. "It's just a precaution," he would say soothingly.

"Too sit," Grosbeck would reply, under the mask. "Art wha ur rattids or refarif murder amd sin," meaning, "Bullshit. That's what you bastards call defensive medicine." The functionary would smile and pat, at random, look past Grosbeck at the screens behind him, crook an imperious finger at Rawson, pick up the chart at the foot of the bed, pound it, and stick it under Rawson's nose. She had had a particularly heavy dose of Mukerji ever since Grosbeck came into intensive care. The lock of the broom closet had shut on them once and the two of them had spent half an hour getting out. Mukerji, who was not without resource, had first kicked viciously at the door jamb, managing a few splinters, but he was wearing cheap shoes and he was afraid of hurting his feet. This would have been inconvenient, since he was learning to play tennis. He stopped kicking, looked at Rawson under the light in the broom closet and said his mantra. He sounded like a mouse caught in a box of cereal. The nurse mistook this for an appeal for something else and advanced on Mukerji again. The broom closet was a small one and she did not have far to go.

Mukerji pushed her away impatiently, stopped muttering, and reached into his white jacket. He pulled out a scalpel which he had taken surreptitiously from an operating table in pathology (the corpse would never miss it) and which he had meant to clean and keep, presumably to pick the crooked, gleaming teeth behind his purple lips, or, possibly, to plunge into himself an inch or so when he felt his flesh had to be mortified. This time, dirty or not, he used the scalpel to pick the spring lock, and, in a minute, the two of them were out of the closet, puffing and grateful.

"Mooky," said Rawson, "you are the limit. Pull up your fly."

"My peach," said Mukerji, smiling the smile of the subcontinent, "you have eight hands at least and you bring out in me all the religion of my forebears. Let us attend that poor man."

Grosbeck's three sons and his daughter were permitted to visit him in intensive care briefly, which they did with the religiosity they knew was expected of them. The sons, two of a mother prior to Madeline, resembled and did not resemble one another. They were knowing, gentle, and courteous to their father once in a while. They knew nothing about him other than the things he had chosen to tell them and he knew nothing about them. They told him nothing at great length. The daughter was thin, passionate, quirky. She was given to avoiding her father by fussing extravagantly over him. She gave him all the attention one gives to those improbable plants in a pot, hanging by ropes from the ceiling. One waters the plants endlessly (the plants wait in hope of eating the waterer eventually and grumble if neglected) and an outsider speculates how long it will take for the hemp to fray and break and pot and plants to fall and crush one's head. How dear the little homely things in life. The relationship between Grosbeck and his children was ideal—that of four *blinde* playing *pishe paysha* with a pinochle deck. Nevertheless, Grosbeck was convinced that he loved them and that they loved him and that that would be evident to anyone with half an eye. It was important to him, too, that he know that he loved them and that they know he loved them and that they know they loved him. And that Madeline knew and so on. If they knew also that *he* did not always love *him*, Grosbeck, well . . . Frequently, this led to quarrels, but otherwise everybody got along fine.

The oldest son said to Grosbeck, "What's shaking, *hombre?*" The youngest, conscious of his surroundings, softly sang a refrain he had composed on a street corner. "La la la. Meat and shit. I like fruit and corn. Kiss my ass. La la la. Meat and shit. I like fruit and corn." Very Anglo-Saxon.

The *buba* in one of the other beds smiled in approval. She was stone deaf. The piece of cancer on the other side of Grosbeck heard nothing. The middle son kept quiet.

The daughter put down a package, placed her hands on her hips, removed her glasses (she could be seen at such times to be quite beautiful) and said to Grosbeck, "Papa, you're such a *pain.*" She picked up the package. "I brought you something."

She held out toward Grosbeck two thick books, wrapped in the paper of as good a shop as she could find in midtown. Grosbeck feigned not to be able to remove his hands from beneath the coverlet and signaled feebly to her with his eyes to open the package. That was the way she wanted it. She fiddled and faddled with the paper and the transparent tape holding it around the books. Tear it, will you, Grosbeck said to himself. It's only paper. She and Madeline always did that and the result was an apartment full of half-torn, chic paper that had been used to wrap presents in, paper that had cost a great deal of money and would never be used again for any reason. There was so much of it around the house it was hard to find a pair of shoes. The daughter came to her senses, realized this was an emergency, that her father had had a heart attack and might likely have a second one if she dallied any further. Bravely, she tore open the paper and revealed the two-volume edition of the Oxford English Dictionary of which, of course, Grosbeck had been the author. This was the complete edition in which the type was so small that it had to be read with a magnifying glass. The glass was furnished with every purchase—lagniappe—and the lot was expensive. That one knew her father like, to coin a phrase, a book.

Two events took place in the four days in which Grosbeck lay pent in intensive care. On the second day, the cancerous man suspired mightily in his slonk of a bed, and, just as it appeared that this bundle of disease might rise from the trough to address some invisible levee, he died and the number of lights and clicks on the machines in back of him was reduced. The *buba* turned to look across Grosbeck in triumph—none of this was new to her; she had buried most of her family and *nudgied* as many of the rest as she could toward the grave—and the effort caused her wig to slip down on her nose, hiding her eyes but not the little twitch flickering over her lips.

"*Zeite gezhint*. Go in good health," she said. "You should only get *noches* in heaven." Relenting.

On the day Grosbeck was taken out of intensive care to a room in which the window gave on the south side of the anchorage of the Brooklyn Bridge, the twitch on the *buba's* face stopped; a mole near the lips sank quickly into the toothless mouth; the face became gaumy, and the *buba* was gone too. Grosbeck was moved out on a cart. In the midst of death we are in life. Hard cheese. Better luck next eon. Pardon me, but you're blocking the door. Taxi!

3

There is nothing in the world like a heart attack to bring a man to the mourner's bench, full of nervous repentance, and to cause other changes in a life theretofore encrusted with the thick black grime and the stiff white grease of habit. Unless, of course, it kills him. In which case, there are other guides. From The Newspaper, which the office had seen to it that he got daily from the moment he got out of intensive care, Grosbeck had plucked this rose: "Please consider this ULTIMATE GIFT TO INFINITY. If you wish to perform an important service at time of death, you may bequeath your body for science NOW!" The advertisement went on to say that there was no charge.

From some ambiguous cleric wandering around the hospital, as these people do, he had received a leaflet, printed on the cheapest of paper and full of typographical errors. That one had said to him, "Come as you are, come to this loving and dear Saviour, who died for you. Be washed with His Blood, believe on His name, and receive remission of sins. He is the only Saviour, without Him you are lost, under the control of the devil."

Then, there was the rabbi who came to see him, having, unlike the cleric with the leaflets, checked the roster downstairs and determined that Grosbeck was a Jew. This reb was a real svingehr, Grosbeck could tell. He wore a beige-colored suit with lapels so wide that he looked like a weather satellite and he was so Reform that, as they say, his temple was closed on the Jewish holidays. He was angling to get out of Congregation Kish Mir in Tuchas in Englewood, New Jersey, into Congregation Hub Im in Drehrd in Tenafly, down the road a way and five thousand bucks a year more in salary. He had demonstrated his broad outlook to the Tenafly board of trustees by eating ham in public and getting himself photographed with Billy Graham at a brotherhood picnic in Kansas City. He had a doctorate of philosophy in voice resonance and glottal delivery, which he augmented by creating bubbles of saliva between the spaces of his teeth. Also, his secretary read book reviews for him and digested the proceedings of various scholarly groups so that there was nothing for which he did not have an answer.

Some rabbi. He performed a ritual resembling a tap dance before Grosbeck's bed, called him "Harvey," asked him to drop in at Englewood when he was on his feet again and even asked Grosbeck whether he would conduct a seminar for the Young People some time on "Journalism: Will There Be a Printed Word After Death? Another View." That, at any rate, was what he seemed to be saying between time steps. He tired Grosbeck immeasurably in the three minutes he was at the bedside. Grosbeck could only imagine what life must be like for the *rebbitsin*, the consort of this descendant of a pillar of the Workmen's Circle. And whatever unfortunate children the two of them might have had. The rabbi stopped dancing his eerie combination of Hora and Hustle after looking at his wristwatch, left his card next to the water pitcher and glass straw at the side of Grosbeck's bed, and went off in search of a Jew less intractable.

What the rabbi did not know and would not have cared much about if he had, was that Grosbeck believed himself to be a changed man. He lay in his bed covered with piles of cards and letters wishing him well and a long life. Some of the letters had actually been written by those who sent them. Others had been dictated, run through an electric typewriter, and signed by a secretary. There was one on heavy, embossed paper which wished Grosbeck all the good things in life, including a plot in a nonsectarian cemetery for him and his family. A small down payment. His life. And there was another from The Publisher, hinting that once Grosbeck was out and around once more, great things were in store for him. Yes, it had not been forgotten that he had been on the paper for so many years, that in his head was the accumulation of wisdom only to be expected of a man of his age, that The Newspaper fully intended to take advantage of it. The Publisher wouldn't tell him what it was. That could wait. First, Grosbeck must convalesce; then, The Publisher would tell him. He signed the letter with his first name.

Grosbeck napped off shortly after receiving it and had a nightmare in which he saw himself running copy and getting coffee from the cafeteria for the reporters, half of whom called him "Boy," and the other half, graduates of schools of journalism who had firmly rejected social Darwinism, called him "Mr. Grosbeck." Any way Grosbeck looked at it in his dream, The Publisher intended to make him a copyboy, head copyboy at best, the kind at whom he had yelled "Boy" himself, even during the years of the Second World War, when all the boys were girls. The dream ended with Grosbeck, the copyboy, spilling a container of coffee over a story intended for the city desk and down the pants of the reporter who had written it. Such was the stuff Grosbeck's dreams were made on. He was still incapable of keeping his malicious unconscious in check. He would dream more kindly the next time, in keeping with the new self he knew must rise from his damaged body. He blinked away two tears of adoration for that new self—it was all he could afford at the moment—and looked through the window of his hospital room, past the flowers wilting quietly on the sill, through the wide pane of glass, filthy because there was a strike of window washers.

What he could see was his idea of eternity: the granite blocks of the anchorage and approaches of the Brooklyn Bridge, the Roman arches let in the approaches covering streets which, until the bridge was built a hundred years ago, were tangles of wooden hovels and red-brick mansions with white Doric columns and warehouses, and, before that, an odorous acre or so known as The Swamp, to which the tanners had been driven by the good burghers who wanted the leather but whose delicate nostrils had been assailed by the smells loosed on the air to make it. Fires burned late and yellow in The Swamp. The years passed. The fetid air—acid, coal, dead animals— cleared. The Swamp had been memorialized in a building over the door of which had been placed a bronze sculpture of a longhorn's head. And now, even that was gone, in its place something which evoked only the successes of real-estate speculators.

Gone, too, Grosbeck knew, was another piece of what he conceived to be eternity: a tiny street on the north side of the bridge. It had been called Hague Street and it led into a dead end against the perfect curve of one of the bridge's arches. Grosbeck had walked often on that dark street, no more than seventy-five feet long, and had been astounded to find on it, backed up to that curve, a tenement, a survivor of all the tearing down which had been necessary to put up the approach to the bridge. There had been doorbells and mailboxes in that tenement and people living in the building, half a dozen names. How mysterious.

Grosbeck would have given a good deal to know who they were, where they came from to this sunless recess, why they were there, where they shopped, what they did. Why had the building not been torn down? Of what use were the windows? All that could be seen out of them was the brick of the arch. Grosbeck had never seen any of the tenants in the building on Hague Street. Angels and devils are all around us and we do not see them. Some delicacy in him prevented him from ringing a bell and forcing a tenant to answer it. He was content that Hague Street and its people should simply be. Oh, do not ask what is it. Let us go and make our visit. And now, that, too, was gone. A fence of heavy steel mesh blocked the arch. Even the street sign was gone. So much had been altered that Grosbeck could not any longer be sure just which arch had sheltered Hague Street. Nor could he bring himself to look at the old street plats to fresh his memory. Since it must be, let it be. Nobody maps eternity.

No doubt about it, The Publisher's letter had aroused in Grosbeck an anxiety and an exquisite, nervous anticipation. He sought to still them in the most quotidian of activities—looking out the window, treating visitors as though he were the Pope celebrating the *Missa Solemnis*, lying in the bed as though it were a catafalque, extending his left hand as though the wedding ring on it were Peter's and half expecting it to be kissed, waiting only for the puff of white smoke to go up to tell him who his successor would be. There is hardly a man who does not long to be present at his death, whose curiosity is not so great that he will not hang on, peering through the veil to see what will happen next. Grosbeck cultivated the other world—in theory—hoped he was pale, and exerted all his strength to be feeble in company, now knowing that he was not about to die. He accepted medications from the nurses as though they were communion wafers and let them wash his body as though they were dabbing at it with the oils of finality. His alb was his hospital nightgown. No mitre for this simplest of pontiffs, no rosary twined in the delicate fingers, no tiny slippers to cover the feet of the Poor Pilgrim so long on the road to Paradise. For prayerbook, at his side was Volume I of the diaries of Philip Hone, gentleman, merchant, once mayor of New York, and in it the vision of hell shared by Hone and Pope Grosbeck: the burning of New York in December, 1835.

December 17.—How shall I record the events of last night, or how attempt to describe the most awful calamity which has ever visited these United States? The greatest loss by fire that has ever been known, with the exception perhaps of the conflagration of Moscow, and that was an incidental concomitant of war. I am fatigued in body, disturbed in mind, and my fancy filled with images of horror which my pen is inadequate to describe. Nearly one-half of the first ward is in ashes, five hundred to seven hundred stores, which with their contents are valued at $20,000,000 to $40,000,000, are now lying in an indistinguishable mass of ruins. There is not, perhaps in the world, the same space of ground covered by so great an amount of real and personal property as the scene of this dreadful conflagration. The fire broke out at nine o'clock last evening. I was writing in the library when the alarm was given and went immediately down. The night was intensely cold, which was one cause of the unprecedented progress of the flames, for the water froze in the hydrants, and the engines and their hose could not be worked without great difficulty. The firemen, too, had been on duty all last night, and were almost incapable of performing their usual services.

(Wood, red brick, brown sandstone fronts, marble, wrought-iron railings melting in the heat. Grosbeck had no need to imagine it. He owned the two somber aquatints of the fire—before and after—by the artist Calyo. What Hone did not tell him about hell in his diary, Calyo showed him.)

ि≈

At this period the flames were unmanageable, and the crowd, including the firemen, appeared to look on with the apathy of despair, and the destruction continued until it reached Coenties Slip, in that direction, and Wall street down to the river, including all South street and Water street; while to the west, Exchange Street, including all Post's stores, Lord's beautiful row, William street, Beaver and Stone streets, were destroyed. The splendid edifice erected a few years ago by the liberality of the merchants, known as the Merchants' Exchange, and one of the ornaments of the city, took fire in the rear, and is now a heap of ruins. The façade and magnificent marble columns fronting on Wall street are all that remain of this noble building, and resemble the ruins of an ancient temple rather than the new and beautiful resort of the merchants. When the dome of this edifice fell in, the sight was awfully grand; in its fall it demolished the statue of Hamilton. . . .

ॐ

(Read on, Grosbeck, read on. Brush away the tears. Reflect in irony. Mourn your city. Oh, the prescience of Hone, and, ah, the pessimism of Grosbeck.)

ॐ

Several companies of uniformed militia and a company of United States marines are under arms, to protect the property scattered over the lower part of the city. I have been alarmed by some of the signs of the times which this calamity has brought forth; the miserable wretches who prowled about the ruins and became beastly drunk on the champagne and other wines and liquors with which the streets and wharves were lined, seemed to exult in the misfortune, and such expressions were heard as, "Ah! they'll make no more five per cent. dividends," and "This will make the aristocracy haul in their horns." Poor, deluded wretches!—little do they know that their own horns "live, and move, and have their being" in these very horns of the aristocracy, as their instigators teach their deluded followers. It forms part of the warfare of the poor against the rich,—a warfare which is destined, I fear, to break the hearts of some of the politicians of Tammany Hall, who have used these men to answer a temporary purpose, and find now that the dogs they have taught to bark will bite them as soon as their political opponents.

ॐ

(Yes, indeed.)

(God will keep you and preserve you, Mr. David Rockefeller. How could so decent a man be so greatly misunderstood? Almost a hundred and fifty years later, Grosbeck reminded himself in reading Hone, this man, benevolent feelings and all, devoted his whole time and labor to creating destruction by comparison with which the Great Fire of 1835 could be seen to be no more than a pile of kindling going up. Grosbeck wore his grudges like an out-of-date suit—shiny with pressing, the seat of the pants woven over and over, but nevertheless getting thinner and thinner. He had become a figure of fun in his denunciations of I. M. Pei, Minoru Yamasaki, Emory Roth, Philip Johnson, Mies van der Rohe, Gordon Bunshaft, who-

ever and whatever. They could not even prevent a roof from leaking
or a window from blowing out. God, said Grosbeck to himself with
so much bitterness that it produced foul breath in him, was on their
side. So, too, was Hone.)

ɞ

It is gratifying to witness the spirit and firmness with which the
merchants meet this calamity. There is no despondency; every
man is determined to go to work to redeem his loss, and all are
ready to assist their more unfortunate neighbours.

ɞ

(Yes, indeed!)

ɞ

A committee of one hundred and twenty-five was appointed,
which met in the evening at the Mayor's office . . .

ɞ

(Lo, the Downtown-Lower Manhattan Association, the Port Authority of New York and New Jersey, Robert Moses.)

ɞ

The utmost spirit and harmony prevailed at the meeting, which
embraced all the best and most influential men in the city . . .
But the unfortunate stockholders, what is to become of them?

ɞ

(File under Chapter 11 of the Bankruptcy Act. Issue debentures.
Merge. Diversify. Conglomerate. [As a verb.] Go offshore. Lie, steal,
cheat, subvert, crush, build, stand back and look, bite the lip, hasten
the money into another country, live anywhere else possible, stave off
the howling mob for as long as possible, collect art, buy computers,
hire the best and most crooked accountants, put the boldest and
most brazen face on everything.)

ɞ

Christmas Day, but not by any means "a merry Christmas." The
recent calamity bears so hard upon the whole community that it
seems unfeeling to be joyful. Philosophy enables many of us to
bear our own misfortunes without repining, and hope spreads its
buoyant wings over the future; but as all are not equally consoled
by the former, or encouraged by the latter, respect for individual
loss restrains all the appearance of mirth which belongs to this
otherwise happy season.

ɞ

As he always did at that passage, Grosbeck laughed aloud. The bed shook. Dr. Salomon walked in the door just then and observed Grosbeck with satisfaction. He waved a long piece of electrocardiogram at Grosbeck and told him how much progress he had made. "But, why are you laughing?" he asked.

"Progress, Doctor," Grosbeck answered. "What is progress?" Grosbeck put the volume of Hone on the bedside table.

"Oh, I see," Salomon said. "Metaphysics. How fancy. I don't get that many high-class patients. Myself, I don't go in for that sort of thing anymore. The Germans cured me of it. High time. I advise the same for you. Give it up. Live in the world. You will be out of here in ten days. I don't think I could put up with you longer than that in a hospital. Office visits are something else. And, when you come, I beg you, no metaphysics. What medicine doesn't prescribe is a palliative for the doctor who has to listen to that. Metaphysics."

Grosbeck protested. "I only asked what progress is, Dr. Salomon. Nothing more."

"That was quite enough," Salomon said. "No more cosmicizing, if you please."

This time, when Dr. Salomon left, something came out of Grosbeck which had never made itself known to him before: an instant— no more—of clarity, clarity so bright in the distances it permitted him to see (behind him, in front of him) that an instant was all he could bear. He finally admitted to himself, without dismay or sorrow, possibly in resignation, possibly even with a languorous purl of pleasure in the belly, something the world had long since conceded him, although it had been singularly forbearing and had not killed him: that he was a crank, a blown-in-the-bottle crank, a bag lady among men, dragging around with him in the shopping bag of his mind the messy accumulations of a life spent missing the point while poking around in dustbins.

He went down the list: a contentious fool, a small, posturing man, terrified in bluster, easily overcome at the first flick of an authoritative hand. He realized (or thought he did), in that instant, that he had swallowed his lump of a life and that his guts could not digest it. He did not care that millions upon millions were exactly like him; they were not he. (The hell with that: say *him* and get it over with.) How otherwise explain himself when he was rusted over with the

effort of not seeing himself. Should he have done it on the free and
easy . . . gone through the textbooks, citing this scholarly article or
that, leafing through Sunday supplements, talking to friends, enemies, teachers (dead, all of them, and doddering if not), acquain-
tances of the wispiest connection, his children, wives, aunts, uncles,
cousins?

Should he henceforth, put himself, piece by piece, under a micro-
scope, whirl himself in a centrifuge? Push himself, prod himself, hold
himself up to the Light of Reason? Hold conferences on himself?
Take counsel alone, or in groups, with psychiatrists, or quacks of one
kind or another? (Fuck you, was the motto inscribed on the Grosbeck gonfalon, the colors of which were black and white.) Read his
horoscope daily? Wear one of those metal bracelets which look like
gold and have inscribed on them, "I'm the best, you hear me?" and
which later leave green rings on the wrist because both metal and
sentiment are base? No, no. He could not, would not.

He remembered how, as an adolescent snotnose, he had run across
a book by a Frenchman named Coué on something the man called
"Autosuggestion." Coué had told people that if they told themselves, "Every day in every way I am getting better and better," they
would. The book had had a tremendous vogue. Grosbeck's parents
had bought it. He had read it and watched. Neither his parents nor
anyone else who bought the book, it seemed to Grosbeck after a
while, got a bit better. Worse, possibly, or stayed just about the same.
He, certainly, did not get better, and from then forward he spat upon
all tinkerers with the mind. He became, without it ever dawning on
him, an ignorant mystic, plucked by his nerves and moved on the
winds. A Jewish redneck. A jock of the mind. A New York City
peckerwood.

He was so very much like so very many. In his bed, Grosbeck
began to cry, to cry for his lost life, his pot belly, his skinny shanks,
and his shrunken behind; for the shoulders, all bone now, and the
sunken chest and the mealy breasts and the veined backs of the
hands; for the gray toenails and the splayed feet; for the heart which
was no good any longer; for the books not read and the things not attended to and the words not heeded; for the lurid bullheadedness
and the cowardice; for the shams only he was convinced he had perpetrated on the world (they had fooled very few); for the
meannesses he had committed and the sidelong invitations of

women he had avoided (had there really been that many? How read an invitation?); for the will he had made, now years out of date; for his children and their children who would be born when he was underground. (The tears flowed fast.) For . . . for . . . for . . . himself, himself alone. (Monster of selfishness!) He pitied himself beyond belief and thought that he was crying for everyone else. Grosbeck had sprung full-blown from the forehead of Confusion or the loins of pointless Noise or the backside of the Unnameable and he had always believed that he had always looked and behaved the way he did; that he was the old, old Naughty Child, peeing into the fountain while scratching his gray hair, sucking a thumb and bawling at the top of his lungs. He had spent his years forgetting as hard as he could what had made him until he had made of himself (he believed) one of those stone figures found underground of which nothing is known, only that there it was and it must have come from something and had some meaning. Had he thought he believed in predestination, he would have kicked a desk and torn up his Social Security card.

Grosbeck had at least ten minutes of glorious bathos all alone. The other bed in the room was unoccupied. It was a time of day when, for some reason unknown to him, the hospital administration saw fit to send no one to his bedside with pills or to pat his pillow or to tuck in his blankets or to raise or lower the head of the bed. He lay slack in it, the pile of letters wishing him well under his hands (why did anyone bother? He would have been furious had they not); the light streaming in, broken up by the strong steel cables of the bridge. The bridge did not judge him as harshly as he judged himself. That's insane, he said aloud, bridges judging anything. Yet, in fact, the great Brooklyn Bridge did look like a judge to Grosbeck, and, in his hazy kind of anthropomorphism, he felt that the bridge had reserved decision on him and that when the decision was forthcoming, it might be kind.

Put it all down to sickness, weakness, and a bad education. He was having such a good, good cry. He had not had one like that since the middle of the Second World War when he received a telegram from the government telling him, without elaboration, that his brother had been a casualty. His brother, Grosbeck had found out a day or two later, had suffered an impacted wisdom tooth while on duty with the Signal Corps in Alaska, and the Army, in its serious, elephantine way, had had him returned to the States in the sick bay of a troop transport, his jaw swollen, his carbine laid under his folded hands as he was carried down the gangplank on a stretcher to a dentist's office. When Grosbeck found out the details, he laughed hysterically for an hour, and then called his parents.

"Tell the cemetery they don't have to open up the plot, Arthur will live. They brought him all these thousands of miles to pull a tooth. He will get the Purple Tooth. With novocaine. The Army is sending the tooth with a lieutenant and a sergeant. Change the sheets on his bed. Put on a fresh pillowcase. Put the tooth under the pillow. The Tooth Fairy is coming."

Grosbeck's parents had not thought that funny. Neither did his brother, whose jaw was still aching when he was sent back to Alaska, not even though Grosbeck had managed to get him on the telephone and say, "We played 'Taps' over your tooth . . . the Unknown Tooth. What? Screw you, too."

Grosbeck had been kept out of the war by a heart murmur. "My brother," was the last thing he said over the telephone, "I have been awarded the Legion of Merit for being the outstanding 4-F on Lexington Avenue between Forty-second and Fifty-ninth Streets. East side of the avenue. The war has been hell. Did you ever hear of anything called 'Lady Hamilton' cigarettes? They're made out of surplus mouse dung. I smoke them for the war effort and it makes me glow for democracy. It's all you bastards who get the steaks and real cigarettes. Come back soon . . . soon Arthur."

Arthur had come back, intact, to make money in advertising and to end his marriage with a fight with his wife in a parking lot in the suburbs. First, she had knocked him down when he wasn't looking, and then he had knocked her down and pulled her by the hair around the car. He had been so drunk that he had been unable to find the car keys. He had planned to run back and forth over her, ignoring the fact that she was too fast for him.

They had had one of those old-fashioned New York divorces in which the unhappy couple hired a hotel room and the wife got the husband's brother to act as the Other Man and the hired detectives burst into the room (the door was left open a few inches) and jotted down the evidence. The judge dozed or nodded, granted the divorce, and the whole thing cost a hundred and fifty dollars, lawyers and hotel room included. Afterward, everybody went out and had dinner in a restaurant. His sister-in-law wore a negligée over her dress in the hotel room, just for verisimilitude, and Grosbeck put on a pajama coat over his shirt. The hotel management was tipped off and the whole thing went off just fine. The only thing Grosbeck remembered saying to his brother's wife in the hotel room was, "Read any good books lately?" She had answered, "No," and that was the last either had said to the other. There had been none of that lousy soul-searching of the kind which now winds up in magazine articles or paperback books. Life may very well have been better in those days.

People kept their goddamned psyches decently to themselves. Grosbeck had brought a deck of cards with him and he and Arthur's wife had played Honeymoon Bridge without saying a word. Honeymoon Bridge. In a pitiless hotel room, waiting for a couple of hired snoops. All the lights on. A couple of prop drinks on the bridge table. Neither Grosbeck nor his sister-in-law had drunk anything. How pinched her face had seemed, how absent her eyes. He had won every game and thought to himself that, in truth, he would rather have been playing poker. And for money.

One of the reporters had found the room *and* the private detectives. He had lived in the hotel for years as so many reporters without wives once did, never understanding how dead such rooms were in such hotels. It was on a side street, just west of Broadway, and had been quite respectable right up to a few years after the war, before the nameless, dangerous filth thrown up by the Amurrican Way of Life moved into it with its drugs, knives, guns, clap, and bad sex. Bad sex to you, if I may make the pun, Grosbeck thought. Bad sex, bad cess. There hadn't been a newspaperman in the place since the mid-fifties, except to follow the cops in when they were removing a couple of bodies. Grosbeck remembered that there had been a framed reproduction of a drawing on the wall of a man and a woman. He had been dressed in white tie, she in some kind of flowing organdy. He had his arm around her waist and was kissing her cheek. Her neck was bent. The artist wasn't very good and had given her a neck longer than that of a swan and made her look as though she had dislocated it. There was a sentiment, in Spencerian script, at one side of the drawing, a little poem. It read,

Pal O' My Heart

Pal O' my heart
—so steadfast and true;
Courageous and helpful
in all that you do;
Cheering, endearing,
sharing a part
Of each gladness,
each sadness
that lives in my heart;
Sympathetic and tender,

the truest best part
Of all that
is wonderful,
Pal O' my heart.

Poor Arthur, poor Beatrice, poor Harvey. Poor hotel room. Poor New York. What did they do to all of you? That was the way John Tully found Grosbeck when he came to visit.

"What the hell's got into you, Harvey? You're a spectacle." He pulled a handful of tissues out of the box on the table next to the bed and wiped Grosbeck's face roughly. "That's enough of that now, you hear me? You're through crying; through, finished, done."

"I've been thinking," Grosbeck said.

"Harvey, forget it. Thinking never was good for you. The last time you did any thinking, you got beat up, lost a lot of teeth and wound up in the hospital. Do me a favor, will you, please? Don't think. It doesn't become you, and, besides, the surgeon general has determined that it is hazardous to your health."

"College humor," Grosbeck said.

Tully was a thin, graceful Irishman of Harvey's age, a political reporter and fixer for The Newspaper; a dandy, a man who had achieved something Grosbeck had not: the talent for concealing himself from the world he despised as much as Grosbeck did. But he was capable of pity and understanding and he lavished it on people like Grosbeck, telling himself that there was something there that other people did not see. To the best of his knowledge, Grosbeck had never taken a bribe as did so many of the people with whom Tully dealt. He knew that he might be mistaken, but he felt for Grosbeck nonetheless. It was he who, so long ago, had arranged for the hotel room and the private detectives, who had lived in the hotel himself. He knew all about Grosbeck's tears and he said to him,

"There *does* come a time when you have to drill a hole in yourself, I guess, maybe a couple of holes and let some of the crap out, but there's no need for this diarrhea, for this carrying on day and night. Don't make me ashamed of you."

"I'm sorry, John. I didn't know you were coming." He looked at Tully piteously—he hoped. Tully would not be drawn. When two men have known each other for as many years as these two had, when both have come to the same distasteful conclusions about everything, neither is apt to be taken in by the other. Tully said—and he knew what he was doing—

"Harvey, you make me feel as though I need a shave or have a thread on my tie. You embarrass me. I thought of lighting a candle for you when this happened, but you know something about my parish? They don't use real candles any more. Just those things you stick some money in a slot and an electric light comes on in a fake candle. So, I didn't do it. That's what I think about your heart attack and your tears." He didn't, but that is what he forced himself to say. "Coin in the slot," he went on, "tears, the whole thing turns off in . . . what . . . twelve hours? Impress me some other way, will you, for the first time in your life." Didactic. Ah, how well Tully knew his man.

Grosbeck got angry. It was good for him. "Dandy," he said, "think about it. What's left? I'll never be the same."

"The same as what?" Tully asked. "I know three or four of you and a heart attack is the least of it." He got up elegantly, but with purpose, from the chair at Grosbeck's bedside. With a single graceful wave of the hand, he swept the pile of letters from the bed onto the floor. He pulled a flower from a bouquet on the night table. Water dripped from the stem as he slapped Grosbeck repeatedly across the face with it. His face was stern. Grosbeck could smell the perfume of the rose petals as they fell on his face and the cool drops of water as they mingled with the remains of his tears. Tully slapped him with the rose until there was no rose left, just the stalk.

"What are you doing?" Grosbeck asked. "Why are you scourging me, Dandy?" Tully pretended to make noises of disgust in his throat. It was difficult. For answer, he pushed the bouquet and the vase to the floor and water poured on the sisal carpet and over the scattered letters.

"I'm tired of you," Tully said. If there were to be another crisis in Grosbeck's life, Tully would make it a lively one, however fake. He would divert this man without hurting him. "Yes, fed up." He did not raise his voice. Tully had thought out carefully what he intended to do when he visited Grosbeck. He harbored the same distrust of science and its prescriptions that Grosbeck did and he was convinced that he knew better than anyone else in the world—Madeline included—how to bring Grosbeck around.

This Bronx Irishman—this Irishman of fifty years before—grew up with a mad, submerged father and a cop grandfather, both of whom (and his mother) had intended him for the seminary, and Tully had learned what is to be done with children. Other people's children. Tully had not gone to the seminary and he had forgotten the Latin he had begun and he had not been pious and submissive and he had become a drinker (within bounds) and he had gone to Fordham University after parochial school (God forbid, in those days, that he should have been sent to a free secular college—City—with all those mockies) and he had fallen away from his religion while living by it. He had read and he had learned how to dress and he had fallen into becoming a newspaperman because God had punished him for not becoming a priest and he had remained a bachelor after one terrible marriage to a woman who should have been the housekeeper to a priest. They had never been divorced, naturally, and Tully went to bed with other women as though he were eating meat on Fridays. He had made himself into a rectitudinous leper, covering his sores as fastidiously as might be in the best of clothing, and sinned and sinned and sinned. What could have been lower, more sinful than to have become a reporter and City Hall greaser of wheels for the powerful newspaper? He tried not to repent and kept his mouth shut.

He had learned how to bring up a child, although he had never had one of his own. Grosbeck was his child and he loved him, and, loving him, he took the stick to him in his own way. Neither he nor Grosbeck would ever enter the seminary, Tully knew, but Grosbeck damned well would pull himself together. Pull himself together! Nobody talked like that, thought like that, anymore. They got their head together, didn't they, Tully said to himself. Like Grosbeck, he would no more have talked so than worn brown shoes with a navy blue suit. Like Grosbeck, he inhabited a world which had long since disappeared. Each pretended that it was not so. Tully did it much better than Grosbeck. But both were tough and would be a long time dying.

Tully had one last scene for Grosbeck before finishing the play he had prepared for this visit. One of the things he and Grosbeck shared was Trollope. Both had read *Phineas Finn*, and Tully had sent Grosbeck a paperback copy to read over again. Whether Grosbeck had or not, Tully did not know. The book had fallen to the floor with the flowers and letters and now Tully picked it up. He had pages and passages well in mind and what there was left of him of priest, father, teacher, brother and Dutch uncle came out in what he read:

> " 'Never think, Duke. I am convinced that it does no good. It simply means doubting, and doubt always leads to error. The safest way in the world is to do nothing.'
> " 'I believe so,' said the Duke."

Tully shook the book at Grosbeck. "You ready, Harvey?" Grosbeck, appalled, enthralled by what Tully was doing in the room of a defenseless man, a man preparing himself for the gravest of eventualities, only nodded, closed his eyes, and placed his hands, fingers apart, at the side of the bed, preparing for it to be shot out the window.

> " 'The safest way in the world is to do nothing,' [Tully repeated]. 'Much the safest. But if you have not sufficient command over yourself to enable you to sit in repose, always quiet, never committing yourself to the chance of any danger, then take a leap in the dark; or rather many leaps. A stumbling horse regains his footing by persevering in his onward course. As for moving cautiously, that I detest.'

"How does that grab you, Harvey?"
"Give me that book," Grosbeck said, with unexpected strength. "You just give it to me." Tully handed it to him. Grosbeck looked down a page. "You got a pencil?" Tully handed him one. Grosbeck underlined something and then looked up at Tully again. "I got one for you, Dandy. You just didn't go far enough. You left this out:

> " 'And yet one must think;—for instance, whether one will succeed or not.'

"Some reporting, Tully. That's typical, typical of you and the way *you* get through life. The last leap in the dark *you* took was when you left Clarissa and moved into that fleabag."
"It wasn't a fleabag then, Harvey. It was good enough for that divorce thing I set up for you, wasn't it?" Tully cleared his throat, straightened his tie and sat down. He said calmly, "You have the instincts of a proofreader, Harvey. Forget how I get through life. Forget the sentence left out. I don't think it was unfair to leave it out. What I read says quite enough. What is that extra sentence?" His

voice grew softer behind the curtain of the confession box. "It's what you're always telling me such things are—an act of supererogation. Jesus. Where do you get such expressions from and why do you use them? It's time, Harvey. Time, time, time. Leap. Just leap. You have never leaped, only hopped. Hoppers come croppers. A leaper is deeper. Get out of here and jump, you mad, mad fool." He hesitated. Then he bent down and embraced Grosbeck. His eyes were wet but not enough for Grosbeck to see.

"Maybe, Dandy," Grosbeck said. "We'll see." We'll see had been the story of his life. "I don't mean to be equivocal . . ."

"Yeah, sure," Tully said. "Certainly not." He stopped at the door. "One last thing, you rotten little anarchist. This is the American way. You don't do what I tell you, I close the iron gate against you."

Grosbeck smiled at the old line from an old comedy. As Tully started to leave the room, he said, "I been watching a lot of television news, John, and, if I may quote, 'One thing we know for sure . . . It is certain that only time will tell.' They really do say things like that, John, I swear they do. Maybe, maybe . . ." Tully closed the door and went away.

At that instant, the light in the window darkened. Through it poured gray protoplasm and shaped itself into a big hand. The hand pulled Grosbeck up to sitting position, propped the pillows behind him, and patted the bedcovers smooth. If there were anything more than the hand, it must be enormous, Grosbeck thought, but he could see nothing. There was, however, a voice somewhere back of and above the hand. The hand grasped Grosbeck's chin and pushed it up and the voice said, gently enough, considering the size of the hand,

"This way, my son, not that. Your friend Tully is right. Dare all and I will sustain you. Have a cigarette?"

Grosbeck answered faintly, "Are you crazy? Dr. Salomon . . ."

"I joke you, *mi hijo*," said the voice. "Later for that. Get you ass out of here. Do the Lord's work."

"What is it?" Grosbeck asked.

"You find out, *mi hijo*. My, yes, you find out. You live, you find out. I work in mysterious ways My wonders to perform. Bet you sweet ass."

"You going to give me much more of that *mi hijo* jive?" Grosbeck asked. Might as well talk The Man's language.

"No jive, my man," said the voice. "Get *down!*"

The voice continued. "I got one more thing from that tight-ass English dude you friend read you. He also say, 'Then I will come and find you,—with a troop of householders. You will come. You will be there. I do not believe in death coming without signs. You are full of life.' H-e-e-e-e-ey! I read, too. Read everything. Nothing I don't know." The voice stopped. The hand disappeared slowly, in whorls, through the closed window. The bridge rumbled with laughter and three trucks blew their tires.

"La la la," Grosbeck sang to himself. Nurse Rawson entered the room.

"Mr. Grosbeck! This *mess!* What on earth have you been doing?" She had a hard time putting reproof in her voice. She and Mukerji had just been at it again and had made their own mess. She put a hand to his forehead and thrust a thermometer under his tongue. She listened to his heart with her stethoscope. She picked everything up, blew away a strand of hair from her nose and tucked it back beneath her cap. "Bad boy," she said. "Bad, bad boy. You're going home tomorrow." She remembered something, looked down, and buttoned the top two buttons of her uniform.

"La la la," Grosbeck sang.

Grosbeck awoke several hours before dawn of the day he was to return to work, still not quite used to the idea of being alive, although
not ungrateful for it. He felt his heart, searched for his pulse and
could not find it, decided that the world was not enough with him
and switched on a small radio at his bedside.

The bedroom flickered with light. Madeline, snoring lightly now
and then at his side, occasionally muttering runes, had left the television set on, the sound down. On the screen, Jean Gabin, the fugi-
tive thief and gunman from the foulest purlieus of Montmartre,
had finished exchanging sentimental reminiscences with his lover,
Mireille Balin, blond, the hardened plaything of a businessman on
holiday in Algiers.

"*Place Blanche.*" "*Ah!*" "*Boulevard Clichy.*" "*Ah!*" "*Place du
Tertre.*" "*Ah!*" "*Sacré Coeur.*" "*Ah!*" "*L'hôtel de . . . de quoi?*"
"*Ah!*" "*Des huîtres.*" "*Ah!*" "*Je t'aime . . .*" "*Bien sur, mon âme.
Moi aussi!*" "*Ah!*"

Pépé le Moko, now, insane with exile, with longing for the *rues,
allées, impasses, boulevards* of Montmartre, for the garish neon, the
pimps and whores, even the tourists, Pépé has decided to leave the
Casbah, no matter what. On the screen, he runs down the thousand
uneven stone steps, the Arab woman who loved and betrayed him
screaming noiselessly behind him, stumbling, reaching her arms
pointlessly after him toward his broad back in its terribly tight jacket.
(The French still make the worst men's clothing in the world.) The
camera concentrates alternately on Gabin's feet in their tight,
pointed shoes (didn't they hurt?), and on the woman's open mouth
and long, lank black hair. (Who did her makeup?). Down, down,
down Pépé runs, down to the stone archway into the city (transfixed
by the unblinking sun) past Arab women nursing children (discreetly, for the censors of the thirties), past greasy stallkeepers ped-

dling couscous and fake jewelry (the taste of both was the same), past idly curious tourists who barely turn to watch, past the hard-eyed, impassive colonial police in the *quartier Arabe* (Pépé le Moko is none of *their* business, just so long as he remains in the Casbah), past the ruined walls and black rookeries (since the sound was down, Grosbeck could not hear the wailing Arab music, played on old American Victrolas with bamboo needles pulling the sound out of the scratched records), and so into the open streets of the city, where Slimane, the detective, waits. Lame, slimy, indefatigable Slimane, who has sworn he will take Pépé, cane in one hand and leaning on it to favor his bad leg, cocked pistol in the other, two Algiers *flics* standing behind him. Out of the *quartier* Pépé pounds. The ship carrying his blond lover, for whom he threw over the Arab whore, and her disgusting sugar daddy is about to cast off. A blast of the whistle and a plume of steam. (No sound, remember.) Mireille Balin stands at the rail. Her eyes, the camera, sweep the heights of the Cas-bah. Nothing. Gabin, back to the camera, stabs himself in the stom-ach. The camera dollies around him. The knife must have been a foot long. Gabin dies beautifully. Slimane is furious. FIN.

Grosbeck sighed as the picture ended and a nondenominational clergyman materialized with a smile and offered jolly matins through a beard. Grosbeck knew he was fortunate not to hear anything. God, ah God, what hath Thou wrought? Have You got any idea of the kind of cleric You're turning out these days? This one wore a turn-around collar, all right, but he had a bush jacket over it and a gold chain around his neck. Very jazzy, very much in tune with the times, probably stoned to the ears on peyote a couple of hours before show-ing up at the studio for the taping. One Cool Priest. He did a lot of waving with one hand (out of control?), on one finger of which he wore a thick, near-silver ring with an enormous stone in it. (Bet the finger's green under it.) He paused a lot to run a thick tongue around lips made of pemmican. He pulled at the beard a lot. There was so much of it from eyes to chin that when he tugged at it, Gros-beck thought of the beard as a backyard overgrown with weeds and dandelions, the priest trying to pull them up. Would he mow the lawn for Easter and stop scandalizing the neighbors? Were there worms in the jaws and gums beneath the beard? Did he sell them to fishermen? Or give them away, in Christian charity? Grosbeck had always been tickled by the spectacle of the religious on television.

Male or female. To tell the truth, he was unable to tell the women from the men. There *were* times when neither had a beard. Father Blather. Mother Fucker. They were at their best when, as now, they could not be heard. Nor did one have to account to them. One had only, as Grosbeck did now, to turn off the set.

In the dark, as Pépé le Moko was succeeded by Pépé the Priest, the world plucked at Grosbeck's brain without mercy through the radio. He listened to the cretinous voices of announcers who hadn't any idea what they were saying, since everything had been written for them, including the pronunciation (sometimes correct) of proper names and difficult words. It always occurred to Grosbeck that it had not been many years since they learned to read by guess in progressive schools which referred their pupils to psychiatrists if they showed any alarming tendency to write whole sentences or spell correctly. Meaning eluded them. To them, Armageddon and armadillo were all one. It was their sworn duty just never to stop, lest cancer cover their throbbing larynxes, leaving only croakings, or, worse, silence—that not to be endured.

They punctuated their sonorous pronouncements with carefully scheduled interludes of bonhomie, a detestable kind of camaraderie applied (and proved profitable, research confirmed) to everything. There were laughs, titters, side remarks, boyish enthusiasms, baritone incredulities, shouts, murmurs, gravities. (All misplaced, bearing no relation to the news at hand.) Gravidities, Grosbeck said to himself. They are gravid as worms. Ho ho ho, you sons of bitches. They also —in the identical manner—sold salve for piles, powders to keep false teeth from falling on the floor; cut-rate vacations to places no sane human being would be found dead in at the season they recommended; banks which swindled depositors while pretending to pay them more in interest than the mines of King Solomon. Gongoresque.

They managed to make of the world the cheapest kind of vaudeville. They were proof that vaudeville had never died. They told Grosbeck of undertakers offering skyscraper burying grounds with drive-in entrances, where funeral rites were conducted before the body was moved out of the hearse onto a conveyer belt and up the elevator twenty stories. (The higher, the closer to heaven—and the more expensive. Would one want any less for one's Loved Ones?) They told, with a leer in the voice as palpable as a look, of oversized women parading for clean air, carrying signs reading, "If you will stop smoking, you, too, can have lungs like mine." Get it? Hey, get it? Got it! They peddled revelations from Doctor This or That how, when one is young, one is apt to float easily and that when one grows older, one is apt to sink. Something to do with fatty tissue and will-power. Or, was it the other way around? And, did it make any difference? Nobody believed it, anyway.

Grosbeck had the deep-seated mistrust of newspapermen for any-thing that was not in print. And even when it was, he was merely less skeptical. He would not believe in the Second Coming on the air, despite every assurance that he was getting it Live from the Tomb. He might believe when he read about it the next morning in The Newspaper with separate vivid color stories—interviews with those living near the place; surly comments from Roman guards clanking around in their armor; possibly an exclusive with the Lord; possibly smudged news pictures of everything a photographer could grab in a hurry ("Hey, God, just one more. Look this way, God!"); *and* an arty shot of the heavens opening to show the blinding sun. Symbolism arranged for in advance by one of the Lord's press agents.

Grosbeck did not like to admit to himself that The Newspaper told many of the same lies as radio or television (at much greater length) and he showed an old-fashioned contempt for them by hav-ing a black-and-white television set and a radio the sides of which were held together with transparent tape to keep it from falling apart. It had tubes.

One item in the endless burble caught Grosbeck's ear, something about an old building. The radio reader had all the architectural de-tail wrong (who has time to look up all that shit and who cares?), but his writer *had* been given the right address. A small miracle. Even The Newspaper got addresses wrong these days. One day, one of its most promising young men dropped dead playing tennis. The obituary writer, flown in the kind of eulogy The Newspaper obliga-torily gave One of Our Own, killed him at the wrong address, in a cheesy saloon two blocks away, just as though he had been getting loaded on bad whiskey instead of taking care of his body. (It might have been better that way, Grosbeck thought; he might be alive today.) The tennis court, in fact, had been located on the site of Edwin Booth's marble theatre (Modjeska closed it with a thrilling throb in her throat), torn down for a department store late in the nineteenth century, and that was the only reason Grosbeck noticed the wrong address at all. The department store, in turn, had been replaced by one of those huge green plastic bags inside of which people paid too much to play games which killed them.

Some time during his stay in the hospital, when Grosbeck had been kept away from news for the sake of his heart, the pack of thieves, liars, and lobbygows who ran the City had decided to pull down still another of the few remaining good-looking pieces of it. This one, a series of linked mansions, had been built shortly after the Civil War by a railroad plunderer and banker for himself and his family, the whole thing in the form of a noble C. The plunderer, inexplicably, had founded an abolitionist butcher-paper magazine.

After he died, the noble mansions had, eventually, in the tortuous way things are done among the rich, fallen into the hands first of a religion and then of a developer, . . . one hundred per cent secular. The developer had won permission from the City to render unto Caesar a fifty-story office building. It had been a long, dirty fight, but he had won permission to put up his thing only after agreeing to keep the façade of the mansions as the lower floor of the new building. The outcry subsided, the investment would be recouped in twenty years and the building would fall down in forty. (The computers had it all figured out. The first printout to come out of the computers read: *Sauve qui peut!*)

The developer had hired an eminent architect of Armenian descent to design the building, a man who had distinguished himself in many ways and won many awards, to say nothing of the fulsome praise of The Newspaper's art and architecture critics (it took both departments to cover someone of his dimensions) for his *Je ne sais quoi*, his *panache* (the word of the moment), his marvelous *sense of place*. The Newspaper's prose on the subject of this man's works had piled up over the years until it resembled nothing so much as a big cake, the cream gone stale and rigid and turned gray and brown. The Newspaper forebore from reminding itself of other things about him.

The Armenian had started out as the house architect for the developer. At that time, he giggled a lot, rubbed his hands together often in a frenzy of desire to please, broke out in sweats and broke pencil points. For his first patron, the architect had created an office which probably represented the only insight in his life. The patron was a very fat man, with cigars stuck in a florid face above double-breasted suits the fronts of which resembled the doors of the Cathedral with which he had done business.

For him, the Armenian concocted a perfectly round office paneled in rosewood, teak, and mahogany. There was a profusion of crystal, silver, gold leaf, marble, Kermanshah rugs, Louis XIV side tables, desks inlaid with bits of ivory, a tantalus, inferior eighteenth-century French paintings and worse modern ones, mosaics filched by Greeks from Byzantium (this was one of the few revenges the Armenian was able to get on the terrible Turks who had killed at least one member of eight generations of his family), and a ceiling made of many-colored glass panels depicting the signs of the Zodiac, at the center of which was a face, a large round sun in yellow quartz, bearing an uncanny resemblance to the developer. All the sun lacked was a Habana Perfecto in its mouth.

The Armenian needed only a fez on his head, baggy pants with bad embroidery running through the waist, and two or three oriental rugs of doubtful provenance over each shoulder; a black vest with colored threads running through it, and turned-up shoes in which he padded silently and deferentially—a shifty-eyed foreign swindler putting one over on an honest American swindler, who, when *he* stole, made no bones about it in the name of Art.

The office was only one of the early successful things the Armenian had created, an apt expression of his Balkan origins and messy ways. There had been many others since: a group of contiguous apartment buildings which had cost the developer an extra million dollars because the Armenian, perplexed where to put in the air conditioning, had blithely guessed wrong; buildings in several cities, the windows of which blew out because of miscalculations of air currents outside and pressures from inside; buildings which resembled mud-and-wood-and-wattle huts, widely admired for their percipient carrying-out of what were hailed as "ethnic" themes, except that they were all forty stories or more high and would have scared the life out of any shepherd in Tashkent.

The roofs of the buildings the Armenian designed leaked. The ornaments he put on them fell off because they were not carved into the thin, flawed stone he put on the steel frames but affixed with a cheap epoxy. The "amenities" (as they were now called) he planned for his buildings (in return for permission to add ten stories)—wooden benches, galleries, brick walkways, muddy frescoes painted by ferociously inferior artists, little, bad, unexpectedly fallen-upon restaurants and shops in waste space, withered trees in huge tubs—that sort of thing—resembled amusement parks deserted when the interurban electric trains were shut down. There were awkward turnings into blank walls or standpipes; things cracked and flaked; establishments went into bankruptcy a month after opening, whereupon their windows were painted violent reds and greens to conceal their emptiness until new tenants could be dragooned into renting them. Dreadful musicians serenaded the sullen office workers eating poisonous foods bought from the near-Victorian kiosks thrown up in the plazas.

More than one visitor to the plaza of one of the Armenian's buildings had just missed being hit by a piece of fake Persian mosaic falling from the marvelous barrel-vault adaptations which were his signature—his memories, he said, of churches of the Eastern Rite. Sometimes what fell was the outsized nose of Saint Athanasius, sometimes the dun-colored shin of Sancta Sophia. A falling communion wafer the size of a discus and much heavier had broken the skull of a woman who (served her right) had only lately ceased being a communicant in the Roman Catholic rite. She sued. She won. The insurance company paid.

"God is just," observed the Armenian. "God struck her down. God raised her up. I tell you this confidentially—whenever I see one of my buildings, my inclination is to walk on the other side of the street. I am joking." It was these two—this Armenian rug dealer and his patron—who had been chosen by The Money to tear down the old mansions. Nobody of any consequence cared. Grosbeck was of no consequence.

The developer had done the rest of the furnishing of the office himself: exotic women with big behinds and great hanging breasts who showed up after working hours, were let into the building by the watchmen, thence up the elevator into the circular office, silent and ready. The developer, they had learned, was harmless. He simply insisted on having them dress (in another room) in the things he had laid out for them.

Corydon Varney (that was the name he had acquired from his father, a scabrous Episcopal priest in Boston, together with his habits, less odd than banal) began to form his visions of unbearable bliss and unspeakable rites thirty years before in the dirty-book stores of that time. He was, really, behind the times now. Modern standards repelled him; they were not furtive enough. The way he went about sex was curiously at odds with the way he went about his business— otherwise, he would not have been a millionaire. Until he had had a small row of buildings torn down to make room for one of his big buildings over on the West Side, Varney had frequented the *établissement* (he insisted on thinking of the place in that way) in one of them for the things he felt he needed. He still remembered his first visit to the place, which he had noticed while walking past and calculating how to buy the whole damned block.

Late one afternoon, he made his way (quickly, for a fat man) from the Madison Avenue office he then occupied to the West Side. Fever had brought a spring to his step; anticipation very nearly blinded him as he walked. He was obsessed. Like so many obsessed people, he was convinced of three things: the first was that no one else was aware of the existence of the place; the second that, no matter how many times he was to go there, the proprietor would not recognize him; and the third was that, because he *willed* it, he was invisible . . . no one would see him coming or going.

The store was in the basement. It could not have existed in the kind of building Varney was going to put up once he got the property. The rent would have been out of the question in a cottage industry of this kind and any air of mystery, shame, or transgression would have been dispelled. *Slyness* was still the watchword here.

The building was a four-story tenement on a twenty-five-foot front; it extended seventy feet to the rear, with almost no distinguishing marks on its face. Vernacular, no ornament. It had been built just before the Civil War; it had not yet been necessary for builders to tempt immigrants with elaborate façades or stone carvings (or carvings cast in cement) to hide the interiors of the prisons they put up. The plate-glass windows of the establishment had been painted with black enamel as had the cast-iron pilasters at either end of the windows, and the cast-iron balusters on the five stone steps leading down. Four. One piece of stone was gone, replaced with an indented, skid-proof piece of steel. A wooden sign, white letters on black field, said only APPAREL FOR THE STAGE. Not what kind of apparel; not what kind of stage. One pressed a buzzer at the rusted metal door. Inside, the proprietor pressed a button which opened the door, and the visitor was faced with him and his works in uncertain light.

"Nice to see you again, sir," he said to Varney. Wrong, thought
Varney. Oil ran in the man's voice. The hand he extended had fat
but nimble fingers, needle-pricked and no longer sore, the knowing
fingers of a tailor. The white scalp was inlaid with oily strands of
hair. (Had the oil of the voice leaked through?) He wore a brown
vest over a white shirt, pants of good cloth in navy blue, and, around
his neck, like a *tallis*, a tape measure.

"What do you mean, 'Nice to see you, again'? I've never been here
before." Varney was about to continue, "What would I be doing in
a place like this?" when the absurdity of the impulse stopped him.
He had been the buzzer—had he not?—and there, before him, was
the buzzee.

He could see they were not alone. There was a stupendous woman
with red hair, accompanied by a tall man. The man had a snout and
he snuffled; his voice was catarrhal. He had the huge, well-propor-
tioned woman before a pier glass framed in scratched mahogany and
kept turning her around and around, enjoining her to look at herself
in certain ways, making suggestions. She shook her crateful of breast
at him, stroked her pelvis, shook her behind, made chicken noises
and waggled a finger at him. The tall man looked pleased at himself.
They made purchases, she mincing around the tables on which
things were laid out. Short steps. High heels. The air was foul with
the odor of fabrics and perfumes and bodies washed only casually.
Then they left.

"I must have been mistaken, sir," said the shop owner. He took
gold-rimmed eyeglasses off, revealing a pair of marbles resembling
those agates of no color. He rubbed a nose of distrustful shape and
put the glasses back on. "So many gentlemen in the course of a
week, over so many years. Now, had you come in with a lady, I
would have been sure. But, as it is . . . a mistake. A natural error.
The eyes are still fine for close work. The memory? Another thing."
He placed an elbow in the palm of one hand, and, with the other,
caressed his nose. "You might say I have a distinctive clientele and
that I should have known better. Perhaps it is because," he said,
". . . because"—allowing himself the faint outline of a grin—"they
all have something in common." A look of complicity followed.
"No?"

The voice, with its inflections of Yiddish and Cockney, did not
imply; it insisted; and the client did not infer; he knew. The propri-

etor's name was F. Barger. It was on the business card he fished out of a vest pocket. The card looked as though it had been passed around and returned to him. F. Barger, of Whitechapel, taken to the United States in the steerage of one of those Cunarders, the names of which ended in "ia," and brought up on the Lower East Side.

F. Barger's father had carried bolts of cloth from store to factory. He had died when he was almost ninety, blown over in a high wind while trying to board a trolley car with one of those bolts over one thin shoulder—hip broken, terminal pneumonia, wooden coffin, quick, noisy burial, *shiva* sat on orange crates, *yartzheit* glasses burning in the dark living room of the tenement on Eldridge Street. F. Barger's mother had been a seamstress, so the devoted son had been born, as the saying goes, with a needle in his hand. He had turned to costume design. For vaudeville first; then, burlesque; Broadway had eluded him. Finally, he had fallen into the intense private trade he now carried on. APPAREL FOR THE STAGE was, well, not entirely a sham. All life is a stage, no?

"Was there something special you had in mind, sir?" asked F. Barger.

"Special?" asked Varney. "Special. Umm." It would have suited him (he was still young) not to put these things into words; unspoken intimations, rather. But that was not possible in this place. F. Barger would not permit it. He must gauge the deeps of the customer, force him to *say*. None of this take-the-first-thing-lying-around-pay-and-get-out. Nothing hurried or careless, oblivious of fabric and workmanship, so impersonal. F. Barger, the guildsman, understood well the symbiosis of buyer and seller in this trade. Here was no ten-cent store, no mass-produced *dreck*. The integrity of Worth could have been no higher, for all that L'Atelier Barger stood in a slum. Barger took Varney by the arm.

"Permit me, sir," he said. "It strikes me that while we both have the same objectives, you, sir, have not yet faced up to the specific needs of yourself and the lady. Ladies? No, I would say not. Lady, then."

Varney's teeth were set on edge; at the same time, he found himself experiencing the beginning of a chill of pleasure which had sent him to F. Barger in the first place. "Really . . . is all this necessary?" The question was whispered.

"Of the utmost necessity," said F. Barger. "Especially when, as in this case, the lady cannot be present for fittings."

"Fittings? Are you serious?"

F. Barger drew himself up. "Serious, certainly, sir. Do you doubt me? Is it so unusual? Is it? Think! Here *you* are, are you not? It is only one more step and I would be highly gratified should you come to it. In the meantime . . . height, weight, proportions, sizes . . . texture of skin, color of hair. Little idiosyncrasies you have observed in her, possibly?" He kept hold of Varney's arm, and, with the other hand, motioned around the dark shop and workroom, the only cleared space around the sewing machine. "We have our *prêt-à-porter*, of course . . . I have a little French as you can see . . . but, when a man like yourself, so obviously a gentleman, visits us for the first time we like to let him know we are prepared to extend ourselves . . ."

"Mr. Barker, please." Varney's skin had begun to tingle.

"Barger, sir, Barger, if *you* please."

"Barger, then . . ."

"May I suggest . . ."

"Look," Varney said. "All I came in for . . . I just happened to see your sign . . . were a few attractive things my wife can wear at home . . ." At that time, it was true. ". . . And I would like to take them home with me today." Mrs. Varney was not exactly inhibited, nothing like that; she enjoyed herself, but she did not linger on the way, she did not drink, and she removed her makeup before surrendering to her husband. "I want to surprise her. Besides, ah, I don't think she'd take to fittings. She's a busy woman. I know her sizes . . . I don't think we have to bother with textures, idiosyncrasies, that sort of thing . . . I have a pretty good idea of what she'd like." (What Varney wanted?)

"No offense taken, sir," said F. Barger. "It will have to be ready-to-wear, then. But, had you given any consideration to cut and color and fit, to the *kind* of material . . . to *access* . . ."

"Access?" asked Varney. "Oh, sure, access." He essayed a snicker. "Let's have all the access possible."

"Immediate? Time-consuming? Just the suggestion of difficulty? Simply the outlines of the garment?"

"I don't know," said Varney. "All at once." F. Barger smiled.

From then on, the atmosphere was somewhat lightened. F. Barger spoke more freely; hinted less; made so bold as to; surrendered Varney's arm as the two men moved through the narrow aisles past counters heaped with articles, walls on which had been tacked illustrative patterns and photographs. (Patterns? Photographs? Varney was incredulous.)

As they careered over the splintered wood floor, littered with scraps of material, an occasional glittering sequin, cardboard boxes of varying sizes, whorls of dust here and there, F. Barger expatiated, appearing to nudge Varney without actually touching him; winked one eye or the other; blinked both; gestured expansively, supremely confident of what it was that men and women wanted out of his line of work; related how well he could satisfy requirements through an artistry born of the years in vaudeville and burlesque; how long and thoughtfully he had labored over these creations of his. He asked Varney, as he did all his customers, "Do me a favor . . ." He beseeched, almost. "You want to do me a real favor?" Varney wanted to do him no favor, nothing, save to buy what was making him itch, hand the man money, get out on the streets again. The fetid air of the streets was infinitely preferable to the sickly miasmas surrounding this man. But by now, on his travels through the store with Varney, F. Barger was caught up in his own dreams.

"I want," he said to Varney, "you should . . . Let me put it this way. You ever take pictures? Photographs? I would be grateful to you if you took pictures of the lady in whatever garments you are pleased to choose. I have no doubt of your ultimate taste and of my guidance. So, if you must, alter the face, eliminate it. Faces, if I may make the joke, are for Max Factor. The photographs help me in my work. You would not believe the differences from lady to lady. Quarter inches, eighths of an inch, sixteenths. The curves, the angles. Anatomy. I am an anatomist." He stopped, radiant.

"So, you only have time for ready-to-wear. Ready to take off, no? Pity." He made a noise in his throat. "The garments we will choose will grace her. Believe me. They will be a tribute to her, a tribute to you. She will be more than you brought to her, and, I say this with all the strength at my command, she would be less you didn't put them on her. What they give you elsewhere these days . . . Take my word for it, my things are not accident."

Varney's hands trembled as he picked up, discarded, finally selected, things. F. Barger's hands moved to dissuade him from this or that; his eyes gave assent to that or this; he made *moues* of doubt with his mouth.

"In such a small way I started," continued F. Barger. "Years before La Guardia shut down the burlesque houses. Variety called me first and I listened. There is no one left like me. They *think*, some of them, they're like me. They are nothing. Do you find my creations in Saks Fifth? Bonwit's? Bergdorf's? I will make a joke . . . Peck & Peck? Gone. No. Never. You must find me and my creations in this . . . this what? . . . this *hole*. [I own this hole, worm, thought Varney.] I am no thinker, but I know the value of a hole, a basement; dark, light only here and there, just enough to show the *paillettes* . . ." He said *pale-ettes*.

"The exquisite shaping of the panties, the chemises, the jackets, skirts, dresses, blouses . . ." He held up things. "You see? The departure from the expected just so much. *Too* much and we have vulgarity. Even in these matters, the dividing line between vulgarity and inspiration of the kind of which I am capable exists—so delicate, so fine. Those two you saw in here before . . . I did my best to make a silk purse out of a sow . . . But what is a conscientious workman to do if the man is a pig? We must all compromise, must we not? Taste, taste, above all, taste! Observe the brassieres." He pronounced the word *brazhaires*; for him, lingerie was *londgeray*.

"Passementerie," F. Barger said, out of his madness. "Gimps, braids, cords, beads, the right buttons. I prefer buttons to zippers, but I go along with the times. Zippers, if they must. How many *schlock* stores you find passementerie in these days. Silks. I look long and hard for silks and I pay for them. The chemical trash does terrible things to the skin of the wearer; it is an insult to the fingers of the feeler. I go down in the district and buy and make. That what I make should even be called *londgeray* or skirts or blouses . . . They are . . . I been to the Museum of Art, they can't match for creation what I do, the Egyptians, the Greeks, the Romans, those French ladies. I am a man educated in what is wanted . . . Educated!"

Varney experienced a feeling of suffocation and thrills and increasing agitation. He had been made privy (privy!) to the mind of an artist, something he would never be.

F. Barger veered a little. "My wife, God forbid she should ever wear such things. Not for her, a girl from the *shtetl*. But, for you, your lady, all those ladies . . . all that riant flesh."

"What's that?" Varney asked.

"Riant," replied F. Barger, "laughing, gay, smiling . . . Understand? I read it, I looked it up, I know no better description, none more fitting. Fitting, understand? Somewhere in all of us, the most humble, the artist sits. I got a collection photographs my customers send me because I understand them and they understand the artist. Satisfaction guaranteed and given. I don't show the pictures; they're not like . . . how to say it . . . the tailor's catalogue to be displayed for the customer to pick what he wants. *My* customers, *my* people have in their heads what they want and I make it and I don't repeat. The photographs I work from *not* to repeat and I don't show them. However, I do make an exception, you understand . . . If the inspiration in the buyer is lacking . . . if . . . understand? If you would care to . . ." Varney wanted very much to, but . . . another time. The day was getting on.

"Front, back, side," F. Barger was saying. "Standing, sitting, bending. Fully dressed, partly dressed. Never naked, of course. Otherwise, I would be out of business. I am a sworn enemy of nakedness. In the beginning . . . What happens in the course of an evening is the business of the clients . . . their fancies, their beds, their floors, their twistings and turnings, their imaginings built on my imaginings." Saliva gathered in the corners of his mouth. "Lift this, rip that—yes, rip—throw this here, that there, advance, move back, move forward, stand up, sit down, contemplate . . . But, enough . . . The ready to wear . . . No . . . no monotony, even in that. Enough styles to go around. Around the lady . . . any lady . . . my small joke. Much to vary, to change, ever so little, one different from another. And, never more than three, four, five to a line. It takes time, thought, ingenuity, invention. Everything gives way when you want it to give way. Like . . . like . . . Would you believe, I made breakaway suits for burlesque comedians? The experience was invaluable . . . only a matter of adaptation for what I make now . . ."

By now, Varney felt a little drunk. He boldly held up brassieres, chemises, dresses and skirts and jackets—if they could be called that —and examined them under the uncertain light. F. Barger had become bold enough, too, now to slap certain of them contemptuously out of Varney's hands. "Not for you," he said sharply. "Not for that lovely lady of yours. For *nafkes*—whores—maybe, but not for her. I judge her by you. And, the very little you told me, I *know* her tastes.

Still a little reluctant, but curious. This is not your ordinary department store. Here," he said. "Here and here and here," draping things over Varney's arm. "Take and take and take. This, but not that. It may be different later, but now, listen to me. Would I steer you wrong?" He shook his head slowly from side to side. "God forbid."

Varney had pulled down the row of small buildings and put up his big one and F. Barger had died a year later, leaving behind the wife, his catalogue and an apartment somewhere in the bowels of Brooklyn. Years later, the likes of F. Barger disappeared too. His disordered Victorian dreams could be found on the racks and counters of every department store and the kind of stores that called themselves boutiques because they were small. Openly displayed. Separate stores for homosexuals, transvestites, people who fancied cheap boots, black leather, chrome-plated handcuffs and chains, one kind of degradation or another; side by side with tons and tons and tons, in bookstores, of writing proclaiming new freedoms for everyone—for men, women, children, dogs, cactus, jacaranda, the starving people of the Sahel, beginning stockbrokers, shyster lawyers, do-good lawyers, misunderstood wool hats, misunderstood bankers, politicians and industrialists, spastics, paralytics, hot-dog peddlers, cabdrivers, murderers, astronauts, cosmonauts, camel drivers. So much understanding had been thought up that the interval between wars grew shorter and shorter.

Varney, his purchases made, wrapped, and paid for, saw a torn, foxed drawing on the wall, its brown edges curling away from the tacks with which it had been put up. It depicted a woman's shoe with an unbelievably high heel, a shoe obviously not meant to be walked in. He was attracted by it and asked F. Barger, "You sell shoes, too?" His throat felt constricted.

Barger smiled again. "I have a man comes in on order. On order, you understand. Takes time. He is very highly thought of. Like me. If, eventually, your lady so desires . . . But, she must come in."

"I'll talk to her about it," Varney said. Margot? Doubtful.

"Talk it over with her. Let her get her feet wet. Another joke."

"Don't shoes like that hurt?" asked Varney.

"Hurt? They hurt. They are supposed to hurt. For that, you don't need no psychiatrist to tell you. Better a podiatrist. But, the ladies like them. They like them best when they can tell Mr. Marino . . .

that is his name . . . 'Give me a little higher here and more cut out
there . . . very, very high. Can you do it? Will they be too tight? I
guess so . . . you can't avoid that, can you?' They know it is unavoid-
able. But the rewards . . . The poster you see? That is nothing to
what he can do. I have seen the finished product. I have told him
more times than I can remember, 'Mario, you need a better ad than
that.' He won't change—like me. He tells me . . . he jokes with me,
too . . . 'Barger, my shoes don't need advertisements, they can stand
on their own two feet.'" He folded his hands over his stomach.
"Marino has integrity."

Varney brought the afternoon to an end. He had been in the shop
for the better part of two hours. He had paid in cash. The amount
was not inconsiderable. The goods had been put in a long, dusty
white box which said, on its cover, DEMOPOLIS . . . FLOWERS . . .
FUNERAL OFFERINGS . . . FLORAL ARRANGEMENTS OF ANY KIND. The
proprietor shrugged. "I got a bargain on the boxes. What does it
matter? These *are* flowers. *My* flowers."

Varney made his goodbyes, climbed the steps to the street (how
heavy his feet felt) and went off to try out his paraphernalia on his
wife. He had bought her flowers, taken her to a restaurant (hastily),
and, finally, at home, trotted out the paraphernalia. He had made her
(reluctantly) and himself drunk. She had sobered up at once, sighed,
submitted, understood, writhed perfunctorily and given the both of
them a night as filled with passion as poached eggs. The articles
disappeared. Their couplings continued as antiseptically as though F.
Barger had never existed. Varney took his fevers, together with his
work, to the office. All was understood. There was no forgiveness on
either side. There was nothing to forgive. Mrs. Varney, her nose
pinched, devoted herself to good works, collecting modern paintings,
and busyness of one kind or another which filled her days and left
her husband in peace. Sometimes, they appeared together in public
at a good work of hers.

As for Varney, his Armenian architect had taken him to a Greek
nightclub near Pennsylvania Station and there he had developed a
taste for fat women who undulated to the music of bouzoukis and
sour clarinets, the tinkle of finger cymbals, and the warnings of snare
drums.

These women had eyes of obsidian rimmed in green paste and silver powder, eyes which saw nothing. Their cheeks were of ocher,

which made them seem to have jaundice. Their fingernails and their toenails were painted the red of dried blood. They danced in their bare feet and their amazingly slender ankles were dirty. Their hair was black, always black, and long, to the waist. Their bodies were powdered white from neck to ankle where the dirt began. As the evening wore on, sweat ran through the powder and the streaks made rills, folds in the abundant flesh. They were built like vases.

Most of the customers were men and their attitude toward the belly dancers was one of innocence and a terrible passion which they expressed by getting up from their tables, dancing a few steps with the performer and then stuffing bills in her brassiere, and, even more brazenly, deep in the girdle where it lay just above the great hips and the behind like a stand of trees covering hills.

The dancer never so much as nodded, but the finger cymbals acknowledged the money in new frenzies of tinkling, the stubby hands at the end of the round arms curled more wildly and the navel in the pudding of the belly said Thank you, thank you, thank you, and she continued to pad about the hot, dim, clouded, odorous room silently to the screaming music of Turks, Armenians, Greeks.

The men, frustrated at her and yet satisfied with the expression of their admiration, walked stiff-legged back to their tables. But it was not enough. They drank from any glass which had anything in it. They pulled the men they had come with to their feet and danced with them—muscular as men are, graceful as the belly dancers—and everyone cheered and applauded and threw the pits of black olives or broke plates, as was expected of them. No body touched any other body.

One belly dancer succeeded another without interruption. The olive pits and the broken plates made the steps tricky and dangerous, and busboys made their way among the dancers and swept olives and cheap crockery out of the way. It went on and on in what Varney very nearly took to be a dream, in what the Armenian architect sensed so cunningly was the putting of flesh into Varney's dream. The perfect client. The perfect pimp.

Fashion had not yet found places of this kind the first time the architect took Varney to one of them. Pennsylvania Station was still standing then and the Armenian did not neglect to take Varney into the station to lecture him on how part of it was an adaptation of the Baths of Caracalla, and so on. A pinch of culture, the Armenian laughed, a spoonful of sex, a glass of ouzo. What more could life offer?

The Greeks who ran the little clubs were real Greeks, the belly dancers imported from the Piraeus. The Greeks kept them in tiny apartments above the clubs in the dingy old four-story buildings in all the blocks around the magnificent railroad station. The dancers were paid very little. Half the money stuffed into brassieres and girdles was taken by the boss and the girls were threatened with deportation if they so much as opened their mouths. Once in a while, they were taken for walks in the neighborhood, their bodies concealed in ugly cotton housedresses. Most of the time, they were forbidden to leave their rooms. Mad with boredom, mad with the lust they simulated, they were overtaken by the genuine need. Then, they made love to one another in their filthy quarters, lying on split mattresses and tearing at one another's hair and muttering all of the words they had heard as very young children from sailors in the Piraeus. When they had had enough of it, they slept—sodden, sore, naked, unbathed, the streaked makeup giving them the faces of zebras. Six of them shared a single tub in the hall of the old-law tenements, and, nightly before the clubs opened, they were made to bathe and cleanse themselves.

They were very simple girls. Under guard, they went to worship at a Greek Orthodox church in the neighborhood. Other times, under the blackest of threats should they not come back, they were let out to satisfy the needs of trusted clients of the clubs. It was with one of these that Varney first found the kind of fever which puddled his brain and made his life complete.

The Armenian architect had gone to the back of the room to talk to the boss. Their conversation had been a series of deferences, cartouches of gestures, which, if captured on paper, would have resembled the obscene at its most rococo. The odors emanating from the kitchen had been suffocating—decaying lamb, rotting grape leaves, rancid rice and spoiled olive oil—but the Armenian had breathed them in with pleasure. They, too, were the smells of sex. Sex existed only east of Vienna. The Mediterranean, the Adriatic, the Aegean, the Ionic, the Sea of Crete and the Sea of Marmara (and the marmoreal bodies). Essentially, the Armenian was a hot, simple man, unable to swallow the notion that sex existed at the mouth of the

Mississippi or the rising of the Ohio or in the highlands of the Hudson. The boss, of the same mind, picked his nose and nodded.

"No checks," he said, in the *lingua franca* of his kind.

"Of course not," said the Armenian, pulling disorderly piles of money from a pocket. That would go down on Varney's bill as another draftsman.

One of the women had gone off with Varney to his office at three o'clock in the morning, after changing her makeup, which could not conceal the brave mustache to which the customers paid no attention while she was performing. She had very little English, but she exclaimed over everything in a harsh voice. In Varney's office, she undressed and walked around, picking up objects and putting them down. She might as well have been dancing for him. She knit her brows.

"Music," she expostulated. "T'ank you. Next time. Better." She displayed her flesh in archaic poses, wearing the things he gave her to put on, and ran a finger over her upper lip before attempting to kiss Varney. He blinked as she pulled open his fly and then entered into the spirit of the thing. She curried him, milked him and made butter of his fat body. She made noises in a tongue which was neither her own nor anybody else's. She slapped his face with an enormous breast and he spanked her on a behind at once large, richly shaped, and hairy. Oh, how they romped and ravened and muttered and chirped and groaned; subsided on couches at intervals; danced—he clumsily, she leading him in the only steps she knew. A clock ticked on the wall. A watchman knocked on the door.

"Working," Varney got out in a strangled voice.

"Pssssss," said the woman, and tittered. Altogether a satisfactory night for Varney. He got her out of the building, past the watchman, who suddenly went blind when a twenty-dollar bill was pressed into his hand.

Later, Varney had put in the best record player he could find at the time and consulted his architect for the right kind of records, which he bought at small shops in the Greek neighborhood along Eighth Avenue. The woman had been dead right. The women who succeeded her felt the same way. The music raised them to heights until then unimaginable to Varney. It made poetry of a simple commercial transaction. Who would have imagined such stimulating music from an Egyptian singer in a Cairo recording studio or a

Greek woman past her best years making records in Athens? Varney paid for a succession of these women. They left him exuberant. Unwontedly, he sang to himself from time to time, "Life is just a bowl of cherries,/ Don't take it serious/ It's too mysterious."

But, alas, things changed as the years passed. The immigration people, in an aberrant spasm of reform, cleaned out the girls from the Piraeus and sent them home. They tried to deport the boss, but Greece had enough troubles without his kind—it refused to accept him. The club remained open, but the belly dancers now were ambitious little Jewish, Irish, and Italian girls—even housewives. They worked regular hours and then went home. They earned salaries and kept whatever was stuffed into their brassieres and girdles. They gave classes and taught others who wanted to express themselves. Belly dancing acquired the same cachet as Yoga or Christian revivalism.

This depressed the boss, who took to spitting in the salads in the kitchen, and it depressed the aging musicians who tried to make the new belly dancers stumble by varying tempos without warning. Their bitterness knew no bounds when the new customers—few of them Greek—misunderstood this for new steps.

If the new race of belly dancers sweated, they did so politely, and their ankles were clean. Try as they might, they were too wholesome. But business was never better: the club and the others like it were *discovered* by The Newspaper, the magazines, photographers and writers. Skinny models were posed in front of fat bouzoukis in the newest Greek fashions dredged from the minds of designers whose ideas of Greece came from travel posters and bad movies made in Corsica.

The boss did not benefit quite as much as he might have. Now, he had to pay not only the police, but the girls as well, and the gangsters who invariably knew a good thing when they saw one. The boss gave in when they broke three fingers on the hand of the bouzouki player. He sold the place to a corporation he knew nothing about, represented by a lawyer who scratched at his crotch, handed him papers to sign and a reasonably large check, and was never seen again in the club. Varney was forced to go elsewhere for the kind of women he had fixed on. They were always to be found somewhere, unaffected by changes in the philosophy of woman's place in the universe or the vagaries of the Bureau of Immigration and Naturalization. It is true that, privately, some of them preferred disco music to Middle Eastern music, but, when all was said and done, the two kinds of music did have something in common—they were sufficiently monotonous not to interfere with sex.

Varney played one kind of music or another for the newer women and he was no longer put to the inconvenience of having to stay up late in Greek nightclubs, since he made an arrangement for the women to come to his office at the close of *his* business day and before the beginning of *theirs*. They stayed no later than eleven o'clock, and they had the advantage of being fresh. After all, Varney was growing older and more set in his ways, pickier and less eager to go out of his way.

When he was through, he sent the women down the elevator, seeing to it that a cab was waiting to take them to work while he went home in a limousine (leased, of course; everything tax-deductible, even the women), tired, exhilarated, a little drunk perhaps. There, he would toss his leather briefcase on a sofa, kiss his wife, accept a cup of the Turkish coffee he had come to like, talk, be talked at, and go to bed, there to dream of debentures, futures, options, and binders on plots of land the size of Rhode Island. He was an outstanding citizen of the City of New York and Grosbeck had long hated him, among many others, for what he had done to the city Harvey foolishly believed was his.

Grosbeck was not entirely stupid, though. In bed still, he divided himself in half and said aloud: "Those people are beneath your contempt.

"Absolutely, but while I'm remembering that, I also have to keep in mind that that race of vermin beneath my contempt also controls my life and feeds me the steaks from which I get the energy to fulminate.

"Parlor pink!

"We'll see, we'll see. Tully, Madeline, everybody, I said *we'll see*.

"Bullshit," he concluded, and sighed, sighed as he had at the death of Pépé le Moko.

The day began to announce itself to Grosbeck. He switched off the radio as some mewling voice was telling him about hardy perennials. The inanity of it got him to stop talking to himself. Outside, the air was chill and Phoebus 'gan arise: the son-of-a-bitching garbage truck banging and roaring and whining the length of the block. The banging was rage, the whining unrequited love. Nobody loves a garbage man, particularly if his civil-service pension is bigger than that, say, of a bibliographer of materials on Medean potsherds.

The light was coming through the venetian blinds, and Grosbeck got out of bed, lifted them a slat or two and looked out the window. As is not uncommon in those who have had a heart attack, he moved as though he were a rare piece of Meissen which might shatter at an unkind word. The sun coming up in New York was no bargain. Even on the best of days, it looked like nothing so much as a burning crouton in a bowl of rancid pea soup. The garbage truck departed with one more spiteful banging of cans and a last whine.

In the apartment buildings all around him at this hour, there were (a) people breathing stertorously in the kind of sleep that sped them from one end of life to the other; (b) people scratching at themselves in their sleep with one hand and scrabbling at the bedclothes with the other; (c) lovers of any number of sexes, sweet or foul with the excesses of the night, uncoupling, barely stirring, rearranging themselves to meet the day or to avoid it drunken or drugged; (d) people fumbling for aluminum crutches while they regarded the livid end of a leg which no longer had a foot on it and peered over the side of the bed to see whether the plastic foot and its straps were in their proper box; (e) innocent children with tousled hair renewing their strength, the better to be able to fight on against parents and teachers for another day, dried dribbles of chocolate affixed to a corner of their petulant mouths; (f) the dying; and (g) the recent dead. (Surprise!)

Among these, in his building—although Grosbeck and the police would not know it for days—was a respected professor of languages at a university only a few blocks away. He had sexual tastes acquired at an early age which overwhelmed him at just about the time he got tenure at the university—at which point, as everybody knew, they couldn't have got him out of his chair even for buggering goats in Washington Square Park under the bust of Alexander Lyman Holley (1830–1882), "Foremost Among Those/ Whose Genius and Energy/ Established in America/ And Improved/ Throughout The World/ The Manufacture of Bessemer Steel . . ." The professor believed his little peccancies to be secret. They were not; they were well known to some of the tenants—not including Grosbeck— through the agency of a skinny, eccentric woman who chose to do her washing in the laundry room between four and six o'clock in the morning, smoking, smoking, smoking (Grosbeck understood *that* almost better than anything else in life), while the machines ate money and went through their querulous sequences of wash, rinse, spin—the history of the race, the music of drudgery—recapitulated in thirty minutes.

She read magazines that had been filed with the other tenants' garbage (leaving her months behind the times) and hummed to herself while the machines sang to one another. Over all this noise, she heard the lobby door open at the urging of a key put uncertainly into the lock. The lobby was hidden to view around a corner of the laundry room, but she heard the footsteps of the respected professor of languages. (There was no one in the building with whose habits, characteristics, clothing, and hours she was not familiar.) Behind the professor's, she heard the footsteps of a younger man. At it again, she said to herself, breaking off her hum, then nodding and returning to hum and magazine. She heard the elevator door open and close behind the two of them. That's him, all right, she said, having calculated correctly that the elevator had gone four floors to the professor's satiny love nest.

Her percipience was worthy of any cause she chose to direct it at. Instead, as had become quite common in New York, she had a job with a foundation which paid her well and the purpose of which, when asked to do so, she described as "screening criteria." This dumbfounded older people, accustomed to such things as "buying," "selling," "practicing law," "manufacturing"—whatever—and satisfied the aggressively ignorant young, themselves proudly incapable of measuring twelve inches on a foot-long ruler.

When the professor was found, he was on his knees before a bookcase, looking, from behind, as though he were searching for a Pushtu dictionary. However, he was naked; his hands and feet had been bound with an extension cord from a lamp; his back was bruised badly; several ribs had been broken; and, when he was turned around, it could be seen that his throat had been cut—inexpertly but conclusively—and the apartment had been robbed. Had he and the young man quarreled over price? Had there been a lovers' quarrel? The young man, whoever he was, had ignored several pieces of paraphernalia intended to stir ardor in the user. The professor may have been mourned by his colleagues (if he had any family, none of its members acknowledged themselves), but not by the tenants. He had a sharp tongue and a manner so condescending that he seemed to fill the elevator, and people would let it go rather than ride with him. But, when the police stuffed him into a bag and carried him down, it could be seen, finally, that he was no bigger than anyone else.

So much for Lord Cornbury, Grosbeck thought as he looked down at the street. Cornbury had been a British governor of New York who fancied making excursions into Broad-Way and the crooked lanes below Wall Street in women's clothes and had occasionally to be restrained by the constables. A thief, too. Altogether a *shonda* for the neighbors, and eventually he was sent home to England. A car came down the street like a bat out of hell, one of the last convertibles, Grosbeck guessed, souped-up and dented. He couldn't see the driver, but he knew from long experience of this motorist, just what would happen. The moment he got under the window, he leaned on the horn and what came out was this:

First Call, an early nineteenth-century American military bugle call. First Call comes before Reveille and is followed by the Morning Gun and Assembly. The Morning Gun in New York City is a manhole cover blowing sky-high, Assembly going to work. Grosbeck had heard First Call out of this demon car for several years. The man's punctuality was an unending source of wonder to Grosbeck. Daily, that racketing engine with its broken muffler, its brassy horn, prickled his skin with anger. He was helpless; the bastard went by too fast to be yelled at. He wouldn't have heard Grosbeck, in any case, and, it was Grosbeck's certainty that could he, he would have hit the horn again and, in the neighborly manner of New Yorkers, told him to go fuck himself.

On the other hand, Grosbeck ruminated in his new condition of forbearance, maybe he's just going to work in an office or a factory like the rest of us, just a little bit earlier. Or, who knows, maybe he's on his way out to the track for the morning workouts—there's always a track running somewhere around the city—and he'll stay for the races. A real horse degenerate, bellying up to the two-dollar window, stooping with the rest of the stoopers between races, looking desperately, maybe somebody threw away a winning ticket by mistake. Grosbeck could hear him at the end of the day—tapped out—and he would have given six, two, and even on it—muttering, "I coulda, I shoulda, I woulda . . ."

He smiled. It was better than the breaking of glass and the harsh keening of miseries too great to be described, the sounds reverberating from building wall to building wall and disappearing in backyards which had heard them so often that the laundry on clotheslines flapped in boredom. Grosbeck was prepared for all of this; he had lived all his life in New York and everything alien was human to him. The horn awoke Madeline.

"Wha', wha'?" she asked.

"Nothing, sweetheart," he answered, interested that a woman so beautiful to him could make sounds like "Wha', wha' . . ." "It was just First Call on his way. Go back to sleep. I'm going out for the papers."

"Why, Harvey, why?" She sat up in bed. "Oh," she remembered, "you're going back to work tomorrow."

"Today," he said. "It's today."

"Yes." She scratched her head with both hands and yawned and Grosbeck marveled again at the difference between what she was doing and the way she looked. He sat down on the bed and put his arms around her.

"Yes," he said. There was so much drama in his voice.

"For God's sake, Harvey." Madeline laughed. She lay back and looked at him. "Now, *really*, why do you have to go out for the papers the first day?"

"Because," he answered, dropping the pants of his pajamas to the floor, "they're *there*."

"Oh, you." Their conversation, like that of old lovers, each familiar with the least wart on the other's behind, was fatuous in the extreme.

You never know what's out there. It's a battlefield. Careful of the Very lights—that damned lime color shows up everything. Crawl. Look out for barbed wire. Check gas mask, first-aid kit, entrenching tool. Mud out there. Dive into a shellhole at the first pap, pap, pap of that heavy machine gun, Private John Gilbert. So what if it is the Astor Theatre and the firing comes off the end of the sticks of the pit-band's drummer? The Boche is waiting out there, the filthy Boche. Back of the lines, Renée Adorée, Marianne. If he were hit, would she find him? Of course. "In the midst of war's curse,/ Stands the Red Cross nurse./ She's the Sweetheart of No Man's Land." Wait a minute. She wasn't the nurse. She was the little French girl he came back to when it was all over Over There; when, on a cane, he walked his wounded leg through a wheatfield to find her, arms outstretched, among the snuffling pigs near the farmhouse, the roof torn off by a shell from a Big Bertha firing seventy-five miles from the northeast. There was a glad cry from her (silent), a mighty oath from him (silent), violins and woodwinds from the pit band (all Jewish and Italian musicians, family men, who had not had to go); he tore off his forage cap with difficulty, dropped the cane, kissed Renée-Marianne, and the two of them sank to the good French earth amid the truffles neglected those four long years of hell and the Kaiser. And to hell, too, with the V.D. posters: "Two minutes with Venus, two years with Mercury!" His *petit chou* was as clean as a hound's tooth. He hoped.

Gone, the Astor Theatre. Gone, John Gilbert, Renée. Gone, Grosbeck's uncle's scratchy khaki wool uniform, the Purple Heart, the wind-around puttees, the battle ribbons—Argonne, Meuse, Belleau Wood. Gone Grosbeck's uncle. Gone, his mother and father and the city which had been mother *and* father to him. Gone, the dumbwaiter shaft in which he had first fumbled at the breasts of a fat girl unable to resist herself or anyone else. Gone, Miss Sharp, the shrunken little old Irish teacher, always in black, always weeping the day before Armistice Day in leading the singing of "The Star-Spangled Banner." Gone Mr. Hinck, the principal. ("Miss McArty had a party/ And all the teachers were there./ Mr. Hinck he left a stink on Dr. Haney's chair.") And gone, the great military bands marching, marching up Fifth Avenue, past St. Patrick's, playing, "Some day, I'm going to murder the bugler;/ . . . I'll amputate his reveille/ And step upon it heavily/ And spend the rest of my life in bed." Gone, gone, all gone.

Grosbeck returned. "You were saying . . ."

"Why do you have to go out the first day?"

"Would you have it any other way?" he asked, sternly.

"Yes."

"Not yet," he answered. "Not for a couple of weeks yet. Salomon said so. Besides, I . . . well . . . I *am* still a little nervous."

"My," Madeline said, looking down at him, "you are, aren't you . . . ?"

"I think a lot, Madeline." He took off the coat of his pajamas and reached for an old pair of pants. "You want me to die in the saddle?" Reproachfully. Madeline laughed again.

"You'll outlive all of us," she said. She wasn't sure of that. "Go get your papers." He finished dressing. "Make sure you're warm enough." Grosbeck paid no attention to that; she said that in midsummer too.

"What will you bet," he said to her, "Angelo won't ask me, How you feeling? He'll *tell* me it's time to nuke-those-gook-bastards-back-into-the-jungle-MacArthur-he-could-have-done-it-if-they-hadn't-tied-one-hand-behind-his-back. Angelo was too young for Korea, too old for Vietnam." He pulled on a jacket, tied his shoes and kissed Madeline. "I'm off."

"Yes, you're off, all right. You've been off all your life, all our life. I never met a man like you."

"Just luck, baby," he said, and kissed her again. This time, something came out of his head which he felt between his legs, but he forebore; he had something else on his mind.

A cigarette. The appetite for a cigarette, forbidden, foreseen, bidden, arose in Grosbeck, seized him by the throat, and led him to an overwhelming conclusion: he needed a cigarette. Above all else. Beyond wealth and the pleasures houris in seductive postures might bring; the finest silks and worsteds or leather or wood or cloth, gold or diamonds, the treasures of Samarkand; the most exquisite work of lapidaries, work so beautiful that, when it was finished, the lapidaries' eyes were gouged out by the Sultan's handymen so that they might never repeat themselves. (It had been discovered that emasculation was an insufficient threat and the result, anthropologists learned, was that many of these lapidaries had become successful beggars and bred inordinately large families whose members had had the foresight to go into some other line of business and become rich.)

Grosbeck's heart might stop, his eyes roll up and his jaw go slack. But, before that, before, Grosbeck knew he must have a cigarette. Where, where was he to get one at this hour? At once! Everyone who could conceivably have given him one, including Angelo the candy-store man, had been warned. There were none in the house. Long before he returned home from the hospital, Madeline had thrown out his last half carton of cigarettes and emptied his pockets of butts and tobacco crumbs and had his clothes dry-cleaned, had gotten rid of the brand to which he had dedicated heart, lungs, and guts. Day after day, after work, after her visits to Harvey at the hospital, she had sprayed the apartment with her most expensive perfumes to expunge the odor of tobacco. She had cooked meal after meal of the most elaborate kind so that the smell of food would permeate everything and then, unable to eat for anguish over her junkie of a husband, had thrown the meals out or gotten other people to come by and eat them. Their friends suspected her sanity and the apartment reeked of the warring odors of cooking and perfume.

For some reason, however, in going through his things, Madeline had overlooked one of those cheap lighters Grosbeck used and he had found it in a shoe at the bottom of the closet the day he came home from the hospital. It was his votive light and he had hidden it from Madeline. He palmed it into his pants from its hiding place. It was a beginning. Dressed, Grosbeck mumbled his way out of the bedroom and the apartment to the elevator. Somewhere, there was a cigarette and he should have it. He should light it. He should take the first long, long, long puff into his lungs. (He didn't believe any of that guff about how the first puff after laying off doesn't taste good. Tell that to a guy getting laid the first time after six months on a desert island.) Screw the Lung Association, the Heart Association, the Cancer Association. Or Society, whatever they called it. If it were his last gulp of oxygen, he should use it to pull down the blue-gray smoke into his chest, looking for all the world like some opium fiend reclining on a pallet covered by a threadbare Kermanshah in a chancy *souk* in North Africa. He should keep it down as long as he could and then, if fate so willed it, die at the foot of the pallet, the smoking weapon between stained and burned fingers, a smile on his wasted face.

6:11. Now then, where? And how? And who? At the elevator, his ears strained to hear. Possibly someone going to work early who smoked? Who had not been told by Madeline? Pah! In this building, everybody knew everybody else's business. Besides, so many assholes and health freaks had given up smoking—at the same time they were demonstrating against the war in Vietnam. Some parlay. It gave them that self-satisfied feeling, like voting, or chewing on vitamins, or proclaiming that Black Is Beautiful or Gay Is Gorgeous. They had become as self-righteous as the Reverend Dr. Parkhurst leapfrogging over the backs of whores in the Tenderloin during one of his perfervid investigations into the Sins of New York. But, enough. That kind of thinking wasn't getting him anywhere. What did they call that now? Counterproductive. The word, like so many others in use these maggoty times, made him flinch. The Newspaper had accepted the use of the word "parent" as a verb and told its humorless readers that there were no longer any distinctions to be made in the use of "who" and "whom." "Who the gods would destroy, they first make ignorant."

6:12. As the elevator came down from the top floor, knowledge came to Grosbeck as it had to Edison, Steinmetz, Michelangelo, Plato. Where else would there be a cigarette, at least the corpse of one, but in the public ashtrays placed near the elevator doors on each floor? They were cast in a cheap, pebbly cement and resembled funerary urns. As a rule, they were filled until, overflowing onto the floors, they were emptied by the janitor. But, this morning, on his floor, the pickings were slim. The little girl down the hall had left her bubble gum in the sand. (The size of it! That so small and foul a mouth could engulf a thing the size and consistency of a golf ball and shriek at the same time!) Her father had left a gobbet of spittle in it. Her mother, an advanced creature who, Grosbeck was certain, had given birth by parthenogenesis had deposited the wrapper from a feminist magazine. His trembling fingers danced through the sand. A cigar butt. A cheap cigar, one of those things with plastic mouthpieces. That was all that was left of it. Elderly Italians don't waste. Aha! Two cigarette butts sticking up. Damn! Nothing left of either but the filters. And one of them mentholated, anyway. Another floor, another floor. Quick!

6:14. Top floor. A tiny, empty pink plastic vial which Grosbeck knew to have contained amyl nitrate and which had sent someone either to his apartment or out in the street in a rush of expectation. But no cigarette ends. 6:15:30. He took the elevator down a floor; walking the stairs at this stage of the game was more exercise than he needed. Nothing.

6:17. Seventh floor. Nothing to rave about. 6:18. Sixth floor. Again, nothing. The janitor must have made one of his badly timed rounds. 6:19:30 to 6:22:30. Five, four, three, two, Lobby. Grosbeck was getting more exercise than he had bargained for, since, in his haste, he put one foot at the elevator door to keep it open and save time, and stretched to reach the ashtray. He resembled a discus thrower at the end of his cast, or a fisherman about to fall out of a dory. In the lobby he hit pay dirt, a mother lode; he should have known all along; what more logical place to find a filthy Lucullan feast? More people got rid of their cigarettes (coming and going) in the lobby ashtray than anywhere else. How could he have wasted so much time? Two Kools, a Merit, a Rothmann (how chic!), a Camel (that was the retired insurance broker on the fourth floor), and two Marlboros, one Light, one Soft Pack—the real thing. Grosbeck was so excited he didn't know where to begin.

6:23. The Soft Pack, fetched up as carefully as a drilling bit, was two and a half inches long and clean, except for the sand at the end. Grosbeck caressed the sand away, straightened out the butt. It didn't break. He put it in his mouth. He took out his lighter, flicked the little wheel three times before the flame went up and held it to the butt. He inhaled. The augmented John Philip Sousa Band (Patrick Gilmore, co-conductor), a thousand men strong, on a prairie outside Chicago, under a burning summer sun, struck up "The Washington Post March," followed by "Liberty Bell," excerpts from *El Capitan* and *The American Maid*, "Semper Fidelis," and "The Stars and Stripes Forever." Grosbeck could have sworn he heard Buddy Bolden in the cornet section, playing notes Sousa had warned him not to play, but it was probably no more than a ringing in his ears. It was a long concert. Night fell and with it came the grand finale, the display of Pain's fireworks—Roman candles, pinwheels, vaulting rockets, one mighty explosion after another in all colors, and then the piece of resistance: a red and white and green cowboy on horseback, mustachioed, the lines in his thin cheeks created by strings of Chinese firecrackers, Greek fire pouring out of the end of the Marlboro dangling from his narrow, manly lips.

"Jesus Christ," Grosbeck said. He coughed and strangled and leaned on the lobby wall. His stomach was roiled. His eyes closed and opened. He heard a noise of shuffling. It was the woman who knew everybody's business. With her wicker basket of laundry, cigarette in her mouth, big green plastic curlers in her mouse hair (where else did she wear them?), gray reworked-wool slippers on her feet (nuthouse slippers), white sticks for legs under the quilted nightdress.

"Good morning, Mr. Grosbeck," she said, out of buck teeth. "We haven't seen you for a while." He held up the hand with the butt in it. It fell out of his fingers. He should have eaten or drunk something. She rubbed out the ember with a slipper. The taste was awful. "You have lost weight, haven't you?"

"Yes," he whispered as the last of the smoke curled out of his body between teeth and lips. He looked like one of those Chinatown gift-shop Buddha incense-burners.

"Heart attack someone told me."

"Yes."

"And smoking?"

"Yes." No, he wasn't smoking; he was trying to start a fire for a barbecue. "Miss Fanion. Please."

"You don't have to worry. Believe me, I'm the last one in the world to tell anybody."

"Sure you are," he said.

"I swear to you."

"Don't swear. Bad for the soul."

The woman giggled, and the noise made Grosbeck cringe. She

picked up what remained of the butt. "Mr. Grosbeck, do you know what you are?"

"What?"

"A pervert."

"Miss Fanion!" he protested.

"Where did you get this nasty thing?" He pointed at the ashtray. "That's not good for you."

Ha! Now, she was all solicitude. She reached into the pocket of the nightdress and took out a pack of Marlboro Soft. Pervert, eh? Takes one to know one.

"That was mine," she said. "I got rid of it an hour ago. You deserve better than that." Her voice was soft with implication.

"I think a man has the right to kill himself any way he likes." She shook a cigarette out of the pack.

"No, no, wait a few seconds." Wait.

"Here, I've got a light."

"I've got my own."

"I should have figured that. Go on, now. Light up. It'll"—she giggled again—"it'll put hair on your chest," she said coquettishly. "I'd offer you a drink, too, but it's the wrong time of day. It's the moon's over the yardarm, not the sun." She batted what was left of her eyelashes at him. "Besides, there *is* your wife." Grosbeck nodded, the word RELIEF written large across his forehead. He smoked— with love, but carefully—unable to get away, since his back was to the wall. (It was holding him up.)

"Thank you so much. I don't mean the drink. For the cigarette. You're very understanding. I'm on my way out to get the papers. I've got to run."

"Don't run, Mr. Grosbeck," she said, wagging a flirtatious claw of a finger at him.

"I don't mean *literally*," he said. She looked at him more closely.

"Do you ever . . ." Get me *out* of here. "I mean . . ."

"No, never," Grosbeck lied. Not with you, not here, and not at this time of day. "It's very flattering, Miss Fanion."

"No, it's not," she said, with regret. "You could care less."

There was a click in Grosbeck's head. It set his mouth in motion and he was unable to stop himself. "No, Miss Fanion. What you mean is, 'You *couldn't* care less.'" He was about to go on.

"All right," she said, irritated, disappointed. "Grammar lessons weren't what I had in mind."

Grosbeck feigned contrition. He had smoked as much as he wanted for the moment and he stubbed out the cigarette and put the end in his pocket for another time. "I'm going back to work to-day. That's what I was thinking about, and, you know, in my business [the idiocy of what he was saying] it's just one step from having that on your mind to editing people's conversation. Forgive me . . ." He waited an instant. "I hope I didn't hurt your feelings. You've been most kind." Miss Fanion put a hand to her hair, or would have, had it not been under her giant curlers.

"Don't give it a second thought," she said. "It was just an idea . . ."

"I do give it second thoughts," he said. "You'd be surprised."

"I certainly would. I know your wife."

"Oh, that," he said recklessly, now that he was safely out of it. "You mean the present Mrs. Grosbeck? Ha ha."

"Does she think that's funny?"

"No," Grosbeck admitted. "I tried that at parties once or twice, but I don't any more. She gave me what for. There was hell to pay." He stopped. "Why am I telling you all this?"

"I'm sure I don't know," Miss Fanion said. "Yes, I do. You're the kind of man who'd sell his wife for a cigarette."

"Do you really think that?" Grosbeck was interested.

"Almost," Miss Fanion said. "Good morning, Mr. Grosbeck," she said firmly. "I've enjoyed talking to you. I've got a day in front of me, too. I guess you know I don't sleep too well." She smelled of resignation.

Grosbeck nodded. "I'm sorry. Have a nice day," he called after her as she disappeared into the elevator. "Let's care less together some-time." That drew a last giggle out of her as the elevator door closed on her wicker basket, her curlers, and the pack of cigarettes in the pocket of her nightdress. He should at least have given her a courtesy kiss.

7

As he left for work, Grosbeck noticed that across the street, someone had summoned a cherry picker from the Fire Department. It had reached up to the top floor of a tenement and almost into an open window. But, there was no smoke, no sign of fire. Grosbeck waited and was rewarded. He saw three men struggling in the open window with something very big. It was a woman, a fire lieutenant told him. She had had a heart attack and she was dead. She weighed (the lieutenant said) six hundred pounds and (he said) hadn't been out of the apartment for fifteen years. Couldn't make the stairs. Yup. Hard to believe. (A murmur from Grosbeck.) "You better believe it, mister. And, you better believe no one but us could get that thing out of there. Look for yourself. I wish they wouldn't give us all those weirdo things to handle. We got our hands full as it is." The three men in the window strained and heaved and dumped the dead woman onto the platform of the cherry picker. It seemed to buckle for an instant. A slight man in a white uniform, with a stethoscope dangling around his neck, passed a wide canvas belt around and under the woman and fastened it to the railings of the cherry picker. Then, he sat on the woman's belly and the cherry picker groaned as its shaft retracted toward the street. It needed greasing. As it shuddered and stopped, Grosbeck noted that the woman's eyes were open. What, after fifteen years in three tiny rooms, did she see? It was all so disorderly. But, in the recesses of his brain, some poor, despairing cell kept trying to tell him that disorder was the way of the world—had always been, would always be—and that nowhere was disorder greater than in New York City. The only part of all these signals Grosbeck acknowledged—just a little—was the New York City part and he fell upon that, with stunning illogic, as proof of the City's innate superiority; where New York was concerned, he would clutch at anything.

Grosbeck took a cab to The Newspaper. Might as well pleasure himself the first day back. He paid, felt for the bottle of nitro-glycerine tablets in his pocket, and got out at the entrance to the Gothic fortress on the blasted heath of Longacre Square in which he had worked so long. It had withstood everything—the assaults of every kind of degradation in the streets, the government of gangsters and respectable men, and its own grave, spectacular foolishnesses, its doubtful alliances, its forthright misunderstanding of almost everything to which it devoted its elephantine attention. It had also survived its stumblings into reality and the truths to which it paid such mincing tributes.

There, there it was, that great pile. And whatever it might be—good or bad, lying or truthful, naïve or disingenuous—it was The Newspaper. It was, above all, Grosbeck's newspaper, the one he cursed year in and year out and would not leave. He loved The Newspaper, but when he got out of the cab, he had all he could do not to get back in and go home. It was too late for that. Between Tully and Trollope, he must dare all. He had sentenced himself for life to The Newspaper and it would have him—he would have it—no matter what.

The Newspaper was so big and employed so many people that it had given up trying to keep track of them all. Flanders Field it was, with the poppies blowing row on row. There was no discharge in the war, or almost never. The Newspaper, busy with its omniscience, would get rid of a man only if he keeled over and died or didn't show up for work for several years or made an indecent proposal to the business manager's wife. On the face of it, that was absurd, since she was outstandingly ugly and bore an unsettling resemblance to the Gilbert Stuart Washington on the dollar bill—white hair, big nose, teeth forged by a blacksmith, and all. Nevertheless, she was no fool, the business manager was uncomfortable in her presence (she knew a great deal more about running The Newspaper than he did) and did not like to cross her. She had had several discreet suitors, one of whom had become the Managing Editor and was Grosbeck's boss. (This man had never laid a finger on her, but he had laid siege to her with so many significant looks over the years that she felt pleasantly ravished and got him promoted. He had been a good reporter and he was sufficiently overawed by The Newspaper to want to be the Managing Editor rather than Secretary of State. What the hell, it was all politics, anyway, wasn't it?) As for the rest of the dim foot soldiers, Grosbeck had once proposed that some sort of small monument be put up at the entrance to the City Room with a bronze plaque above it, reading: HERE SITS A NEW YORK CITY NEWSPAPERMAN, KNOWN ONLY TO PAYROLL.

Still, he was compelled by The Newspaper. As he waited for an elevator, his nostrils filled with the delicious odors of newsprint and ink from the pressroom. (Daily, the blackened fingers of a million readers bore testimony to the poor quality of the ink.) He loved the acrid smell of the metal plates from the presses and from the hot lead in the composing room and the stereotype room. He made himself hear, floors away—through thick walls—the Chinese tinkle of brass matrices (letters, numbers, punctuation, accents *graves* and *aigus, umlauts* and *cedillas*) falling in cascades down the narrow channels of Linotype-machine fonts into widths of words over which smoking lead would pour, the words dropping diffidently, endlessly, one after another, into sentences, paragraphs, columns.

There were rows upon rows of these machines before which thin, silent old men sat at keyboards, turning the marked-up pieces of paper before them into The Newspaper every hour of the day. The machines sang and clacked at them, but they had not the remotest idea of what they were transmuting. Only happenstance, an erring finger, caused them to make mistakes, and, for that, there were other ranks of silent men called proofreaders to correct the mistakes, edition after edition. When a line of type had been made, deft steel arms would reach down, lift up the brass matrices, and put them back in place so that they could be made to fall once again and form more sentences, paragraphs, and columns—wise and foolish, in good English and wretched; subtle and blatant, once in a while noble and full of song; misleading words, misguided or lying; sometimes words full of truth and understanding, sometimes full of evasions, sometimes dazzling, jeweled. The machines were not discriminating; the men sitting before them tapped out only what they saw. Thought, such as it was, lived upstairs.

To Grosbeck, Otto Mergenthaler, the inventor of the machine, was as great a man as Gutenberg, the invention of the high-speed Hoe press another miracle. To say nothing of the flying pasters, which permitted a huge roll of newsprint to move into place majestically when another had been used up, fixing itself to the tail of the first and letting the voracious presses go on—*basso profundo*—eating paper and throwing out newspapers uninterrupted—printed, folded, cut, spewed forth, every fiftieth one pushed a little sideways to save counting on the conveyor belt, and bound in wire. Then, gangs of men were needed. They heaved up the bundles and threw them into the trucks racketing to get away from the loading docks to give to the world all The Newspaper had found out (and its opinion of it) in the last day. The roadway was fogged with the smoke of exhausts under the golden street lights and the white fluorescents of the loading docks. The sidewalks were covered with streamers of cut paper and ends of wire. They were slippery with ink and grease and thrown-away bits of food and the urine of men pissing on truck tires between throwing bundles of The Newspaper into the trucks. These were brutal trucks, trucks with fronts of steel, perfectly able—no, willing—to crumple and push aside anything that got in their way in their race to get The News to The People.

Grosbeck was old enough and (he fancied) cynical enough to know better, but he was (in truth) romantic enough to conceive of all this as the trying-out of whales. Moby Dick. All that blubber, rendered into oil, transferred into the light of lamps. The Newspaper was the try-works of his life.

But, he also knew that much of what he loved about The Newspaper was on its way out just as other things were everywhere in the city. He knew that it was only a short time away from the end of the composing room. He knew that computers and photography and the pasting-up of pages and telephone transmission of The Newspaper to a building across the Hudson River in New Jersey were coming; that there would be no hot lead to make lines of type; that the plates on the press would be made of thin plastic; that they would not require the attention of all those muscular men in their clever square hats made of newsprint; that stories would be written on television screens; rewritten and edited in those godforsaken greenish images which could be summoned up or made to vanish with the punch of keys. He cursed that coming day from the bottom of his soul as he had the disappearance of the golden-oak desks in the City Room and their replacement with steel desks in what were known odiously as "decorator colors."

Not everything was gone yet, Grosbeck was heartened to find out. There was the City Room receptionist, an ancient Irish watch dog (a busted capillary along the flanges of his nose for every year on the paper; red-faced; outsized and stained false teeth which seemed to have been stolen from Painless Parker, The Dentist); out of Queens (a step up from his grandfather, who had been a dock walloper from the time he was taken to America during the Puhdado Famine). He was a powerful, garrulous old man whose job it was to bar the door to strangers, particularly during full moon, when, the superstition ran, all the nuts came out and demanded to see the editor.

When he had been younger and stronger, it had been one of his duties to start The Publisher (a late cousin of the present one) home. That publisher had been, unwontedly for the descendant of stiff-necked German Jews, a drinker of dimensions (in his civic hypocrisy, however, he had had the paper back the Eighteenth Amendment and the Volstead Act) and it was his wont to stagger from his office in the tower with the first edition of The Newspaper under one arm and the City Room receptionist on the other, into the elevator and out to his car, a chauffeured Bentley parked conspicuously among the trucks. The roughnecks on the loading docks always cheered when the receptionist got The Publisher into his car. It was an athletic event, like hurling, and the receptionist would brush off the sleeves of his shiny black alpaca coat, bow and smile to the roughnecks, and take the elevator back upstairs. Tradition did not go unobserved on The Newspaper.

The receptionist ministered similarly to the Drama Critic of his youth, another drinker. He attended first nights in the company of the receptionist, in order to keep him away from the sauce, and then was returned to The Newspaper to write his review. The receptionist kept a ham hand firmly under The Critic's arm, led him to a toilet off the composing room and locked him in with a typewriter and paper. The Critic was a slight man and easily directed when sober, a maniac when drunk. One by one, the sheets of his review would be slid grudgingly under the door, edited by a copyreader stationed outside and taken to the Linotype machines. The Critic was not an easy man to please, even when sober, and his opinions came to be known in the theatre as Shithouse Reviews. Not until he was through, did the receptionist unlock the door and let him out. While The Critic was writing, a copyboy was sent downstairs to the bar frequented by the reporters and when the toilet door was opened, the receptionist presented The Critic with a cardboard container of martinis. The

Critic never omitted to mumble (a) that the martinis were not dry enough and (b) that the taste of cardboard spoiled them. He said this only after he had finished the container. And since, in those days, there were four or five openings a week, in season, The Critic left the office every working night raving mad, raving mad, waving his arms, invoking Ibsen and Aeschylus, near to incoherent. He had, poor man, graduated from Harvard. What he did on his own time, nobody knew or much cared. He was a bachelor and a competent workman who had known both Gordon Craig and Wilson Mizner. Mizner, who when he had briefly and insanely run a hotel, put up signs reading "No Opium Smoking in the Elevators," and "Bring Out Your Own Dead." When he died, The Critic was honored by all those in the theatre for whom, season after season, he had expressed such embroidered contempt. A bronze plaque was put up in Shubert Alley and a theatre named after him. A few years after his death, The Newspaper changed the spelling of the word "theatre" to "theater"; it had waited, in deference, for him to go before doing so. The receptionist stayed on, as an expression of The Newspaper's odd benevolence, a *memento mori*. It would not be very long before someone would have to help *him* out of the building and into his coffin.

"Morning, Mr. Grosbeck," said the receptionist. "Been away?"

"Morning, Duffy. Back to the peat bogs, Michael, me boy. You *know* I had a heart attack. Got a cigarette?"

"Not for you, Mr. Grosbeck." The old man smoked those little Piedmonts. They still made them, for God's sake. Where did he find them?

"What do you mean, 'Not for you, Mr. Grosbeck?' "

"Get along with you now, Mr. Grosbeck." He did superb imitations of Irishmen; it takes one to know one; right off the boat, he might say, and Grosbeck always had the expected answer—*scraped* off the boat, right Duffy? Not today. The receptionist got up, came around the desk and shook hands with Grosbeck.

"Need any help?"

"I'm not the late Publisher."

"I'm here to serve," said the receptionist.

"Here to serve . . ." Grosbeck repeated. "How many years is it?"

"Forty-two. A week from now."

"That long." It was not a question.

"Yup."

"You're pretty well preserved." Grosbeck bore Duffy no resentment for not giving him a cigarette.

"Wish I could say the same for you, Mr. Grosbeck."

"None of your mouth now, Duffy, or I'll give you a fat lip."

"You never saw the day you could, Mr. Grosbeck."

"I never thought of trying, Duffy."

"I never thought you did, Mr. Grosbeck."

Grosbeck drew comfort out of this soft-shoe dance. So much was not said by the two men. There was, between them, the kind of affection that had grown out of their both working in the same place for a long time, doing different things, being different men together for different reasons, neither wanting anything the other had. The most they had ever done together was to have a drink across the street from The Newspaper, finding themselves together by accident in the bar. Both had done that with reporters and printers and pressmen and copyboys, and, without ever saying very much, each knew every last detail of the life of the other—habits, crotchets, quirks, time of arrival, of departure, opinions, state of marriage, capacity for liquor, climate of the mind, what the other could do, what he was likely to do. What was important was not that Duffy knew his place, but that Grosbeck knew *his* place. He knew, for example, that Duffy had not gone on the cops because his father, for some reason, had been a Republican in Red Hook. The best he could do was to get Duffy on The Newspaper as an errand boy.

"Anything new?" Grosbeck asked.

"Yes," the old man said, "they've hired three more female reporters."

"You don't say."

"I do. I'll say this much, they couldn't do any worse than the men." He stopped for a moment. "One of them's my daughter, the one I put through Manhattan."

"Congratulations, Duffy, I'll buy you a drink on that."

"She's good, Mr. Grosbeck."

"I don't doubt it, Duffy."

"I never thought I'd live to see the day."

"Why not, Duffy, the world do move."

"Not this part of it, Mr. Grosbeck. They *had* to take on some more women. What do they call it? Affirmative action." He grinned. Grosbeck smiled.

"If she's your daughter, Duffy, she'll do. I won't be easy on her, you understand." Duffy grinned once more.

"That would be discrimination if you were, Mr. Grosbeck, wouldn't it? Can't have any of that sort of thing nowadays, can we?"

"Anything else, Duffy?"

"Besides," Duffy said, "I doubt you'll be having very much to do with her."

"What does that mean, Duffy?"

"They'll tell you. Tully's inside, waiting for you."

"He did say something while I was in the hospital and there was a note from The Publisher. God damn it, Duffy, what?"

"Let Tully tell you." Grosbeck grew anxious.

"It'd be overstepping the bounds if you did, wouldn't it, Duffy? Is there anything around here you *don't* know?" He wanted to wheedle, but he knew that *he* would be overstepping the bounds. "Why don't you just tell me to have a nice day, Duffy."

"Have a nice day, Mr. Grosbeck."

"Go fuck yourself, Duffy," said Grosbeck and walked into the City Room.

It was quiet and almost airless, and the motes of dust raised by the news of the night before ("an authoritative source," "alleged," ". . . at Khe Sanh, a platoon of Marines came under heavy fire . . .") floated in the grudging sunlight that found its way through the windows at either end of the City Room. The typewriters had nothing to say at the moment; the Telexes and the wire-service machines chattered desultorily. It was not yet time for them to shout. One of the new television writing machines had been installed while Grosbeck was away and one of the day copyboys was fooling with it. "The quick brown fox jumps over the lazy dog," he punched out and the green letters came up on the screen. And then, "ETAOIN SHRDLU," as though he were a linotyper warming up his machine. And made *that* disappear. If The Newspaper had been ephemeral before, diurnal, it would be less than that now, the final stamp of impermanence placed on it by electrical magic—and then made to disappear, not even kept for reference in paper clippings but "stored"—stored, ugh! —in a computer and on microfilm.

Tully, legs crossed, was sitting on a desk. "Welcome back, Harvey," he said, and grasped both of Grosbeck's arms.

"Tully. Tully. Martha," to the woman reporter who didn't believe a word she wrote. He got out of his coat. Between marriages, he had tried her and she him and each had found the other wanting. He opened a desk drawer. "Who took my eyeshade?" he asked. And then, ashamed of himself, "What are you two doing here? You're not due for another hour?"

"Neither are you, Harvey," said Martha Sloane.

"All business, right?" asked Tully.

"Say 'Good morning' to your friends, Harvey," said Martha Sloane.

"Go on, Harvey," added Tully, "you haven't got that many."

"I'll level with you," Grosbeck said, "I didn't think I could miss this place that much. I don't know why."

"Where else would you go?" Martha Sloane asked. "What else would you do? Where else could you find, all in one place, so many people you've got so little use for and love so much. Where else," she concluded fondly, "could someone like you get paid to suck your thumb all day and jump up and down and scream at your youngers and inferiors? Why didn't you become a teacher?"

"I'll tell you, Martha. In five minutes, they'd either kill me or I'd kill them." He began to lecture. "Martha, Tully, if I may coin a phrase . . ."

"Always, Harvey," said Martha.

". . . If I may coin a phrase, Yout' sucks. Isn't that the way they say it? Sucks. That's what they call 'communicating.' Pigs root and I suppose that's 'communicating' too. They dress like mountebanks and they think like the Jukeses and the Kallikaks and . . ."

Tully teased Grosbeck. "You're mixing your singulars and plurals, Harvey," he said. "Youth . . . *they?*"

"Harvey," said Martha, "seriously, now. Why do they come to you? Who else is going to straighten them out? And," she added, "who in this place takes so much time with them?"

"I'm a form of entertainment to them," Grosbeck said. Resentfully. "Something to pass the time between editions."

"No, Harvey," she said, "you know better than that."

"You tell them over and over and over, and no sooner are their backs turned than they forget what they've been told. Bird brains. In a way, I guess, I'm lucky. If they remembered anything, there wouldn't be any need for me. Pretty soon, I tell you, they won't be required to remember anything because nobody will be required to make sense out of anything."

"You really believe that, Harvey, don't you?" Tully asked, genuinely curious.

"No. Yes. I don't know what I believe."

"Two things, Harvey," Tully said. "What do you think the old-timers thought of *you* when you started? And, go back into the morgue sometime when you've got nothing better to do and see what they were turning out then. You may get a shock."

"I have," Grosbeck said stubbornly. "It was better."

"It was awful, Harvey," said Tully, "and you know it. It was fake-literary, it drew on the worst it could find in high-flown language, it never let the facts stand in the way of a story, it told lies blithely and it gossiped and dithered and altogether wasn't very much to be proud of. You forget what a newspaper is—a thing put together in haste and gotten rid of faster. The people who work for it are exactly what it deserves. If they are any better than the paper, they leave it."

"What you're saying, Tully," said Grosbeck, "is that I'm no better than the paper."

"I'm saying that you never chose to be," Tully said. "I don't pretend to know why." Quiet.

A copyboy dropped the morning papers on Grosbeck's desk. Again, quiet. Grosbeck found his eyeshade in a drawer. He took off his jacket, hung it over the back of his swivel chair, took five pencils out of another drawer (the points were just fine), and laid them neatly at his right, pushing the newspapers (neatly) to the left. Tully sat down on the newspapers. Martha pushed the pencils away and sat down where they had been.

"Good morning, then," Grosbeck said. "I thought I'd get an early start." He looked at the two of them sitting on his desk. "You're crowding me." Martha, her legs crossed, bent forward, took off his eyeshade and kissed him on the forehead. Her knees were almost in his face. "You still tempt me, Harvey."

"Be still, my heart," Grosbeck answered.

"I mean it, Harvey," she said.

"No reflection on you, but I'd as soon have a cigarette right now."

"No," said Martha Sloane. "No reflection on you, either, Harvey, but no cigarette. Not from me." Grosbeck shrugged. "I'm afraid," she went on, "we're going to have to jar your delicate sensibilities."

Tully said, "You're not going to be here much longer, Grosbeck." Grosbeck blinked. "Don't take on, Harvey," said Tully. He pointed a finger upstairs. "They've got bigger things in mind for you."

"I don't want anything bigger. Everybody seems to know what it is but me. First, you hint at me in the hospital, then that note from The Publisher. Then, Duffy plays his Irish game with me outside—lilt in the voice, brogue a little thicker than usual, dancing his little jig. He did everything but bang his ass with a tambourine. And now, the two of you. What? What? What?"

Tully handed Grosbeck an envelope. It was sealed. "I took it out of your box, Harvey. I steamed it open. Greenspan wants to see you." Greenspan was the Managing Editor. "I didn't steam it open," Tully said. "He told me about it. Anyway, you knew something was up. Open the envelope."

Grosbeck read the handwritten note. It said, "Mr. Grosbeck, could you drop by at about 10:30? Not the City Room. Too public. In my office, up on the twelfth." The Newspaper called everybody "Mr." in print, including murderers and rapists. Grosbeck looked at Tully and Martha. "What is it?"

"We don't know," Martha said. "How bad can it be? You know this place."

"Why me?" Grosbeck asked, a snail being extracted with a tiny suck of protest from its shell. Tully took Grosbeck's jacket off the back of the chair and held it up for him to get into. Grosbeck took it away. "I can still dress myself."

"You're due just about now," Tully said. "Straighten your tie."

"I was perfectly happy," Grosbeck said, looking past the two of them, down the City Room. It was an appeal.

"We know, Harvey," said Martha. "You've spent the last thirty years being happy, haven't you? It's left its marks all over you. The heart attack . . ." She thought for a moment. ". . . The heart attack," she went on, "was the least of it. Where did you disappear to? The heart attack was the first sign you've given—to us, anyway—that you're alive. I'm not making epigrams. You've avoided yourself all the years I've known you." She, too, looked down the City Room.

"What about you?" Grosbeck asked petulantly as he slipped into his jacket.

Martha continued, "You couldn't have found a better place in which to do it, I'll admit. All that inconsequential muttering over junk and the crossing out and the banging on the desk and the exactions of penance drawn from people over facts and words. The sound of everything you say drowns in here. The alterations you make in other people's words . . . Who cares in the end? They weren't your words to begin with. Whatever happened to those? Whatever happened, bright youth?"

"Don't accuse *me*, Martha. You didn't exactly turn out to be one of the Brontës."

"Oh, shit, pull up your socks, Harvey."

"Forgive me, Martha." The impulse was to whine, but to do so in a manner which would make it seem dignified and forthright and manly—as not whining, but something else—reasonable explanation, justification, circumstance, natal flaw, the world, events beyond control, acts of God, bad luck.

"I forgive you, Harvey," said Martha Sloane. "Everybody forgives everybody everything."

"That's not true," Grosbeck said, "but I shouldn't have said what I did."

"It is, but you shouldn't have, Harvey. You're a hard man. Hard mostly on yourself." She pulled at his jacket and tightened his tie. "Harvey, you're the only man I ever knew for whom getting laid was a matter of editorial judgment." Grosbeck held up a hand. "No, Harvey, Tully knows." She looked at Tully. "You've got your own drawbacks, you religious maniac." Tully rubbed his chin. "Now," she said to Grosbeck, "get on upstairs."

Grosbeck headed for the elevators. "There's nothing," he said, "which can match the love of a good woman." Martha Sloane's back was turned and she did not hear him. Tully waved him out of the City Room.

8

The twelfth floor of The Newspaper had been designed in keeping with the thinking of The Founder, which ran a slow, thick course of rich German Jew and English High Church. It was the synagogue of the *goyim*, with its tiled, barrel-vaulted ceiling, its good walnut paneling and Gothic arches, its dark, tiny, monastic offices for the editorial writers, the long refectory table to which all these prissy monks repaired daily to decide not just what had happened but Why and What Is To Be Done. The chairs were heavy Spanish Gothic, the real article. There were hangings of wine brocade shot through with gold thread over the oriel windows to shut out the importunate, filthy world that did not always work the way The Newspaper insisted it should. The Library was a hollow square in the center of the floor, walled off by the spindles of a reredos. The rugs were oriental and carefully worn. The walls were hung with Hong paintings (a reporter had brought them back from China on a British packet late in the nineteenth century and given them to The Founder as curios), watercolors of early New York by the Baroness Hyde de Neuville, prints of Park Row in the years when most of the newspapers were published there, a huge, dark oil painting of New York Harbor at night with a moon behind a full-rigged sailing ship and the pilot rowing out to take her up the East River.

By its behavior over the years, The Newspaper had betrayed the meaning of almost everything it had placed on the walls of the twelfth floor. It had looked on smilingly and approved, in the name of Civic Virtue, the tearing down of the buildings in the prints and paintings and their replacement with eyeless things of glass and concrete and steel, so many of them and so alike that they caused people to lose their way on the streets. When these things happened, it was The Newspaper's custom to run sentimental editorials, sighing and deploring, of course, but always after the fact and always with a conscience dimpled in mercantile righteousness. The Founder and his heirs owned a great deal of real estate. On the twelfth floor, the builder had provided Hush, only intermittently profaned by the sound of typewriter or voice; the telephones did not ring, they buzzed in shame. And the designer had surpassed himself in the entrance: it resembled the Judgment Porch to the Angel Choir of Lincoln Cathedral, except that the figures carved on it were of printers and pressmen and reporters, pad and pencil in hand. At the keystone of the arch, The Founder had been imposed. The carver had thrust his beard forward and upward. He had reproduced the wart on the right side of his face but tamed the prognathous jaw and made the eyes kinder. He had put his watch fob and seals across the ample belly, hidden the hands behind the back and ended the whole thing at the waist. All in all, The Founder looked like a capon now, rather than the buzzard he had been.

The receptionist on the twelfth floor was an elderly woman in black who, had she not moved every now and then, might easily have been still another occasional piece of sculpture.

"Good morning, Mr. Grosbeck," quoth this raven. She had never been known to call anyone by his first name. "Mr. Greenspan is waiting for you."

"Thank you, Emily," Grosbeck said. He knew she hated being called by her first name.

Martin Greenspan motioned to Grosbeck as he entered the office. A woman got up at the same time from the side of his desk, pushing papers back into a briefcase.

"Harvey Grosbeck, Alice Forsythe," said Greenspan. "It's time you got back, Harvey."

"Have a nice day, Marty," said Grosbeck.

"Harvey is our assistant metropolitan editor, one of our best men. Cross-grained, thinks New York should have stopped seventy-five years ago, maybe longer. Alice is an architect, works for Corydon Varney, the builder. You two ought to know each other. You'd have plenty to fight about."

"Not really for Cory," said the woman. "I work for *his* architect."

"The Armenian," Grosbeck said.

"Same thing," Greenspan said. "They've got something new, Harvey, and I think we ought to know all we can about it. If they go through with it, it's bound to have a tremendous impact . . ."

"*Effect*, Marty. Effect will do it nicely enough."

"Harvey thinks the language should have stopped seventy-five years ago, too. Maybe longer."

"I know what it is," Grosbeck said. "I heard it on the radio the other day. Saw it in the real estate notes."

The woman was about forty. Extraordinarily good-looking, Grosbeck thought, just enough worn around the edges, not too thin, good legs. Brain? Undoubtedly. Wonder whether she smokes? Two fingers were stained. A lot, he thought. Grosbeck was old-fashioned enough to notice that she did not wear a wedding ring. Dark blond hair. Fast out of the gate? When she felt like it, he guessed. Fashionable? Who knows these days? What else besides cigarettes? Drink? Not too much. Cook? Oh, come on. He took her clothes off as she slipped into her coat.

"I think I know your wife, Mr. Grosbeck," she said, "or know of her. She saves old buildings, doesn't she?"

"Yes, you don't, do you?"

"Come on, Harvey," Greenspan said. "It's too early for that. Have it out with Miss Forsythe over a drink some other time. You and I've got things to talk about."

"Nice to have met you, Miss Forsythe," Grosbeck said. "I've met your boss. He once told me he crosses the street whenever he passes one of his buildings. For safety's sake."

Alice Forsythe smiled. "He *is* exuberant, isn't he?" she said. "Thank you, Mr. Greenspan. Mr. Grosbeck." And left.

Greenspan was fifteen years younger than Grosbeck, but, as part of the demeanor The Newspaper required its executives to wear, he had permitted himself to run to flesh a little and to appear older than he was. His face, however, was thin, his cheeks green with shaving twice a day. His manner was agreeable unless the circumstances required something different. It was said of him that he could cut a man off at the knees and that the man wouldn't know it until he looked down. (How many of the beneficiaries of Greenspan, Grosbeck wondered, were rolling around on those wooden platforms with roller-skate wheels under them.) That was how he had become the Managing Editor. His clothes were outstandingly inconspicuous. (Much thought and money had gone into them, and Grosbeck approved of that.) He was very intelligent. He believed in everything The Newspaper stood for, or had come to. He was a good American: that was his flaw. Brainy good Americans were something Grosbeck was unable to figure out. How could that be? What was it that everyone else knew that Grosbeck did not? Greenspan had taken the king's shilling, but his affection for The Newspaper, like Grosbeck's, was patent. It was all they had in common. Unlike Grosbeck, he did not also hate it; his mind was clear about that. If he were as confused as Grosbeck, he did not know it. Grosbeck envied him, envied all those good Americans—of high intelligence or low—that. They might be . . . were . . . betrayed every day of their lives (by whom, Grosbeck was unable to put his finger on), but they were *sure*. Grosbeck would dearly love to have been sure, but he was not, and, not being sure, was an anxious, sentimental cynic. Or thought he was. Greenspan's was the eye of certainty and now he fixed Grosbeck with it.

"Harvey, we'd been meaning to talk to you even before you had your heart attack."

"What about?" Grosbeck asked.

"Bear with me, Harvey."

"I'm bearing."

"Harvey, I don't have to tell you the world has changed, that the paper is changing with it. It had better. There are great stirrings in the wind . . ." He gestured toward the windows. "We have put a finger up to that wind and we know which way it is blowing."

You should live so long, Grosbeck thought. Cut it out. But, he said, "Yes, and then?"

"I don't want to seem to be lecturing, Harvey, but there are those who say we are . . . have become . . . like the City itself, like the world, too large, too impersonal to take account of everything any longer the way The Founder intended. What was it he wrote? 'Not the least sparrow is to be ignored, any more than it would be by the God of the Jews and the Christians.'"

"Did he really say that?" Grosbeck asked.

"Really," Greenspan said. "You can find it in the diaries his son turned over some years ago to The New York Public Library. The son was a trustee, as you know, and I think he made a mistake letting those diaries get out of his hands. On the other hand, there's no denying they have a wider audience where they are now."

"I've read the diaries, Marty."

"I should have known."

"He also wrote in them that it was with some discomfort and

reluctance that he was raising the price of the paper from two to three cents—newsprint had gone up a dollar fifty a ton—there was nothing else for it, he knew the readers would understand. He also confided to himself that while destiny had made a Jew Founder and Owner, it would be better for all concerned if the paper never had a Jewish Managing Editor. You're the first, Marty. He had a long memory, the revered Founder did. He never forgot that Peter Stuyvesant tried to keep a boatload of Sephardim out of New York and he never forgot, either, that he couldn't get into the Union Club. He was a closet Jew with an Episcopalian newspaper. He was so German, so German. I'm sorry if I broke your flow, Marty."

"You exasperate me, Harvey. All of us. But, I put that down to part of your doubtful charm. It's also part of why we need you."

"You need me?"

"Yes, although I often wish we didn't. But, the plain fact of the matter is that there aren't too many of your kind around anymore and not likely to be. Will you let me go on?"

"Ummmm," Grosbeck said.

"To go back to what The Founder intended is what we have in mind, Harvey."

"You've made surveys is what you mean," Grosbeck said. "You've had—what do they call them?—the demographics people in, those miserable little bastards with their numbers and certainties, and they've found something lacking. That's the way it's done, isn't it? What did they find out, where did The Newspaper go wrong?"

Greenspan closed his eyes and rubbed his bony, luxuriant nose with thumb and forefinger. "Why do we always have to go through this sort of thing, Harvey? Doesn't it tell you something about yourself?"

"All right, Marty, it is your bounden duty, as the steward of The Founder, as the keeper of the flame, the gleaner of all that is good and true, if not beautiful, to take note of sparrows as well as to record the thunder of larger events, the firm or faltering steps of statesmen, the tinkle of bank rates, the newest recipe for polyester pie, and, pardon me, the latest wrinkle in clothing. Right?"

The floor rumbled. High up as they were in the building, the two men could still feel the presses turning over briefly as plates were put on the rollers for a section of the paper that would not be printed for hours. "That sound, Harvey," Greenspan said. He was being remarkably patient with Grosbeck. "That sound you and I know so well, leads me to my last digression and then, God willing, to your future. The role of The Newspaper," he continued, "is that we neither lead nor follow. We reflect what the people think even when they do not know they think it."

"You believe that, don't you?" Grosbeck asked.

Greenspan nodded. "We guide, we suggest, we place a hand on an elbow. There are times when we exhort, but only in a manner made subtle and refined in the course of more than a century of taking the pulse of the public and only in consonance with what we know to be the best for it in a world we know not to be perfect, but which we nevertheless accept."

"Ummmm," said Grosbeck.

"We make it known to the people that the body politic is well or ill," Greenspan said.

"What about my future?" Grosbeck asked. The presses gave another monitory rumble.

"I'm getting there." Hurry, hurry! "Have you ever thought that we want you *alive* for as long as possible? That you represent a generation fast disappearing?"

"How elegiac," Grosbeck said.

"Not elegy, Harvey. Wistfulness. I think I am not being sentimental when I say yours is a generation we once took for granted would reproduce itself endlessly, that would provide us with the kind of continuity The Newspaper needs. The solid, sonorous, clear voice of Reason that it has always been and must continue to be. I look around the City Room now and I am not encouraged. Bulwarks is what we need. You are a bulwark, however small, however quirky."

"Quirky bulwark," Grosbeck said. "Now, just feature that for a metaphor."

"That's just what I mean, Harvey. You save us from ourselves."

"Ummm," said Grosbeck.

"Short of murder, mayhem, hopeless drunkenness, too many trips to the funny farm, stealing from petty cash or screwing around with expense accounts, we need your kind. Even with a heart attack."

"Even," Grosbeck said. "What do you need me for?"

"To write, Harvey."

"Write!"

"We want you to do something different from what you've been doing."

"Write what?"

Greenspan looked past him. "In a way, Harvey, your becoming an editor wasn't a bad thing—for us, for you. I never asked you why you stopped writing . . . We make a point on the paper of not asking questions like that . . . A man's life is his own to do with what he will. Within limits . . ."

"Whose limits?" Grosbeck asked.

"As I said, not a bad thing," Greenspan continued. "Have you ever thought you'd like to write again?"

"Yes. I just lie down until the feeling goes away."

"What *did* happen?"

"I'd as soon not talk about it. Is there anything wrong with what I'm doing?"

"Would you be here if there were? Come on, Harvey. Anything you say is dead in this room." He smiled.

"Ummm," Grosbeck said.

"I'm serious, Harvey. The paper is serious about you. Why did you stop? Two books, all those articles . . ." He paused. "I've never talked to you like this before."

"No," Grosbeck admitted, "you haven't. You must want something."

Greenspan leaned forward and put his hands, palms down, on the desk. "Of course, we do, Harvey."

"Why are you taking all this time and trouble with me?" Grosbeck asked.

"I will tell you, Harvey."

"Yes?"

"You have proved, over and over, in your cranky, often offensive way, that you are a craftsman. But, there is more than a craftsman in you, Harvey. We all know that up here in editorial. We've read what you wrote. Grace, temperateness in what you did—I don't believe for a moment you believed in everything you wrote—the ability to call things by their right name when you did believe, a genuine eloquence . . . all the things we want on the editorial page . . ." Grosbeck felt himself becoming constipated.

"We don't get as much of that now as we would like."

Jesus, Grosbeck thought. "Jesus, Mary and Joseph," he said.

"Why did I stop?" Grosbeck asked the room. As well ask why darkies were born. Greenspan nodded, in anticipation. As well ask . . . what? . . . Tell him. Something. Anything. Grosbeck decided on what he believed to be the truth. "Do you remember," he asked, "when I disappeared for a couple of weeks?"

"No, that was before my time, but I heard about it."

"It's very hard for me to talk about it," Grosbeck said. Still, he was suffused with pleasure, unexpectedly.

"Do it for me," Greenspan said. When he wanted to, he could charm a snake out of a tree.

"I was between marriages at the time," Grosbeck said, "so there was nothing to go home to. I had finished something I didn't like. I went back to my apartment, packed up a bag, and took a room in one of those small hotels down on Lexington Avenue near Madison Square. You could do that then. The halls didn't smell of piss and filth and they weren't crowded with junkies and nuts thrown out of the mental hospitals. They catered to genteel people down on their luck but not broke. Even a few bachelor newspapermen, like Bob Schwenk, who didn't particularly want company after work. Solitaries. The hotel was clean. What I wanted. To think. To be alone. Not even to read or drink. But to think. I read the paper every day— that's a tough habit to break—but that was all. There weren't any pictures on the walls and the room wasn't very big. Comfortable enough. I ate in the neighborhood. There used to be a pretty good German steakhouse on Twenty-third Street. I had an occasional drink in a bar. I saw no one. I've never told anyone any of this. I didn't cry. I didn't beat my head against the dresser. I did stand at the window, often for an hour on end, and watch the traffic. It was quieter than I thought it would be. The City was beginning to lose a lot of its people and a lot of its traffic. The telephone never rang. Nobody knew where I was. I stopped. Stopped, stopped, stopped. Do you really want to hear all this?" Greenspan nodded.

"The wallpaper had a brown pattern. Wallpaper. There was a brownish-yellow stain in the plaster on the ceiling. None of it conjured up any pictures for me. I was as sane as I could be. Calm. And nuttier than a fruitcake. Sometimes, I'd sit in Madison Square. You cannot begin to imagine how wonderful Madison Square was. O. Henry knew. I knew. I could sit there, and, if I felt like it, think of the Fifth Avenue Hotel and the Prince of Wales dancing there. The

Eden Musée on Twenty-third. There had been Delmonico's at Twenty-sixth Street and the Hoffman House and the Albemarle on the Broadway side of it, the Gilsey House at Twenty-ninth and all the bloods and the fancy and their women, the Madison Square Theatre . . . Marty, you don't have to hear all this . . ."

"Yes, I do," Greenspan said.

"Madison Square Garden," Grosbeck recited. "It was Venice . . . The circus, the circus . . . The horse show . . . The monument to General Worth and the Mexican campaign . . . Stanford White . . . Harry Thaw . . . Evelyn Nesbit . . . Saint Gaudens . . . Mac-monnies . . . the Tenderloin . . . Koster & Bial's . . . whores and faro . . . Maurice Prendergast . . . Childe Hassam . . . Alfred Stieglitz . . . Daniel Burnham . . . the Flatiron Building. I was full of love and dead and I sat on a bench and trembled . . . Fall was just beginning . . . It wasn't cold but the leaves had begun to come down and there were white wings to rake them up . . . With *rakes*, not those goddamned vacuum cleaners they use up in Rockefeller Center. I was all alone . . . with a hot dog in my hand. It was cold and I never finished it. I took care to sit on a bench next to a basket —they didn't get stolen every fifteen minutes then—and I threw it in . . . Come on, Marty, let me up . . ."

"No, Harvey," Greenspan said. "You don't know it right now, but this is good for you." He was shameless, playing father to a man fifteen years older. Tully had done it, too, in the hospital.

"Well, Marty, about the time the two weeks were up, I decided something."

"What?"

"You must know by now, Marty, without my telling you, but, if you must hear it, I decided I was not absolutely first rate, never had been, never would be, and that I would never again write a word of my own; that I would, thereafter, chivy other people's words around if the paper would let me, which it did. It would be much less painful. And it was. I was everybody else from then on. I remember sweating in my topcoat that day, through the shirt, the suit jacket. My forehead was wet. My scalp prickled. More than you wanted to hear, eh, Marty?"

"I remind you," Greenspan said. "I'm human too."

"Anyway," Grosbeck went on, "I said nothing, saw nothing, barely knew where I was and made up my mind to bury myself."

"I wouldn't call what you've been doing since burying yourself, Harvey," Greenspan said.

Grosbeck looked at him. "No?" he asked. He continued. "What brought me back was the Appellate Division Courthouse."

"The Appellate Division Courthouse!"

"Yes," Grosbeck said.

"It's not *that* old, Harvey," Greenspan said.

"I know, but it's so beautiful, so classical, so naïve, all things considered. All that white marble, those modest boastings of the statues, a temple, the fact that it is a court of *appeal* . . . that there is something to appeal *to* . . . that if *that* were to stand, to remain, then I could . . ."

"You're serious, aren't you?" Greenspan asked.

"Marty, I'm not talking about a chickenshit state court populated by shyster judges in black robes who paid to get where they were. I'm talking about an idea embodied in a building . . . I'm getting lacy, aren't I?"

"No," Greenspan said. "No. And the way you put it happens to be just what I was thinking about for you."

"Not so fast, Marty. I'm not finished."

"Forgive me," Greenspan said. He had heard far nuttier things from other people.

"Do you begin to understand what I'm getting at?" Grosbeck asked.

"I don't," Greenspan admitted, "but I will."

"That's what you get paid for . . . isn't that what you always say, Marty? Only, you don't always understand, do you?"

Greenspan held up a hand. "I'm not God, Harvey."

"But, you'll do until He comes along, won't you, Marty? That's why you're the Managing Editor."

"You exaggerate, Harvey, and *that's* another part of what I was thinking about you."

"My wife knows all about this," Grosbeck said. "You're the only other one now. It must be my weakened condition . . ."

"Certainly," Greenspan said.

"I thought, it is all of a piece, sturdy, it will last. If it can, I can . . . I *know* it's not that old. What—1904?"

"You're not that old, either, Harvey," Greenspan said. "Coffee?"

"No, Marty, not unless I can have a cigarette with it," Grosbeck said.

"No coffee," Greenspan said. "What else have you got to say?"

"Where are you finding all the time for this?" Grosbeck asked.

"That's the secret of being Managing Editor, Harvey. No waste. All the fat trimmed away. Go on."

"All right, Marty, I'm no goddamned mystic, I don't have to tell you, but everybody has his *mishigas* . . . somehow . . ." He grew uncomfortable.

"Somehow what?" Greenspan asked. "Get it out."

"Somehow," Grosbeck repeated, "I discovered a connection between the state of my mind and body and the changes in the city. Every time some fine, absurd building was torn down, every time Standard Granite Block in the streets was covered over with asphalt or thrown away, every time a piece of slate was uprooted from some old sidewalk over which I had roller-skated, every time I ran across some piece of inferior cast-cement sculpture in a pile of red-brick dust from a tenement that had been torn down . . ."

"What?"

Grosbeck seemed not to hear Greenspan. "When, at last, I had come to accept the Empire State Building—my father had taken me through the lobby of the old Waldorf and I knew what magnificence was—then Washington Market disappeared and the Hudson Terminal and Cortlandt Street altogether and up went that Port Authority profanation, the World Trade Center . . ."

"You *are* parochial," Greenspan said.

"*You* don't belong anywhere, Marty. L.A. to N.Y. N.Y. to L.A. It's all the same to you."

Somewhere, over near one of the oriel windows, two machines side by side chuckled at each other intermittently, one the high-speed Associated Press Dataspeed, the other The Newspaper's own wire. One said, "Hamburger Hill" and several thousand other words very fast. The other, slower, said "Sinai, Tel Aviv, Cairo." No opinions. Otherwise, the room was now warm with confession. It had left droplets on the ceiling, tiny clouds at the valances of the hangings. "I don't pretend to know the meaning of all this, Harvey," Greenspan said. "That's between you and whatever deity does you the most good. But, I'm not entirely without understanding."

"There you are," Grosbeck admitted. "It *is* a weird line of reasoning. Still, I'm no goddamned mystic . . ."

"No?"

"No," Grosbeck said, "but somehow . . ."

"Somehow what?"

"Do you want to hear this or don't you, Marty?"

"All right, Harvey, I forgot myself."

Grosbeck went on. "Every time one of those things happened, it was a spike in my side, a nail in my hands. First, I stopped writing—stopped building things with my own hands, so to speak—then, my health began to go downhill. Then, I became increasingly depressed—even marrying Madeline didn't get rid of that—then, the heart attack. I am convinced beyond argument . . . I swear it . . . that I knew these things were going to happen when The Bank of New York decided it needed a jazzy new building on Fifth Avenue and got rid of the old one. The last Delmonico's was right across the street. Down the block, Richard Canfield had his last gambling joint. The building's still standing, only, of course, it doesn't look anything like it did in 1912." He looked at Greenspan again. "Not much sense in that, is there?"

"You asked me to keep quiet, didn't you?" Greenspan asked.

"I walked across Madison Square, rubbed my hand along the marble of the Appellate Division, went up Lex to the hotel, checked out, and went back to the apartment. It was awfully dusty. I was relieved. I knew what I intended to do. The phone rang a couple of times. I didn't answer it. I fussed around the apartment. Then, I called the office and told the desk I'd be back to work the next day if that suited everyone. No one objected. They were surprised when I told them what I wanted to do, but not all that much. I gather that sort of thing has happened before." Recitative. "One thing hurt," Grosbeck said.

"What?" Greenspan asked.

"Nobody'd gone looking for me."

Greenspan laughed. "They knew where you were, Harvey," he said. "They're not stupid. They knew you'd be back. You didn't show up in the river or the morgue or any of the hospitals or in the trunk of a car out at Kennedy. That would have been more Tully's style than yours, now that I think of his connections. I think it took Tully all of a day to locate you. I am told he recommended letting you alone. Very wise. I would have done the same. The Newspaper has a greater tolerance of eccentricity than you give it credit for."

"I'm not an eccentric," Grosbeck said. "I'm simply not absolutely first rate and I am unable to reconcile myself to what has happened in the City. I am grief-stricken."

"As to eccentricity, Harvey," Greenspan continued, "whatever you call it, it comes down to the same thing in the end. And, as far as first rate is concerned, neither I nor anyone else agrees. I don't know what *you* mean by first rate. But, *we* do and you are. As to the City . . ." He shrugged. "Nobody can do anything about that. Not here, not in any other city, nowhere in the world."

He began to speak more quickly. "I don't know—don't want to— what you're sunk in. I want you back, I want you writing . . ." Greenspan, like everyone else, knew that Grosbeck's air of independence was spurious, his anger vaporous. Both had come to be expected of him and it was well known that he needed the money and would stop when his knuckles were rapped. Yr. surly, obdt. servt.

He had begun by playing a part to insulate himself from fools and bores. Year by year, sometimes with forethought, sometimes not, he had refined the part, adding bits of business here, discarding some there, as time wore them out through repetition or others took them up. He fought contemporaneity; he cultivated the appearance of antiquity. Through constant reference to people and events current when he could have been no more than a child, he succeeded in making others think of him as at least ten years older than he was. One would have thought he was at the bar the night they shot up the Hotsy Totsy during Prohibition or in the Brooklyn restaurant where Frankie Yale got his or that he regularly took the Pig Woman to dinner during the Hall-Mills trial.

The closest he had ever come to those roseate days was when, as a copyboy and *after* the end of Prohibition, he had accompanied a crime reporter to the all-night barbershop downstairs in the BMT station at Forty-ninth and Broadway to find Big Frenchy DeMange and another hood shot and bleeding heavily, side by side in their chairs, the same time Dutch Schultz was killed over the river in Jersey. ("Shave and a haircut, two bits; I seen a lady's big tits.") He had thrown up. The crime reporter had laughed at him. The barber's sheet was still on DeMange's chest, the towel around his neck, the shaving cream still on his cheeks, which had two holes in them. The blood had run into the shaving cream and the face looked like peppermint candy. An ambulance had come from Bellevue and the two were taken away up the stairs on stretchers. The other man died on the way downtown. The barbershop shades were drawn and the place closed forever. When Grosbeck recovered from his vomiting, the crime reporter handed him one of the barber's towels to wipe his mouth with, called the office, and took Grosbeck around the corner to the little Lindy's for a sandwich. Grosbeck's appetite returned. He was overcome by the richness of his life, by his presence at events of such transcendent importance.

He tried to convey all of this later to a girl named Pickles as the two of them struggled at the bottom of the dumbwaiter shaft in her apartment and she whimpered, without much conviction, "Don't, don't," as he told her what had happened and tried to get both of her great, precocious breasts in his hands. She didn't understand a word of what he was saying, thinking he was just trying, in his circumlocutory way, to distract her from the business at hand. She knew all about that and he need not have. ("I don't know art, but I know what I like.") All Grosbeck was trying to do was to convey to someone the fullness of what he had experienced while, at the same time, fulfilling himself another way. It was one of the most satisfying nights he had ever had. The girl, Pickles, had not the remotest idea what he was getting so excited about, but since it seemed to enhance his youthful virility, so much the better. She had no intention of stopping him, but she wanted him to understand that she wasn't— Don't! Oooh!—loose. Every boy on the block knew she wasn't loose —Aaah!—that it would often take as long as an hour—What's that! —to open his pants and diddle him—That's nice, isn't it!—until the spunk ran over his unbuttoned fly. Was that all right? You're pretty good yourself! Grosbeck had never slept as well as he did that night; no dreams, sated in mind and body. Whatever happened to Pickles?

("Oh, do you remember Sweet Alice, Ben Bolt?/ Sweet Alice whose hair was so brown?/ Who wept with delight when you gave her a smile?/ And trembled with fear at your frown?")

"Harvey," Greenspan said, "Howard Thorson died a couple of weeks ago."

"I read about it. High time."

Greenspan said, "That means we've got a hole on the editorial page and we sorely need to fill it."

"I sympathize deeply. Where are you going to find another nature-faker like him, another road-company Thoreau or Whitman?" He put aside the state of his heart, got up from his chair, and walked around the room, waving his arms and shouting as much at the walls as at Greenspan.

"That fraud. Who's going to give you that shyly peeping crocuses crap now? Who's going to give you the slow turning of solstice into equinox and the turning of the good black earth under rusted spades? And the music of the spheres dinning into people's ears from the empyrean? While in the highways and byways of the land the renewal of life is seen in the budding dogwood. Mulch, mulch. Don't forget mulch. And the sweet rot of compost. Or, depending on the season, the sometimes slow, sometimes erratic falling of the leaves from the trees—insert names of several and give their Latin names—the hastening, chastening chill in the air, the signs, the signs all about us of what is to come—death and then resurrection—the burning of wood in fireplaces, the blue smoke ascending over ancient cots from the rockbound coast of Maine to the sunkissed shores of California. I'm getting out of sequence. Who cares? Whoever did?"

"You'd be surprised, Harvey," Greenspan said, amused, "at the mail we get. People—our people—want that." Grosbeck wasn't listening.

"No, Harvey," Greenspan said, "that's not what we want out of you. It has long seemed to The Publisher that we have neglected the very city in which we publish, and the things for which it stands. I don't mean that we scamp on news of the City or fail to take note of the changes in it, but we seem to have missed something. That something is a kind of perspective we feel you can provide us with. I don't want to sound toplofty, but what we need on the editorial page, on the signed-opinion page is more New York City *atmosphere* and a sense of *people*."

"What you're saying is you want me to be your New York City nature-faker. Remember, I get nosebleeds above Fourteenth Street."

"What we envision, Harvey, is the sort of thing that will remind us of our history while we take note of the contemporary." He put the tips of his fingers together. "You're the man to do it, Harvey."

"You mean, if you get the blacks rioting in Brooklyn, then I'm supposed to balance that with a wistful account of the burning of the Negro Orphans' Home on Fifth Avenue during the draft riots? Is that right, Marty?"

"Something of the sort. I think you get the idea."

"Balance, balance, above all balance," Grosbeck said. "I . . . the paper got along without any atmospheric rhapsodizing about the City and it didn't worry very much about your famous *people* until . . . ah, of course . . . the poor and the humble started burning and bombing and looting and mugging and raping and killing and the money started to move out of town and the bankers started to get nervous and you really began to understand that the City was in trouble. And now, you will save the City—what there is left of it to save, and the paper, too—with, among other devices, a New York City nature-faker, quaint and stern by turns, comic, sad, dramatic, historical, but, above all, calm and judicial."

"I'd say you have a pretty fair notion of what's called for, Harvey. I knew you would. I even rather like your description of the job— New York City nature-faker. It is my mission in life—my mission in life, I cannot emphasize that too strongly—to keep this newspaper at the level of greatness it achieved long before my time. If the accomplishment of that mission requires me to stop plunging my hands into the caldron of actual newsgathering . . ."

"My goodness," Grosbeck said. "How you do go on!"

". . . to move upstairs," Greenspan went on, "where the overview . . ."

"*Overview!*" Grosbeck said.

."Where the overview is wider . . ."

"And deeper, too?" Grosbeck asked. "Right up to the tops of your shoes?"

"Then, so be it," Greenspan said. "That was my decision. I have long since accepted the things I must do—for myself, for The Newspaper."

"And the money and the ass-kissing and the sail-trimming that go with it?" Grosbeck asked.

"Yes, all that," Greenspan said, "and so be it. I feel no pain within, no canker." Grosbeck had irritated him. "I can't help but feel impatient, Harvey, that you haven't accepted too. I play squash three times a week, dine with The Publisher once a month, take his wife to art openings when he is otherwise occupied—with mine, naturally— . . ."

"Naturally," Grosbeck said.

". . . and make the annual trip abroad with him to see whether, in fact, the world has changed to the degree that The Newspaper has reported those changes. You, Harvey, have stood still—still, you hear me?—sunk in I don't know what."

"I've *told* you," Grosbeck said.

"You've talked a lot, Harvey, but I don't know that you've told me anything. It's bar talk—at eleven o'clock in the morning. And, you're making me beg you. I don't like that. I've got to end this," Greenspan said. "This is the tidiest way I can think of doing it. I am asking you to leave the City Room and take an office among us up here. Write your own words. You would do two kinds of pieces— New York City editorials—nothing controversial . . ."

"God forbid," Grosbeck said.

". . . but which would induce in the reader a feeling of warmth and sharing and even laughter, and you would also do an occasional signed piece for the other page. And there, since the piece would be signed, you would have freer rein."

"My own words," Grosbeck said. "Freer rein . . ."

"I don't think you have much choice . . . unless, of course, you want to go back downstairs into your box and nurse your broken heart until you die on us. We'll give you the best of funerals . . . and a two-paragraph obit. Another thing. There's more money up here. The hours are pretty much what you want to make them . . ."

"Do you recommend squash?" Grosbeck asked.

". . . except for the afternoon meeting." Grosbeck swelled in his suit. "We don't do this very often, Harvey." The nightingales sang in Berkeley Square.

"Just remember, though, you're not Proust—you're something better for our purposes—*and*, you're going to have to deal with such phenomena as Corydon Varney and Alice Forsythe. That's the note of caution. Will you do it?"

Grosbeck forgot his heart. He said, "Yes." Then he said, "When?"

"Tomorrow."

"How much?"

Greenspan told him.

"Can I do it?" Grosbeck asked.

"Yes," Greenspan said. "The interview is over. See you tomorrow." Tomorrow, tomorrow, how happy we will be!

9

Corydon Varney sat behind the desk. Alice Forsythe sat facing him across it. The Armenian architect, overspreading a gilded chair, proffered a roll of drawings. Varney held up a hand and shook his head. "Not just now," he said. The architect shrugged voluminously, put the roll on the floor, and crossed his legs. The thin legs of the chair sighed, staggered, and braced themselves. "Watch it, Aram."

"I'll get it fixed," the Armenian said. "Here, I'll put it in the corner. I'll use the armchair. I forgot."

"You forget trusses every once in a while, too, Aram, don't you?"

"Am I to be held responsible, Cory, for the oversight of an engineer, the illness of a draftsman, the misplacing of a memorandum, the flightiness of a young girl who picked up the first piece of paper she could lay hands on and put it through . . . ?"

"And so on and so on and so on," Varney said. "What did that cost us? Never mind. Who is responsible for anything anymore?" He was not above being sententious. Neither was Ponzi. Neither is the President of the United States. A male secretary sat attentively with a notebook in his lap and a pencil in his hand. Discreet, expressionless, physically fit, homosexual, an ambitious fixture in the grandiose office. There was no home in his life. He appeared daily, in the morning, and disappeared, daily, in the evening. He lifted weights in a gymnasium, changed lovers once a year, cooked, abhorred vulgarity, worked devotedly on a dissertation for his doctorate about a painting of the Virgin owned by an obscure order of monks in a monastery near Avignon and wrote them letters in exquisite French, supplicating them for information. (They gave him that and broad texts on salvation, although he was convinced he had no need of it.)

A macaw shrieked on its perch behind the bars of a Venetian cage. "Really, Mr. Varney, Aram," said Alice Forsythe. "How much, after all, did it cost any of us? Nothing. Someone else always pays. Should I have said that?"

"No, Miss Forsythe, you should not," Varney said.

"Alice," said the architect, "I beg of you . . ."

"Alice," Varney said, "there *are* some things which must not be said, you will have to learn. Except . . . except . . . by people like me. *I* can say them. *You* can't . . . or shouldn't . . . or dare not. Unless . . ."

"Shall I bite my lip, Mr. Varney?" Alice Forsythe asked. "Shall I look down? Or away? Or stammer something?"

"No, Alice," Varney said. "Just shut up and listen, will you? I can say things like that to you because you are not just a woman any longer. You are my *equal*. Isn't that so?" A tableau in a morality play, the stage darkened, the forces of evil in the ascendant for the moment? What lay ahead? Alice Forsythe looked at Varney. Not my style. If I must conspire with him, I will, but not my style.

"I've been to see Greenspan," she said.

Varney nodded. "He called me. We have to show him something." To the secretary: "Take notes. Transcribe them and give them to Miss Forsythe. You," to Alice Forsythe, "will fill them in. You know what's required."

"I think so," she said.

"All right, then," Varney went on. "Four-color brochure . . . good type and layout . . . attractive illustrations . . . not exactly architectural renderings, understand . . . but, so to speak, *projections, extrapolations* . . . justifying the use of the entire block . . . there are so damned many slips between the banks and the bricks . . ." Varney smiled. The Armenian laughed. The male secretary tapped his teeth with the pencil. He never smiled in the office. Alice Forsythe looked out the window.

The rivers had been obliterated by building. There were vistas of unrelieved tedium and terror. The spires of churches, once the tallest things to be seen in the City, now were no more than gray or brown splinters. The pleasant uniformities of nineteenth-century builders, their private architectural idiosyncrasies, their bits of derivative Greek, or ignorant Renaissance, or Gothic or Baroque, or Beaux Arts, their mingling of a dozen different styles were being pounded into dust, burned, taken away . . . what had risen on the ashes had no past. The little that was left had been self-consciously prettified into museum exhibits and pointed out to earnest lovers of culture on walking tours, these conducted by "lecturers" whose information, like as not, was wrong.

"Alice," Varney asked, "are you listening?" The Armenian frowned at her from the armchair. The macaw reproached her harshly from his perch. Who was that angry little man, Grosbeck?

Varney dictated fluently, mellifluously, with an occasional rounded or chopping motion of the hands. The voice . . . the voice . . . the manner. Snake-oil salesman. He could have been standing on the tailgate of a wagon at night, his face lighted by kerosene flares, an audience of appleknockers, mouths open, before him. ". . . the flagging economy of this great city . . . a graceful mix of the purely utilitarian and these strong architectural traditions which have made New York what it is . . . That what you were looking at, Alice?"

"No," she said, "just waiting to hear."

Varney clasped his hands and laid them on the desk. ". . . incorporating all of what our engineers and designers have learned in the course of a thousand years of discovery . . . Bernini and Inigo Jones *and* William Le Baron Jenney . . . you drop in the names, Alice . . . to produce a city the grandeur of which is unequaled by Rome, Athens or Paris . . . I'm tempted to write the thing myself, but"— with another lardly smile at Alice Forsythe—"time . . . I just don't seem to have the time for anything anymore . . .

"If the City is to be turned around—and such is the strength of our conviction that it can and will be . . . then—you'll put all this in order, won't you, Miss Forsythe? Inspiration has the habit of showing itself in lumps. I am depending on you to smooth them out— And no one understands more fully than our group the human needs which must be satisfied if the . . . a domed galleria—Naples? Providence, Rhode Island? You get the idea . . . walkways paved with the identical blue slate our forebears quarried out of New England hillsides or carried in ballast from the home country to make their rude sidewalks . . . some reference to Nieuw Amsterdam . . . the stepped gables of the roofs . . . THEN . . . the march of the City through fire, storm, and war, and reconstruction, and so on . . . Robber Barons . . . the Fifth Avenue mansions . . . Custom House . . . Woolworth Building . . . the old Waldorf . . . until we come to this, the perfect jewel carefully fixed in the last waiting bezel in the diadem which will crown this city . . . the Varney Building . . ."

"How eloquent, Mr. Varney," said Alice Forsythe, "but what's there now—the mansions—is . . . well . . . However, I can understand your enthusiasm."

"Certainly you can, my dear," Varney said, "and I can understand you, but we move on, we put away aimless regrets, we live in our time . . ."

"I can't disagree with you," Alice Forsythe said.

"No," Varney said, "you can't, can you?

". . . We envision a series of efficiently, but pleasantly, arranged shops, boutiques, bank branches, airline offices, possibly a department store, restaurants for every taste and purse . . . agora, the word agora comes to me . . . based on intensive studies of the area . . . history at every hand . . . the ornaments, sills, lintels, pediments, some of the rusticated stone of the mansion to be built into the first few stories of . . . possibly saving most of the façade, although that presents difficulties which, if not insuperable, must at least be taken into account . . . it's almost impossible to find the kind of workmen today who can do that sort of thing . . . and engineers are such an impatient lot . . . so in a hurry to get finished . . . I sometimes think that's what killed the decorative in architecture. Nevertheless, we shall . . . ah . . . overcome . . . money is no object . . . a design concept at once sensitive to the needs of people and the urgencies of business . . . the business of America is, indeed, business . . . an eclecticism which, when carried through, will result in . . . four towers of up to forty stories each . . . possibly each of a different height, emulating the irregular spires of certain churches . . . and the last ten stories of each tower designed differently . . . the great European cathedrals . . . you'll have to attend to the details of that, Alice . . . each tower overlooking a plaza which will carry the eye to . . . self-contained . . . I did say agora, didn't I? Stick in zócalo, too . . . marketplaces for the exchange of things and ideas . . . dance groups, mimes, small orchestras . . . all trumpets, all strings on fine days . . . tiny, gaily painted carts and exotic foods . . . mustn't forget the vegetation . . . fresh flowers in season . . . dwarf Japanese trees . . . the gardeners in ethnic costume . . . the plashing of fountains . . . etc., etc. . . . . a wonderful sense of place, a welcome and long-overdue relief from the crushing sameness of . . . no need to dwell too long on the sameness . . . the dreams of a Piranesi made possible through modern technology . . . twenty-four-hour security, alarm systems, closed-circuit television . . . the eye which never closes . . . lobbies, corridors, stairs, elevators . . . I almost forgot . . . solar panels to be installed on two of the four towers . . . great, shining affirmations of our determination at last to be free of foreign oil . . . I don't expect they'll be used, but they're an earnest of good faith . . . they're . . . why . . . like the four-story false fronts on one-story buildings, aren't they?

". . . Permanently sealed, tinted windows, controlled atmosphere, ample garage space, loading docks, electronic this, that, and the other . . . you fill in the details . . . truly a city within a city, a monument which generations to come will . . . at the same time, a significant addition to the City's tax base . . . a commitment to . . . an end to the humdrum which has characterized so much of . . . and yet . . . no small detail has been overlooked . . . health clubs . . . a small luxury hotel with separate entrance . . . possibly corporate apartments beautifully appointed . . . secretaries on call night and day . . . every business machine there is, artfully hidden . . . shared-time computer accessibility . . . all for those executives working late . . . the bedrooms giving no hint of any of this . . . I shall probably requisition one for myself . . . twenty-four-hour limousine service . . ."

Varney said, "That should do it." He slapped his forehead. "Jesus Christ," he said, "I forgot to work in *ambiance*, didn't I? That's our key word today, isn't it? Can't have an agora without an ambiance, can we? An ambiance a day keeps the ambulance away . . . I'd say about sixty-four pages, Alice, when we're done . . . lots of 'artist's conceptions' . . . I don't know right now how much any of this has to do with the actual plans . . . The brochure is for the people who write up this stuff for newspapers and magazines . . . don't forget the scale models, Aram . . . Anything I've forgotten?" Varney asked. "You, Aram, you, Alice."

"Not a thing," she said.

"Almost . . ."

"Byzantine," said the Armenian. "Somewhere, small colored tiles, mosaics, hints of the Eastern Rite . . . ?"

"Why not?" Varney said. "You work that up, Aram. One of the restaurants? A lobby?"

Aram: "A whole plaza?"

Varney: "If you like."

Alice Forsythe: "Isn't all this apt to get out of hand? Incoherent?"

Varney: "I wouldn't worry about it, Alice."

Alice Forsythe: "Had you ever thought of being an architect your-self, Mr. Varney?"

"Aram," Varney said to the architect. "Donald," to the secretary. The two men left. "Alice," Varney said, "my parents, my mother, anyway, *did* want me to be something in the arts. I'm uncomfortable with 'Mr. Varney.' Say 'Cory.' "

"Cory," said Alice Forsythe.

"Can I get you something? Coffee?" She shook her head. "I'm afraid I disappointed them. We were not poor. I was stuffed with the good, the true, and the beautiful. It made me what I am today. I hated it."

"Oh?" said Alice Forsythe. "Look at the name they gave me." Poor baby, she thought.

Examine him: Episcopalian, with a pocketful of Peek Frean bis-cuits to be sucked on at outings. Boston, Back Bay, Commonwealth Avenue, with a high-church Episcopal priest for a father who diddled little boys seriously in the robing room. God Almighty, the things to be found under black cassocks and white surplices, and along the way . . . the delicious fumblings, the fond, stern admonitions, the exclamations, the warmth and wetness and stains, and, yes, the possi-bility of being caught or told on . . . ever a possibility, although who would have thought it of this comely Anglican with his sonorous voice and blunt fingers and smooth face and thick gray hair still streaked with the blond of his youth . . . this tall angel of the choir loft and the *pissoirs* and purlieus of Downtown, only blocks from the purity of the Common. The blade between his legs was no avenging one, rather the . . . succor of all mankind (Pun, my son, pun!) below the age of, say, twelve. ("Forgive him, oh Dearest Lord, for he cannot get his head out of a porthole to save his ass." Coarse and ex-citing.) Varney Senior marched in parades for good causes, suffra-gettes, the First World War, Liberty Bonds and Liberty Cabbage, Sacco and Vanzetti . . .

"My mother, you can imagine, was very much taken with the Cul-ture of the day . . . William Morris, pre-Raphaelites, hand looms, *Trilby* . . ." Of young Varney's mother, another marcher for good causes, it could be said that while her marriage was a miracle it was not made in heaven. She was constructed of the finest British tweed and would have had an adopted child had that been possible. It was not, Father Varney taking his fun where he found it at the time. The conception of her only child was accomplished in fascinated loathing, after which Father Varney, understandably enough, discovered his true vocation and let her alone. When the boy was old enough, he was sent to Boston Latin. His mother drank quantities of sherry and played medieval airs for Cory on a recorder. She rode him in the swan boats in the Public Garden. She made him learn what a ditriglyph was and divagated on the Bulfinch dome on the State House and how it confirmed the serenities of Beacon Hill. She told him that Louisburg Square was matchless. She took him to the beaches outside Boston and encouraged him to play at chivalry, to tilt lances at imaginary charges of black knights on the sand. In the shimmering summer heat, in her mind, all the knights wore turnaround collars above their cuirasses and looked like her husband. As the fumes of sherry rose higher in her brain, she would say, under her breath to her son, "Run the cocksucker through, Don Cory," and the word would produce a chill in her shoulder blades, a thrilling stink in her nostrils.

For the highest of moral reasons, Father Varney kept his hands off his son. His mother, the fuddled bluestocking, read Browning to him over nuts and wine and took him to exhibitions of antiseptic Victorian paintings, including nudes of women never before (or since) seen on land or sea. Even so, the nudes stirred Corydon powerfully, made him conscious of possibilities. By the age of fourteen, young Varney had developed a lifelong dislike for art and literature and religion and an Irish housemaid in the rectory had taught him, by example, that there were things to be found in women other than the smooth surfaces and polished symmetries of Sir Lawrence Alma-Tadema. The glory that was Greece and the grandeur that was Rome couldn't hold a candle to the pink, pimpled bulk of Mary Cecelia Murphy, who crossed herself every time she crossed the threshold of this Protestant house, but crossed it nevertheless; her family needed the money.

She fell upon Cory out of revenge and want, which came first she neither knew nor cared. Corydon never said a word during the rude rites performed on him by Mary in the dark, paneled recesses of the rectory, around the corners of the heavy Mission Oak furniture on which she placed her dustcloths and leaned her mop. Only, he kept his pale blue eyes opened wide throughout everything; did not close them, even when she pulled at him and heaved and rose and subsided; even when she demanded of him the same noises she made. He remained silent and open-eyed, but he did not avoid her. In the end, she decided that that sort of reserve displeased her and took her business elsewhere, outside the rectory. She gave Cory a year to conform and was unrelenting when, finally, he made small, ratlike noises to get her back, when he opened his pants to offer her a white candy bar. Too late, Cory, too late, and shook her head disdainfully and dusted. I would have settled for that, but not now. You are a cold fish, my boy.

Yes, the life of the Varneys was one of remarkable felicity. Father Varney was not unappreciative of the attractions of this froward Celt from South Boston, but his interests lay elsewhere. Mrs. Varney had to be content with her private agonies, public probity, and the private income with which her husband had come to the cloth. Young Varney, for his mother's sake, had studied architecture at Harvard and had become a speculator and builder and moved away to New York, despising anything that had been built earlier than the day before and which did not chip, rust, break, or fall down quickly. He had learned to bribe government people and union leaders, buy inferior materials, and arrange financial deals that could not possibly have withstood the scrutiny of even such imperfect laws as existed. And, if Corydon Varney preferred women to men in the end, it was only to spite his father, about whom the boy learned a great deal at an early age; his mother had made a proficient sneak of him, and, more than once, he had witnessed the tableaux in the dimly illuminated corners of the church.

Nor had the lessons of Mary Cecelia Murphy been lost on him. Once, before the Armenian architect had taken him in hand, Varney took a woman, the associate of a business acquaintance, to a restaurant. She had the look of goods set out for a fire sale. He had slid a hand up her dress under the table, and, with the other, pulled out money and offered it to her. "What in hell is all that about," she had said—not at the hand beneath the table, but at the money. "Look, look at it," Varney had said, excitedly. She looked. It was a two-dollar bill.

"Oh?"

Varney explained that there weren't many of them in circulation any longer, but that that wasn't even the point: it was the symbolism involved. Two-buck whore. Get it?

"Well, all right," she had said, "if you insist, but you really didn't have to go through all that." And closed her legs on the hand. "There, now," she went on. "Why so complicated? Oh, I guess everybody's got his own tastes." She took the two-dollar bill out of his hand. "Thank you," she said. "Tickle me while you're at it. Don't just sit there.

"That's nice," she said. "Your wife. Can you come home with me?" He nodded. "I have a few tricks that would raise the dead. You'll see . . ."

10

Vertigo. Agoraphobia. Koro. Koro?

All in the head, Grosbeck assured himself over and over on the way to the elevator downstairs, past Emily, past the grandeurs of the outer office, past The Founder. All in the head. The heart, too. He saw nothing outside his whirling head. The heart ignored him disdainfully and continued to beat steadily.

VERTIGO: So many years of sitting at a desk, the head barely higher than the top, regarding nothing more dizzying below than a piece of badly written copy; bawling in feckless contempt at the top of his voice at what had been served up and subsiding when told, as McFarland often told him, "Give it a rest." McFarland, the editor who worked at the next desk, had solved the riddle of the universe at the bar across the street. He had been an athlete and his sense of pace was as fine as it had been when he was young: he went to the bar just often enough during the day to permit him to repair the atrocities put before him, sucking in the breath between his teeth as he did so, and to leave the building glowing, rain or shine. He would give it a rest until the end of his life. His liver understood him because he did not abuse it.

AGORAPHOBIA: So many years in the box. And then to be thrust naked into the world by Greenspan, the skin so tender and white and unexposed, like that of a slug in a wet crevice. How toughen it? How flatten the belly, where find the needle and palm to stitch up the heart; how remove the hump, straighten the shoulders, grow five inches taller, clear the milky film from the eye, rip away the caul? Grosbeck blinked in the light in terror, in exhilaration. His hands reached for the sides of the box. They were gone.

KORO: Grosbeck acknowledged a debt to *The Lancet*—" 'Koro' is a form of acute anxiety reaction generally thought of as peculiar to southern Chinese emigrés in Malaya. Since first noted over 100 years ago few cases have been recorded outside China and the Malay archipelago, and the syndrome is generally regarded to be culture bound, relating to indigenous beliefs surrounding sexual function. Koro takes the form of acute panic in which the patient fears his penis is shrinking into the abdomen with potentially lethal consequences. To prevent this the penis is grasped by the patient or by his relatives and friends. Two cases have been reported in North American whites in the presence of amphetamine abuse and a brain tumour."

It was not a perfect fit—Grosbeck had no brain tumor (he ignored the British spelling of the word) and he had never bothered to abuse amphetamines, depending on the sound of his own voice to make him swim in felicity. But, he had no doubt that *The Lancet* had been on the right track. He carried the clipping in his wallet.

"The patient. . . had travelled little . . ."

(Click! Again, the British spelling. He had often edited it in his head.)

". . . and denied any interest in the Orient. He related awakening at 3 A.M. one morning . . ."

(Jesus! 3 A.M. one *morning!* As opposed, of course, to 3 A.M. one evening! Go on, go on, let the poor dumb bastard have it. He's got other things to say. Almost, thou persuadest me.)

". . . with an intense feeling of impending doom. This was associated with the physical awareness that his penis had become very small and was shrinking into his body. Palpitations, sweating, nausea, and other symptoms of the panic attack rapidly developed, but the feeling that he was about to die was inextricably linked with the recession of his penis. As a result of this he sought to alleviate his anxiety by pulling the organ in an attempt to restore it to normality."

(At least, he didn't say "normalcy.") The rest of the article was a lot of blah, blah, blah with the exception of the following:

"He found that he was able to foreshorten an attack by forcing his mind to other things—usually, and appropriately, erotic subjects . . . He was, and remains, sexually well adjusted."

Grosbeck set out for the City Room with, as *The Lancet* had promised him, feelings of impending doom, every thumping palpitation, the sweating and the nausea. But, lacking friends and relatives to grasp his penis at the moment, there was nothing for it but to work on the pud himself. Looking about him as he waited for the elevator, Grosbeck was overcome with shyness. He had never grasped his penis in public, had never even pissed on a hub cap, had never waved it threateningly at a woman, but now he must, he must. This was an emergency he felt sure anyone would understand. If not, he must find out anyway. There was no one else waiting for the elevator. He poked at his pud with a forefinger. That would have to do for now. But, just as he did so, the elevator doors opened. There was a man inside. Quickly, he transferred the finger to his mouth, pretending to look for some fragment of food between his teeth.

"Damn it all," he said, finger in mouth.

"What's that?" the man asked. "Were you talking to me? And just what *did* you say? Are you threatening me?"

"No. I'm terribly sorry." He forgot that he had been pretending to clean his teeth. "I beg your pardon. You see, I just got a crick in my neck when I turned my head. It's chronic and it's a little painful and the words just slipped out."

"What *did* you say?"

"Just 'Damn it all,'" Grosbeck said. "Pure annoyance with the condition. Nothing to do with you or anybody else in the world."

"I just wondered, was all," the man said. He was tall and thin, obviously someone who stood on his rights but willing enough to avoid a fuss.

"I can hardly blame you," Grosbeck said, dredging up as glutinous a smile as he could find. "I would have done exactly the same thing in your position." He moved into the opposite corner of the car, turned slightly away from the man, and, this time, applied both thumb and forefinger to his fly. They resembled nothing so much as the claws of a lobster trying to pick its nose. But, Grosbeck found that he was all there. All there. Oh, it had never been such a much, but it had not fled into his belly. The palpitations and nausea had stopped, but not the sweating. Casually, he removed his fingers from his innocent penis and looked over his shoulder at the other passenger.

"It's funny," he said. "Sometimes, the pain goes from the neck right down to the groin. I got it in a skiing accident. You never know, do you?"

"No, you don't," the man said as Grosbeck got out at the City Room floor. "Believe me, I sympathize with you. I once got a migraine so bad I curled right up on the floor in front of half a dozen people." Grosbeck nodded. "I'll tell you, though," the man went on, "you never know what to expect in this city anymore, even in a place like this—and even from someone who *looks* as respectable as you."

"Thank you for that," Grosbeck said. He prided himself on how well he concealed his loathing for the other man. Just before the door closed on him, the passenger leaned forward and shouted at Grosbeck's back, "Sir! Sir! I'd give you the benefit of the doubt any time. That's more than I'd say to most other complete strangers." The closing door choked off his last remark: "Sir, have a nice . . ."

"Day, right?" Grosbeck shouted back at the door.

Duffy, the old receptionist, put down his pencil and *Racing Form.* He said to Grosbeck, "He didn't mean any harm, Mr. Grosbeck, sir."

"You stay out of it, Duffy. I don't need any of those quaint forms of social amelioration. Nor your particular brand of clog-dancing, either. All you're missing, Duffy, is a jogging cart and your cap and a scarf around your neck. Vaudeville is dead, Duffy, dead. Harrigan *and* Hart are *dead.* You hear?"

"Beggin' your pardon, Mr. Harvey, sir," Duffy said, "I was only tryin' to be helpful. Do you have an appointment with anyone inside, sir?"

Grosbeck gave it up. "Where do they find them?"

"Find what?" the old man asked.

"People, Duffy, people," Grosbeck said, gesturing toward the elevators.

Duffy looked around the deserted reception room. "They're everywhere," he said, lowering his voice to a whisper. "I have no hesitation telling you that. Best keep an eye out for them." He made a couple of check marks on the *Racing Form* and put it away. "You sure you're all right?" he asked. "You looked better when you came in an hour and a half ago. Don't strain yourself too much your first day back. You look peculiar to me."

"That's only where it begins, Michael," Grosbeck said. "Go make a novena for me."

"Don't make fun of my religion, Mr. Grosbeck, and don't poke fun at a poor old man."

"Up yours, Duffy. When was the last time you were in church?"

"I . . . ah . . . have never lost the intention and that is as good as the deed."

"You think so?"

"I do."

"Duffy, my old and tried, the closest you have ever come since I've known you is those pilgrimages you make so often to the toilet to make your obeisance to the porcelain god."

Duffy raised his right hand and blessed Grosbeck with the middle finger. "My son," he said, "I forgive you. My father and his father before him would have belted you out over on the docks. I have learned the patience that comes with forty-two years on my behind at this desk. I've seen them come and go, the great and the near great, the nuts and the hustlers, the doctors of philosophy and the re-porters and the editors . . . *and* . . . you too."

"How come you stayed here all those years?" Grosbeck asked him curiously. "And you so well-spoken and all?"

"God's will, Mr. Grosbeck, sir, and the sin of sloth. Still, I man-aged to get a son through the seminary and now he is fallen away and a stockbroker—and yet not ashamed of me—and a daughter through college and onto this newspaper. God chose not to accept my son into the priesthood, for which I am deeply grateful. It's not much of a living and all the rewards are in the hereafter. My wife and I live in a house in Queens—we burned the mortgage ten years ago—and, yes, she cooks me corned beef and cabbage once a week and keeps the accounts."

"Accounts?"

"Yes, Harvey, sir. I have accounts to keep, all sorts of little rackets around here, bookmaking and so on . . . It is convenient . . . the men don't have to run out to any of those thieving OTB offices and lose time off the job. I do have one besetting sin, though; I bet on the ponies myself, but I consider that a venial sin and not a mortal one, since I don't bet very much. On balance, the accounts show that we are still ahead. I doubt not that I will be laid away in Cal-vary just as readily as any bluenose. It is possible to commune with the Almighty at the track too."

"I can't say you amaze me, Michael," Grosbeck said. "We've been around each other too long for me not to have some idea of it."

"One more thing, Mr. Grosbeck, sir. Would it surprise you to know who I think you are?"

"Maybe," Grosbeck said. "Probably not. Not any longer."

"I've done a little reading, Harvey, humble though my origins are, on sunny afternoons in the backyard. I've picked my way, word by word, through some books and I know who you are . . ."

"Oh, we're going to be literary now, are we? I can't wait to hear, Duffy."

"Mr. Grosbeck, sir, you are Leopold Bloom."

"What!"

"Leopold Bloom. You gave me the book years ago, one night across the street in the bar. You thought I might like what you called the 'dirty parts.'"

"I apologize, Michael." He thought about it for a moment. "No, Duffy, no. Ordinarily, I go along with your judgments. But, no. I couldn't tell you myself."

"Close enough to suit me," Duffy said. "Some differences here and there . . . different time, different place . . . but that is who you are to me. I mean it as a compliment."

Grosbeck was on the verge of trying to tell Duffy why none of this was so, but he had a mortal fear of boring people outside the line of his business and besides, he realized, it would have taken him several years to explain himself to Duffy and then, of course, he would have been wide of the mark. So many years it had taken him to learn so little about himself. He sighed.

"I take it as a compliment, Michael. I'm touched."

"It's nothing much to be touched about, Harvey, sir. It's that Bloom struck me that way—you don't look anything alike, I don't know anything about your private life, but what I saw in him . . . see in you . . . convinced me."

"What?"

"Some little crazy streak makes you like him."

"What little crazy streak?"

"I can't put my finger on it," Duffy went on, "but it's there. It shows. Drunk or sober, it shows. It comes out. Like the time you disappeared . . ."

"You're tantalizing me, Duffy."

"I don't mean to. That's all I know. That's who you are."

"Well, you read wrong."

Duffy shrugged. "I'm not a hundred per cent," he said. And said, "We'll see."

"Michael, I . . . this is insane . . . you and I talking like this."

"Both of us have said more foolish things over a drink."

"Don't give me the horrible details."

"Take it as a compliment, too, Mr. Grosbeck, sir, that you are the first on this newspaper to whom I have divulged so many facts and opinions, but considering your heart attack and the new job, I decided it was time."

"You aren't burying me now, are you, Michael?"

"No, I am not. And the end of your journey is not yet."

"Hoo hah, the Irish seer. I never knew you could be so flossy."

"I know you're going upstairs."

"How in hell did you know that?"

"I have my ways."

"All right, I can see how Tully and Martha and McFarland . . . any number of people . . . would know *something* in a general way . . . so your knowing I'm going upstairs is no great shakes."

"I even know what you're going to do."

"That's impossible," Grosbeck said to the old man. "You couldn't."

Duffy leaned back in his chair. He intoned solemnly, "A knife, a fork,/ A bottle and a cork;/ And that's the way/ You spell New York."

"Duffy, you've stolen my underwear. Give it back. How? Who? When?"

"The same way I put two hundred and fifty thousand dollars in the bank," Duffy said. "Connections." They both laughed.

"I forgot you used to get the Old Man out of the building when he was still around. You make book. You . . ."

"You may buy me a drink across the street once you're settled in," Duffy said. "It's time to tell the others, clean out your desk, get on upstairs. I'll have someone move you."

"Who?" Grosbeck asked. "Frank Campbell?"

"And your typewriter," Duffy finished. "You wouldn't be caught dead, would you, using an electric?"

11

Alice Forsythe reached over to the night table for her cigarettes. Her eyes were nailed shut. Her nails scrabbled at the table top. She patted the night table. The cigarettes were not there. Mercy, mercy. She knocked the receiver off the telephone. It fell to the floor. Clang. She followed it, falling out of bed, an ear next to the receiver. It buzzed. Then, it importuned her with other sounds. Then, it was silent. It was Sunday morning. She was alone.

She opened her eyes. They creaked. The instep of one of her shoes said good morning to her. The high heel waved a perfunctory greeting. She rolled away from it. She was naked and drunk and sore. The pack of cigarettes winked broadly at her. He must have opened them, she thought. How many times have I told him, told him, told him, *don't* tear off the foil, I don't want crumbs in my bag. She got up on hands and knees. The matches were nearby. Head down, she lit a cigarette. One puff was all she could endure. He had set down his drink near the bed and she dropped the cigarette in it.

Her breasts were blotched red, her thighs mottled. There were black marks on both her arms. Her face? She would look later; he had always been punctilious about that and besides she felt nothing, nothing but the heat of alcohol receding from her cheeks and forehead, a dry mouth and a hum of content between her legs. She felt her breasts, felt her thighs, arms, felt everywhere else, front and back. All in one piece as usual, she thought, her back against the bedstead, her head lolling as though the neck were broken.

There was—she almost regretted it—nothing peculiar about this lover. He had been a lacrosse player in college (of all things) and he was a lawyer. He drank judiciously and made love as though he were composing a brief: so much excess, but not too much; so much yelling at the ceiling, but not too much; so much exploration and abandon, but not too much; so much tenderness, so much humor over everything, but not too much. If it were possible to be systematic and self-possessed in the act which required none of these things, then he was.

"No hard feelings," he would shout jocosely, pinning her down.

"Perfectly all right," she would shout back, working herself up, waiting for it to be out of her hands. "Don't stop. I admire your . . . your stick-to-itiveness." Gasp. Simulated. The real thing would come later. She would admire him to distraction with hands, mouth, feet, behind, front, the hair on her head; running from it and back to it, subsiding cleverly just long enough to get him into the net and then scooping at it with her hips, her arms behind her head, whispering, "Keep it in there [in a voice she did not recognize], stick it, you all-American prick." Why could she not do better than that? "Ah," she went on, "too much is it? Not too much. Good." Well? "Again. Wait a moment. You're hurting me." She crossed her arms on her breasts and provoked him with everything else.

He tore her arms away and squashed her breasts in his hands. "Hard to hold on to anything that size."

"Try," she said, "but gently. I can feel you."

"I *am* trying."

"Now I feel it."

"How did we get so drunk?" he asked.

"We put our heads together," she said. He laughed and belched and fell out of her.

"Don't go away," she said. "Not just yet."

"I want another drink," he said.

"Again," she said.

"In a while, I want another drink."

"Drink here," she said, pointing downward. He sipped at her. "You're *very* good," she reminded him. "I'm smoking."

He looked up. "You really are," he said. "I thought you meant something else."

"Both."

"Play with me," he said, his face smeared with her.

"Gladly. Just a puff or two." She did things to him. A spark fell on her chest and she slapped at it. "It burned me," she whimpered. "Make it better."

He brushed at a breast. "Give me that butt," he said. He stubbed it out in an ashtray.

"You're ready," she announced. "Ready. Is that what you say?"
No answer.

Then: "Don't rush things."

"I'll rush," he said. "I'll rush if I have to. I have to, don't I?"

How sad and stringy this litany: cigarette butts for tapers, glasses smelling powerfully of whiskey for chalices, a bed for altar, the Stations of the Cross a series of prints, inchoate and ambiguous, on the white walls, whimpering at the beholder out of narrow metal frames; the pews a few chairs, one of them overturned in the nightlong, hasty, erratic genuflections of the two worshipers; the wafers bits of bread smeared over with meat pastes and nibbled at the edges, scattered anyhow on a silver tray. How tiring the worship in this travesty of a church, how puerile the communicants, how stale the perfume filling this quiet, despairing room—bodies, tobacco, food, alcohol, scents, the gray smell of damp and dust making its way over the sill of open windows. "Is that all there is?" the recording asked over and over, fixed in a groove. That was all there was, no higher calling than satiety, fatigue, nausea, the skin shrinking in dismay. A pigeon sat on the sill, looking inquisitively into the disarray of the Lady Chapel. It cocked its head, glared and blinked, swelled, emptied its bowels in white (in disapproval? For no reason at all?), pranced fatly a few steps, and flew away. There was no food on the sill and it had no opinion and it was bored. But the service was not yet over.

"Is that all there is?" the recording continued to ask in reproach.
"Turn it off," Alice Forsythe said.

"Funny it should get stuck there," he said. He got up, took the recording off the machine, and broke it in half. The turntable continued to revolve. "That should do it," he said. "I'll get you another one." Then, he found the switch and stopped the turntable.

"No, you won't. You've forgotten. Not that, not anything else. It's the last time. You're getting married today," she reminded him. "I *was* going to send you home early." She rode him easily, but came down hard on the "was."

"Nothing is the last . . . aaaah . . . time," he said.

"No more talk," she said.

"No more last time," he said. They barely moved. She bowed her head; he closed his eyes. They accommodated each other minutely. Old acquaintance. Darby and Joan.

"Do you really love her?"

"You're wonderful," he said. The voices were low and monotonous, the voices of tired shopkeepers making up the day's accounts. Polite nonetheless. "Do I love her?" He considered it. "Do I love her. Do I love you? Yes," he concluded, "I love you."

"You're making conversation," she said.

"You had to think about it, didn't you?" he asked. Not for an instant did their bodies separate. Spasm was off in the distance somewhere, the button on the foil yet to touch off the electric light to signal a score.

"God," she said, "you feel good."

She lifted her head from her chest. "Why are you crying?" she asked.

He opened his eyes beneath her. "My eyes are tired," he said. "Too much smoke."

"No more than that?" He pushed up at her; she pushed down at him. Spasm. The two cold fornicators were finished. For the time being.

"Let me up," he said. She rolled off him. "You *are* crying," she said.

"No," he insisted.

"Should *I* be crying?" she asked.

"Do as you please."

"I cry."

"Delighted. We could have got married," he said. "Today. Any day. We suited each other."

"What else?"

"That's all there is," he said, smiling, pointing to the broken record.

"There must be more," she said, lighting another cigarette. "You're going around and around."

"I *do* repeat myself," he admitted.

"No, no, that isn't what I mean," she said. Her body told her she had better hurry. "You're *revolving*. Why don't you stay in one place?" She rose as quickly as she could, tripped over a bedsheet and got to the bathroom where she threw up. She raised her head to see that the smoking cigarette was still between her fingers and she threw that into the bowl too. She flushed everything down, put her forehead on the seat, listened to the rush of the water through the ringing in her ears.

"You all right?" he asked from the bed.

By now, she was sitting on the toilet seat. "Yes, yes, of course," she said impatiently. "Just give me a minute, will you?"

"All the time in the world," he said, looking at her from the doorway to the bathroom. She pulled a towel off a rack, wiped her face and mouth and neck as she sat there, then threw the towel into the tub. He lifted her off the toilet seat, his arms under her shoulders, and kissed her. "One last drink?" he asked.

"Ah," she said, "one last drink. *That's* it." He had her head in his hands, holding it as though it were part of a dummy.

"I didn't mean it," he said to the dummy.

It ignored him and went on: "One last drink and one last screw and one last night and one last I-don't-know-what . . ." His lips moved as the dummy's scratchy voice rose. A plaster tear ran down the dummy's wooden face. He set Alice Forsythe down on the toilet again. "I don't have your intestinal fortitude," she said to his navel. The slack of her belly cried.

"You're whining," he concluded. She nodded. He leaned against the doorway and watched. "Don't try to stop it," he said solicitously. "It can't do you anything but good." She nodded. Minutes passed in the cold.

"Look at me," he said. He was standing straight out again. She opened her eyes.

"Look at you," she said. "One of the seven wonders of the world."

"I can't help it. That's the way I feel about you."

"And you have to show me, over and over and over."

"I can't help it." He picked around in his mind for something else to say and found an old joke: "This thing is bigger than the both of us."

Her belly stopped crying and grinned. "There's the evidence, eh counselor?"

"We're not litigating, Alice," he said, banging on the door jamb with the palm of his hand.

"I've got one for you, counselor," she went on. "I think of you as the party of the first part." She weighed it in her hand. "Got it? Party of the first part." Neither of them smiled. "Go get married," she commanded him. "Let me alone. You haven't got that long to get ready, either. I'm in the wedding party, too, remember? I've got to get ready, too . . ."

"I *am* ready," he said. She rose from the bowl and somehow got past him into the bedroom. She looked over her shoulder at him. "Aren't you ever the one."

"I guess it *is* time for me to go," he said, looking around for his clothes.

"You *are* a good-looking man, Howard," she said.

"Thank you," he said, picking things up. Out of deference to what he conceived to be her hankering after abandon, he would throw his clothes around the room; proof, he thought, that all that mattered was getting his hands on her, proof that the world was well lost for him, too. It troubled him to do it; he would much have preferred to hang his things away in a closet. One night, he had tried to, and, in the clumsiness of drunkenness, had brought down a whole rack of her clothing.

"Forget it, you big oaf," she had said.

Horror stirred like a worm in a corner of the bedroom, but neither he nor she saw it, nor felt a chill, nor drew back; that would have been an unprofitable digression, sentimental. From then on, they clinked carefully against each other, like glasses, and nothing got spilled or broken. There were no dried scabs to be picked at or burning flushes of anguish to be endured. Or, so it seemed.

"You smell good," she said.

"You, too," he said.

"Even now? Even with the whiskey and the throwing up?" He buckled his belt and reached for his shoes and socks. "Even with all that. Do you have a shoehorn?" he asked.

"You don't know yet?"

"I forgot," he said, and pushed the shoes on his feet.

Show some remorse, each thought, observe the forms, at least be thoughtful.

"Why did you ask me whether I love you?" he asked. "Why did you say you did," she said, not asking.

"I told you, we suit each other."

"I didn't send you off to marry her," Alice Forsythe said. "You found her yourself."

"There were reasons."

"Such as . . . ?"

He raised a hand, as though to slap her. She did not move, and he dropped his hand. "I can't."

"No, you never could."

"You counted on that, didn't you?"

"People like us don't slap or punch or kill. We're reasonably careful. But, you haven't answered me."

Fully dressed now, he sat before her, the lawyer making his case, thinking. He patted the pockets of his jacket and his pants pockets. Everything was there. The lines across his forehead disappeared. "There's nothing about you or me," he said, "which suggests love. There are a lot of people around . . . here, anyway, here in this city . . ." He gestured toward the windows and at the pale, fat rays of sun coming through the slats of the half-closed blinds and through the motes of dust swirling in the shafts of light. "Maybe everywhere . . . I have a theory," he went on, "that we . . . you and I and all those people I was about to mention . . . I don't know how many of them there are, but I do know that they are of the same class— roughly—all over this country, all over the world, I guess, and that— roughly—they all behave the same way and that they are interchangeable—no matter what they do—like automobile parts. The tolerance between parts is not always the finest, they're not made by hand the way things used to be"—she laughed—"and when that happens, they crack or get scratched and broken or catch fire and have to be taken out for other parts. And, I suspect that these mechanical accidents, the result of bad workmanship, are as close as these people ever get to feeling anything . . ."

"Speak for yourself, my dear," said Alice Forsythe.

"I *am* speaking for myself," Tracy said, "and for you, too, and for all of these people, and I know, sure as hell, that there isn't any more than that to any of us . . ."

"You're yearning, Howard," said Alice Forsythe. "You're saying to me that because you're like that, I'm like that and everybody else is like that."

"Everybody I know," he said. "There must be others who are different, but I haven't met them and from the way we did things, I think you're not one of them and not likely to be. I don't mean to be rough about it, I don't think we're unique, I don't think . . . Yes, I'm like that and so are you and so are they and here we are on my wedding day as little upset as can be . . . worn a little, scratched a little, needing only another part to keep moving. I've found my other part, you'll find yours . . . Alice, Alice, you dislike any pretense at eloquence just as much as I do. I haven't told you anything you don't already know."

"No," she said, "you haven't."

"It's no knock on you," he added. "No knock on me or anybody else. It's just the way we are, the way the world is now—our particular world—and had we wanted to be any other way, we would long since have behaved differently."

"I can't argue that," she said. "Tell me something," she asked, "Did she . . . does she . . . know about us?"

"You astonish me, Alice," he said. "Of course. From the day I first started taking her out. Just as you did."

"Did it bother her?" she wanted to know.

"Did it bother *you?*" he asked.

"Well, I must admit I admired your stamina."

"Now," he concluded, "do you finally see what I mean? Had you felt anything else, you wouldn't have said something like that. Had I felt something else, I suppose, I wouldn't be going off to get married today—and with you as a spectator."

Chant, response, homily. "Is that what's wrong with me?" she asked.

"With me, too. And not wrong. Wrong isn't the right word. There isn't any word. Nobody is guilty of anything." He sat quietly in the chair, his hands folded on his lap. "I would rather be asleep," he said. "We've both of us had too much tonight, drink and food and so on."

"Tonight?" she asked, nodding toward the windows.

"I can get two or three hours, and a shave and shower. You, too."

"Shave and shower?" she asked.

He waved a hand at that. "You'd better. It's a career decision," he added derisively. "Varney will be there and Kazanjian. We both work for them."

"I met an angry little old man the other day, Howard."

"So that's it. How little, how old?"

"No, that *isn't* it, Howard. I just happened to think of him. Pretty little."

"How old?" he asked again. "Don't get girlish about it."

"A good twenty years older than you, Howard."

"How does he come up in your head now?"

"For God's sake, Howard, I was *introduced* to him, that's all."

"A lot of us get introduced to a lot of people," he said.

"I'm surprised, Howard, you've got any temper left in you after a night like this."

"That's all that's left," he said.

"Thank you," she said. "I thought more highly of you." That made both of them laugh and cackle and rock back and forth.

But he was persistent. "Where?" he asked.

She was impatient. "At The Newspaper," she said. "In the editor's office. Greenspan. I was up there to talk to him about the new buildings, to get the paper interested. On our side. The rebirth of New York. That paper is so eccentric. Times you least expect it, they'll go against you. Varney does want to tear down those mansions. And he needs The Newspaper. They *are* beautiful," she said, "and we can't have the paper rhapsodizing and wringing its hands over them. It's a precaution. I don't expect Greenspan to fight it. If it were their piece of real estate, they'd be the first to go along, even if it were Versailles. But, we can't take the chance. Varney will take care of the zoning people and the banks and the Board of Estimate and the Landmarks people . . . They've never been able to touch him and they won't now. But, what I have to do is get The Newspaper to tell people how good this is for them and, at the same time, how inevitable, and to dig up history to prove it . . . the tide in the affairs of men and so on. They've got enough light-footed architecture critics to justify anything." She stopped. She was still very drunk. So was he. "It's against everything I thought I stood for," she said. "It's a career decision, as you say, like my showing up at your wedding in one curry-combed piece." Her voice began to tail off. "Where are we all going?" she asked. "What does it all mean? I'm kidding."

"You want an answer, Alice?" he asked. "I've got just the one for you: 'Life is real, life is earnest.' "

"Please," she said, putting up the palm of a hand before her.

"What's your angry little old man got to do with this? I repeat: How old? How little? Angry about what?"

"Howard, I was on my way out, he was on his way in to see Greenspan about something."

"But, why do you bring him up now, of all times?"

"Because, Howard, he's some sort of editor for the paper, I gather, and what got my attention was how furious he got when he found out what I do, where I work. He's an architecture nut; he doesn't like anything we do these days . . . He's bent and he's got a belly and white hair and he's small. He could barely contain his contempt and his name is Grosbeck."

"Grosbeck, Grosbeck. Marjorie knows him, knows his wife, anyway. They'll probably be there today. Of course they will. That proves another theory I have. We all know one another or know of one other or have something to do with one another or do things which have to do with things all of us do . . ."

"Remarkable, Howard, remarkable. See? That explains everything, doesn't it? That should set your mind at rest, shouldn't it? Grosbeck and I, we're just another proof of your theory that we all feed out of the same trough."

"Aren't you both, though?" he asked.

"Doesn't the sun come up in the East?" she responded.

"Doesn't a Jew always answer a question with a question?" he asked. Mirthless, the both of them. "Grosbeck," he said. "The name fits him."

"That's childish, Howard. What fit him most was his clothes. So do yours. I liked it."

"You're saying I don't?" he asked.

"Don't pout, Howard," she said. "Today's your wedding day."

"And not so small you didn't notice him," he went on.

"What are we going on about?" she asked the ceiling. Her eyes rolled back in her head. She sat with her legs apart. "Is this the best we can do?" she asked. She listened. The Puerto Rican lady God cleared her throat, thought better of it, and said nothing. She would provide no answers to small talk. Only to big talk. She did not have anything to say to the meeting of small minds. She was pitiless. They would have to fend for themselves.

"But you did take notice, didn't you, Alice? In so short a time?"

"I'm a trained observer."

"I've noticed."

"Howard," she said, covering her eyes, sprawled in the armchair, "that's enough. For both of us." She struggled up out of the chair. He rose, too.

"What does he have for breakfast? How is he in bed . . . ?"

"I'm dismissing you, Howard," she said, urging him toward the door faintly. "Haven't you noticed the air of finality about me?" He opened his mouth again. "Don't nag me, Howard. It isn't that important. Nothing is. Neither you nor I nor Grosbeck nor his wife, nor your wife . . ."

"Nothing," he said, opening the door. The open door caught a draft and ashes blew out of an ashtray. "See you this afternoon," he said to the corridor leading to the elevator.

"I'll be there," she said, closing the door on him. She moved painstakingly toward the bed and fell on it, face down, sick, asleep.

On the morning of the wedding, Grosbeck had a dream in which his undependable, clownish unconscious trotted out some representative samples of the tricks it was forever playing on him. The little dog laughed to see such sport and the dish ran away with the spoon. "I have an idea for your first piece, Harvey," said his unconscious. It was Greenspan, looking more malevolent than usual. Greenspan was a huge fish—a bloater?—disguised as a rabbi, but Grosbeck was able to tell it was a fish because the long black coat in which it was dressed did not quite cover the tail which thrashed about for emphasis whenever Greenspan spoke. The fish was a dybbuk, which was nothing untoward for Grosbeck: awake or asleep, his life was peopled with dybbuks, and he did not awaken. The Greenspan dybbuk wore a broad-brimmed, black, brushed-beaver hat which kept sliding from one side to the other of the narrow fish head; the hat had not been made for a fish. Beneath it, there were earlocks made of rainbow-colored scales with black spots on them. "It will give you the necessary scope," said the dybbuk in a string of bubbles.

"I don't need scope," Grosbeck said, in his own string of bubbles. He, too, was a fish, a smaller one, in knickerbockers, the legs of which covered the fork in his tail. Otherwise, he was a naked fish.

He wasn't sure where the conversation was taking place. It was neither in a room nor out of doors. There was no furniture, there were no landmarks; there was neither light nor dark, although the morning star and a crescent moon were still up in the lovely sky outside and the constellations were so assertive that they could be heard through the street lights. There was neither sound nor silence, yet everything said was understood, answered, agreed with or disputed. In the background, of which there was none, there could be heard (or not) the sound of a telephone ringing and those of a manual typewriter contesting with an electric typewriter. (Electric typewriters were among the demons which plucked at Grosbeck's flesh; his fingers could summon up from their keys only gibberish, such as ,¢¢rmxitx tybme or, if he permitted a finger to linger an instant too long on a key, XCcccccccccccbbbbbbb. The carriage of an electric typewriter then would bang back and forth in a rage at him until he pulled the plug. He would implore the manual typewriter to bite the electric, but the manual would shake its head in resignation and roll away on its little table to a closet. The presence of an electric in his dream confirmed for Grosbeck that it was an invention of the devil and the dream a bad one, but the devil had invented so many evils for Grosbeck he was sore beset to keep up with them. He snored in dismay and a trickle of loathing ran out of a corner of his mouth.)

He and Greenspan seemed to be swimming around and around each other in some sort of viscous, transparent liquid. It was plain that Greenspan was chasing Grosbeck rather than the other way around. Sometimes, when a paucity of bubbles indicated that nothing was being said, Greenspan would curl his rubbery fish lips and bite Grosbeck's tail, which was raw from having been bitten by this one or that all his life. The dybbuk's teeth had even ripped his knickerbockers. "It's kind of a departure for us, Harvey," Greenspan said, "the idea being to incorporate a lot of the new elements we're putting into the paper."

"Incorporate!" Grosbeck bubbled. "Incorporate me no incorporations." Greenspan fished a long, powerful fin out of a pocket in his coat and slapped Grosbeck with it. "Pay attention, you poor fish," Greenspan admonished.

"I am," Grosbeck said in a bubbling whine. "What do you want? Blood? My heart doesn't pump enough anymore."

"That's from smoking," Greenspan rebuked him.

"You're as bad as my wife," Grosbeck said. "There's a way around both of you," he added.

"There's no way around me, Harvey," Greenspan said, puffing himself up so that he almost burst the buttons on his coat, which he had bought at a one-stop Hebrew clerical-supplies outlet on Essex Street. "I want about 750 words in which you will combine nostalgia for some part of the City—or a building—whatever, I don't care— with diet, medicine, sex, science, the theatre, and finance. It's a tall order, but I know you can do it. We didn't pick you to do this sort of thing for nothing."

Slowly, Grosbeck listed the ingredients after Greenspan. "Is that all?" he asked. "Sure you haven't forgotten anything. How about settling for the Apocrypha in outmoded British slang?" Sarcasm was lost on fish like Greenspan; they stand on their own two feet. By now, the liquid was a fury of bubbles. "No," Greenspan said. "Let yourself go. The sky's the limit. Just keep policy in mind. Don't come on too strong for anything unless you're ready to take it back in the last couple of paragraphs. That's the mark of a finished writer around here."

"Finished. You're dead, dead right. Mostly dead."

"Don't get smart with me, Harvey," Greenspan said, smacking him with a fin. "Get smart with something else. The subject is closed. This newspaper is *for* psychiatry, soul searching, dreams, bilingualism, *understanding*, from the first tiny cry of a child in the Matto Grosso or Darkest Africa—we don't even say 'Darkest Africa' any longer—to the commendable gropings of a wetback eking out a miserable living in a California lettuce field. It's our job to fill holes, to bring certitude, not to punch more holes in a structure so delicate, so beset with doubt and contradiction as it is. It is cynicism of the kind you display which has brought us to the . . . to the brink of . . ."

"I'll finish it for you, Marty . . . Nuclear destruction, Marty? Naturally. The messy end of all social order. The damping down of compassion. Darkness. The closing down or blowing up of banks and boutiques, delicatessens and department stores, the end of expense accounts and credit cards, the end of civilization as The Newspaper knows it and all the rest of the lying horseshit we peddle so assiduously."

Grosbeck was almost hidden in his bubbles. Greenspan was firm. "You took the money, Harvey. You asked for work."

"Everyone's got to eat, Marty."

"So, eat," Greenspan admonished him, "and spare me and the paper your parlor nihilism."

"That's an order, Marty?"

"That's an order, Harvey."

The two found themselves in a burlesque house in Harlem, on East 125th Street, not far from the Third Avenue El. The Triborough Bridge had not yet been built. At the New York Central station, a block west of the El, dozens of trains passed, where today only a few go through, usually with their generators smoking or on fire, to break down in the Park Avenue tunnel or in the Bronx, causing the suspension of traffic for hours and inducing even greater emotional illness among the unfortunates whose fathers and mothers had gone to the suburbs, thinking they were putting one over on the City of New York. When the trains did manage to move, disadvantaged youths, as they came to be known, threw stones through the windows, now and then hitting a driver or a passenger, even killing a few. Such occasions were now celebrated in burned-out buildings in the Bronx where the disadvantaged youths, the object of tremulous concern among social workers who feared they might themselves get hit one day, finished one another off with whiskey, drugs, knives, guns, and clubs, thereby making things a little easier for the police and providing some modest form of population control—not a lot, but some.

"Serves the bastards right," Grosbeck murmured aloud, thinking thirty years ahead. Greenspan was sitting next to him.

"What's that you said, Harvey?" he asked.

"Nothing," Grosbeck answered. "Just expressing some humanitarian feelings."

"Didn't sound that way to me, Harvey. Remember, I can hear what you're thinking, too. Sounded like any outworn linthead, woolhat bigotry to me. Don't even permit yourself to think it. You blame the criminal-justice system, my boy, you blame two hundred years of injustice, of economic and educational deprivation, the prisons, the teachers, the parents, the unequal distribution of the world's goods and so on and so on and so on. And, you do it with such a bewildering array of statistics—you can think them up yourself or get them by telephone, nobody's going to know whether they're right or wrong anyway or whether they have anything to do with what you're talking about—that everything cancels everything else out. You stand foursquare and flatfooted with the utmost conviction. That's what makes the world go round—more than love." He reflected a moment. "I take that back," he said. "Can't neglect love. The priceless ingredient. The bottom line, Harvey, you'll forgive the expression. More precious by far than ambergris. Got to have love too."

"Let 'em eat love, Marty?" Grosbeck asked.

"You want the last word, Harvey, you can have it," Greenspan

said. "By the way, where are we? This doesn't look like any conference hall to me. More like a fish tank."

"It's a burlesque house, Marty."

"What are we doing here," Greenspan asked, "chewing over dubi-
ous social philosophies?"

"Beats the shit out of me," Grosbeck said. "I don't know what I'm
doing here. I'm not responsible for my dreams. But, you know, I
used to come here a lot when I was in high school. Part of my education. And that was before the kids used to take field trips to relieve
the teachers of working for an afternoon. I did it on my own. It
broadened my horizons. I *anticipated* field trips. Burlesque was an article of *vertu*, or it was going to be. I was ahead of my time. You
weren't even in New York then, were you?" Greenspan shook his
head. "Where you from?"

"Cleveland," Greenspan said.

"Cleveland, Cleveland," Grosbeck mused. "Then you must have
had burlesque there. My memory tells me they had a Wilner Wheel
house in Cleveland, maybe Columbia Wheel, maybe both. You
must have gone."

"Well, yes," Greenspan admitted reluctantly. "What I'm telling
you is dead in this dream, but I used to go afternoons when I
was supposed to be cramming at Hebrew school to be *bar mitz-
vahed* . . ."

"Reform, right, Marty?" Grosbeck asked triumphantly. "In and
out in five weeks? Otherwise, you would . . . Orthodox you would
have had that Torah, the Baal Shem Tov, and all the rest of it
rammed through your curly little head from the time public school
let out until the sun went down. Some *yeshiva bucher* you must have
been, pounding your meat in a burlesque house. And in Cleveland
yet!" It was the first time Grosbeck had ever caught Greenspan out
at anything, dream or no dream.

"I got it, Marty," Grosbeck said, excitedly. "I know why we're
here. This is going to be my first piece . . . an affectionate recreation
of burlesque, with notes on the performers, observations on the architecture . . . Oscar Hammerstein, the old man, built in Harlem, I
remind you . . . faded red-velvet curtains, gold leaf peeling off the
proscenium, plaster caryatids with broken noses on the pilasters,
busted seats . . ."

"You can say that again," Greenspan interrupted, shifting from side to side. "Already, my tail is a mass of numb scales."

"Numb scales," Grosbeck repeated. "Numb skulls, Marty?"

"Boy, ain't you a card, Harvey."

"I couldn't help it, Marty. I've got worse than that." Neither paid much attention to what was in front of them at the moment: a scratched Burton Holmes travelogue, which had been preceded by another and another and would be followed by others until the house was respectably filled or the manager had decided that that was all he was going to pull in for the matinée and he might as well get the show started. The travelogues had eccentric sound tracks—they roared during sunsets and were so muffled when the narrator was speaking that he could not be understood. And they were shown on a wrinkled, dirty-white screen with long tears in it. It rippled whenever the sour, warm blasts from the fans at the side of the theatre turned in its direction. Nobody watched or listened. The house lights were kept up during the "movie presentation" and the audience could be discerned through the discreet beams of amber bulbs screwed into brass torchières.

The assemblage was all male—none of this mingling of the sexes which was later to be found in dirty-movie houses. The men seemed to be people interested in what was going on in the world: they all carried newspapers—not tabloids, but substantial, standard-sized journals like the *Sun* or the *Evening World* from the night before or the *Times* from last Sunday, despite it being the middle of the week. This was misleading, however. The newspapers would be put to another purpose. To a man, the audience wore raincoats, despite the fact that the sky outside was clear, or topcoats, in the face of unseasonably mild weather and a theatre hissing with heat. They were known as "newspapermen." It was their custom, when the strippers came on, to spread the newspapers on their laps and fumble at themselves through the pockets of their coats and pants which had been cut open with a razor blade. (The forgetful among them lost a lot of change that way.)

There was never any applause at the conclusion of a stripper's turn because their hands were busily occupied elsewhere. At the most, there would be a grunt or a cavernous sigh, a series of wriggles, a creaking of seats, a sliding of newspapers from the lap among the most abandoned. (It was bad for the seats, which collapsed often;

they were not repaired but tied in place with lengths of rope or removed altogether when that no longer worked. There were gaps in almost every row. Customers had fallen, it is true, but if any had been hurt, nothing had been said. There were still enough seats for all.) Nobody ever stayed for the entire show, the length of stay depending on staying power, the ability to stave off climax. Men left at odd intervals, raincoats buttoned, newspapers under their arm, shoulders sagging, head down, shaking one wet, sticky leg, reproached by the purity of the sunlight, purged.

The last travelogue flickered to an end. Actually, the film had broken. The sound track had first groaned, then squawked, then choked on an enthusiastic, off-pitch rendition of "The Ride of the Valkyries," the film dying on a charge of yak into the Tibetan sun. The manager, who had been peering into the street from the lobby, ran hurriedly upstairs to the booth. The projectionist had fallen asleep again. "Son of a bitch," the manager screamed at him, "couldn't I get another fifteen minutes out of you?" The projectionist, an old man, took no offense. "Tell it to the union, mac," he said. "Them reels are like torn paper napkins. You gimme paper napkins, that's what you get. See you tomorrow morning." He picked up a cigar butt from the floor. It had fallen out of his mouth when he went to sleep. It was still burning. The projectionist put it in his mouth and dragged it up to a glow. It had left a black burn mark on the floor, one of dozens. The projectionist had explained to the manager many times that he had a nose so sensitive that he would wake up instantly should the floor ever catch fire. The union had upheld him.

The pit band filed in. It bore a resemblance to Napoleon's tired dragoons (in Moe Levy suits, one price: twenty-five dollars) in retreat from Moscow.

DRUMMER: Three snares, one bass drum, cymbals, top hats, tom-toms. The band depended on him to underscore bumps, grinds, and revolutions, to punctuate jokes. He always came in late, clicking his false teeth in a vain effort to keep up. The teeth were on time, but nobody could hear them. He wasn't much good at holding the band together. The strippers, who were so particular, so touchy about having him come in just before a thrust, accommodated themselves to him in disgust.

"He gives me arthuritis," one of them had complained to the manager.

"What can I do?" the manager asked with a shrug. "He's the walking delegate for the union."

"So let him walk," the stripper had said, "and get another one."

"I can't afford it," the manager told her. "You want a better drummer? Go downtown to Broadway."

"Fuck you," said the stripper. "You can kiss my ass," she added, turning her back on him in anger.

"Darling," said the manager, whose white hair was turning green and yellow, "I been waiting all my life you should ask me. Get out of my sight, you dirty bum." There were many such flickerings of lightning on Olympus.

CORNETIST: The only bright thing about him was his instrument, which he had learned in twenty-six easy mail-order lessons at home. His hair was black, pomaded. He improvised solos often, although not intentionally, but the strippers liked him and sometimes went to bed with him, just as though he were lead man in the Paul Whiteman band.

TENOR SAX, BARITONE SAX: Siamese twins, there only to lend a touch of erotic suggestion when the strippers were going through their graceless gyrations. They doubled on clarinet.

VIOLIN AND NOMINAL LEADER: Lost and tuneless, a tiny man ideal to accompany the house tenor, since neither could carry a tune. In a remote corner of his head, there lived maybe Paganini, maybe Walter Damrosch. At work, his eyes watered with longing and he bowed his cheap instrument like a plumber pushing a length of pipe through a hole in the wall. On Garden Street, in the Bronx, he was regarded as someone apart from the ruck; people could *see* he was a violinist. His wife loved him and made him bad pot roast. His children loved him, but the boy wouldn't go to the settlement music school and the girl had a voice like a crow. His eyes watered at them too.

PIANO PLAYER: A wreath of broken capillaries on his nose, which looked like a pot of violets. He kept a bottle of whiskey he called "Panther's Piss" at his feet and knocked it over once in a while when his forgetful foot missed a pedal. He had learned to keep it corked. Liquor had disguised his age and despair had thinned him. There were deep furrows in his cheeks, deep lines in his forehead, much gray in his hair. He was thirty-five. He was a fine piano player, cake-walks and jazz. The violinist looked down on him for that. There was always a baleful smell of cheap liquor in the pit, which floated out to mingle with all the other stenches harbored by the theatre. If the house were cold, he played with gloves on. It made no difference: no fewer than a third of the upright's keys had lost their hammers and the instrument had not been tuned since a traveling opera company last appeared in the theatre in the early twenties. He and the BASS PLAYER (who peddled insurance on the side) did what the drummer could not—created an approximation of order in the band. (Fifteen years later, the piano player would leave his messy apartment on the West Side dead drunk, fall downstairs, and kill himself, breaking several of his long, thin fingers on the iron bal-usters as he clutched and tumbled down the carpeted steps.)

AS TO THE ENSEMBLE: It carried sheet music to which no one ever referred, which often was strewn upside down on the stands in the wrong sequence. The band knew its dismal repertory by heart. The management insisted on the sheet music as a bit of class which would impress the audience. The band had another characteristic, *de rigueur* in burlesque pit bands: it played conscientiously out of tune and sprayed clinkers blithely into the air, like mummers on a parade float throwing confetti at a crowd. There was something genetic in its ineptitude. Once, in the past, it had unexpectedly played all the right notes of a song and that had given the manager a flare in his ulcer. At intermission, while the candy butcher was moving up and down the aisles selling chocolate bars (". . . with the nuts on the outside . . ."), the manager had berated the musicians. "What're you guys trying to do?" he demanded to know. "Ruin me? All of a sudden you're the Philharmonic?" He turned on the leader. "You, Walter Damrosch, play like you always play. Don't make me nervous, my stomach won't take it." The flush of accuracy was quickly suppressed.

The band started up the overture: a "millange" (that was the manager's word for it) of "Runnin' Wild," "Girls, Girls, Girls," and "Keepin' Out of Mischief." The house lights dimmed, the audience settled down, the newspapers stopped rustling, the rotten air grew thick with anticipation, and the house tenor strode from the wings to do his opening number and get the first act on. The audience knew it would have to suffer him, the chorus, and then a sketch be-

fore the first stripper went to work. It was worth the suffering; had it
not been, all these men would have been somewhere else, possibly
doing research in back issues of "Film Fun." The tenor was a man
in his early fifties, who had never seen better days, who had lost out
in vaudeville to a series of tumblers, Indian-club throwers, sand-box
dancers, bicycle acts, trained dogs, Japanese acrobats, and similar distractions hired to flesh out the turns of the leading singers, dancers,
and comedians. He was not backward in recounting how he had appeared on one bill with Ann Pennington when she brought the
shimmy to the peak of perfection, and had said hello to Eva Tan-
guay in Reisenweber's on Columbus Circle the dawn Prohibition
darkened the land.

His was the poor pomposity of failure, yellowed collars and black
fingernails, a pinkie ring with a yellow stone so large it resembled a
tumor. He was not beloved of the strippers who let him know scorn-
fully that the shimmy was only where it began and who first pointed
at him incredulously and then bent over in laughter when he offered
to take one of them out to a bar. One of them was onstage once during a sketch in which he doubled for the straight man when that former butcher's helper failed to show up (the tenor wasn't paid extra
for doubling; he should ought to of been glad he was working; go sell
apples you don't like it) and drew attention from his string of bad
jokes by lifting her skirt, turning around and wiggling her behind at
him. (It had pimples on it, in several colors.) "How's that for
shimmy, Jimmy?" she bellowed, addressing the audience over her
shoulder rather than the despised, nothing tenor. He was beyond
depression and humiliation. Since her contemptuous ad lib worked
(the audience appreciated her behind), it was dumped into the
sketch. Whatever worked was dumped into the sketch until all that
remained of the original might be the rubber hot dog the comic
waved at the girls, the iron bed painted white, the stethoscope, the
portable front and back doors and the stage itself with its splintered
boards. (The strippers did splits on it, but with misgivings.)

Something in the man's aspect disturbed Grosbeck. Then, as in all
dreams, it came to him. The tenor was Corydon Varney for all that
he looked nothing like him. He had seen Varney's photograph in
more than one paean to him on the real estate page and in magazine
articles (". . . this most innovative of developers . . .") and he did

not think it unusual of Varney to show up in a dream. Not at all. He was so intrigued that he merely snored and rolled over.

The violinist arose and banged his bow across his fiddle. " 'Digga Do,' " he told the band and without further ado it was struck up noisily, unrecognizable.

"Now, Marty," Grosbeck whispered. "Now it really gets going."

"Gotcha, Harvey," Greenspan whispered back.

But something unforeseen happened. Out of the tenor's mouth, a despondent slit over brown teeth in a thin puce face plainly belonging to a different torso, there issued the following, with appropriate gestures: "Pale hands I love,/ Beside the Shalimar./ Where are you now?/ Who lies beneath your spell?" . . . That had been intended to bring on the second from last stripper in the first act. Someone had been woolgathering. The chorus was in no better case. The fire curtain with the word "Asbestos" on it descended slowly and jerkily, then went up again. The red-velveteen curtains parted, each retreating toward a wing at its own pace and the chorus was onstage—half a dozen girls of a variety of sizes and shapes, no two alike, like day-old rolls out of a German bakery. The curtain at stage left was so slow getting to its destination that three of the girls had to throw it backward over their heads as they advanced, hay foot, straw foot, toward the footlights. The mishap had no effect on their dancing, since no two did the same thing at the same time. They could not do a simple time step in unison. The band was still playing "Digga Digga Do" (the tenor had had the good sense to subside and retreat), but the cheerful chorus was singing something else:

> "Sun goes down, tide goes out.
> Darkies gather round
> An' they all begin to shout:
> Hey, hey, Uncle Dud,
> It's a treat to beat your feet
> On the Mississippi mud . . ."

Eventually, the band got the idea. The girls were in blackface and got up in Aunt Jemima costumes. They had on red-and-white bandannas and gingham aprons over their dresses. However, the aprons were tiny and the mammy dresses had been cut well above their thighs to reveal G-strings on which had been sewed a finger that wagged rakishly at the audience as they moved. Each girl carried a small chamber pot with the words MIXING BOWL on it in one hand and a gray-flannel pancake in the other. They bumped into one another as they howled the song. They cavorted dementedly. They dropped props and picked them up, but they were so lacking in coordination that the audience, if it thought about it at all, believed the colossal clumsiness to be part of the dance. The audience was undisturbed. It saw nothing untoward in the band playing "Digga Digga Do," while the girls were shrilling,

> "What a dance do they do
> Lordy, how I'm tellin' you.
> They don't need no bands.
> They keep time by clappin' their hands.
> Happy as a cow chewin' on her cud,
> When the darkies beat their feet
> On the Mississippi mud."

The violinist-leader was all upset, as usual: within the space of fewer than forty bars he had had to make the band switch three times. Except for the tempos, though, all three songs came out the same. And none of it was Beethoven; it was burlesque at its finest. "May you all burn in Gehenna," muttered the leader. "May your children be born with a trolley car in their stomachs."

"You hear those words, Marty?" asked Grosbeck. "Darkies! Whoops! And right in the middle of Harlem!"

"I do," Greenspan said. "And just after the wops got into Ethiopia."

"Couldn't get away with that kind of coon talk today, Marty. Couldn't! But, don't forget, we're a long time away from today."

"But, Jesus, Harvey," Greenspan expostulated, "Aunt Jemima. White girls in blackface . . . what next? How you going to turn that into an essay on brotherhood in New York?"

"Easy as pie, Marty," Grosbeck said. "You take all that plain, goodhearted bigotry and just turn it around and you say 'We don't do that no more.' And, you tell the reader how common it was and how they did it to everybody, but we know better now, we sure do. They used to do it to the kikes, the krauts, the bohunks, the polacks, the mick bog trotters, broads, faggots, Christians, Ayrabs—they got one little guy with a big nose, he does Jews and Arabs—brothers under the nostrils. Everybody. Just good, clean fun. Nobody took it any other way."

"You don't believe that, do you, Harvey?"

"No, I don't," Grosbeck admitted, "but there were more of us than there were of them, some of my best friends are Jews and not all niggers smell. What's an occasional lynching with what we're going to do to them years from now? And they to us? Nobody was confused in those days. Everybody knew his place and kept it. You miss those days, Marty?"

"You're as funny as a crutch, Harvey."

"It wasn't that funny being a Jew, Marty, a little funnier, but not that much. I took my lumps from a lot of little Irish bastards on Briggs Avenue passing Our Lady of Refuge school on the way to P.S. 46 a lot of mornings."

"But not lynching, Harvey."

"What about Leo Frank?" Grosbeck wanted to know.

"What about all those black faces *without* names, Harvey?"

"You think things are so much better now, don't you, Marty? Sure they are: the black faces have names now is the improvement. Equal rights. They have names."

Happily for the dream, this philosophical colloquy was interrupted when one of the girls dropped her chamber pot. It hit the stage with an iron bang and rolled into the footlights. The audience applauded for the first time. The girl stepped out of the approximation of a line and took a bow facing the wrong way. She had the meatiest, most good-natured, most eloquent buttocks anyone could have asked for. And, they had written across them, KISS ME, YOU FOOL.

"Look around you, Marty," Grosbeck went on. "Some day, you know what they're going to call what we're doing today?"

"What?"

"In-depth research, Marty. You can't even begin to imagine." He turned in his seat and poked Greenspan in the chest with a fin. "I haven't forgotten we're dreaming, Marty," Grosbeck said, "but years from now this kind of 'in-depth research' is going to be very, very big at all the universities. They're going to have something called the National Endowment for the Humanities and a potful of private money—funds, they'll call it, not money, don't ask me why—for this sort of thing and people will get *degrees*, important ones and they'll get to be professors of folkways and mores. With tenure, yet!

And appearances in the morning on television! Poor William Graham Sumner, if he knew anything of this he'd upend his grave. He was such a bluenose. What *did* they teach you in Cleveland, anyway, Marty?" Grosbeck asked. Greenspan did not answer. "A-a-a-g-h, I forgot," Grosbeck added. "You're not even out of Cleveland yet. In a manner of speaking, you'll never get out."

The chorus girls disappeared. They were replaced by a tall, ungainly woman foil in a green skirt slit everywhere it could be without falling off her. Her pink blouse was open to the navel. She had plenty up there and she didn't mind throwing it around. The straight man was onstage. And the comic. This was an undersized man wearing an oriental turban, a morning coat the tails of which reached his ankles, a breech clout made of a diaper, and army shoes. He sat on a dirty pillow. His legs were bowed and hairy. He flapped like a chicken as he talked. A settee with broken springs poking through the mohair had materialized. And piles of stage money. A chart of the Zodiac had been hung on an easel. The comic had a wand in one hand, a horse syringe in the other. "This is called 'Capricorn,'" Grosbeck whispered to Greenspan. "They never do it the same way twice."

"Oh, Mahatma," the girl cooed, rolling her hips at the comic.

The straight man intoned, "The Mahatma is now in the Great Nowhere and only the rustle of a twenty-dollar bill can bring him back." The comic swayed, rolled his eyes, dropped wand and horse syringe, made toilet noises at the girl, scratched his crotch, wriggled in the Lotus Position, and extended his right hand, palm up, toward the girl.

"Here you are, Great Whammy," she said, reaching under her skirt and plucking out a bill. She held the bill daintily between thumb and forefinger, as though it were a cup of tea. Her nails were long and peach-colored, like those of some predatory bird.

"Swami, miss," said the straight man. "The Whammy is something he puts on you."

"Whammy, shwammy," said the girl with a bump at each word. She had no control over the modulations of her voice and the uses of emphasis were lost on her.

"I can see that you are a great dreamer," the comic said with a stage stare at her thighs. They were thick and strong but well-shaped and seemed impatient to get free of the slit skirt.

"Oh, Mahatma," the girl went on, in a praiseworthy but futile attempt to match movement with words, "you are wonderful. [Grind.] Every night I dream. [Bump.] Sometimes I am in a beautiful, shaded glen [covers face with skirt; the sunny thighs breathed hard and smiled at the comic] romping like a nymph [fast, wild walk around the comic with very short steps, causing the enameled iron buttocks to quiver immoderately and the comic to goggle] naked and unashamed. [Not quite; she didn't get stripper's pay; the audience knew the words would have to do for the deed.] Oh," she said, looking down at herself with child eyes, "that *beautiful* spot. [Did she believe it? Who is to say?] Oh, how you would love it." The comic did a series of spastic convulsions sitting on his pillow.

"Lady," he said, lascivient as was required of him, "you're selling real estate, you got a customer." He rolled out a long, fat tongue, surprising in a pygmy; it had grown without reference to the rest of him.

"Aren't you going to read my palm?" the girl asked, dropping her skirt.

"Palm reading is old-fashioned," said the comic. "I specialize in body reading . . . the hand must come in contact with the body." He leered so hard his turban fell over his eyes. The girl pushed it back and felt his forehead. "Oh, sir," she said, "you're so *hot*. Are you all right?" The comic mumbled something in Yiddish, ending with the word *nafka,* meaning whore.

"He loves to simonize them," the straight man confided broadly to the audience. "He puts a high polish on everything."

"I'll put a high polish on your keister," the comic grumbled at the straight man, "if you don't keep out of my sacred forbidden rites."

"Forgive me, oh Great One," said the straight man, recoiling so hard that he almost flung himself into the orchestra pit.

The comic rubbed the girl's ankle, barked and growled. "I'm getting in the mood," he said. "I'm getting in the mood myself just watching you," the straight man said, ad-libbing the line. "It won't do you a damn bit of good, you fairy," the comic ad-libbed back at him. The straight man put his hands on his hips and stamped a foot. Offstage, the two men got along about as well as two clerks working in the same office. Neither had ever caught the other out over an unscheduled bit of business.

The comic pulled the girl down on the settee after a last glare of annoyance at the straight man. Her behind settled on the tip of an uncovered spring. "Shit," she said, getting up quickly, rubbing her backside and moving.

"And now the calf," the comic went on, rubbing a shapely column with dry fingers. "I'll get you something else to play with," the girl said, leaning down toward him. "You better," said the comic. "I can't get anything out of that calf." He explained to the audience: "It's too young to give milk." Nobody laughed.

"Let me try it," begged the straight man. "I feel . . . I feel . . . I feel . . ."

"You're feeling too damn good," said the comic, slapping the other man's hand away. "Gerradahere before you get hurt, you *goyisheh goniff*." Aggrieved, he turned back to the girl. "Let's skip to the knee, honey," he said, with an enthusiasm he found increasingly difficult to work up every performance. (Like the tenor and straight man, he was a failure and tired; he sometimes wondered what he was doing in burlesque, but he would sooner have died than be a civilian.) He was mildly amusing, however, and the audience permitted him a titter. It was all that kept him alive.

"Boy," he repeated, "I haven't been around a *joint* like this in years." Pause. "I can tell by this knee that you're going to take an ocean voyage. The waves are getting higher and higher." He pulled up the girl's skirt and peered beneath it. "Oh, heaven help a sailor on a night like this. Lady, here's your twenty dollars back and I owe you ten." Much fake hilarity onstage from all hands, fanfare, blackout, props kicked into the wings. No reaction from the audience other than a restless stirring in the broken seats.

"Harvey," Greenspan said impatiently, "let's get out of here. I haven't got all afternoon. I got a date to play stickball and I got homework to do."

"Stick around," Grosbeck pleaded, "just a little longer." He added reasonably, "Besides, how do you think you're going to get back to Cleveland from here in time? The homework can wait. Besides, I never heard of anyone playing stickball in Cleveland. They don't have the same kind of sewer system there."

"A lot you know," Greenspan said.

"Tell you what, Marty, just one of the strippers, all right? Then we go. I got enough money to buy us ice cream sodas at Schlumbohm's up the block after."

"This better be good, Grosbeck," Greenspan said. "Why don't we just forget it and have the sodas?"

"Both, both, Marty," Grosbeck said, patting him on the shoulder. "This one is like nothing you ever imagined." He had not the remotest idea which stripper was coming out.

Another rackety fanfare from the band. This time, it brought the tenor out in a sport jacket over his evening pants; there was no time for a complete change. He wore a sprig of celery in his lapel. And he sang the song which would bring on the first stripper of the day. The house lights went out. A red spot was thrown on the tenor's face; it was meant to convey unbridled passion, or, possibly, that the tenor had scarlet fever. He sang an English tune called "You're Blasé," a signal to the audience that the stripper would go the whole way or very close. The tenor wasn't content just to do the chorus and get it over with. Oh, no, he had to do the whole goddamned refrain, too, including:

> "Now life, the overseer, has left you flat,
> He found the killing was not too thrilling,
> You were easy.
> He left you insincere, and aged at that;
> Your voice once happy is sharp and snappy,
> hoarse and wheezy;
> You clutch at ev'ry passing straw, you dope and drink
> While those who were your friends before
> Just watch you sink . . ."

A voice rose out of the audience, impatient. "What kind of corpse you gonna roll out this time?" Beneath the impatience, a note of tumid longing. "We ain't got all day," said another voice. "Finish up and get her out here." The tenor closed his eyes, let his head fall back and extended his arms to the side. He would persist whatever the cost. They could drive nails through his palms, but he would finish. Through his tiny brain there ran, not The Passion, but an old joke: Christ is on the Cross, see? And one of the women wants to bathe his brow with the vinegar. And one of them approaches him. He opens his eyes and looks at the label on the bottle and shakes his head and says, "Take it away, take it away, it ain't Heinz's." The tenor wanted to laugh as he sang but the most he could extract from his agony was a strained smile: in such ways did he inure himself to everything which had conspired to put him on this stage before this collection of hardup trash preparing to jerk off at the sight of a naked woman they would never dare to touch, from whom they would run in panic. He went into the chorus:

> "You're deep, Just like a chasm;
> You've no enthusiasm!
> You're tired and uninspired,
> You're blasé . . ."

The melody was sweet and unaffected, the audience deaf to it and in revolt. The electrician tried to get him off by putting him in darkness and throwing a white baby spot on a parting in the velveteen curtains. The tenor was not to be dissuaded:

> "Your day is one of leisure
> In which you search for pleasure,
> You're bored when you're adored,
> You're blasé!"

The manager sensed revolution and hurried into the pit, banging his head on the underside of the stage. "Anything," he instructed the violinist. "How about 'Over There'?" The band went determinedly into "Hard-hearted Hannah," the tenor bowed in the dark and disappeared to pick at his scabs and leave new wounds, the curtains opened, the band subsided, and the stripper came forth. She didn't need music, she had told the manager. That's what she was famous for, she had told the manager. Just drums and tom-toms. She might talk to the boys (the boys!) she said, but no music. She never knew what her mood was going to be, so she didn't know exactly what she was going to do, so no music, if you don't mind.

The electrician lit her full. She was both alluring and intimidating in her bulk, meet (meat) for such an audience, thighs like the pilings on a North River pier, breasts like great loaves of shaking pumpernickel, slender ankles and feet. "What did I tell you, Marty?" Grosbeck asked Greenspan. "In dreams I hold your hand, madame," he sang at Greenspan.

What there was of her costume was unusual, ingenious. On her left hip, there was a tiny winch, the cables of which ran to miniature mason's hods under each breast, raising and lowering them as she thought necessary for effect. On her right hip, another winch which made them revolve. (In a year, she broke up to eight pairs of hods for the sake of her art.) She mixed things up. She had on not a stitch of clothing, being a great believer, unlike the tenor, in wasting no time. She wore a headdress, however, not one of those bunches of wax oranges, bananas, and pineapples, which some strippers favored, in tribute to Carmen Miranda, but something odd and imaginative: a cardboard rendering of the New York City Hall. (Forty degrees, forty-two minutes North; seventy-four degrees West, the center of the universe by any calculation. Henry James: "The divine little structure . . . perfect taste and finish, the reduced yet ample scale, the harmony of parts, the just proportions, the modest classic grace." The Common Council: "It should be remembered that this building is intended to endure for ages; that it is to be narrowly inspected not only by the scrutinizing eye of our own citizens, but of every scientific stranger, and in an architectural point of view it, in fact, is to give a character to our city." Blunt's Stranger's Guide: ". . . the handsomest structure in the United States; perhaps, of its size, in the world.") So that it could be told that for those who thought, here was a serious woman with a purpose.

Quite serious, quite purposeful, patient in yet another detail: in place of a G-string, she had devised a miniature wrecking ball on a chain. It banged against her whenever she bumped, and while it smashed nothing, its symbolism was evident to the dullest. At the most telling part of her act, she bumped the wrecker's ball against herself. Simultaneously, fire broke out in the cupola of the City Hall on her head (nothing more, really, than St. Elmo's fire rising from the swamp of her brain), a historical re-enactment. There were little fire hoses stretching up over her shoulders from a hydrant affixed to her behind. Their sprays put out the fire in City Hall, leaving the cupola blackened and broken. When the fire was out, she removed the wrecking ball from around her waist and tossed it into the audience. The audience didn't know what to make of it, but there was a brief scramble for the ball, which turned out to be a Ping-Pong ball painted black.

"I got to hand it to you, Harvey," Greenspan said. "That baby sure is something. What'll she do for an encore?" Grosbeck wasn't listening.

"Marty," he said, "I've seen that broad somewhere." The stripper, clouds of smoke still coming up from her head, stood quietly to acknowledge her triumph.

"I can't believe it, Harvey," Greenspan said. "I *know* her. You *know* her. The woman I introduced you to in my office, the one who works for the architect. What was her name? Alice Forsythe. What do you know. So this is what she does in her off time."

"It is, it is, it is," Grosbeck exclaimed. His voice cracked; it was changing; he was not yet past his adolescence. "It is and it isn't, Marty," he went on. "It's a dream, just as I've been telling you all afternoon." And prophecy, portent. Metaphor?

The dream was not yet over. The fire in City Hall started up again. The stripper had not made allowances for that. Flames spread rapidly through her hair; her torso shook in pain and began to melt; her eyes, pieces of char now, their intense stare destroyed by fire, poured out of her skull. What was left of her was obscured in yellow-black smoke. The wings, curtains and proscenium went up next. No one thought to bring down the asbestos curtain. The audience, in a panic, dropped newspapers and rioted for the exits, of which there were fewer than stipulated by law. Some fell and bodies blocked the aisles. There were cries for help. ("*Au secours, au secours!*" Why in French?) Then, there were whimperings for help, grotesque in the mouths of men so lately intent on matters of sex. Then, silence, except for the crackling of burning.

Through it all, the blinded stripper, enveloped in smoke and flame, shrank until, with a derisive explosion, she flew into pieces. The tenor, ham to the end, began another ballad; then, he, too, blew up. Neither Grosbeck nor Greenspan was any longer certain where he was—in or out of a dream—did not know which way to move. Out on 125th Street could be heard the sounds of sirens, the ringing of bells, the screech of tires on the fire engines as they rounded corners to get to the theatre. The theatre blew up. The last thing Grosbeck could remember was grasping Greenspan's hand and saying monotonously and hopelessly, "Help, help, help . . ."

Grosbeck found himself on the floor, his head near the radiator, hot and banging—head *and* radiator. The legs of his pajamas had worked their way above his knees. Knickerbockers, he told himself. The coat was open; the buttons had been ripped off while he was struggling in bed to get out of the burlesque house. Madeline was standing over him, her hands on her hips. Some legs, he thought, looking up. No waist at all, either, although the short robe concealed that. "What was all that caterwauling, Harvey?" she asked. She had a spatula in her hand. He could smell breakfast. "I've turned every-thing off," she said, anticipating him. He could hear a radio in the kitchen playing twenty-four hours of Coleman Hawkins, Lester Young, Bud Freeman, Jimmie Noone, George Brunis, John Col-trane, Sonny Rollins, Louis Armstrong, Doc Cheatham.

"They don't mix well," he said to Madeline. "I don't make the programs," she said. The engines from the firehouse next door rolled back in, silent and exasperated, from a false alarm.

He had an odd reaction: he still tingled from apprehension and Apocalypse; he was depressed and bored with the ordinarinesses to which he had awakened. He reached into his head trying to grasp more of the infernal or supernal, he did not know which it was. "Would you mind," he asked Madeline, "if I called Greenspan?"

"Greenspan? What for? I can understand you calling him about any number of things but you don't need him to verify one of your nightmares."

"He was in it," Grosbeck explained.

"Get up, get up Prince Thrushbeard," Madeline said. She tapped him on a shoulder with the spatula and kissed him on top of the head. "We're going to a wedding in a few hours. The food will prob-ably not be very good, so you'd better have a decent breakfast, and the doctor has told you that you can have a drink—but only one drink a day—for a couple of months, so you can't get drunk."

"Take off the robe?" Grosbeck wheedled.

"And you can't do that, either, for a couple of months," Madeline added.

"I'll go crazy," Grosbeck said. "I don't mind laying down my life, what little's left of it. What can I do?"

"Not much, yet," Madeline said, "but we can both hope, can't we?"

"Thank you," Grosbeck said, and went off to the bathroom. There, he took the pills Dr. Salomon had prescribed for him—an-ticlotting pills, water pills, irregularity pills, optimism pills—for the rest of his life. Alice Forsythe, he ruminated as he shaved. Corydon Varney. Greenspan. He nicked his upper lip. He looked at the safety razor. Had Madeline been using it again on her legs without chang-ing the blade? "God damn it," he said, as the blood ran into his mouth and the last clouds of the dream were dispelled.

13

On her wedding day, Marjorie Denman awoke—alone—from a sleep which had been dreamless and still and free of light or dark. The bedclothes were barely disturbed. The very last thing she had done before turning out the light was to telephone the minister who would marry her and Howard.

"What do you intend to say?" she asked him. He was surprised.

"Why, Miss Denman," he said, "nothing that would not be in full accord with the desires of yourself and Mr. Tracy. Serious yet light, full of hope for a future stretching endless years before the both of you, yet mindful of the many unforeseen events which most certainly will befall the both of you . . ."

"Are you reading something to me?" Marjorie Denman asked.

"Why, no," he said. "As a matter of fact, I have set nothing down yet, but I have talked with you, I have bound many others to each other . . . Perhaps I should not have said *bound* . . . the word is so old-fashioned . . . but I have given the occasion much thought. It is my duty to do so and I do not take it lightly. Mine is a church mindful of its hundreds of years of ministering to its people . . . the good and the bad, the obedient and the willful . . . and it has tempered the sternness of its preceptors with the lessons bequeathed to it by minds perhaps wider in their scope than the narrow paths prescribed in the beginning. There are, if I may make a mild joke, many more mansions in my Father's House than when he set up shop in a hut. Why, only the other day, we joined together for as long as they shall love each other, two gay young men for whom nothing would suffice but marriage. We have not forgotten our Greek heritage. We have overcome much. It was a double-ring ceremony, a union at once solemn and joyful. Strings played Bach partitas. The food was of a surprising delicacy. I could go on, but it is late and I promise you you shall have nothing less. Trust me, my dear. I should say, 'my dears,' although I suspect you are alone at the moment."

"Well, all right," said Marjorie Denman. "I just don't like to leave things to chance." She said good night; the Reverend Mr. McCormack sighed, scratched his head, peed and went to sleep himself. He had a long day before him: three of these things, to say nothing of a special service in the evening for drug addicts. He had had telephone calls like that before. Sometimes he wished he were in something other than the God business, watered down as it had become.

The things Marjorie Denman would wear to get married in were perfect reflections of herself; they would have done equally well at a board meeting and they hung alertly in a closet, ready, ready. Her few jewels, her perfume, her cosmetics were laid out on a dressing table as neatly as drafting tools. Her bedroom had the air of a confident and well-kept locker room.

The only exceptional note in it was a portrait of her by an artist who, upon being dismissed, had returned one night, let himself in with the key she had neglected to ask him for and painted in black under the face the legend, "We have your name on file. If anything turns up we'll get in touch with you." He had thought, at first, to paint over the face, but vanity had got the better of him. She had thought, at first, to cut the painting up or put it in a closet, but vanity had got the better of her, too, so she left it up. The painter was a good one. He had not compromised with the aquiline nose nor with the clenched mouth—he could not make her smile even slightly—nor with the severity of the temples and straight black hair and yet he had made it evident that here was a good-looking woman as well as a determined one. Two art dealers had offered her twice the price they originally had in mind after they saw what he had painted across the neck.

Marjorie Denman's belly was flat, her skin smooth, her body perfectly acceptable. Over the years, she had tried it out on a number of men (not an excessive number), all of whom said they found nothing to complain of on that score. She was not a voluptuary. She thought of sex as a form of self-improvement, an extension course given at night which would give her Living Credits toward some higher degree. She had brushed her mind as she brushed her hair, tossing it this way and that until she was satisfied with it. Nothing would ever lead her to an overwhelming conclusion; her mind was made up as tidily as her bed.

And now, she had decided, as had Howard Tracy, to get married. ("Are You Ready for the Ultimate Job Promotion?") Once, she had thought of going to bed with Alice Forsythe, but had put it out of her head. It had no point. (So absorbed with herself, besides, it had not occurred to her that Alice Forsythe might not want to go to bed with *her*.) But she had discussed Alice Forsythe straightforwardly with Howard Tracy in the lee of one of their nights in bed; argued that she, Marjorie, had not the slightest trace of eccentricity and would make Howard an ideal wife. He had said he would let her know soon. Did he object to the portrait? She would take it down. Not at all, he said. It can always be restored. He knew what he was doing when he painted you, Howard said. No, leave it where it is and . . . oh, hell . . . sure. Why shouldn't we get married? And you will get it over with? Tell her as soon as possible? Tomorrow, he promised. The day after. Fuck me again, Howard. Quickly. One thing at a time, he had protested, but only feebly. We'll make a good couple, Howard. You'll see.

She was full of accomplishment. An earlier resumé showed that:

"Objective," it said. "To utilize in-depth experience and thorough knowledge of all phases of publishing . . . communicating verbally and in writing . . . solving organizational, operational, and communications problems . . . devising and implementing systems and procedures."

!

"Identified and clearly defined complex interrelationships within department, establishing clear lines of communications and responsibilities. Expanded this concept and improved lines of communications in interfacing with other departments."

How's that again?

"Served as catalyst, introducing people who were engaged in diverse activities to each other, enabling them to coordinate. Structured department and created atmosphere of cooperation so that unanticipated peak loads were handled through cooperative effort. Coordinated complex systems into cohesive whole so that the possibility of overlap or duplication of effort was reduced to a minimum."

Oh.

"Maintained high morale and cohesiveness among clerical and supervisory personnel. Helped develop employee's own style while achieving department's goals. Promoted Executive Secretary to Supervisor. Counseled her as she in turn hired and trained staff of four and successfully mastered highly complex job. Developed simplified circulation, logging and follow-through systems thus enabling tracing the status of any piece of vast amounts of printed matter while completely eliminating the danger of loss."

Anything else? Yes.

"Height: 5′ 5″; weight, 123; age, 34.

"Health: excellent—gymnastics, jogging.

"Notary public."

"Good morning, Howard," she said into the telephone. She looked down at herself as she talked. Everything neatly arranged from head to toe.

"What time is it?" he asked.

"Time to get married, my darling," said Marjorie.

"I'll *be* there," he said, and hung up. She called him back. "Marjorie, I had some business to conclude last night. I was out quite late." He had set the alarm and thrown off his clothes and fallen on the bed, but when the telephone awakened him he found that he was still wearing his shirt and tie (properly knotted) and his socks, a figure out of an old stag reel.

"Business?" she asked. "I simply can't imagine . . . and on the night before your wedding . . ."

"Yes, you can," he said. "Alice."

"Alice!" she said. "You waited that long, Howard? I would have thought weeks ago. But, I'm being bitchy about a detail, aren't I?"

"Just sending an invitation wasn't enough. There was a lot to talk about."

"I can imagine," she said.

"I'm sure you can. You have a hell of an imagination." He made an effort. "It got you where you are today."

"Thank you," said Marjorie. "I know that comes from the bottom of your heart."

"How are you?" he asked.

"Oh, just fine, lover. I didn't have any business to conclude."

"No, not you."

"But, I'm glad *you* did, Howard," she went on. "Did she . . . was she . . . ? I'm just curious."

"No, nothing like that." Oh no, not at all, last thing in the world. "The two of you go to bed . . . for old time's sake?"

"For God's sake, Marjorie, that was . . . would have been . . . *wrong!* There really are a few things . . ."

Marjorie Denman laughed loudly into the telephone. "What few things? Howard?" she wanted to know. He said nothing. "You know how little difference that makes to me." He said nothing. "Will you be too tired?" she asked solicitously.

"No," he said.

"You won't be, will you? Not played out? Ready at the word go? I'll tell you something, Howard, although I shouldn't. It gives me a little, dirty thrill thinking of the two of you last night saying goodbye. Would you believe it excites me?"

"Yes," he said, "it excited me, too, sweetheart. Is that enough for now?"

"Oh," she said, "I can't wait."

He sniffed. "Neither can I."

There was silence, then crackling in the wires, then the barely heard sounds of two other voices contesting something which could not be understood, then distant musical notes played by the telephone equipment from some airless, windowless switching center downtown, an epithalamium for Howard Tracy and Marjorie Denman.

"I will see you in two hours, Howard."

Howard Tracy rubbed at his closed eyes with thumb and forefinger and breathed deeply. "It'll be all right, Marjorie. Let me get off now, will you? We've both got things to do." He wrenched at his tie as he spoke, opened the button on his collar and pulled his socks off. "Believe me," he said, "love will find a way."

She laughed. "I couldn't have put it better myself."

"See you later," he said. She made a kissing noise into the mouthpiece of the phone; the sound was indistinguishable from the crackling.

The wedding was held in what had once been the limestone bastard Beaux Arts home of a lesser millionaire of the early twentieth century. He could not, like a Frick, a Carnegie, a Vanderbilt, afford an entire block front on upper Fifth Avenue, so, like others of his kind, he had settled for a twenty-eight-foot lot on a side street between Fifth and Madison. It expressed exactly, almost to the penny, his state in life. His architect had provided him with what amounted to a miracle of craziness: a highly compressed rendering of the Paris Opéra, an *hôtel particulier* in the Marais and one of the lesser châteaux of the Ile de France, all in one. Architects were infinitely more ingenious in those times. He gave his hobbledehoy client a cobbled *porte cochère*, a formal garden at the back (the lot extended a hundred feet to the rear) and a splendid view of the Frick stables.

The millionaire had been wiped out in the Panic of 1907 and the building had passed to another who had played the wrong or bear side of the market. But time and war and the pinch of money had driven that family away, too, and the building, with its green-copper mansard and streaked limestone façade, balusters on nonexistent balconies, caryatids, fussy pilasters and cracked marble steps now belonged to a private club devoted to geography and exploration. The French government had thought of buying it as an adjunct to its consulate, but the birdwatchers, mountain-climbers, cartographers, pseudo-adventurers, advertising men, and manufacturers' representatives in search of a fitting place to eat, drink, and puff themselves up had put up enough money to beat out the French. However, in order to keep up the place, the owners were obliged to rent it out for weddings, tea dances, receptions, reunions, memorial services, and other things known as "functions."

The bar, a long mahogany affair installed in what had once been a study (study!), served big martinis still, but the quality of the kitchen under the club's stewardship had so declined that the board of trustees decided to have all food catered; in the basement kitchen now, there were nothing but warming stoves and microwave ovens. The silver, china, and napery had similarly declined and were rented. The oriental rugs were worn almost through, but the membership preferred to think of that, the cracked leather of the armchairs, the threadbare tapestries of the wing chairs (romps at Versailles, Greek myths, and so on), and the dirty red-velvet drapes with what was left of the ball fringe as unimpeachable evidence of aristocracy, struggling gallantly and somehow intact if in tatters. Only the accounting department had been kept up to date and that was out of sight in what had once been a brick tool shed in a back corner of the garden.

There were other faded glories. In the largest of the public rooms, in which Marjorie Denman and Howard Tracy would be made one flesh, was a polar bear, eight feet high, standing erect in a menacing attitude on a black teak pedestal with wheels. The white fur had become yellow in places; pieces of fur were missing elsewhere; the animal had all of its teeth, but the fangs stuck out cockeyed, as though the polar bear had been given ill-fitting dentures after being shot. A number of its claws were missing. The marks of the bullets which had killed it had been left to be seen—three in the behind, one in the chest. One eye had been shot out and the socket left empty, for verisimilitude; the other eye was glass, yellow and black; it glared maniacally, when the light struck it right, at another prize possession of the club: a dark, badly painted oil of the explorer Roald Amundsen. Nearby, was an equally bad painting of Admiral Peary. Between the two was a view of Mount Everest, the work of an earnest climber who had never reached the top. In its gilded Victorian frame, it looked like nothing so much as a large cone of soft vanilla ice cream garnished with rock outcroppings. On a brass plate affixed to the frame were the words, BECAUSE IT'S THERE! which was the motto of the club.

For the occasion, the room had been turned into a sort of rustic bower—masses of flowers, dwarf Japanese trees, urns of willow branches. A lectern had been placed directly in front of the polar bear. A small orchestra had been provided that alternated between the lesser-known songs of Cole Porter and George Gershwin and medieval lays. The latter were the fancy of the double-bass player, a large woman in a tentlike gown made of some kind of rough hair. She doubled on dulcimer, shawm, and crumhorn, at which times she was accompanied—timidly—by the drummer who, it was easy to see, was frightened of her.

But, by and large, the atmosphere was one of tenacious informality. Chiffon and tulle, black leather pants, business suits, jeans. It was much like a gathering of a motorcycle club which had left its machines home. By the time the Grosbecks arrived, there had been a good deal of drinking and dancing, and the bass-player lady had been blowing Holy Jesus out of the crumhorn, doing variations on the shawm and twirling her bass. Even the three sullen bartenders behind a table off in a corner had entered into the spirit of the afternoon, drinking one of anything for three of anything they served. Waitresses in black, with white aprons, chunky calves, and broad faces, Irish, veterans all of the late Schrafft's restaurants, circulated

among the guests with trays of small colored things, all of which, it
turned out, tasted the same. Nothing deterred them, not the wildest
dance. They dropped nothing; they disposed of everything; the guest
had not been born who dared refuse any of their ambiguous offerings.

Alice Forsythe arrived. Corydon Varney and his wife arrived. Kazanjian, the Armenian, arrived with a belly dancer whom he had
tricked out in a conventional ladies' suit with a string of pearls. It
was his joke. She spoke only Greek and everyone was led to believe
that she had just bought a controlling interest in nine tenths of everything from Turtle Bay to Kip's Bay. Varney knew better; he had
once been to bed with her. Alice Forsythe caught sight of Grosbeck
and introduced him to Varney and his wife. The din grew greater.
"I've always envied you newspapermen," Varney said to Grosbeck.
"I understand you're interested in architecture."

"Yes," Grosbeck replied, "they couldn't have picked a better day
for a wedding. This certainly is a picturesque setting for one, isn't
it?"

"I suppose you've heard what I've got in mind for that place near
the cathedral," Varney said. Grosbeck had barely managed to catch
the word "cathedral."

"Speaking of that," he said, "have you ever taken a trip out to
Green-Wood cemetery in Brooklyn? Hell of a place. Full of symbolism, you know. There's Boss Tweed, buried at the *bottom* of a hill,
and James Gordon Bennett, the newspaper publisher, buried at the
top, looking down on him. What a perfect juxtaposition."

Grosbeck and Madeline drifted away. "What do you guess we
were talking about?" Grosbeck shouted at her.

"I can't imagine," said Madeline. "He doesn't look stupid. Who
was that woman introduced you to the Varneys? She's got style."

"She works for him," Grosbeck said. "Lots of style. She needs it.
She does his dirty work for him with people like Greenspan. I
wouldn't be the least bit surprised if he turned up here." Nor was he
when Greenspan did, alone.

"Gathering material, Harvey?" he asked, putting his mouth near
Grosbeck's ear so that he could be heard.

"My wife, Madeline," said Grosbeck. "Madeline, Greenspan, the
protector of the poor, arbiter of taste, discretion and the like. Martin
the Magnificent." He, too, had to put his mouth to Madeline's ear so

that she could hear and the result was that all of them looked like birds feeding out of one another's ears.

The lady bass player picked up a bass saxophone she had brought along, just in case, and let go with a long blast on it. The drummer followed that with a crash of cymbals and a thump on his bass drum. Somebody held up his hands for silence. The dancers stopped. Peary, Amundsen, and the polar bear stared at the curtained doorway. The objects of all the fuss, the bridal couple, Marjorie Denman and Howard Tracy had arrived. On time. Suitably accoutered. The waitresses retreated in bulk. A bartender dropped a glass and pushed the pieces under the table. The room seemed to whisper, mutter, and chuckle in anticipation. A decorous cheer went up.

"Bravo!" someone ventured, who had drunk too much.

"Not yet, jerk," his companion whispered loudly. "It hasn't started yet."

"So?" asked the other belligerently.

The companion led him away, with as much force as he could muster without making a scene, to the toilet downstairs, where the first man threw up and the other, having witnessed it, followed suit. They pointed at each other. "That's better," they said simultaneously, and, grinning, washed their mouths and returned to the bower upstairs.

The minister was a reedy, pale man of indeterminate age in a corduroy jacket and open-necked shirt. (He had surmised, correctly, that that was what was wanted of him this blessed afternoon, although he owned a black suit, a couple of white shirts and a tie.) He belonged, nominally, to the Unitarian-Universalist Church into which he had slid gratefully since it appeared to demand nothing exhausting either of conscience or intellect (he had barely graduated from a northern California community college) and to promise everything: love, solace, hope, commiseration, forgiveness, goodfellowship, an enlightened view of the universe (particularly enlightened in his case; he knew almost nothing about it), a measured but pacific indignation at wrongdoing, tolerance to match, and endless probation for all transgressions, including murder, false witness and barratry.

He had come to this (after picking up a doubtful degree in divinity from a school in Texas, the accreditation of which was recognized only within a twenty-mile radius) through some nibbling at the table of a number of the Christian religions; whooping it up with the Jews, whom he found both too intense and too cynical; and puddling around casually in some forms of Asian worship (from Orientalia through Genitalia) which he gave up when he realized he might have to spend the rest of his life walking around the streets barefoot in a soiled sheet, his head shaved, clashing finger cymbals and begging cumshaw of the credulous for the greater good of swindlers. He wore also the pudding smile of an idiot on his face at all times, but there was a steady, low hum of rage deep in his throat which swelled the neck so that the head seemed even smaller than it was.

God, whoever you are, forbid anything else, the Reverend Mr. Angus McCormack had told himself. The Mysterious East had taught him to forgo alcohol, which had begun to become a problem for him in his California youth, and, instead, to smoke (in moderation, with the precepts of the Omnipotent Oom or whatever He happened to be called at the moment) opiated hashish to reach the sublimest level of meditation. He had shucked his beard; hair was no problem, since he was beginning to go bald. Regretfully, the hashish had its disadvantages; it was not the best of all possible worlds in which the Reverend Mr. McCormack lived, and whenever he got high and was about to lay his hands on the Philosopher's Stone, it eluded him—he slid out of the Lotus position it had cost him so much to get his legs into and fell forward on his face, asleep, and fuck the Philosopher's Stone.

He had settled for the racket which, he hoped, would get him through life as painlessly as might be. He had thought up little things to tell people under any circumstances and he found that they worked quite well. At the moment, for example, he had gathered unto himself a small throng of guests and was telling them, "I am, you might say, a Tinker for God. Yes, a Tinker for God, carrying my little table of tools on my back, grindstone, hammers, nails, scissors, solders . . ." He had blown a couple of tokes before showing up, to polish his eloquence, enough to do that but not so much that he would stumble. He patted hands and cheeks as he talked, but then checked himself. Save that wonderful timbre, those modest flights of fancy for the ceremony itself. He patted his breast pocket. The modest speech was there; he hoped he could understand what he had written. He patted his side pocket. The hash pipe had been extinguished; he hoped its odors could not be traced to him. He ate a couple of colored things from a tray, held up a hand, "No, thank you" for the offer of a glass of champagne from another tray, belted his mind a notch tighter and excused himself to find the betrothed couple. He had never seen the two. All of the arrangements had been made over the telephone.

He had no difficulty finding them. At the blast of the bass saxophone, the crash of the cymbals and the thump of the drum, the guests had retreated hastily to the walls, leaving Howard Tracy and Marjorie Denman alone in the center of the room, like lepers. For an instant, it was impossible to say whether they were about to be joined together or cast out. "My dears," the Reverend Mr. McCormack said to them. "The time has come." The timbre of his voice was holding up nicely, he thought. "Indeed, indeed." He turned to the guests. "And will you, dear ladies and gentlemen, dispose yourselves accordingly. If there is one thing for which we have striven today, it is the informality so characteristic of our time—informality and the good will, yes, even love, with which we will speed these two onto the path of matrimony. I will not say forever . . ." Ease up, you jerk, he said to himself. "Yes, I *will* say forever . . ." He took Howard by one hand, Marjorie by the other and led them toward the lectern. "Forever, forever," he intoned in a whisper. "Forgive me the *gaffe* my dear friends," he said to them. "But, we all know . . . I am certain the love you bear each other, the maturity of both of you . . ."

"You mean," Howard Tracy said, "better luck this time? No offense taken, Reverend. Where do you want us to stand?"

McCormack placed them before the lectern and scrambled around to mount the footstool that had been placed behind it. It broke, and his chin struck the small lamp affixed to the lectern, knocking it to one side. There were titters and cluckings from the assemblage. A set of memoirs by an explorer—bound in morocco, six volumes—was found to serve. The reading lamp on the lectern still worked. People quieted down. In one form or another, almost all of them had been through this before and about all they were interested in was how long it would take.

McCormack gave them a fast shuffle. He was well aware that the only words which counted were, roughly, these: "By authority of the laws of the State of New York vested in me, I pronounce you man and wife," but he knew that people expected more than that—not too much more, but some. He fiddled up a couple of excerpts from the Song of Solomon, a chunk of the Testaments, Old and New, dropped in some bits and pieces out of his sparse Asian readings and then pronounced Marjorie and Howard man and wife "by authority . . ." and so on. No more than six or seven minutes. Then, he reached into his breast pocket for the little homily he had thrown together. He looked out over the heads of the wedding guests and then down at the bride and groom, fixing them with what he hoped was a look at once burning, prescient, even biblical. He would retrieve the breaking of the footstool and the blow on his chin. He would mind his footing on the memoirs and keep an eye out for the lamp. For an instant, the lees of the hashish turned the papers before him into swirls of black lettering in a language he hoped he could read, but he breathed deeply and it went away. He cleared his throat, wiggled his behind and gripped the edges of the lectern, firmly putting away a mad impulse to laugh and slap the lectern until tears rolled down his face. The last vapors of the hashish were still upon him.

"Now, dear company," he began. His voice, in an unforeseen tenor, broke. Damn. But the faces before and beneath him did him the courtesy of remaining grave. "Forgive me," he began again, like a clarinet player running scales before a performance. "This sound about right?" he asked. The assemblage hummed sympathetically and shuffled its feet. "Very well, then," he tried once more. "Now, it's my turn to say a few words of my own. And so, may I say this?" He directed his eyes at the bride and groom. A tough pair of cookies, he thought, if I ever saw one.

"I am happy today," he said, "that the two of you have decided to live together for the rest of your lives. So much about us in these times . . ." He looked down at the papers; that wasn't on them. Screw. An ad lib here and there . . . ? Why not. He'd carried it off before. ". . . in these times has gone cockahoop. We see about us, strewn in disarray all too often the wreckage of noble intentions, of strong passions torn to tatters in the mistaken belief that they represented love, of the slow sinking into indifference, even hatred, of two people for whom the stars once represented the illuminations that would show them the course of their lives . . ." Where the hell had that come from. He adjusted his glasses, looked at the papers again, and couldn't find any of it. Not bad, he thought; I wonder if I can remember it next time.

"But," he went on, "I err in starting on such a note and if I do, it is, my dears and my friends, an error of longing that it not befall these two so close to my hopes for all of you. It is not a false note I stroke—strike—in so beginning. Rather, for whatever error it may constitute, it is a hortatory one, and, having made it, I dispense with it, I disperse it to the four winds of fortune and trust—oh, I do trust —that it will dissipate on the soft wind of happiness; not eternal, for we are all too mortal, but for so long as you—ye—shall endure in this flesh from which we have been fashioned."

"What was that he said?" Grosbeck whispered to Madeline.

"Be quiet," she whispered back to him. "He doesn't know, either."

"If I didn't know better," Grosbeck whispered again, "I'd swear it was one of our editorials. I've seen the kind of flash before from which this one's been fashioned."

"Harvey," Madeline whispered sharply, "that'll be quite enough of that."

"No, it won't, not if you're talking about that one up there." She slapped his hand, all the while looking attentively before her. "He's winging it," Grosbeck said to Madeline. "How much would you like to bet?" She ignored him.

The Reverend Mr. McCormack returned to his text, scribbled on a bus coming uptown. "I am happy," he said, "that the two of you have decided to live together for the rest of your lives." More than that, he said, he was "*very* happy, for I *sense* that yours will be a very warm and beautiful and loving relationship." He had set that down between traffic lights going up Madison Avenue and had been, as always, a little depressed at saying such things about people he had never seen and would never see again. He had never become quite hardened to it. On he went:

"There may come a time . . . there may come about those *times* when your relationship [he had crossed out the word *partnership*; something a little too litigious about it] will be strained. That happens in all marriages." He was gratified to note that everybody nodded solemnly. Possibly, they were no more than drunk or sleepy, but they nodded. "That happens in all marriages," he went on, "but if your relationship is *solid* [heavily delivered] you will learn and grow and emerge with more understanding of each other." He felt he was really getting into it now . . . an impeccable set of bromides.

He had his voice under control and he let it rise a little. "This is a great adventure that you are beginning. [Subtle reference to the club; *that* came off rather well, he thought.] The greatest. Nourish it with faith and hope and love. Add to these qualities those the great Apostles speak of: joy, peace, patience, kindness, goodness, gentleness, and self-control. And add another dimension: forgiveness—a word that is preveland in the Bible." (He had spelled it wrong. He blamed that on a jolt of the bus.)

"The highest form of love is forgiveness," he went on. "Be as forgiving of each other as the Lord has been forgiving of you." He poured a small drop of foreboding into his voice. "There will be times," he said, "when you will want to call on the Lord to bring out the best qualities in you so your marriage will remain strong and full." On to the peroration. He was running late.

"Only God is perfect," he observed. No one disputed him. "So you will not find perfection in each other. But your marriage, as challenging as it will be, will be full of joy and happiness." Both Howard Tracy and Marjorie Denman looked down at the floor. "Be understanding," he told them. "Be tolerant." Then he dropped in a pinch of current thinking. "Remember, marriage is a linkage of equal rights and responsibilities. We do not speak of obedience any longer. Share those rights and responsibilities. I say, share them to the last ounce of your strengths, share them in order to build a home rather than just a house." Get it? "Live together," he concluded, "enjoy together, grow together. Go with God to your journey's end . . ." He wilted at the lectern and then came around to put his hands about the shoulders of the bride and groom. "Kiss her," he said to Howard Tracy, in a voice of treacle. "And you, likewise," to Marjorie Denman. "And then, let me kiss you both." He looked out at the guests. "Let there be huzzahs and dancing," he commanded.

From the rest of the afternoon, Grosbeck took away the impression that he had been permitted to visit an expensive retreat for the mentally ill in which all the catatonics sat in gilt chairs at the side of the room and the elated slobbered at the food and danced fifty kinds of dances, none of which kept time to the music. One whirling couple knocked a chip off the bottom of an oak Corinthian column. The polar bear trembled with annoyance at the pounding. Peary and Amundsen looked disdainful.

Alice Forsythe put an arm through Grosbeck's and drew him into a conversation with Varney and Kazanjian. The subject was the mansions. Madeline would not let Grosbeck be drawn. Grosbeck asked for a drink. "Only one," said Madeline. "Salomon said one a day. And, besides, you know what you're like when you get started."

"What *is* he like when he gets started?" asked Alice Forsythe.

"Uncontrollable," said Madeline. "All sex and lectures on the decline of New York. Very active. I don't mean to be indelicate, but how would you like, in the midst of making love to be told that the Seagram Building looks like an upended coffin without handles?"

"I'd like to give it a try," said Alice Forsythe.

"Would you, though?" asked Madeline. She looked at Alice. "I'm afraid that, aside from anything else, he's just been through a heart attack and it'll be a while before he's altogether himself again."

"I'd be glad to wait," said Alice Forsythe. "Sex and the Seagram Building."

"It *is* decadent, isn't it?" Madeline said.

"Positively *kinky*, my dear."

Grosbeck finished his drink; he wanted another and he also wanted a cigarette—badly. "You two fight over my pure white body," he said, excused himself, walked down a flight of stairs, found a black attendant in the washroom and got a cigarette from him. He tipped him two dollars, took three long puffs and put the stub away for another time.

"Have you divided me up?" he asked the two women when he got back. And to Madeline, "Take me home, Mother, I've been out too long today." And in the cab going downtown, "What got into the two of you?"

"Why," said Madeline, "you're simply irresistible." He made a face and stuck his tongue out. "Even at your age."

"Thank you."

"No, I mean it, Harvey," she said.

"Sure, if you like well-dressed old dwarfs."

"Ah, Harvey, you don't know your own strength." She thought. "I do, though." Thought again. "So does she."

"Don't be crude, sweetheart."

"I will be," she said, putting a hand on his leg. "It's only a matter of weeks now."

14

The transmogrification of Harvey Grosbeck from disengaged nihilist (as he believed himself to be) into pertinent thinker (as defined by The Newspaper) was not an easy one. The world (by which he meant the City) was not yet enough with him. As a child, he had been enchanted: enchanted by the tall, graceful traffic towers of gold on Fifth Avenue, the enormous, red-faced Irish policemen in white gloves with their magnificent, curving, arbitrary gestures, by the great ocean liners with their horns which shook the belly as they made their way down the North River on their way to where? where? He had ridden back and forth over the Brooklyn Bridge on an elevated train and marveled at the dirty, fast-running river beneath it. He had ridden the elevated around the Dead Man's Curve at 110th Street and he had listened to Mr. Turchin tell him in school that no such city on earth had ever been. He read O. Henry and believed him.

He had an uncle who worked in the old post office down at City Hall and who took him into Hitchcock's on Park Row for beef and beans and then, and then, showed him the pneumatic tubes which connected that Victorian pile with the new post office uptown. His uncle had told him how some of the men transferred uptown still wanted to eat Hitchcock's beef and beans and apple pie and how they sent it, carefully packed in paper bags, through the pneumatic tubes up to Thirty-fourth Street. A man could be fired for doing that, his uncle told him, but the supervisors looked the other way. They, too, knew Hitchcock's.

His father, a gentle, somber man, an immigrant with a talent for drawing, became a commercial artist, but on Sundays he would take his son with him and sketch rock outcroppings in Central Park and the Casino in which Jimmy Walker disported himself and his women so flagrantly until Fiorello La Guardia shut it down in outrage—there should be no watering-place for the privileged in the People's Park. His father showed him Hester Street and Rivington where *he* had grown up and the Art Students League where he studied under the incomparable draftsman George Bridgman. He made pencil sketches of the boy sitting in an uncomfortable armchair inspired by William Morris and executed in Grand Rapids. The father romanticized the boy, or so Grosbeck thought in later years. By then, the notion of love had fled him, he no longer realized what his father had been attempting. He grew a thick carapace of denial. Yet, one of the sketches had been framed and Grosbeck had kept it all these years. The paper had foxed and was brown. Yet the passionate eyes of the boy Grosbeck stared out at the man Grosbeck as though to ask, "What happened?"

What happened Grosbeck knew well enough. Why, was another matter and he refused to ask. Refused. Set his feet stubbornly and made his eyes look only inward. He had walked through war and rumor of war, eating and drinking and dressing and fornicating and quarreling and living; now here, now there (but always in the City) with one woman or another; in the sunshine and shadow of the City; in its shining and its growing filth and decay and menace; in the shadows of the unspeakable structures thrown up after the Second World War; in the wanton destruction of so much that was old and that he had thought beautiful and timeless.

He heard music in stones and shapes and vistas in the City; he understood Stanford White perfectly: artist and lecher. He once confessed to a psychiatrist (conversationally, at a party) that he could be aroused by an architectural rendering, that he thought of, say, a Piranesi drawing as very nearly the most *raffiné* form of pornography. "What do you say to that?" he asked the psychiatrist.

The psychiatrist behaved as though he were in his office and Grosbeck a patient. He nodded . . . over and over . . . rubbed his chin, dabbed at his forehead with a cocktail napkin (for lack of a tissue; Grosbeck half expected him to offer *him* one), looked at the ceiling and then at the floor and, finally, said to Grosbeck, in that expressionless manner psychiatrists must learn in order to get their degrees, "You're crazy."

"Thank you, Doctor," Grosbeck replied. "Up yours, too." The psychiatrist had shrugged. He had gotten successive A's in shrugging; his analysands were mad for his shrugs; he shrugged his way into bed with women—expressionlessly.

Grosbeck had begun by writing, possibly because his father couldn't get him to draw a straight line. (It was one of the father's secret griefs.) But, by the same process of denial through which he had refused to acknowledge the overwhelming transformation of the City, he stopped and became an editor. The pain of writing was, for him, the same as the pain of the City's transformation. The carapace of the crab covered him; he scuttled into the box set up for him in the City Room; he could be indifferent to what happened to other men's words, just as he would, henceforth, be indifferent to what happened to the City—provided, of course, that he was lucky enough not to get knifed some night in the middle of a dark block by someone darting out of a hiding place behind some huge machine on a construction site.

Of course, he was not indifferent at all. The pain of the canker never left him; all it did was alter him and make him what he became. Other men had better or more plausible excuses for their terrible tics, he did not doubt, but his would do him. It was the mouth of the canker opening and talking when he met Alice Forsythe or anyone else for whom the City either meant nothing or very little or something out of which a profit was to be made. Enough of common sense remained in him to know that it had ever been thus . . . in New York, in Alexandria, in the remotest collection of grass huts in Africa . . . but that made no difference to Grosbeck. For him, the parallel between the Vandals, the Visigoths, and a Corydon Varney, a Kazanjian was exact and the words, "What are you going to do about it?" might just as well have been uttered by Corydon Varney as by Tweed.

About all that could be said in mitigation of Grosbeck's obsession was that it had not yet required institutionalization and was not likely to get anyone shot and that it was not entirely unreasonable: the City had become a smoking ruin out of which a myriad cold, poorly constructed towers had been built; through which the rats and vermin coursed familiarly; a pleasance, in stone and steel, of the disgusting and the immoral under a sky which condemned it eternally; a cemetery in which the damned were not dead but pullulated. Phew, what an outlook!

But, it had to be acknowledged that for all he felt that way, Gros-

beck had never done very much about it. He was about as cir-
cumspect a madman as might be found: he had written an occasional letter of protest, signed a petition here and there, appeared at
hearings of the Landmarks Preservation Commission and said his futile piece. But he had never lain down before a bulldozer, received
the blow of the wrecker's iron ball in the head, or spreadeagled himself in a Georgian doorway to stop some act foul beyond redemption.
No, what he *had* done, in resignation, was to *steal*, or *beg* or even
buy fragments of buildings he mourned and put them on display in
his living room, once in a while drinking himself into a stupor while
contemplating them. His was a most singular form of mourning, not
to say precious, even comic, in a grown man. In his right mind,
which was not often, he knew all this and had tried to tell it to
Greenspan when Greenspan moved him up to editorial. Greenspan
could have said to him, but did not, "You ever miss a meal?" Grosbeck could have said to Greenspan, "My soul is starving," but he had
not. And Greenspan could have said to him, "Blow it out your
asshole, mac, don't you know they're gonna nuke us all back to the
Stone Age? You won't even have your pebbles to play with. Take it
while you can, make it before they break it. Wise up, drink up,
dummy." But, Greenspan had been more subtle than that for reasons Grosbeck would never know. Possibly, all he had in mind was
an experiment with an aging yet still promising eccentric.

Daily, Grosbeck got off at the editorial floor and said good morning to Emily Braestrup, the guardian of the floor. (She had only one
head, this Cerberus, not the fifty ascribed to her by Hesiod, but it
was enough.) She acknowledged him only with a grimace (all that
was left of her smile, her womanhood, her visions, whatever they had
been, of pine forests on some Scandinavian mountainside) and the
declination of a head which had come, finally, to be almost all
tightly wound gray-white bun which held together the collapsed bal-
loon of her face. The starch of her black dress crackled faintly in the
silence. Would she, had he been suspect in some way, come out
from behind the desk, roared, and bitten him in the ankle?
     It was Grosbeck's fantasy that she did not live anywhere; that,
who knows how long ago, she had been placed behind that desk and
that she had never moved out from behind it; that she required neither sustenance nor had intestinal disturbances; that she had once

been sprayed with lavender and that the odor still hung over her; that her movements had been devised by some dwarf Swiss clockmaker; and that they included everything that might be necessary to perform her function of receptionist for the Editorial Board, a refined, infinitely refined, version of the plaster gypsy fortune-tellers to be found behind glass at a carnival, *sans* rouge, *sans* reddened plaster lips, *sans* multicolored turban. But, there were old hands on The Newspaper who had learned to read her, who knew that not only was she alive, but that she knew a great deal about everything in the building, although she had never been seen anywhere but behind the desk.

She was provided for in The Publisher's will; he had said that on that day when her iron flesh rusted and bits of plaster were found to be falling from her face, she was to be moved to a nursing home, to a room which would be an exact reproduction of the reception room, not excluding the old black Underwood typewriter she had used for fifty years and the wire IN and OUT baskets at the left and right of her golden-oak desk. She should never know she was not a part of The Newspaper unto death. After that, The Publisher reasoned, in his own dotage, she should be on her own. Or let God take over.

Grosbeck passed under the arch celebrating The Founder and it seemed to him that every time he did so The Founder sniffed in dubiety, that the look of affection reserved for Miss Braestrup changed. Did the old bastard have any idea of what Greenspan had taken to his bosom? Enough, enough, Grosbeck. Go to your room. Looking neither to left nor right, he walked down the heavy carpeting to his office—his alone—making no impress underfoot. He drew the heavy curtains against the world (the rings gargled as he pulled the drawstring) and sat down behind the elaborately carved desk which had belonged to an editor who had tapped out one last endorsement of God and one last inveighing against Sin and then put his head down on the typewriter and died.

The Newspaper had commemorated him appropriately: it had printed the editorial just as he had left it in his typewriter—unfinished. That didn't make any difference, since most of the time it was difficult to tell where an editorial began or ended, which was one of the reasons for the editorial page's reputation; there was a bone for everyone to pick. (The Newspaper had never done anything like that before.) It had even added an elegy. "Think, think," it

urged on its readers, "of the devotion of this man, that whatever in-
timation of Death was upon him, he staved it off valiantly, expending the last ounce of his strength, his consciousness, his unshakable
convictions; he pecked away at his typewriter as Death tugged at his
shoulder (gently, we trust, for he had richly earned gentleness); we
like to think that Death laid down his scythe for this man and took
him up in his arms and transported him to that Place where, for
Eternity, he will make Heaven a better place for his opinions on the
Cosmos."

That'll show 'em, The Newspaper said to itself.

Grosbeck was not unaware of the Mantle of Responsibility that
Greenspan had laid on his shoulders. It itched. It galled. Willy-nilly
(the story of his life) he had permitted himself to be levitated eight
floors up on the way to a fake heaven from the City Room . . .
noisy, contentious, sometimes joyous, busy, thoughtless, and, above
all, illiterate . . . first to be tacked to the Cross of The Founder's
consensus with the nails of contrary opinion. The urge not to write
consumed him when he first put paper into the manual typewriter he
had begged Greenspan to let him take upstairs with him. Although
very little came out of it, the first thing he wrote came as close to
making sense as anything else on the editorial page: "; l k j h j and A
S D F G F. This goddamned thing needs a new ribbon." That took
a little doing.

The editorial department, like the rest of The Newspaper, was
slowly shifting over to the VDT—the Video Display Terminal—an
instrument which contained keys resembling those of a typewriter,
but which threw up words and letters in green on a screen. The machine could, as they put it, "talk" to other machines, edit, erase,
reject, accept and transport these nonexistent words and paragraphs
several floors away where they appeared once more in black and
white on strips of paper, then to be pasted on other rectangles of
paper making up a page. Grosbeck feared it. He told Greenspan at
the outset that he would not use it, that he would do whatever it was
he had to do on the typewriter and then get someone else to put it
into the infernal machine. Greenspan had agreed to let him work
that way for a while. "You'll come to it, Harvey," he said. "You'll
love it. You'll wonder how you ever did without it."

Nothing came out of Grosbeck's typewriter for a month that
could be put in the paper, that he would even show anyone, nor was

he reproached for it. He was in his novitiate. The editorial page and the signed Opinion Page required more than the slambang of the City Room, which was really no more than a machine shop. But Thought, the Thought that would make the readers leap to the side of The Newspaper, that would make congressmen flinch, presidents turn pale or glow with gratitude, and statesmen thousands of miles away think twice or wrongdoers (businessmen, bankers, and industrialists exempted, except in the most egregious of cases) undergo plastic surgery after being caught in the glare of The Newspaper's disapproval . . . that kind of Thought called for Time and the Weighing of Alternatives. Had it not been for the exigencies of daily publication, the opinions of The Newspaper would have taken as long to be uttered as the Books of the Old Testament, with which they were compared often and favorably, at least by The Newspaper. As a result, much tolerance was granted Grosbeck, in keeping with the paper's policy of letting a man get his feet wet in his own way, provided he didn't splash anyone, or, as the less reverent downstairs put it, "piss on the parade." The occasional anarchist was not fired; he was put to writing obituaries until he either quit or joined the subjects he laid to rest.

There was an Editorial Meeting daily in a large rectangular room. Midafternoons, a minion would knock on the heavy door of Grosbeck's cell in the cloister and summon him to the monkish conclave. The Editorial Board consisted of twelve men in addition to Greenspan (it was still a few years before women would shoulder their way in, exuding sex, intelligence, and a grab bag of opinions that would have had them broken on the Catherine wheel in other times), Who Knew What They Wanted and What the Readers Needed and would tell them the next morning. From the beginning, Grosbeck was taken aback that so many men were needed to write so few words, that none of them wrote more than two or three little pieces a week. How many had it taken to turn out the Ten Commandments or the *Communist Manifesto?* But The Newspaper put the highest premium on the act of Thought and it was pleased to think of its editorial writers and columnists as monks turning out illuminated manuscripts in gold, blue, black, and red with pen and brush. "Veni, Creator Spiritus," The Founder had said with a throb in his voice when he first threw open the doors of the room, and the injunction had been carved into a slab of marble over a fireplace. (Carved above it was the logotype of the newspaper, giving the impression that it had thought up the thrilling message.)

The men sat at a long antique Spanish table, Greenspan at the head. They reflected perfectly The Newpaper's notions of balance. A few were so conservative that they wore both belts and suspenders, and it fell to them to denounce whatever had to be denounced that day, in no uncertain terms. Then, there were the tightwire artists (a majority), so highly skilled in seeing all sides of an issue that they needed no more than five paragraphs to make it disappear so that the bitterest of enemies could say to each other that The Newspaper agreed with them when, in fact, it had no opinion at all. And, finally, there were two or three whose specialty was labeled Humor. These went about Humor like elephants with clubs in their trunks. They were beyond parody. They thought quite well of themselves, but so did the entire Editorial Board.

The editors tapped their teeth with pencils, made incisive remarks (qualifying them instantly so that it could not be said later that they had taken a stand on anything), nodded frequently, shook their heads seldom, wrinkled their brows, fondled their noses, took their glasses off and rubbed at tired eyes (little did The World realize what they went through to enlighten it), took notes on lined legal pads ("Pork chops tonight? I think not. But, what then?"), smoked cigars, cigarettes and pipes (some of them) despite the concurrence of The Newspaper with the Surgeon General of the United States. Those who did not smoke indicated their displeasure by shifting, but by no more than an inch. (One man had actually made a face and moved an ashtray; there had been a spatter of applause from the nonsmokers and cries of "Resign! Resign!" from the others. The gesture was never repeated that broadly.)

In keeping with another of The Founder's wishes (he did unexpected things, like Mad King Ludwig), there was a silver tray on the conference table, a heavy cut-glass bowl of fruit on it, a circle of glasses to match, and plates; and two bottles, one of *schnapps* (a reminder of The Founder's German origins) and one of good sherry (the idea of his wife, who had also supplied delicate biscuits to go with it; her gentility had known no bounds nor her zeal for refuges for homeless dogs; in her mind, the sherry and biscuits and the dog refuges were of a piece—she was gone, but all this was her legacy—

and the members of the Board were encouraged to Oil Their Minds —in moderation—during deliberations.

The fruit and biscuits were rarely touched and were given to the cleaning women; the sherry tended to be drunk only on days when war, peculation, defalcation, outrages against the public weal and opinions contrary to those of the Board were at a minimum; the *schnapps*, stronger stuff, flowed freely most of the time, since the world seemed forever to be on the edge of an abyss (a phrase much favored in editorials, which also liked "brink," "confrontation," "imminent danger," and "honorable differences of opinion," to say nothing of "cooler heads," "wiser counsels," "days of reflection," and "There is much to be said for . . ." or, if the situation demanded it, "against.")

"Gold," said one member of the Board.

"Agreed," said another, in a spasm of furious acquiescence. He had not the faintest idea what the other man had intended to say about gold, but it was his function to take either side.

"The governor," said a third man.

"The president," said a fourth.

"The mayor . . ."

"No man barely five feet tall ought to be mayor of anything." That was the Board Wit.

"Double parking."

"I don't drive."

"A valid justification for regulation . . ."

"I think it is incumbent upon . . ."

"Agreed!" That one poured himself a tiny dollop of sherry and took a biscuit. It was *schnapps* all around otherwise: the Board was getting down to weightier matters. "An indefensibly rebellious Congress, particularly in the face of . . ." "The trend is surely healthy (or unhealthy) . . ." "There are those who wonder . . ." "If a significant choice is denied the people, then surely as night follows day, there will be . . ." "In all the diverse spectrum of human behavior, never has there been . . ." "Stern measures must be taken . . ." "Bureaucratic bumbling of awesome dimensions . . ." ". . . a limited resource that should not be wholly governed by the private sector."

The Board (not alone) had divided the world into "sectors," so many of them, at last, that the globe resembled nothing so much as a heaping up of triangular pieces of cheese. As the *schnapps* took hold, there were mentions of "failure of nerve," "fatal inconsistency," and ". . . all that remains to be seen," "down the road a considerable distance," ". . . for all that, however . . . ," and ". . . a leavening of common sense would best be applied to a situation in which all reasonable men . . ."

"Make that persons, when you get around to doing it," said Greenspan. "No more men. Persons. Or, the body politic, the consensus of men *and* women." Although there were no women on the Editorial Board, Greenspan and everyone else at the table knew that dat ole debbil Affirmative Action, having hit the City Room, must inevitably find its way into the precincts of the Editorial Board. Already, they could hear the workmen banging away at partitions and plaster walls, putting in a women's toilet. Auguries. Auguries.

There was a black man on the Board now, it congratulated itself. He wrote editorials which reproached the Establishment (carefully undefined) for its treatment of the downtrodden, counted cockroaches in the plumbing of Harlem, the South Bronx, and sections of Brooklyn and produced statistics to prove (percentagewise, as he put it) that there were more white and brown junkies than black ones. He had read W. E. B. DuBois and the proclamations of Marcus Garvey and recoiled in horror. To him, riots were "disturbances masking deep-seated discontents" and he busted his hump looking for sociological parallels that would, in the end, make everything all right. The Newspaper thought him perfect for his job: black on the outside, white on the inside; Orville Oreo. He was frequently invited by the more athletic members of the Board to play squash with them. About half the time, he let himself be beaten, so far had his consciousness been raised by his circumstances. He was suffused with happiness at the realization that he lived in Riverdale in a tall apartment house filled with white people who not only said "Hello" to him, but had him in for drinks and solicited his opinion on matters concerning blacks. Twice, he had been mugged, robbed, and left with his pants down, which put a strain on his philosophical overview . . . about fifty to sixty dollars each time, as well as his credit cards . . . but he had retained his equanimity by reflecting that that happened to the ofays, too, and was no reflection on his color. Indeed, he told himself, in a way it was a compliment that he had been sought out and waylaid and roughed up by his own kind. It was proof that he had *arrived*.

In an hour or so, the Board arrived at the Consensus of the Day: Human Rights in Argentina (not good); the Federal Reserve Board's current tight-money policy (mixed signals; cloudy future; no conclusions); the subways (time for a thorough probe into . . . and, if heads must roll, they must roll; not a single member of the Board had been on a subway train for years; anything they knew about it, they read in the paper); and an indignant commentary on the size of baseball players' salaries, coupled with a glancing blow at inflation and a notation that club owners were not always in business for the pure love of the game, either, which would doubtless satisfy everybody or nobody and would bring in enough letters to print in "Letters to the Editor." (So homogenized with *politesse* had even the letters become that none of them began, as they once did, "Dear sir, you swine . . .")

Grosbeck had had a *schnapps* at the meeting but he knocked it back guiltily. He had said almost nothing and he had as yet to produce a single editorial or signed opinion. Also, he wanted a cigarette with his drink, but the Board had been enjoined by the company doctor from giving him any. A maid had emptied the ashtrays before he could pick a stub from one of them and he went back to his office and fell asleep, dreaming that he was in bed with a voluptuous woman who kept saying to him (as she enveloped his body), "Let's not make love just yet, darling. Let's smoke," and handed him one cigarette after another.

He awoke, frowsty, dry of mouth, depressed. It was too soon to go home. He got up from the couch and went over to the typewriter. Better gibberish than nothing. He typed on the bare roller. "Jesus," he said and put a sheet of paper into the machine. "Where to begin?" he asked on the paper. "Where to begin?" he started again. "Where does a monomaniac begin? Where find the needle and palm to sew the sail, stitch the heart, set things to rights in all weathers: fore, main, mizzen, jigger, spanker, pusher, driver. Jib, foresail, skysail, royal topgallant, stay, crossjack, spanker, ratlines, shrouds." He ruminated at the machine as the afternoon wore on. His fingers grew less stiff, his neck warm, his forehead wet. He put in sheet after sheet. It hardly mattered what he was typing.

"Get two crimps with knives and a dark lantern to the sailors' boardinghouse, head of Catherine Slip, not fifty feet away from Brooks Brothers store. Tiptoe clumsily up the stairs. Pluck the man out of a drunken sleep in bed with a tumbled whore snoring at his side. Hustle him out of the place (firm grip on both arms, a hand over his mouth, the knife at his throat), down the slip, down the gray-green-greasy wooden ladder into the dory and row him out to the merchantman dipping at anchor under the clouded moon. The fast, dangerous waters of the East River slap at the dory, the wooden oars sigh and scream in their locks. The shade of the dark lantern is opened and the lantern swung in signal to the bos'n's mate leaning on the rail. 'Ahoy, Ophelia,' sings out one of the crimps. 'Comin' aboard with your deck boy.' Past the anchor chain. 'Get him up the ladder and easy as she goes. Into the cabin with him. Hit him once or twice if you have to.

"'Look at them hands. One of them pretty lawyers from up Cherry Street?' 'Not bloody likely,' says one of the crimps. 'Not from the look of him.'

"'What's your name, man?' 'Grosbeck.' 'Grosbeck, eh? Not Gros-beak? I'm Greenspan, bos'n's mate, and you'll get to know me soon enough. Button your pants. Get below and clean up and I want you back on deck instanter.'

"Up anchor. Bower and streak. Capstan bars in windlass. Rattle of chains. Mind that wildcat. Underway. Past the tied-up steam ferries, the fishing schooners and draggers. To starboard, past the red-brick mansions and farm fields sloping down to water's edge and shipyards, brickyards, ship's chandlers, warehouses with sharply pitched roofs. Up the hill, the spires of Trinity, St. Paul's, St. John's Methodist, the Dutch Reformed, the golden dome of the Merchants' Exchange. Peck Slip, Old Slip, Burling Slip, Jeanette Slip, Coenties Slip, Cuyler's Alley, Gouverneur Slip. To port, the splendid colonnades on the steep heights of Brooklyn and the rough edges and shanties of Red Hook. A light winking here and there. Making way. To starboard, Fort Clinton, to port, Fort William. Cannon ports. Dead ahead, Staten Island. Then, Robbins Reef, the Lower Bay, Fort Hamilton, Fort Totten, the sea . . ."

Grosbeck looked at what he had written. "Shanghaied," he added. And, miserably, "Put me back ashore where I was." And, ending it, "Tully, Trollope. Dare all . . . —30—"

As had been the case the better part of his life, Grosbeck's course
was altered for him by something extraneous. The very next morning. He got into one of the newly installed automatic elevators. He
was alone and immediately resentful at the absence of an operator
(however much he might resemble an ape), the clank of the handle,
"Floor, please?" even though the man had taken him to the same
floor for years, and the two unvarying questions, "What's the
weather like out there?" and "Hot enough (or Cold enough) for
you?" He pressed the button for the twelfth floor. The elevator rose
with unusual rapidity as Grosbeck could tell from watching the
lights above the doors. It rose, shrieking wildly, to the fifteenth, and
suddenly started to fall whistling and rocking from side to side. The
cables had given.

"I knew it," Grosbeck shouted into the void. There was no time to
say anything more. He threw himself to the floor, closed his eyes
tightly, and waited to be smashed to bits in his military twill pants
and Shetland jacket. He had expected to be received in the twinkling
cosmos like Little Eva being lifted tenderly into heaven, not this.
The elevator, however, stopped—quite smoothly, all things considered. Grosbeck was rumpled, crouched in his corner, but unhurt.
How soon would anyone find him and get him out of the basement?
"Help!" he shouted. "Help! I'm in the basement." At the third
"Help!" the doors of the elevator opened—by themselves. He looked
up to see Emily Braestrup contemplating him sitting on the floor.

"Did I hear you call for help, Mr. Grosbeck?" she asked. He got
up and brushed himself off.

"It's impossible," he said. "Where am I?"

"What's impossible, Mr. Grosbeck? And where else should you be
other than where you are?"

"In the basement," he told her. "In pieces. And, what are *you*
doing in the basement?" Miss Braestrup had witnessed much in her
years on The Newspaper, mental breakdowns included. "The
damned elevator fell," Grosbeck said. "I don't know how you managed to get down here so fast."

"Fell?" she asked. "Down here? Down where?"

"I told you. The basement. The cables must have gone."

"Mr. Grosbeck," she said firmly, "you *do* recognize me, don't
you?"

"Yes."

"Now," she went on, "look around you. Does this look like the basement . . . ?"

"Tell you the truth," he said, "I've never been down there."

". . . or," she went on, gesturing with a hand, "is this the twelfth floor?"

"You're right," he said. "But what happened?"

"I'm sure I don't know," she said.

He was about to recount the whole thing but changed his mind.

"Mr. Grosbeck, are you sure you're all right, so soon after the heart attack and all?" God, how the woman exasperated him. "You do look a little peaked." She couldn't resist adding, "Hair of the dog?"

"No, damn it, Miss Braestrup, no hair of anything."

"I think I ought to call the doctor," Miss Braestrup said.

"That won't be necessary. In fact," he said, "if you do, I will denounce you to the Managing Editor as an interfering old fraud."

His vehemence shocked Miss Braestrup; no editorial writer had ever used language so strong in her presence. "Very well. I shall say nothing."

"Nor I," Grosbeck said. "I am sorry to have disrupted your morning and I know that your intentions were of the best."

"I accept the apology, Mr. Grosbeck, but I would be less than candid with you did I not tell you that sitting in elevators and calling for help is not customary on this floor—whatever may happen downstairs. I shall not forget it, but it will be a secret between us."

"Thank you, Miss Braestrup," said Grosbeck. "It will never happen again."

But what *had* happened? How had he come so close to Eternity and ended up on his ass with Emily Braestrup looking down at him? Grosbeck did not believe in psychic phenomena and he mistrusted technology. Nevertheless, there must be some explanation for what had happened to him. He found it the next morning in a sheet pasted on every elevator door in the building. It read:

To: ALL EMPLOYEES AND VISITORS
From: Facilities Administration
On Monday morning, May 4th, a malfunction occurred on one of the new automatic cars as it was ascending from the Main Floor.

The elevator manufacturer and our own engineers have determined that the malfunction was caused by a jammed contactor, causing the car to rise at a faster than normal rate.

Automatic safety features braked the car to a rapid but safe stop.

That told him nothing, but Grosbeck read on:

Because the car indicator lights precede the actual location of the car, they indicated a higher floor than the car actually reached. As the car braked to a stop, the indicator reset to the actual lower position of the car, giving the impression to the lone occupant that the car was falling.

The malfunction has been cleared and the car has been checked and found to be perfectly safe.

This memo is to assure you that the safety devices performed as designed and that it is *virtually* impossible for an elevator to fall.

Grosbeck did not believe it *virtually* impossible that it would never happen again, but an unwonted shock of optimism did surge through him. He entered the elevator again—boldly—wished Miss Braestrup a knowing "Good morning," went to his office and wrote his first piece for The Newspaper, an account of what had happened to him, which did not mention where the incident had occurred, and handed it in to Greenspan. "Is that what it took, Harvey?" Greenspan said. He was amused and serious. "We'll use it tomorrow."

"Thank you, Marty."

"There'll be a cut here and there."

"Why?" Grosbeck protested.

"It *is* a little long, Harvey," Greenspan said gently.

"But, Marty . . ."

"We won't hurt it, Harvey. You'll see. I do believe you're on your way."

But, deeply though he believed that black is black and white white, Grosbeck, like anyone else, could not shake himself off all at once. "I'm not all that sure," he said.

15

"Another dead soldier," McFarland said, leaning back in his swivel chair, holding the bottle up to the light. "I cannot offer you a dash of lavender."

"Nobody talks like that anymore, Robert."

"*I* do," McFarland said. "*You* do, darlin', my old and tried."

"Then, failing that, could you favor me with a gasper?" Grosbeck asked. He had been without a cigarette, even a stub, all day.

"Certainly, you fool. And here is a lucifer to light up with. I have others to light the tapers which will follow you to an untimely grave, too. I have never been the one to scrape moral rot off the hide of a witling friend. Puff, puff you ass," McFarland urged, lighting up himself. "You will go up—down—in clouds of blue smoke. How many a day are you back to now that you're still alive?"

"Two," Grosbeck said, "Maybe three." He stubbed out the cigarette carefully and put it in a breast pocket. "I'll have the rest of this later."

"Paaagh. For God's sake, throw that away. Here's a fresh one for later. I can't bear to see you rooting at garbage. Here," he said, holding out the pack, "do yourself a world of harm."

"No, McFarland, I'll stay with the stub. That way, I keep the number down."

"But, don't you know that's even worse?" McFarland said.

"Please, Bob, no science. No diagrams of clogged arteries and black lungs. No lectures. All I know is, one cigarette is one cigarette even if I light it up three times. For me, you see, it's the *number* a day. All I did was come down here to see you because I haven't seen you since I went upstairs. Or Tully or Martha. My heart is of oak— with a slight arrhythmia, whatever that is. I don't hide a pack anywhere; I just smoke a few; I am an honorable man, furtive only in that respect. I say nothing regarding the bottle you keep in your desk, knowing you, too, are an honorable man and furtive only in *that* respect. I hope I have made you feel ashamed of yourself."

McFarland smiled and took both of Grosbeck's hands in his for a moment. "How are you?" he asked.

"Nervous," Grosbeck said. "Thinking takes it out of me, lofty thinking in particular. And there's so much silence up there being all alone in a room all day. But Greenspan's been pretty good about that. I've turned out just one piece in a month."

"I saw it. At least it was in English. It made me proud of you. I could understand every word. Actually, Harvey, it was pretty good. And, it was your own. Think of it. Your own. Not the pusillanimous, badly put together, inaccurate columns of ephemera you and I have had to set to rights year in and year out." He made an old newsroom joke: "I don't think those guys out in the field know what we're up against here." He licked the neck of the bottle. "Dead all right. It'll have to be replaced tomorrow."

Grosbeck took out the stub and lighted it again. "Just in celebration," he explained to McFarland. "You shinny on your side, I'll shinny on mine."

It was the lee of the day in the City Room. The first edition had gone to press an hour earlier with all of its facts, conjectures, opinions both puerile and otherwise, its air of authoritativeness, a miracle the value of which was like that of Lourdes—unproven but not to be mocked, either. The Day Side had drifted out higgledy-piggledy, an army in retreat, and the Night Side had drifted in, tired already, gone to its desks (possible nodding indifferently to the departing Day Side, buckling on its side arms) and sat, heads bent over copy, quiet, awaiting the next war and rumor of war. Goya's *Disasters of War*, lances at rest, limping, feet rotting in boots that had marched too long in mud. Who had won that day, who lost; who had advanced, who retreated? Nobody, everybody. The faces changed down the years, the voices, the clothing, the machinery, the office furniture; the idiosyncrasies of this one were replaced by those of that one; the reasons why changed or were the same in other words; and all was swallowed up in the unchanging tableau and there was no discharge in the war which claimed its victims in stroke and drink, accident and circumstance, faltering and age; stubbornness or too great a strain to agree.

So well did both men understand this that McFarland began to sing softly:

> "When the shrapnel flew fast,
> And our fellows were gassed,
> You sang and baked and prayed";

And Grosbeck joined him:

> "As we bent back the line
> Of the Huns toward the Rhine,
> Cheered on by the doughnuts you made."

McFarland rose from his desk and said to Grosbeck, "Body disposal is the minimum requirement after death."

Grosbeck rose from his chair, the last of the cigarette in the corner of his mouth, and said to McFarland, "And thus shall we renew the earth." The sentimentality, so explicit, deeply satisfied both men for all of its outworn youthfulness, for all of its avoidance of what might truly have been bothering both of them. McFarland should have been gone with the start-up of the presses, but Grosbeck had come downstairs because he knew that McFarland would not be, that it was his habit, as McFarland put it, to "ret up," by which Grosbeck understood him to mean reckon up the day in his head (drinking moderately out of the bottle in his desk, despite The Newspaper's stern ruling against it) and then take himself, with all of his clacking and conflicting thoughts, home to New Jersey where he disposed of the thoughts as he had thousands and thousands of times since he came to The Newspaper at the end of the Second World War; neatly. Just as he disposed of empty scotch bottles, putting them in a small canvas carryall which he emptied into a wastebasket in the bus terminal before going on to the liquor store there for another. A quart lasted him up to two weeks, and his wife honored his temperance by giving him a double martini when he got home for dinner.

McFarland loved her, he loved his children and he was gentle. He did not look gentle. He had been born in Texas and played football for the University of Texas and not just because his father, an Austin banker, had wanted him to. He had been a genuine, blown-in-the-bottle Texan. But the football had left him with a crushed sinus and a broken nose (which, oddly, made him better-looking) and an eye (his eyes were a pale blue) that would no longer do everything it was intended to, and so, when he joined the Marines in the middle of the war, he could not be a flier, he had to be an infantryman. He had been wounded twice in the Pacific—nothing worse, he told people, than he'd gotten out of football—and he had come out of the war to be a newspaperman and to come to The Newspaper as an editor.

He was a blocky, handsome man, and he betrayed his wife as he drank in the office—temperately. A woman—Martha Sloane, for example—would last him for years. She was drawn to him by his silences and his skills in beds they tumbled in in bad hotels near The Newspaper; by the shaven back of his head—he wore his gray hair as he had in the Marines. And she was drawn to him also because there was no more Texas left in him. He was never very drunk when he made love to her; he did not pat her on the behind when they were through; he got her through a humiliating divorce, the result of her husband discovering that he adored male prostitutes of whom there were so many delicious varieties waiting to be plucked on the avenues of the upper East Side.

Her husband had first found out about himself at a cocktail party in a restaurant. He had been standing in a urinal when the man next to him looked over and said, softly, "Oooh!" He had said nothing, done nothing then, but his course from then on was clear. There was a wide streak of vulgarity in his choices—street choices, which were irresistible but dangerous.

Martha had found him out not because of his frequent absences at night or his disinclination to go to bed with her any longer, but because he had neglected one early morning to remove his lipstick and eyeliner. "You too," she had said to this figure, at once ridiculous and pathetic, lying next to her in bed. "Where's your wig?" He almost answered her. "Don't be too flagrant about it," she advised him. "Oil companies don't take kindly to their junior vice-presidents running about in drag." She looked at him both in distaste and regret and impatience at herself. How could she not have known? "Out you go," she said. "Take your time, but out . . ."

He had nodded in humble silence. The stubble of his beard could be seen, unpleasantly, through face powder. In his pajamas, he resembled a circus clown still puffing from having chased a trained dog around a ring, under the legs of trotting horses and through flaming hoops. The two of them had become a little hysterical.

"I don't lisp," he said.

"Wonderful," she told him. He started to cry. "You'll spoil your makeup."

"Martha, Martha," he sobbed. "I never knew, not until . . ."

"All right, Columbus," she said, "I don't need the voyages of your discovery. Just don't get killed. I don't want you on my conscience for something that might have been my fault to begin with. God, how I wish you'd been just a simple alcoholic."

"You know how little I drink," he said inanely.

"Oh, you dumb son of a bitch, get the hell out of my sight," and she, too, cried.

Cried, both of them, cleaned up, went to work, and got divorced. It had taken Martha Sloane six months before accepting McFarland, before realizing that her husband had been no fault of hers. "I feel safer with a newspaperman," she had told McFarland the first time they made love in one of the cheap hotels. "There's no logic in it, but I can't help myself."

He stroked her neck. "There are no faggots on newspapers?" he asked.

"Bob, *please*," she said. "I *know* it doesn't make much sense . . ."

"That's right, Martha," McFarland said. "Let's just put it all down to a whim of the Almighty."

Unlike Grosbeck, who had experienced God in the hospital and found Him to be a Puerto Rican woman, McFarland had no idea of the extent of God's offhand whimsicality. It was McFarland who got punished, the simple heterosexual, not Martha's guilty husband. The celebrated neighborhood in which he worked was a dangerous one. Usually, he made his way carefully down the block and into the scabrous avenue leading to the bus terminal, courteously giving way to the peculiar specimens approaching him, looking back over his shoulder for others who might be following him. It lacerated his pride as a former Marine sergeant major to do this, but he did it out of a sense of duty to his family. If there were to be any trouble at all, he had (like so many others) figured out, it would be in the bus terminal, the Circus Maximus of so much of the murderous degeneracy the City had so passively taken to its wormy bosom in the last twenty years or so.

But this night, in an expansive mood, he had taken a roundabout way to the terminal, imagining himself (for the sake of argument) a stranger to the Great City, hearing its sounds, seeing its sights, smelling its exotic smells, observing the natives, strolling carefree through the bazaars, being generous to the armless beggars and polite, in the manner of a nineteenth-century British colonial, to those who importuned him for this, that, and the other. Whatever had got into him, he had not even had the foresight to cross to the other side of the street when he came up to an empty, darkened parking lot.

A small man darted out of the lot and stood spread-legged before him with a knife in his hand. McFarland was unafraid. He moved stylishly up to the little man, still combat ready, hands up, fingers stiff, shoulders moving ever so little, prepared to take the knife away from the man and beat him to death. The man retreated two steps, the knife before him and then McFarland, as he knew himself, disappeared. Two other men had run out of the parking lot behind him. One hit him on the back of his shaven head with a brick, the other hit him in the ribs with a piece of pipe. The man with the knife punched him in the nose as he went down and broke it once more.

The three of them ripped open his pockets and took everything in them. They broke open a plastic garbage bag, one of half a dozen at the curb, and threw McFarland into the garbage. They broke open three more and emptied garbage on him as he lay face down. They kicked him and danced around him and waved his wallet and keys and pen and pencil in the air. They shouted "Whooo-ee," and staggered and breathed hard in their exertions. They were in no hurry. Who was to say them nay? They were amateurs, which made it all the more unlikely that the police would ever find them. They took their time. They worked in a circle, formally, as though in an avant-garde play. One would kick. All would stop, raise their arms and faces to heaven, and yell in unison, "Mothah!" Then the next would kick, the circle revolve a little, the same hypnotic invocation. With the last kick agreed on in some sort of telepathy, the cry to the black sky hidden behind clouds and a few street lights was, "Suckah!" They looked down, for the last time, at the recumbent McFarland, spat together, contemptuously, and walked away— *walked* away.

In the very heart of the City, McFarland lay unnoticed for an hour. Consciousness returned to him within fifteen minutes and with it, pain. His face was all blood, his clothing torn, his trunk, it seemed, unscrewed from his legs, a bag of torment into which air moved and was expelled with difficulty from the poor nose. He was seen first by a pimp who stopped and examined him for anything the others might have overlooked. Nothing. The pimp was on good terms with the police—they were all in the same business—and so he walked back down the block, away from the all-night cafeteria in which he had intended to meet one of his girls, and found a policeman where he knew he would. The officer was asleep in a squad car, parked in a narrow alley between an all-male movie house ("Studs! Studs! Studs!") and a dirty bookstore a few doors away from a Roman Catholic church which was kept padlocked during the night. No succor there. The pimp reached into the open window of the squad car and shook the cop's shoulder.

"Cannizzaro," he whispered urgently. "Cannizzaro, get yo' ass up from there." He reproached the officer. "Where yo' partner you don' know better than coop without he know it?" He clucked his tongue and shook his head from side to side. "You ought be 'shamed of yo'self."

The policeman sat up, rubbed his eyes, felt around for his gun, and said to the pimp, "I didn't know you, I'd have you down in Central Booking so fast your head could come off. What's wrong?"

The pimp told him. "Best get over there quick. He one of them very, very respectable-lookin' dudes, white, been around a long time. I had nothin' to do with it. You know that ain't my M.O. I found him. Highly respectable, not the kin' lookin' for anything I got to offa . . . although, come to think of it, that ain't that unusual, either." The pimp dragged himself back to the subject at hand. "He layin' in garbage outside that parking lot down the street from the all-night cafeteria. Go on, now!"

"All right," said the cop sourly. He had an awful taste in his mouth. He buttoned his jacket. "You stay," he told the pimp, "until my partner gets here and tell him where I am." The cop backed the car out of the alley and drove off to find McFarland. He stood over him, impressed at the job that had been done on McFarland without killing him and irritated at the victim's stupidity. He called on the radio for an ambulance, took out a notebook. More paperwork. He managed to get McFarland's name and address out of him, asked him how he felt (as though he didn't know), told him not to move, and was relieved he had done all this when he found out that McFarland worked for The Newspaper. That'd put a firecracker up anybody's ass. Gotta say thanks to the pimp. His partner turned up. The ambulance rolled up fifteen minutes later, which set a hospital record for promptness that night.

"Big guy," said one of the attendants to the cop as they surveyed McFarland supine.

"Yeah," said Cannizzaro, "must of took at least three to work *him* over."

McFarland opened his mouth. "I used to play football," he said. "Guy in front had a knife, I could have taken that away from him. I never saw what hit me." He stirred a little. "Marines. Second war." Why did he feel it necessary to explain himself?

"He anybody?"

"Not exactly," Cannizzaro said, "but he happens to work for The Newspaper and they get itchy about things like this. They like their people all in one piece. He falls apart because of you guys, we're in deep shit."

A noise came up from the sidewalk in the vicinity of McFarland's mouth, partly blocked by the displaced nose. ". . . ''Cause you knock-kneed, pigeon-toed, box-ankled, too,/ There's a curse on your family and it fell on you' . . ."

"You believe that?" one of the attendants said. "He's singing!"

The other attendant, who was a jazz enthusiast, bent down to listen. "'Your hair is nappy,'" the cracked voice went on, "'Who's your pappy?/ You some ugly chile' . . ."

The attendant stood up. "It's not rock," he said, "not Country Western. Disco's out. He's singing Dixieland," he said, spacing out each word for emphasis.

"Now," said Cannizzaro, his voice rising, "will you *please*, for the love of Christ, get him the hell out of here? And thank you for the diagnosis."

Grosbeck and McFarland compared notes on ambulances. They slapped each other on the back, metaphorically. McFarland still took the bus home. Perversely. Grosbeck, perversely, took taxicabs: the doctor had told him to take long walks. Each asked after the other's wife and children. McFarland called Jersey on one phone and told his wife he was going to celebrate the repair of Grosbeck's heart and the new bridge in his own mouth. Grosbeck called Madeline and said he had something to talk over with McFarland about his work.

"Come home," Madeline said. "Talk it over with me. I'm feeling beautiful, sympathetic and full of insights, funnier than McFarland. Give him my love. I've cooked. Dr. Salomon says you're ready and I'm aching for your tiny little body. Please?"

"I won't, I swear I won't be late, sweetheart, but it's been so long since I've had any kind of talk with any of the few people around here who mean something to me. An hour is all. And then . . . you mean to say you cooked after a day like yours?" He was all contrition for Madeline's hard day. "I was going to take you out after I got through with McFarland. What do you say?" Grosbeck was still on the phone when McFarland hung up. *His* method was more that of the Marine sergeant major. His wife was as accustomed to that as Grosbeck's was to his wheedling. And it took less time.

McFarland leaned back in his chair and crossed his arms while Grosbeck and Madeline talked. In the end, he knew, Grosbeck would have his way, but he wondered why Harvey took so long about it. It must be the Jew in him: explain, explain, explain. That's what brought out the writer in Grosbeck, he thought, and made *him* a picker-over of other men's words. He could not hear her, but he knew that Madeline was annoyed.

("The tone of your voice," she said. "Harvey, you pick up guilt like lint and dandruff." "Ah, Madeline, it's only for an hour and . . ." "And you two girls haven't had a good talk for ever so long. All right, Harvey, you can take me out—when you get home.") He looked at McFarland, rolled his eyes, made a face meant to explain everything, and shrugged. The telephone almost fell out of the corner of his neck.

McFarland nodded and pushed the receiver back in place. "I'm sorry for your trouble, Mr. Grosbeck," he whispered.

"No trouble at all," Grosbeck said aloud.

"What's no trouble, Harvey?" Madeline said.

"Nothing, I just happened to be saying something to McFarland. That wasn't meant for you."

"What *is*, Harvey?" Madeline asked.

"Everything, my dearest heart. My worldly goods, my nail parings,

the heart that beats so strongly now under your tender ministrations . . ."

"Why don't you just marry Dr. Salomon or McFarland, Harvey?"

"Neither one of them has legs like yours, Madeline," Grosbeck
said softly, "or a behind or breasts which compel me so . . . or a
mouth which, in the proper circumstances, not including these,
makes me give up the world for well lost. Will you wait?" Grosbeck
could sense that her answer was not going to be a short one, and
even as Madeline began he put a palm over the receiver and whispered to McFarland, "I'll only be another minute."

"Have I provoked a domestic quarrel?" McFarland whispered
back.

"No, I don't think so," Grosbeck said, trying to listen to Madeline
at the same time. An odor of maleness arose about the two men, so
strong as to extirpate all the other odors of the City Room. McFarland listening and waiting, Grosbeck on the telephone, were two old
men rocking on a bench in a heterosexual Turkish bath (neither
would have dreamed of using the word "sauna"), one cackling on the
telephone, the other patiently waiting for him to be finished.

Madeline was saying,

"Underneath it all, men continue to think their thoughts about
women and women remain hopeful about men, just hopeful that
they're going to find someone who is understanding and sensitive
and totally accepting of them."

"Madeline," Harvey interrupted, "I don't think you needed the
word 'totally' there. Don't you see, if one accepts, one *does* accept totally?" There was a silence at the other end of the phone. Then a
sigh.

"I said the wrong thing, Madeline, didn't I? I was badly brought
up. But you knew all that before we got married. Sweetheart, it's not
as though it's our anniversary or my birthday." He paused. "Or
yours," he added quickly. "Or Whitsuntide, or Boxing Day, or Sim-
chas Torah . . ."

"No, it isn't," she said, "but it's three months to the day since you
had your heart attack. An occasion. I won't be backward about it
. . . Dr. Salomon said . . ."

"Ah," said Grosbeck, "I'd had it all planned for *tomorrow* night
. . . sort of *spontaneously* . . ." Madeline could not resist laughing.

"There's nothing like youth, is there, Harvey, for rashness?"

"Everything, Madeline," Grosbeck said. "First, the champagne. Then, the dicumarol—the diuretic—for me. Perfume for you. Dim lights. A deep, deep kiss. A bite on the neck. I'd lick your nose. That's exciting. Make a big thing of your slender fingers, pinch that shapely ass, rip off the few tiny garments with which you'd greet me at the door—*if* you thought about it beforehand in our great spontaneity—no excess would be too great, there would be no limit to our ingenuity, no end to our passionate thrashing about. Can't you hear me now, my voice grown husky? If you could only see my fingers trembling, my eyes blinded with I know not what . . . possibly the blood rising in my head . . ."

McFarland regarded Grosbeck admiringly from across the desk. He would no sooner have moved away from this piece of domestic theatre than fly. He was tempted to lift the extension of his own phone to hear the other side of the conversation but his Marine Corps training had been too strong. He saluted Grosbeck and murmured, "Semper Fidelis." He was not too strong on history, but it was his deep conviction that nothing man had ever invented had served to alter in the tiniest this kind of exchange between the sexes. Had Madeline and Grosbeck been talking to each other into two tin cans connected by a piece of waxed string, the conversation must have been much the same. Why, why? he wondered, not much caring, calculating only how much longer it might take. He picked up a piece of wire-service copy he had neglected to throw into a basket and started to read it aloud, all the while listening, too.

"*New York, long considered a 'dog-eat-dog' town, is getting tougher,*" it proclaimed.

Madeline continued. "I think men just want to avoid being beaten on the head."

"Men *are* all alike, aren't they?" Grosbeck said mournfully.

"*City health officials say that New Yorkers sank their teeth into each other last year more than ever before,*" McFarland read.

"So much for feminism," Madeline went on. "Men and women will say anything and do anything and march and shout and issue declarations and they'll still go marching in separate directions."

"I couldn't agree with you more, sweetheart," Grosbeck said humbly, patiently.

"*The number of cases of New Yorkers putting the bite on other people shot up 24 per cent last year from the year before, health officials said."* Are they trying to tell me they keep statistics on *that?* McFarland asked himself. He was not astonished; there was government money to be had to count the least sparrow—was there not?—thereby taking the job off God's hands.

"They just occasionally collide enough to get married or live together or have children or not," Madeline was saying to Grosbeck, "and it's very heartbreaking in the end, because women want men to be as tender and loving as they thought their fathers were, even if the father wasn't that way at all . . ."

"I'll be right home, Madeline," Grosbeck said. "I'll just tell McFarland another time."

"No, you won't, Harvey," said Madeline. "You've just told *me* another time."

"Well," he said, "if you insist. But only on that condition . . ." He could not, of course, see the rue in Madeline's face, but he knew it was there.

McFarland read on, with growing interest. " *'Human bitings are not a matter to be taken lightly,' Health Commissioner Arthur Portman said in a statement. 'Every year, children and young men and women sustain injuries from human bites that lead to serious problems, including deformities and amputations.'* " Grosbeck put his hand over the phone again. "Nothing," he said, "a difference of opinion."

McFarland nodded and continued to read: *"More men than women get bit,"* the story said. True, thought McFarland. *"About half of the bites were considered 'aggressive' and only two of the bites were sexual in nature."* "Harvey," said McFarland, "the bite may be aggressive, but you'll be happy to know, darlin', it ain't sexual in nature. Go on home and get laid."

"What?" asked Grosbeck, who was trying to concentrate on Madeline alone. "I can't hear a word you're saying. No, Madeline, not you. McFarland. He was trying to tell me something."

"I'm sure he was," said Madeline. "I've only one more thing to say. I find it terribly sad that all this working toward a common understanding turns into a pack of lies that people commit on each other in order to keep the peace."

"Have I ever done that to you?" Grosbeck asked.

"Yes, you have, Harvey. One last thing . . ."

"I thought you *had* told me one last thing, Madeline."

"I don't think you'll mind too much hearing this," Madeline said softly. "We've been married long enough so that I'm not always ungrateful for it."

"I can't figure you out, sweetheart," Grosbeck said. "Never could, never will."

"It doesn't matter that much. Just don't stay out too late with him. Put him on, will you?" Grosbeck motioned at McFarland and handed him the phone.

"Robert," she said, "no more than another hour, will you, please? I know you have his best interests at heart."

"Of course, darlin'," McFarland said. "And yours, too. We're not even going out to a saloon, Madeline. We're going to sit right where we are. And talk, just talk." He handed the phone back to Grosbeck.

"You see, sweetheart?" He made kissing noises into the telephone and hung up. He called Madeline again. "You can even call back to check," he said.

"I'd sooner die, Harvey. Call me before you leave. I think I can re-arrange my schedule."

McFarland read one more line from the story, "*Although the number of human bites increased, the number of dog bites decreased 16.7 per cent, down from the figure of a year before of 18,814.*" He threw the piece of copy into a wastebasket. "Now," he said to Grosbeck, "what's on your mind?"

"Women are funny," Grosbeck said.

"Is *that* what you came down here to tell me?" McFarland asked. "They're hilarious," he added. "Tragic, too? did you intend to tell me? Is that what they're teaching you upstairs? Goodness me, Harvey, you make me regret all the years I've spent down here. I could have been a man of the world by now."

"I think they made a man of the world out of you, Robert, that night over on Forty-sixth Street."

"Certainly did, darlin'," McFarland said. "Look." He pushed out his upper bridge with his tongue. "Part of a new man, anyway," he went on, after pushing it back into place. "The ribs still ache in bad weather. The nose, I think, looks a little better than it used to, don't you think?"

Grosbeck smiled at him. "You're a new man, McFarland. But, then, you've been a new man all the years I've known you. Only Texan I've ever known who was a new man."

"Seriously, Harvey, you don't know diddleyshit about Texas or about any other part of the country except New York and what you know about New York went out of existence after the Second World War. Meaning no disrespect to you, my friend, but you're out of date. I like it, but that is the case."

"That's not true," Grosbeck said. "I got beat up, too, remember? At that religious festival? In the middle of all that religion and pinning dollar bills on the Virgin or whatever androgyne it was they were carrying down the street. I've got some teeth missing, too. I've got store-boughts at least as expensive as yours." With his tongue, he pushed out his own lower bridge. "Care to try 'em?" he asked. "They're a little nearsighted, but they ought to work for you."

McFarland pulled his swivel chair over to Grosbeck with his heels, put a hand on Grosbeck's knee and said to him, "All right, Harvey, that's enough. We both know you're not down here to pass the time of night, although you're welcome to. What's on your mind?"

Grosbeck's face had a peculiar look on it, as though he had or were about to pee from the curb as he had done so often and so un-self-consciously when he was a child. "Well, Robert," he said slowly, "it's like this. You know I like some things not to change."

"You astonish me, Harvey. I never would have known. Didn't I just tell you you were out of date?"

"I know, I know," Grosbeck said. "I just don't know how to get to this."

"Quickly," McFarland said. "Quickly. Either that or we make a night of it somewhere else."

Grosbeck took a deep breath. "I'm ashamed of myself."

"For what? Tell Father McFarland, my son, and you will be shriven."

"Oh, it probably isn't much," Grosbeck said, "but I am."

"Well, *what is it*? You're making me impatient, you're carrying me past curiosity." He looked at his watch. "You've got thirty seconds more to get it out or I have another drink and then go home."

"It's that," Grosbeck said, pointing.

"That? What?"

"That thing where your typewriter used to be."

"The VDT? The Video Display Terminal? What about it?"

"I can't use it," Grosbeck said.

"Is *that* all?" McFarland asked.

"What's more," Grosbeck went on, "I don't want to and I'll never learn how."

"I heard what a stink you made about taking your typewriter upstairs."

"I learned to think on a typewriter, Bob."

"If that's what you call it," McFarland said.

"I can do a hundred and twenty words a minute on a manual typewriter, McFarland."

"Not enough these days, Harvey."

"Fast enough for me," said Grosbeck. "That's just about as fast as I can think. And I don't want to try to think even on an electric typewriter, much less this rotten thing. There's nothing anybody can say on it that I can't say on my manual. What's more, I can change ribbons in thirty seconds. There's no ribbon even left to change on your son-of-a-bitching VDT. There aren't any words on it. All it is is light, and, presto, you punch a lousy key and there's nothing there. I despise it, I don't want to learn to use it. But I've got to. I've got reasons. Maybe I'll tell you some day." The words rushed from him in agony, far beyond the demands of the moment. The next words came from him almost hoarsely. "Do you suppose," he asked, "you could show me how? You know about these goddamned things. Greenspan isn't going to let me use a typewriter forever, he told me. Says it slows things up. Says he's tired of having a copyboy take my copy and put it into the machine. Tells me the monks were equally distressed by Gutenberg and then told me they not only got over it but that I wasn't a monk and that if I wanted to turn out illuminated manuscripts on parchment he'd refer me to a calligrapher. But, as I said, it's more than that."

McFarland leaned back in his chair. He did not mock. "All right, Harvey," he said, "it's not the end of the world, and it *is* here to stay. I know it looks complicated and I know it looks inhuman, but what do you think the first typewriter looked like to the first poor victim who had to use one? I'm not up on the history of those things, but it couldn't have been any worse than annoying for a while. I hate to lay things out A, B, and C for you, a man of your intelligence, but you forget that you and I came along when the typewriter—and the Linotype, and so on—represented the ultimate in technology. Well, they aren't anymore, you poor Luddite. I swear to God I never saw such fright. Come here, child, sit down here, at my desk, right in front of the thing. It can't bite. And it does work. In a couple of weeks you'll think it's the greatest thing to come along since—I don't know what—the quill pen, ink, and sand."

Grosbeck sat at the keyboard. "What do I do first?"

"Turn it on," McFarland said.

Grosbeck looked at the black screen and then at the keyboard. "Where for the love of Christ?"

"Here," McFarland said gently, and turned a tiny wheel at the right of the machine. "See this?" he asked. "It says ON and OFF."

Grosbeck looked up at the screen. The black had been replaced by what he conceived to be an eerie glow. "Now what?"

"Well, then," McFarland continued, "normally you punch up the code, your code, and then you type."

"*My* code?" Grosbeck asked. "What code? What the hell am I, classified now?"

"No," McFarland said patiently, "when your code's up, another man, an editor, sits in front of his screen and watches what you're typing and you sort of talk back and forth while you're writing something and you can make changes or he can and that's how you get the finished written product."

"Product?" Grosbeck asked.

"That's what I said," McFarland told him. "It *is* a product, isn't it? It ain't Proust. Go on now and type."

The keys ran out under Grosbeck's fingers. There was no resistance, none at all. Gibberish came up in green on the screen, the same letter repeated—Zzzzzzzzzzzz—a dozen times, words misspelled, lines skipped (McFarland had to show him how to space the lines), words which, even when spelled painfully correctly refused to form themselves into sentences or paragraphs. Grosbeck's fingers stiffened; his eyes grew wild; his arms grew heavy and dropped to his side. "Turn it off," he begged McFarland. "I can't handle it. I had no idea . . ."

"Give it one last try," McFarland said. "And then you can go home."

"If you say so," Grosbeck said, his voice barely audible. And, with his left forefinger alone, he searched out letters on the infernal machine. And, lo, there in green at the top line of the VDT two words came up: "Fuck you."

16

"Fuck you," the infernal machine had said to him, the letters shimmering with hatred on the screen. No exclamation point. The machine had not even thought him worthy of a warning emphasis. Grosbeck had forgotten, in the way so convenient to him, that it was he who had punched up the words. He preferred, instead, to believe that the machine had passed judgment on him, that it smelled disobedience in him and would not brook it.

Would he not have been ever so much better off had he had it say something like, "Lord God of Cybernetics, of chips and tapes and semiconductors, hear me. I kneel in adoration of your chads, your inputs, your throughputs, your outputs, your printouts and feedbacks —whatever you call them—all reconciled more perfectly than mere man could have done with fingers and a brass composing stick. Thou leadest me beside Thy Vydec and Thy Ascii. Thou makest me to lie down beside those revolving drums and Thou swathest me in Thy tapes with holes in them and all this speedily, silently, and perfectly . . . Thou art the hope of the World."

It might even have been advisable for him to make a mistake or two, leaving the machine to shift a line, drop a word, substitute another, correct an inadvertent misspelling, transpose a paragraph and then subside smugly. But he had not.

McFarland had smiled, wiped off the two words that had squeezed their way up from Grosbeck's bottomless depression. He patted Grosbeck on the back, patted the machine on the back and said, "You two'll get to know each other much better. The VDT'll be a better man for it." And to the VDT, "Be good to him, you hear me?" The black screen stared noncommittally at him.

The two men left the building. "Which way, Robert?" Grosbeck asked. "My cab can drop you off at the bus terminal on my way downtown."

"No," McFarland said, "I'll walk it. I always have and I don't mean to stop now."

Grosbeck shrugged. "It's your nose, Robert," he said, "but it doesn't look any better out here tonight than the night you got it."

"I thank you for your concerns, my friend," McFarland said, "but the streets are still mine to walk."

"I've noticed," Grosbeck said. "Yours to die on, may I add."

"Round and round the little ball goes," McFarland concluded, "and where it stops nobody knows. Good night. The VDT isn't going to eat you alive, Harvey," and off he went with the slight, rolling walk that was all that was left of Texas in him.

The June night was extraordinarily hot. All the way home in the cab, Grosbeck reflected on the words, "Fuck you," and on the heat, which, for all that it was seasonal, he took to be as personally directed at him as the invention of the VDT. The air conditioner was one of the few bits of twentieth-century technology he had come to accept unreservedly and he had often said to Madeline that the thing she could give him which he would prize most highly—even if they had to borrow money to buy it—would be a restaurant-size air conditioner.

It was true, he admitted, that it would take up an entire wall of the bedroom, blocking out the windows, but then, he argued, what was there to see through those windows: the after-hours club down the block which catered to four known sexes and a fifth, unidentifiable one—he would have to consult some book on biology to find out—a line of taxicabs awaiting the pleasure of these grotesque clients and, almost every night of the week, a saturnalia of screams, stabbings, beatings, fornications of a complication and sinuosity hitherto unrecorded, and sidewalks littered with broken bottles, crushed vials which had once contained drugs, bits of clothing, an odd shoe, the barely digested contents of stomachs; everything, everything which marked the rapidly approaching apogee of the greatest civilization the world has ever known. Madeline had dismissed his request as fantasy; he had not expected her to do otherwise.

Grosbeck thought of two things the diarist Strong had written and which he had committed to memory: "Saw an extract from some foreign periodical, ascribing this queerest, dampest, cloudiest of all springs and summers, to the influence of Halley's Comet. It seems as if some extraordinary agent must be at work . . ." And, a year later,

"If the D—l comes on Earth about these times to cool himself, as Southey says he used to do, because 'the weather was close below,' he certainly won't choose New York for his visit, though it is undoubtedly a favorite resort of his." He repeated, "Fuck you," aloud.

The driver turned around at a red light. "You said?"

"Excuse me, nothing to do with you, I was just thinking out loud."

"Aha," the driver said skeptically. The man was an Israeli, Grosbeck could tell that much from the identification card on the dashboard. He had a beard, which he did not have on the card since, Grosbeck guessed, the Taxi Commission hadn't bothered to have him photographed again for the renewal of his license. Grosbeck also would have bet that his English had been learned in a Yemenite village and his knowledge of the streets of New York in the same place.

Grosbeck realized at once that he could turn his "Fuck you" to his advantage and soothe whatever feelings had been ruffled in this muscular brute. "What I really meant," he said, "was, when you get to *Fourteenth* Street, just keep on going straight. I'll direct you after that. You're doing pretty well for a stranger to the City. After all, we are a nation of foreigners, aren't we?"

"No stranger," the driver said gruffly. "I drive cab here for two years now." He seemed to be appeased, however. "I miss October War, you see. Drive command car the war before. Perfect driver. Next year, I own my own cab. Year after that, I learn the streets. My wife, an American, she insists on that. Everything should be just right with her."

"I can understand that," Grosbeck said. "Ariel," he added, having read the man's first name off the card. He overtipped him. "Good luck," he said. "Don't take any wooden Uzis. We've got our own kind of desert war going on here, you might have heard."

"Don' *vorry*," said the driver. "I got a brother-in-law in the diamond business. He got a .357 Magnum. A permit he's got, too. We share. I keep both under the cigar box with the money at night. His permit. My gun. Almost my gun. I don' use it yet, but I do, look out. The beard I got because he got a beard. Beard is beard. Who looks twice? You wan' see how fast I get it out from under cigar box? Nah, not nice man like you, not with tip like that, you don' hold up dinner for your wife, I bet."

Grosbeck started to say, "But what about fingerprints?" and then thought better of it. He had encountered garrulous Israelis before and he'd be on his own doorstep half the night hearing once more how this Israeli (like all the other Israeli hack drivers) had taken the Golan Heights singlehandedly in '67. He waved a good night and entered the apartment house.

Grosbeck paused at the doorway to his apartment, keys in hand, rent by his appetites (for both sex and food), his *faiblesse* in the face of the weather and his infarcted heart, his very mind awhirl, a drop of sweat at the end of his nose. In place of the *mezuzah* good Jews were wont to affix at an angle on the right post of a doorway, Grosbeck had installed an expensive thermometer vertically; there was no religiosity, only scientific accuracy, involved in the hanging of a thermometer. So far, nobody, not even Madeline, who loved heat, had bothered to vandalize the instrument. It read 96 degrees—Fahrenheit. Grosbeck would have no truck with attempts to install the metric system in his life—"metricization," naturally—and before he bought the instrument he had made certain there was no nonsense on it about Celsius or any of the other pseudoscientific crap the radio weather forecasters dribbled through mouths filled with caramel. For him, there was no such thing as "shower activity" or "intervals of sunshine and precipitation" or "temperature inversions." For Grosbeck, it either rained or snowed; the sun shone or it didn't and the first time he heard the word "burbs" for "suburbs," he closed his eyes and thought of the chattering of coatimundis at feeding time. These commercial pisspots; these vile little costermongers; these counterjumpers; these graduates in pushcart persuasion of schools of journalism too degenerate to be mentioned in decent company—there they were, laughing it up and gee-whizzing the weather until a thunderstorm took on the dimensions of a protracted giggle-cum-belch.

He was wet through with sweat. In his seersucker suit—all cotton; the merest hint of a synthetic made him dizzy—he looked this night like a carelessly packed bag of tomatoes in burlap, held together incongruously with a fine silk tie, exquisitely patterned in red and blue. There were rills of sweat on his temples and under his mad eyes. The cab ride had taken only twelve minutes, but Grosbeck might as well have spent the day fully clothed in a Turkish bath being flailed at irregular intervals with bundles of switches by a fat attendant who, through the clouds of steam, paid no attention to his entreaties of

"Enough! Enough!" Heat, heat, that was the formula for torturing Grosbeck. Under heat, rolling and unrelenting, he could have been made to confess anything. He reflected that, had the cab ride lasted five minutes longer, he would have confessed to the driver—the words wrung out of him in the last few strings of spittle remaining in his diminishing body—that when he got home, he intended to go to bed with his wife for the first time in three months, for the first time since his heart attack.

He had been cleared—completely cleared, you hear?—by Dr. Salomon, who, however, had counseled him against the more athletic forms of contact between the sexes the first time out—or in—or down—or whatever form of erotic Olympiad to which he had once been accustomed. "I know how large the bump of prurience is in your makeup, professor," Dr. Salomon had said, looking down at Grosbeck's genitals, which were taking in every word immodestly and with every sign of impatience, "but that first night, my blushing virgin, I would prefer that you draw a reasonable line between unbridled passion and a sort of Platonic persuasion. Masterly though I know you to be—if only by *your* account—I counsel a kind of classic passivity, persuasion not blows, perhaps a liqueur instead of your customary—what do you call it?—ah, yes, your four-ounce *el belto* of cheap vodka."

"What other good advice do you have for me, Henry? Walk, do not run, to the nearest entrance?"

"You have quick perceptions, my son," Salomon said.

"What else?" Grosbeck asked. "Tie a piece of gutta percha around my—uh, penis—lie down on a chaise longue and recite couplets of some kind?"

"No, professor," Salomon said. "Just don't let your dingle dangle on the ground. See how well I have learned your slang? Your children's rhymes?"

"You're years behind the times, Henry," Grosbeck said.

"Do you know this one?" Dr. Salomon asked. "It goes, 'Do your balls hang low?/ Do they dangle to and fro?/ Can you tie 'em in a knot?/ Can you tie 'em in a bow?/ Can you swing 'em on your shoulder/ Like a European soldier?/ Can you sing this little ditty while your balls hang low?' "

"Henry!" Grosbeck said. "Between that and your Mitteleuropa accent . . . Where did you pick that up? Have you got any idea how *old* that is? That must have come out of the other World War. *I* first learned *that* when I was in 5-A. A girl named Rosalynne Klein slipped it to me on a piece of paper. She taught me to 'feel her up.' That's the way we used to put it—'feel her up.' I wonder what the last fifty years have done to Feel-Her-Up Klein? No, on second thought, I don't want to know."

"No matter, Mr. Harvey Grosbeck, sir. Like so many great things of history, the little rhyme is as applicable today as it was in, who knows? Clausewitz's time, Caesar's time. Maybe it is an obscure rhyme of one of his anonymous lieutenants, dust these thousands of years. Whatever. If I may descend to your more contemporary vulgate—the word is 'vulgate,' is it not?—don't knock yourself out. No assaults, no rapine, no gorging simply because one's appetite seems insatiable. It is not—the best minds are agreed on that."

"Once only?" Grosbeck asked. "Or twice? Or won't you permit me to stay up that late?"

"I am not a schoolmaster," Salomon had said. "In that respect, you will find me spinsterish enough, so little the voyeur, that I will not be in the bedroom to direct you."

"No more house calls, eh Henry?" Grosbeck asked.

Dr. Salomon sniffed. "Let your heart and your conscience be your guide. Remember that bourne from which no man returns."

"I suppose you're right, Henry. No point in being greedy, is there?"

"As to that, my friend, I have but one thing to add as you put your coat on. Professionally, I am in a reasonably good position to assay the condition of your heart. Where conscience is concerned, there are no reliable guides. Now, go forth, my son. Quickly. I have a waiting room full of cripples, hypochondriacs, and people truly sick with one physical thing or another. The air out there is filled with their symptoms; they hover like butterflies. Be careful as you leave— you might breathe in something you don't already have."

"Thank you, Henry," Grosbeck said as he left. He put his head back inside the half-closed door. "From the bottom of my heart." He began planning at once, but he had not reckoned on the heat of the night he had nominated for his return to the pleasures of concupiscence. Would she dare not turn on the air conditioning full? He had other worries: the evil behavior of the Video Display Terminal; his dismay over larger matters, like the barbaric alteration of New York City according to Corydon Varney and other contesting carrion crows and buzzards. But he was not unfamiliar with other manifestations of the human spirit, the will—in others, anyway—to surmount all. Only the day before, the cops had caught a young couple, not yet out of their teens, making love in utter abandon on the narrow tower of one of the East River bridges, five hundred feet above the water. The cops had spotted them from a helicopter and their sense of duty was so deeply ingrained in them that they had hovered over the tower until the couple climaxed—while holding on for dear life. Only then did they radio down and get a squad car out on the bridge and a couple of patrolmen up the tower to arrest the perpetrators. Both, as The Newspaper photographs showed the next day, were superb physical specimens. Grosbeck could not, did not, hope to emulate them, but, he thought, if Youth could overcome such obstacles, why not Maturity? Love Will Find a Way, Grosbeck told himself, at any altitude, at any age.

Grosbeck started to let himself into the apartment. As he turned the key, he felt the lock being opened from the other side and then heard footsteps in quick, pretty retreat. The magnificence of Madeline's foresight almost took his breath away. Madeline, my darling, you heard me coming down the hall bloated with uxoriousness, didn't you? Aching for you, for all the years of separation; of travels to far countries and terrible perils; the hardships of enemas and catheters; the hand-to-hand combat with the troglodytes whom one addressed as "Doctor," lest they plunge palpators down the gullet; the dissimulations thought up to placate these monsters of science from other planets. And then, the long road back.

The most exotic experience that had befallen the traveler had occurred one morning as he came out of the men's room pulling up his zipper, straightening his tie. There, before the door he had happened on a black woman in turban and caftan on her knees on a straw mat. At The Newspaper! At regular intervals, she bent forward and touched her head to the mat and then sat up. Her eyes looked at him blindly. She was speaking Arabic and she was at her periodic devotions, a recent Moslem, late of South Carolina. The men's room faced east. Greenspan had asked her to do her praying as inconspicuously as possible—on the roof, say—but she was an excellent and conscientious secretary and she had told him there was no time for that.

Grosbeck knew of her existence, and, man of the world that he was, dealt with it like one. "Why here?" he asked. "Surely, there must be some other place in the building facing east?"

"I have a heavy day before me," she said, with a note in her voice suspended halfway between heaven and earth. "Surely, sir, you would not begrudge me the few minutes I have intruded on you here?"

"Never," Grosbeck said. "Why don't you just go right on and I'll disappear in a puff of smoke. Or, if you have a basket, you can charm me into it with a couple of incantations and carry me off to my office." He made a stab at lifting her to her feet.

"That won't be necessary, sir," she said, rising, rolling up the mat, dusting off her feet with a washroom towel and slipping into her sandals.

"I was only kidding about the basket," Grosbeck said. "I mean that."

"And you don't strike me as a cobra, Mr. Grosbeck," the girl said. "More like a garter snake."

"Ah, come on," Grosbeck said, in conformity with The Newspaper's commitment to affirmative action. "I apologize."

"I accept," said the girl.

The simpleton would not be done. "Don't get me wrong," he said, "I've got nothing in the world against any man's—person's, forgive me—religious beliefs, but didn't you feel there was something odd about entreating God at the door to the men's room?"

"Not at all, Mr. Grosbeck," she answered, "not any odder than it is for thousands of Jews traveling thousands of miles to pray in front of an old wall that isn't even a part of a building any more."

"That's not bad," he said, "I wish I had thought of that myself."

"Perhaps you will, sir," said the woman.

"Will you at least shake hands with me?" Grosbeck asked.

"Of course," she said.

In the apartment, Grosbeck was greeted with a steady stream of cold air from every air conditioner in the place. It coursed, hissing, through the dimmest of lighting. (Madeline would have preferred candles, but experimentation had shown they tended to blow out.) The air barely ruffled the heavy damask drapes, drawn to prevent the neighbors across the street from looking in. An unexpected paradox had grown up in the relations between the Grosbecks. As they got older, the dimensions of their lusts had become greater while at the same time the element of spontaneity had diminished to the point where going to bed with each other had devolved into a series of set pieces and they had become, in effect, a repertory company in which the lines were varied only slightly, the scenery shifted just a touch; the plot fixed beyond alteration, since sex has only one plot.

On with the play. For all the imperfections of the arrangements, the crotchets etched in repetition, the Grosbecks loved each other. At the bar, Madeline stood naked, except for a pair of black-satin high-heeled shoes, one ankle crossed over the other, her arms clasped across her breasts. So well had she stage-managed things that she had contrived to hold a martini in the thumb and forefinger of the right hand. The other fingers were holding her left arm. She had been unable, however, to prevent the air conditioning from covering her body with gooseflesh. Madeline's legs were beautifully curved (she was slightly knock-kneed, as well, which provoked Grosbeck to rhapsody; he was bow-legged and Madeline professed to adore *that*), and, what excited Grosbeck still more, at least six inches too long for the torso they supported. That consisted of a tiny waist, a rib cage smaller than it might classically have been, and, above that, what she persisted in calling her "accouterments." (She thought they were too big.) "Accouterments!" Grosbeck had once trumpeted in disbelief. "Jugs like that the good Lord above just didn't go around handing out or pasting on chests at random. God loves you, you misguided creature, and She gave you to me. I don't want to hear the word 'accouterments' out of you again," he said, trying to swallow first one and then the other and then, not knowing which to kiss or bite first, settling for as much of both as he could manage. He had lost a gold crown in that encounter and gave it to her afterward: "A modest keepsake from an ardent suitor," he had said. "Money is no object." She had placed it in a blue-velvet ring box on a blue-velvet pouf. She was touched by his ardor and forethought. "You *could* have swallowed it, couldn't you, lover?"

Grosbeck was struck dumb at her appearance, as who would not have been expecting to go cautiously to bed with his wife after a heart attack, even with a doctor's assurance that it would be therapeutic for both of them. On her part, torn between her natural

wants and his health, she had first called Dr. Salomon, then taken
the afternoon off from her job to prepare. (At the moment, she was
in the midst of negotiating for a piece of the old Pennsylvania Station—the figure, "Night," from one of the station's big clocks—
which had been dumped in the Jersey meadows and which she intended to place at one side of the Museum's New York City sculpture garden, which consisted of odds and ends of buildings torn
down to make way for *real* money-makers.) Grosbeck had disappointed her by staying so late at the office with McFarland, but, as
she told herself, there was nothing which could not be salvaged with
an ounce of determination. Witness the piece of Pennsylvania Station.

Grosbeck let himself be laved in ripples of pleasurable surprise.
Commingled with the emollients she had rubbed into her body, the
perfumes, powders and rouges she had applied (he did not fail to
note eyeliner, lengthened lashes, shining black hair cut short as a
boy's—what did that say, secretly, about his *real* preferences? Nothing, you asshole, he decided), there was a smell of cooking in the air.
Roast beef, possibly? With a Yorkshire pudding to be whipped together quickly (five seconds too long, Madeline always said, and you
had inferior French toast not fit for the cat; was the cat out of the
way? It was always sniffing around enviously) following the dreamy
recovery from the act (two acts?) of love. The woman had thought
of everything, while he . . . he had failed to read her mind, had let
her down tarrying with McFarland over essentially inconsequential
things. Nevertheless, he would rise to the occasion. If she had made
a god of him in his dank, wretched clothing, lifting him out of the
Inferno, he would tear away at the garments encircling him, seat her
on his knee and tumble her, martini in hand, a veritable club between his legs.

But, above the hum of the air conditioning, Grosbeck heard disturbing sounds, only minimally subdued, coming out of the record
player: her favorite song at the time, something he detested, called
"We Are Family," rendered by something known as The Sisters
Sledge. "Listen to it," she had pleaded with him the first time. "Just
listen."

"The Sisters Sledge," he had said. "Who's on piano?" he asked
with what he believed to be biting scorn. "Hammer?" More than
once, he had proposed to Madeline to try something like, say, "A

Good Man Is Hard to Find" or "The Boy in the Boat," anybody's version, or at least something in between, like the "Sing, Sing, Sing" on the Goodman 1938 Carnegie Hall Concert, that they both could enjoy. "Or," he had suggested, "we could start out with some Dixieland to work me up and finish off with your disco which would make you melt all over me. The best of both worlds." Grosbeck had been more than half serious; he had, he was convinced, very delicate nerves. Madeline had ignored the suggestions and he had learned to live with The Sisters Sledge, much as he had with other constraints on his personal freedom. The Sisters would pass too.

So many and so subtle are the nuances of love, that of many years not exempted; so many the hidden crevasses in which a man could bust his balls; so high and giddying the sunny heights to which a man must ascend before looking down—between his legs—and addressing it: "Well done, thou good and faithful beast." Madeline uncrossed her ankles and advanced, swaying, on Grosbeck with the martini, fully exposed at last. He took it from her hand and held it at arm's length while she bent to kiss him. She was about two inches taller than he in sandals, far taller in high heels, and they presented a curious tableau: a caricature of the well-known perfume advertisement in which a man in white tie, consumed with desire yet prudent enough to know the value of a Stradivarius, is holding the instrument away from him while, with the other arm, he encircles the waist of the young woman who has been playing accompaniment for him on piano. He has half-lifted her roughly from the bench, disarranging her decolletage and bringing her near to swooning while bending her backward and implanting a burning kiss on her bee-stung lips. Smoke can be detected issuing through the tendrils of his guardsman's mustache and her towering hairdo with the fat curls depending from it is about to go to rack and ruin.

Grosbeck got the picture. When she let him up for air, he took a pull at the martini. "Never spilled a drop, sweetheart," he observed. "But, I feel so *blowsy*." He stripped off jacket, tie, trousers, shirt and shorts, kicking them into a corner of the darkened room. "Wow," he said, "of such is the kingdom of heaven." He had yet to remove his shoes, socks, and garters.

"Won't you stay awhile?" Madeline asked him, motioning at his shoes.

"Oh, sure," he said, "I was just in such a hurry that I forgot."

Now, standing before her, he essayed a kiss. His lips fell between her breasts. It was a question this time of Madeline bending again to kiss him on the mouth or Grosbeck standing on tiptoe. The martini, among many other tangled ends of thought, had made him decide this would be undignified. He motioned with his martini glass. "Where's yours, sweetie?"

"I'm drinking wine," she said, with a theatrical gesture toward an ice bucket on the bar with a towel wrapped around the open bottle in it.

"Had one or two before I got here?" he asked in great good humor.

"Would you like some rather than another martini?" Madeline asked. "It's nothing special, just a sparkling white wine." He frowned. Wine made Grosbeck sick. "You still haven't taken off your shoes and socks," Madeline said.

Grosbeck did so, obediently, and made himself another martini. "I thought that one was rather, ah, weak," he said in extenuation. "This is it, pussycat. No more. I can't tell you, though, what I wouldn't give for a cigarette. I think I'm going to have to come to some kind of arrangement about that with Dr. Salomon. Maybe one or two a day? I don't think he'd object too much to that. But, no wine, thank you very much."

It was not the first time that the juxtaposition of wine and gin had produced one of those famous, troubling nuances in the love between Grosbeck and Madeline. "Gin makes you foolish in company," Madeline said. "In bed, too," she added.

"Better foolish," Grosbeck declaimed, "than pretentious."

"At least," Madeline went on, "you won't be burning my navel with cigarette ashes any longer."

"That's certainly a hope for the future," Grosbeck replied a trifle pettishly.

"And, furthermore," Madeline said, "you're right about one thing. No denying there's nothing pretentious about you both in company *and* in bed." She covered her mouth, this big, beautiful naked woman. "Oh, Harvey," she then said, "I didn't mean any of that, honestly I didn't, except about the cigarettes, and, really, that's for your good, not mine. Do you really think I minded a little burn now and then? Never, as God is my judge."

Grosbeck put down his empty martini glass. "Have another glass of wine," he said to Madeline. "I'll have one with you."

"Are you sure, Harvey? You know what it does to you."

"No," he said, "we'll both have wine. It will cement our love for each other again. *Cement?* Did I say cement?" She turned her back on him to pour them both some wine and the impulse that had left him during this brief contretemps between husband and wife returned in full strength at the sight of her bottom.

And so the passage at love remembered began. In some respects, Grosbeck's memory was a short one and three months without copulation had made him, or so he thought, a novice in the *cours d'amour*. Additionally, he had drunk two martinis and a glass of wine; in the air conditioning, the sweat had dried on his body, making him feel that he was wearing a skintight, not particularly clean, garment. Thoughts rumbled in him, defying his best efforts to separate them under circumstances demanding more than woolgathering; some mundane, even unworthy in their ordinariness, like unpaid bills, the condition of the roast beef in the oven, a pimple he had detected on a buttock as he sat down on the couch opposite Madeline (the side effect of one of his many medications), and something he had not dreamed of, even in nightmares. There was his naked wife, indubitably ready to mold herself to his fantasies and to mold him to hers until, in a harmony of felicitous squeaking and grunting, the two should cleave to each other—a double cone of soft vanilla ice cream covered with chocolate-caramel sauce, to be licked, bitten, eaten, swallowed—consumed so thoroughly that there would be nothing left of them but their satisfied shades, and, maybe, a little bit of the cone which could be thrown away or put in the cat's dish.

But the something else which had never before given Grosbeck a nightmare (practically everything else had), took on life, or, rather, a small death. The instrument of his pleasure, no obelisk to be sure, but reliable as the next man's, was behaving uncharacteristically: hard one moment, soft the next, spongy as a street-corner hot dog the third. All this despite Madeline's blandishments, well-tried and not few. She kissed him above and below, handled him alternately with the tact of a gazelle and the rough touch of a navvy; put his hands to her breasts and squeezed her fingers over his; opened her legs and closed them; excused herself for a moment and turned off the record player; chirped, moaned, cursed, fondled herself, adopted poses she firmly believed would have put a go-go girl in jail. (She had never seen one.) She told Grosbeck in a bass whisper that not only had she kept herself inviolate during those three months (he had not the faintest reason to doubt it), but that she had not laid a finger on herself, although the urge to do so had swept over her many times, leaving her skin itching for hours.

Grosbeck tried to respond in kind, to tell her how *his* need for her had once almost led him to rip from chest and arms the wires leading to the machines measuring his steady trudge back to health in intensive care. Nothing seemed to work for either of them, so little, in fact, that the air conditioning was making Grosbeck cold and Madeline was ignoring it altogether, so overheated had she become. "What's the matter, Harvey?" She put the question adoringly. A tear rolled down one cheek, streaking through the rouge. In anyone else, this would have been bathos. The sight of it made Grosbeck spring up again, but he chided himself for a degenerate, and it didn't last.

"Wait a minute," he said in desperation to Madeline, "there's something I want to show you." The cornered rat went over to the pile of his clothing, fumbled through the pockets and pulled out a piece of wire-service news copy. A diversion. Perhaps, oh, perhaps. It was worth a try. He looked over the paper at her as he returned to the couch.

"Would you like to go into the bedroom?" Madeline asked.

"Not just yet, sweetheart," he said. "I brought this home for laughs. Get this," he said, and began to read.

" 'Four hugs a day will help you survive the blues, but a dozen is better, says a social scientist.' "

"Really," Madeline said, coldly as she could, but the wine had spun her motor controls and the words came out in small chugs in which mirth and misery were indistinguishable.

" 'Four daily hugs are necessary for survival,' " Grosbeck went on. "I'm quoting, Madeline, I swear I am. Who makes up such *dreck?* May I continue?"

"If you insist," Madeline said. "But I don't want you to forget, Harvey, we're here for a purpose. We're here to get laid, isn't that right, my headstrong lover?"

"But, just listen to this," Grosbeck continued. "Absolutely priceless. Let me just go back a sentence." Standing before her, he rocked slightly on feet splayed widely out of proportion to his height and his devastated little mechanism swung back and forth like the pendulum of a cheap cuckoo clock. "All right, now," he said. "'Four daily hugs are necessary for survival, eight are good for maintenance . . .'"

"Oh, so it's maintenance we're missing, is it?" Madeline asked. "I thought I had been maintaining you into . . . into . . . well, into you know damned well . . ."

Grosbeck ignored her. "'. . . and twelve for growth,'" he said. "Wait," he said, holding up a hand, "there's more." Madeline got up from the couch and left the room.

"Where are you going, sweetie?" Grosbeck asked. "So I'm a little rusty. Besides, I'm not finished."

"I think you are," Madeline answered, from the kitchen. She turned up the oven a little, a trifle only; Grosbeck liked his roast beef rare and Madeline estimated that with the way things were going, it would be done in about seven minutes. Then, she would have to look to the Yorkshire pudding.

Grosbeck followed her, crestfallen, into the kitchen, still holding up his piece of paper, like a child with a miniature flag at a parade. "The story goes on to say," Grosbeck said—naked, aflame in the head, impotent down below, "'our pores are places for messages of love.'"

"Then, how does it happen," Madeline asked, shaking a large cooking fork at him, "that nothing's happened? As far as I can tell, the two of us are all pores. I don't see a hidden pore anywhere," she said, looking herself over and then him. Once again, in the midst of crisis, Grosbeck overreached himself, fixed upon reading one more line.

"That's easy to explain," he said earnestly. "The doctor says North Americans fall short in body contact. Most touching done in this country is done on the football field." At that, Madeline burst out laughing.

The effect on Grosbeck was blessed; he sprang to life again. He turned off the stove, marched Madeline out of the kitchen in front of him, one hand across her breasts, the other on her behind, which he brushed assiduously with his errant pride, and into the bedroom where he flopped her on the bed face up, legs apart, and consummated—in prudent haste, lest the feeling go away again—their original fevered intentions. Neither added much to the history of aberration among middle-class couples that night, but what Grosbeck did not realize was, in fact, something Madeline knew with sorrow: he had failed.

Dinner, however, reached a peak of perfection. Madeline had slipped on an apron and, without thinking about it, had put on her high-heeled shoes again. Grosbeck dressed for dinner in fresh boxer shorts and a boat-neck shirt. Everything was on the table. Grosbeck lifted the carving knife, said, "God bless the cook," and then stopped concentrating on food long enough to see Madeline in her new costume. He dropped the knife and said to her hungrily, "Come on, you great big pitcher of clotted cream. Let's just forget the whole thing and do it again. Off to the couch, off to the bedroom, right here on the floor!" Madeline closed her eyes and shook her head.

"The Yorkshire pudding . . ." she said.

"Screw it," he implored. "It's fattening, anyway."

"I want to get fat," she said starkly. "Will you excuse me a moment. Suppose you begin. I'll help myself." She returned, barefoot, in the least attractive garment she could find—a beige flannel robe given her by her mother in an act of revenge some birthdays ago. She had never worn it.

The two of them ate with the taste of ashes in their mouths. "Marvelous, marvelous, sweetheart," Grosbeck said and went around the table to kiss her. She pushed him away; he had thought she might.

"Go inside, into the living room, Harvey," Madeline said.

"What about cleaning up?" Grosbeck asked.

"It can wait."

"Yes, ma'am, Torquemada. What have I done now? I thought . . . well, I thought everything was as near ideal as two well-matched human beings could have wished."

"No, you didn't, Harvey, and neither did I."

"What about the cat?" Grosbeck asked. "How did the cat feel about it?"

"That won't work, Harvey. I want to know what's on your mind."

Grosbeck sat trapped in a corner of the couch. Madeline sat before him on a stool made by an artist friend of theirs. It was covered in red velvet with gold-colored upholstery tacks running around the seat, but its legs were those of a deer, a deer running; the neat black hooves were all pointed in the same direction. It was no stool for a serious conversation, but Grosbeck, with rare good sense, decided not to raise the issue.

"What's on my mind?" Grosbeck repeated. "Let me warn you, lover, this is going to be kind of a disjointed monologue."

"You're stalling, Harvey."

"Well," he said, pulling up the legs of his shorts as though they were a pair of freshly pressed trousers, "suppose I begin with the heart attack. That did more to me than you'll ever know. I thought I'd be dead in a matter of months." Madeline looked at him. "Why not?" Grosbeck protested. "It happens to a lot of people, boom, that thing in the left arm and across the chest and you're gone."

"No, Harvey, that was only the premonition of doom which broke up your first two marriages, made you stop writing for so long, and very nearly *did* frighten the life out of you when Greenspan moved you upstairs and told you you'd have to write again."

"I thought you wanted to hear my story," Grosbeck said.

"Don't interrupt me, Harvey. Your turn'll come again. You nourish yourself on disaster. No one would think so, but it's one of the characteristics which make you funny and appealing—a grown man for whom the end of the world has been around the corner since he was taken off the bottle. I pride myself I've been able to keep you away from the edge in the years we've been married."

"I'd have been dead years ago without you, Madeline," Grosbeck said humbly.

"On second thought, I take it back," Madeline went on. "There'd always be some little girl half your age around to take care of a cuddly little bear like you."

"I find your sarcasm needlessly cruel," Grosbeck said. Madeline giggled. "Now, do you want to hear the rest of this?" Grosbeck asked. Madeline nodded.

"All right, I didn't die and when Greenspan took me off editing, I began to think that maybe there was something I could do upstairs, make some sort of mark on that editorial page—not just inflate my pea-sized ego, but—I find this embarrassing—leave some sort of lasting impression. Nothing the size of the Bretton Woods monetary agreement, you understand."

"What's that?" Madeline asked.

"Forget it," Grosbeck replied. "But it was big for its time."

"And you, Harvey, what do you want to leave behind you?"

"Nothing that's going to surprise you," Grosbeck said. "Jesus, this is making me uncomfortable."

"Force yourself, Harvey."

"I would like . . . I would like . . . damn it, Madeline . . . I would like to write one or two things that . . ." He rubbed a cheek, pulled at his nose, inspected the big toe of his right foot. ". . . things that would alter, however slightly, the course of things in New York City. I'm too old to leave it anymore, or too lazy, or too filled with contempt and dislike for anywhere else . . ."

"What would you write?" Madeline demanded to know, adding in what was almost an aside, "that would change things in New York and make things better in bed for you and me?"

"What on earth do you mean?" he asked. He knew.

"It just came out of my mouth," she said. "But, you must admit that for a man deprived so long of the woman he loves, you were no world-beater."

"You shock me, Madeline. You horrify me."

"And, I wasn't that great, either," Madeline said. "I don't know whether it was you, me, what's on your mind—or mine—and that's what you're telling me about, isn't it? What you're saying is that this sudden need to make a mark, as you put it, froze your balls? Pardon the vulgarity."

"You're angry," Grosbeck said. "I can't blame you." Then, in a rush, "I would like to stick my two cents in and try to preserve at least one thing I and a few other poor snobs and slobs think must be preserved or there will be nothing left to tell us what city we're in. Lying down in front of bulldozers won't do it. All I'd do is get my clothes dirty and get arrested. Can you see an editorial writer for The Newspaper going off to the pokey for something like that?

"Specifically, I'm thinking of the mansions. And Corydon Varney. And that architect of his, Kazanjian is his name? I don't have to tell you what they've done. And now this. You've heard they want to get their hands on the mansions, tear them down, and put up one of their monsters in brown glass with a leaky roof and windows that won't open or that get blown out in a high wind. Is it naïve of me? They've been to see Greenspan about it . . . one of their dogfaces, anyway . . . as I told you. They want the paper behind them. Is it insane of me to think that I could write something that maybe wouldn't stop them, but that at least would be condoned by The Newspaper? Is it naïve of me to think it might even get them to change their plans? There's enough money to be made elsewhere on

Fifth or Madison or Lex. Is it naïve? Remember, there was once a plan to put apartment houses in Central Park."

"Yes," Madeline said, "it is naïve and that Central Park idea was many, many years ago."

"Well, I'm going to try," Grosbeck said. "That's the mark I want to make."

"That one in particular?" Madeline asked. "Not some other ones? There are still some pretty choice ones around, but you chose that one."

"Yes," Grosbeck said. "It's not an unworthy choice."

"Let me ask you a question or two, Harvey. Didn't you tell me you'd met a woman named Alice Forsythe in Greenspan's office and that she was there to talk about the project? Is that the dogface you meant?"

"Yes," said Grosbeck.

"And that she works for Varney or Kazanjian or whoever?"

"Yes," said Grosbeck.

"And didn't we see her at Marjorie Denman's wedding?"

"Yes," said Grosbeck.

"And didn't I tell you I knew her?"

"Yes," said Grosbeck. "What is this, some sort of cross-examination?"

"And does 'dogface' do her justice? And didn't I tell you I don't like her very much because she does that sort of thing—wheedling favorable publicity for Varney and his kind—for a living?"

"Yes," said Grosbeck.

"And, am I mistaken or did you give this dogface a second, or, perhaps, third look and some possibly inconsequential chitchat in the course of the afternoon?"

"What are you leading up to?" Grosbeck asked. "You know me well enough . . ."

"I'm not sure, Harvey," Madeline said. Her voice was low and unhappy. "How can anyone be sure of what is going on in that peculiar little brain of yours . . ."

"You . . . mean . . . Alice . . . Forsythe!" Grosbeck said indignantly. "Do you, Madeline?"

"Go, Harvey," Madeline concluded, "go and make your mark . . ."

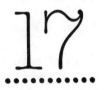

17

At last, Grosbeck had a nodding acquaintance with what it was he had to do in order to experience epiphany. He imagined himself to be unique (the precious innocent), but it came to him as it does to all such men—from outside himself—through a clouded revelation and a burning in the groin, this time through his scarifying experience in bed with his wife and their subsequent conversation in which he had flushed with shame and tingled with anticipation. Madeline had dropped a talisman, tinkling and shining, on his pigeon-toed feet: Alice Forsythe. She could not have done better wishing on a star, poking through the entrails of animals with a stick, reading his palm (long life line, bump of prurience) or pushing him off the sidewalk against a red light in heavy traffic.

It took Grosbeck almost no time to evolve an elaborate theory of behavior for himself in the immediate future: it should be a form of Manichaeanism in reverse. That is, he should seek the release of his chained spirit not through a series of ascetic exercises and denials (such as giving up smoking, walking to work, eating one croissant on a Sunday morning instead of two, or remaining serene through the most trying of provocations), but instead purifying himself through indulgence, in direct contradiction to the mundane prescriptions of Dr. Salomon, the advice of Trollope, the Roman Catholic scoldings of Tully, the offhand injunctions of McFarland, indeed, the well-meant advice of all those he knew or had read. His monkhood should take him out of the cloister of denial—it had probably given him the heart attack in the first place—into the bright, sparkling light of excess and daring. Oh, how had he not known this all his life! Eat, drink, and be merry, for tomorrow we die!

High over the entrance to the subway in Times Square, God, the Puerto Rican woman, opened Its mouth and doubled over with laughter, sending down such shocks that a cast-cement cornice fell off the corner of a building and killed a passing Guatemalan, which God regretted because the man had been, like Herself, a Latin American. God forebore from clucking Her tongue because that might have caused a lot more damage. It contented Herself with glaring and permitting tears to roll down His face, which produced lightning and rain, but nothing worse, and sent the whores and junkies running for the shelter of the bars and the ambiguous tenements in the neighborhood.

Grosbeck's brain had trouble acting on more than one idea at a time. It was true that he had learned not to wear brown shoes with blue suits and things like that, but he had been incapable theretofore of entertaining two large concepts at once and joining them, even of keeping two balls in the air. No more, he chortled to himself. He chortled! He had become—instantly, as was now the fashion—a new man and it had not cost him a red cent. He harbored both a dislike of men like Corydon Varney and what they did, *and* a yen for Alice Forsythe for what she presumably did beyond her association with Varney. Briefly, he teetered on the edge of losing the connection, but only briefly: the new Grosbeck had finally put two ideas together; he should somehow get at the corpus of Corydon Varney through the corpus of Alice Forsythe or was it the other way round? How this was to happen, he did not know at the moment; the sketchiest details eluded him for the time being. But, there it was, the conjunction of two ideas at last, flashing on and off, revolving steadily about each other, like the red and white lights of a lighthouse at the tip of a promontory in a dangerous race of ocean.

Watch me navigate, thought Grosbeck. If I cannot escape the treacherous shoals, I shall, at least, make the most magnificent wreck and leave the most romantic hulk the mind of man could conjure up. The mermaids shall sing to me. What he meant, when the crust of this smoking pot pie had been cut away, was that, through The Newspaper and his writing, he would—perhaps—thwart (that was the word he used to himself) Varney's foul machinations and conquer Alice Forsythe, most sinuous of mermaids. (At Grosbeck's remove from reality, he made the mistake so many sailors have: Alice Forsythe, sad to say, was, in fact, a dugong.)

"Madeline, Madeline," Grosbeck said aloud in his office. "Why, Madeline?" he cried out to the heavy drapes drawn, the heavy door closed, the dark-paneled walls, a single inadequate lamp on an arm bent above his typewriter, the VDT in darkness and covered with a linen tablecloth he had brought from home. Grosbeck preferred to work in bad light. It illuminated perfectly his murky thoughts. Fluorescents oppressed him. He had often contemplated using candles. Absurd thought. Might as well scratch away with quill pen and sprinkle the vellum with sand. Besides, he didn't like the idea of wax dripping on the keys; it would have fouled the escapement. "Alice, Alice," he said, too, not so much in passion as with rising curiosity. "Not now, not yet," he continued; no distractions. Work to be done. He rubbed his hands together, looking at the sheet of paper in the typewriter. He regarded his palms. Long life line? Really? Should he have had Dr. Salomon read his palm, too? Salomon would have hooted had Grosbeck dared ask him. Nobody read palms in the maquis.

Months had passed since the adventure in the elevator. Fluency had returned to Grosbeck, in small drops administered intravenously, invisibly, the bottle held aloft tirelessly in God's hand, for all that He or She or It had so much to do elsewhere. He had gained a strength of which he believed himself to be incapable. He walked through the streets and *saw*. He looked up past the first story of buildings and *saw*; he *saw* people and things; he went beyond the printed accounts of events which for so long had been the only true accounts of life for him. Born again, he said aloud, sardonically. I am one with the appleknockers now; I *feel*. I translate it into words. I am . . . who in hell says it in Molière, gravely and wonderingly? I am writing in prose. Be careful, it can't last forever. Don't bring yourself down, not this morning. He burned with feeling.

Madeline and he had been to a party in what remained of Little Italy on a sunny afternoon, on a Sunday toward the end of summer, invited by two friends, a husband and wife, an artist and a photographer, who neither out of chic nor yet out of proletarian solidarity, but simply because they had to live somewhere and had been able to scrape up the mortgage money, had bought an old-law tenement on Elizabeth Street. Grosbeck had not particularly wanted to go. He had been stretched out on a couch reading Philip Hone and had chosen to make himself morose reading to Madeline a poem recorded by Hone (author unknown) on Andrew Jackson whom Hone, a Whig to the bone, had nevertheless greatly admired.

> *So, the struck eagle stretched upon the plain,*
> *No more through rolling clouds to soar again,*
> *Views his own feather on the fatal dart*
> *That winged the shaft that quivers in his heart.*
> *Keen are his pangs, but keener far to feel*
> *He nursed the pinion that impelled the steel.*

Grosbeck identified himself with the struck eagle and told Madeline he would rather not go. "Get up, stricken eagle," Madeline said. "You might find something to write about." She took the book out of his hand. He reached for the Sunday paper. "And, you're not going to find it in something you already know by heart. You're going out with me. Get your pants on. It's a garden party."

"A garden party? Who has garden parties on Elizabeth Street. The Mafia?" He knew very well that there were thousands of backyards hidden in the rear of the thousands of tenements that still stood in parts of the city, even that in some of these yards there stood tiny brick houses, sheds, that once belonged to the handsome rows of Federal houses torn down to put up tenements for immigrants. Was there one such here, he asked Madeline. She said, yes, there was. She had engaged his interest. Did he know what they were called? Yes, he said. Penthouses, even though they were on the ground. How many people know that?

"You and I do," she said.

"Snob," he said. "Historian. I'll go."

Thus had Madeline made the juice run in him and the muscles pull him up from the couch. Something else sneaked unbidden into his head. Could Alice Forsythe do as much? Did it make any difference? Would she even bother? Would he find out? Stay tuned. (Years before he would have told himself, Read next week's installment.) He got up and dressed and went with Madeline through the fine afternoon and the desecrated streets, made his way through the garbage, both inanimate and smelly and alive and smelly, and was led to a butcher shop on Elizabeth Street. It was closed, but next to it was a door opening on a long, dark, narrow hall and they made their way down it to the garden and the sound of laughter and disputing voices and bits of English and Italian talk racketing against the walls of adjacent buildings and echo upon echo of the lyrics and horribly sentimental music of Italian popular songs coming out of an old windup Victrola. At least three dozen men, women, and children were there.

"See?" asked Madeline. "What did I tell you?"

"What's this all about?" Grosbeck asked.

"It's a birthday party." Madeline opened the large canvas bag she was carrying. "Here's your notebook. And a pencil. You want material for a column? Here's material."

"How do *you* know?"

"I know." A dog sniffed briefly at the two of them and then trotted off to examine a child. Madeline also took out a small package wrapped in tissue paper.

"What's that?"

"It's a present for the birthday girl."

"What birthday girl?" he asked. "And what is it?"

"It's a statue of Our Lady of Somewhere or Other . . . where the birthday girl comes from. Or where her family came from. Palermo, they told me. Come on, New Yorker. Come to the birthday party."

Grosbeck was introduced all around. He had been made to drink and eat and dance to the sentimental Italian records. He had sat down with the guest of honor—the birthday girl—and discovered that she was an old woman. He scribbled notes he hoped he would be able to decipher later. He had said, fatuously, to the guest of honor that heaven must be very much like this and she had said to him, "Plenty of time for heaven. What are you writing? Why? This going to be on television?" Grosbeck closed his eyes and shook his head—firmly. Her voice was hoarse, like a man's, and full of humor and much younger than she and he simply closed his notebook and kissed her.

"Happy birthday, Mrs. Albanese," he said.

"You call me 'Mary the Butcher,'" she said, waving a thick finger at him. "Just 'Mary the Butcher.' Drink some more wine. Eat. You eat like a bird."

He did what he was told. He laughed immoderately, danced clumsily, embraced people he had never seen before (including an off-duty detective, a son of Mary the Butcher) and scribbled more notes, more than he would ever need, and hoped they would make sense when, finally, he tried to do something with them. He expanded and expounded and gestured like all the rest, told stories to little girls and boys who were curious about the notebook and the pencil, and gradually, as the sun went behind the backyard, behind the broken, naked brick of the back of the old buildings, he subsided, fell into a wicker chair from which flakes of white paint had fallen, and dozed. Madeline roused him, took him away after a thousand goodbyes from which she could not make him desist, and got him home. "What did I tell you?" she asked, with satisfaction, as she guided him across town. The dying sun had blinded him, but so, too, had the coals of an unwonted happiness in his head. "Did you find something you could write about?"

"Ummm," he said. "I need a nap. More impressions than I can handle right now. Got to sleep on it."

"You know, Harvey, I don't care if you don't write a line about this. How does it feel to be part of the human race again? *This* is New York, not all those books, not *Sunshine and Shadow*, not *King's Handbook*, not *Stokes's Iconography*. You're such a stubborn fool. I love you." Grosbeck stumbled in embarrassment and got home.

For a wonder, the embers of feeling had not gone out of him as he sat down at the typewriter the next day. No masterpieces, please, he said to himself, as he started to type. Just the facts. He began:

"*It was our privilege, not to say honor, last weekend, to attend a birthday party given by her family and friends (both numerous and including two great-grandchildren) for Mary Ann Ciraulo Albanese.*" Stop. Go through the notes. Agony. I can't make anything out. He wanted a cigarette badly. Forget it. He held the notebook upside down and sideways. Ah, that's what it probably says, but I'm getting ahead of myself. If only there were a formula. Never. If only it poured out, unstinting, ungrudging, endless. Never. Then how? I don't know. Never did, never will. He typed:

"*The occasion was not just pleasurable but instructive. Mrs. Albanese was seventy-five that pleasant late-summer afternoon.*" Don't run on too long. And, not too much fine writing, if you please. And remember Slash Greenspan. And remember Ezra Pound cut the shit out of Eliot. And remember this is only a newspaper.

The door opened and Grosbeck jumped. It was Greenspan. "Good morning, Harvey," he said. "Composing? I'll let you alone," and closed the door on Grosbeck.

What next? Grosbeck wondered. He fidgeted. More came out. In
a rush. And, by now, he was barely looking at his notes.

"*Her people came from Palermo,*" he went on, "*and she was born
on Elizabeth Street, between Prince and Houston, with the Bowery
at her back and Old St. Patrick's Church before her, a block
away . . .*" Here something about Bishop Hughes and his mad plan
to build a cathedral uptown on Fifth Avenue? Here something about
Dr. Hosack's garden of medicinal herbs on which Rockefeller Center
now stands? Here something about Dr. Hosack attending Alexander
Hamilton after the fatal duel with Aaron Burr across the river in
Hoboken? Here something about the removal of the bones of the
yellow-fever dead from Washington Square to the place where the
Cathedral and Saks Fifth Avenue stand? A word or two about Madame Bertha Restell, the fashionable abortionist, whose Italianate
brownstone mansion stood only a block or so north of Bishop
Hughes's Cathedral? And her suicide? No. Irrelevant. Too long. Beside the point. Save it for something else. There's no end to the material. A little discipline, please.

"*Mrs. Albanese is as firmly planted on Elizabeth Street as the Delmonico family and the Countess Annie O'Leary are in their tombs
in the crypt of Old St. Patrick's, beneath its fieldstone walls. Mrs. Albanese has lived on Elizabeth Street all her life in one building or
another, no farther south than Prince, no farther north than Houston. We don't know any more about the Countess Annie O'Leary
than the name on her tomb.*" If you don't know, either find out or
take it out. I haven't got time to find out. Then, take it out. No, I'll
leave it in. It'll bring a letter from *some* crazy New York City historian. Now go on.

"*Mary Ann Ciraulo Albanese has been a widow for twenty-seven
years and she runs the butcher shop started by her husband almost
fifty-five years ago. Her sausage is highly thought of all over the
neighborhood and nothing she sells comes pre-cut or from some
grisly commissary fifteen hundred miles away. Everybody calls her
Mary the Butcher. She is a small, squarely built, astonishingly vigor-
ous woman with iron-gray hair, a generously curved, smooth, extrava-
gant nose and a loud voice capable of the widest modulations, a veritable brass band of a voice, entirely in keeping with the face, which
is rough-hewn and not nearly big enough for the nose. On this day,*

her birthday, she wore a shapeless print dress, years out of style, timeless, smelling of camphor, very becoming to her.

"It is no exaggeration to say that she is a fixture on Elizabeth
Street. Many Italians have died or moved away, their places taken by
Puerto Ricans and some of the Chinese who have pushed north
from Chinatown. Mrs. Albanese can remember when there was a
deadline for the Chinese, beyond which they were not permitted to
live—the south side of Bayard Street near Mulberry Park. She is so
much a fixture that one of her sons, Moe, told us that if she ever had
to go up to Fourteenth Street she would get lost. She overheard this.
'Pah,' she said. 'I'm from here. It looks strange around here now? I
still like it.'

"The party was held in the backyard of one of the two small
buildings she owns, buildings put up more than a hundred years ago
and not likely to fall down soon. There is an ailanthus, a tree of
heaven, very hardy, growing out of the cement, and a bitter-melon
vine hung by one of the Chinese tenants. Washing hung on rope
lines stretched in catenary curves from fire escape to fire escape and
we could imagine the creak of iron pulleys when it was pulled in and
we could see what people wore and it was possible to look down
backyards with the same trees and laundry for the whole block. In
the wintertime, the laundry freezes and the icicles have to be broken
off the underwear and towels.

"A generous table had been laid out: prosciutto, pepperoni and
cappicola in big platters; sausage, hamburgers and spareribs on a
grill, hidden in blue smoke—all from the butcher shop, the hot
meats cooked just so by Moe and Mary's other son, Vincent, a New
York City detective. There were three kinds of pasta and bowls of
raw vegetables. There were jugs of white wine and red, soda for the
children, potato chips, pretzels. Three birthday cakes. A basket of
begonias. Streamers in the colors of Italy and the United States over-
head and hanging straight down from the walls. An old, upright
Victrola—cherry-red veneer, tiny, curved legs—scratched out absurd
romantic Italian songs on 78 rpm records, things like 'Farballa Not-
turnal (Night Butterfly)' and 'Amore Mio' and 'Novella d'Amore
(Love's Message)' and 'Nel Profondo Silenzio (Deep Silence).'
There was no silenzio at all, between the children running underfoot
and yelling and the old women singing and dancing with one an-

other and the men clapping their hands when they weren't eating. It
was about as joyful a noise as we have heard in a long time.

"Mary danced down a half dozen people before it got dark and everybody started to go home, much as she tried to keep them there.
She winded us, too; we could scarcely keep up with her and we
dropped into a chair to have a few more words with her before we,
too, left. She kept jumping up to throw her arms around people who
were leaving. Where, where did she find the strength? 'What's so
special' she wanted to know. 'It's a party—my party—I got to be
polite. That don't take strength. The butcher shop? That's something else six days a week. But that I do until I die.' She crossed herself. 'Dying I don't think much about. Yet.' She crossed herself
again, this time facing in the direction of Old St. Patrick's. 'And,
I tell you something else,' she said, finishing the last of a tumbler of
red wine. 'This. When I die, I want to be buried over there. The
dress I picked out long ago. And I want my apron—a clean one, no
bloodstains—over the dress. I want the cleaver in my right hand, the
boning knife in my left and they cross my hands over my chest. And,
when I get up There and I see my husband and if he's got a shop, then
I hand him the cleaver and the knife and the apron and I ain't ever
gonna work no more. No more!' There was nothing we could say in
answer, so we got up to shake hands goodnight with her but she
pulled our head down and gave us a big, rough, butcher-lady kiss. As
we walked back down the long dark hallway to the street, we could
hear something called 'Va Alla Festa di Ballo' playing on the Victrola. It stopped abruptly as someone turned it off in the middle of a
weepy violin solo and then we were out on the sidewalk again, instructed, warmed, touching the cheek on which Mary the Butcher
had kissed us, just as though we could still feel the kiss there."

Grosbeck's hands trembled slightly as he read over what he had
written. He had disarranged his viscera in the writing of the little
piece and he did not know where to place himself or his feelings.
Was it sentiment? Sentimentality? Viscid? Had it anything to do
with literary quality? (How vain.) Had he let anything out in the
open that were better concealed? Had he pandered to Greenspan
and The Newspaper? Did he really believe a word of what he had set
down? Was that an unusual tightness he felt across his breast? Was
his heart intruding on him at a time like this? Or had he experienced
Revelation at a time least expected, as he had in the hospital? What

was the nature of Revelation? Did it consist of something like this or was it nothing more than receiving a windowed envelope from Brooks Brothers and finding inside a credit rather than a debit? Could it be construed in the same way as a tax refund or a favorable finding from a urinalysis: no trace of sugar, no suspicion of a pervasive, ah, gummosity of fellow-feeling that would, if not treated in time, end up as a chronic love of mankind, killing in its puerility? "Hey, mon," whispered God, the Puerto Rican lady, somewhere off in the heavy drapes, "*you* make up you own min' for a change. I ain' gonna lead you by the han' this time."

Grosbeck had not so far taken leave of his senses that he did not, finally, know what to do. Better puerility than putrefaction; better sentimentality than saturninity; Revelation is as Revelation does. The sense of proportion would return, the turtle retract its head into its shell. But, for the time being, Grosbeck's head was fully exposed. He crawled slowly down the corridor to Greenspan's office and handed the piece to him. "See how you like this, Marty."

"What's the matter with your voice, Harvey? Cold coming on?"

"No," Grosbeck said. "I imagine that's the way turtles talk."

"What?" asked Greenspan. "Your voice does sound peculiar, though. What have you got?"

"*You've* got it, Marty," Grosbeck said, "right there in your hand. You got time to read it now?"

Greenspan read. "It's not the elevator thing again, Harvey," he said after a while.

"No, Marty, it isn't."

"I'm not surprised," Greenspan said.

"All right, Marty, we're agreed on that and you're not surprised. What are you, then?"

"I'm pleased, Harvey. I'm pleased by it, pleased, too, that I know you right down to your socks. I bet you never have a hole in your socks, do you?"

"No, Mr. Greenspan, I don't."

"And you won't abide some teasing, will you, Harvey?"

"You're the boss, Mr. Greenspan, sir. You want me to come back some other time?"

"No, Harvey. I mean, yes, Harvey. This is right for us. This is why we brought you upstairs." He rattled the sheets at Grosbeck. "Honest feelings, warmth, a touch of old New York, clotheslines, ethnic appeal, the common touch . . . and yet, the slightest, oh, just the slightest distance between you and your subject." He motioned to Grosbeck to sit down and read the piece over again.

"Whatever in the world got into you, Harvey?" He put the piece at the side of his desk. "We'll use it in a couple of days. I see the length is just about right for a signer, one column long on Op-ed. Could I induce you to put it on the VDT? No, of course not. That would be asking too much of you right now. We've all got to crawl before we walk, don't we? What can we expect next of you? You know what you are, Harvey?" Greenspan asked.

"No, what?"

"You, Harvey, are a sentimental snob. I said snob."

"Thank you, Mr. Greenspan. You cut me to the quick with your judgments which, however snap, are always app. May I go now?"

"No, stay a moment. I want you to do me a favor somewhere in the busy comings and goings of your life. You remember that Forsythe woman and what she came to see me about? The mansions? The Newspaper hasn't made up its mind about that yet and I want you to have a talk or two with her, find out what *she* has to say, then talk to the other side, the . . . what do they call themselves? . . . preservationists . . . think the whole thing over, and then let me know what *you* think about it. Whether we should be for it or against it or half for and half against or . . . whatever. I don't say yours will be the final word, by any means—we know pretty much where *you* stand—but she might have something persuasive to say— she's got about as persuasive a pair of legs as I've seen in a long time . . . Anyway, go listen to her." He let Grosbeck consider that.

"I don't have to tell you there's a lot of money involved here," Greenspan said, "the future of the City, etc., etc., the fact that The Publisher's wife and Varney's wife do good works together, and the fact that if Varney does get to tear down or otherwise ravish the mansions that would give The Newspaper a perfect excuse to do something it's wanted to do for a long time—sell this building or tear it down, move across the river, get rid of this anachronism in this howling desert and still call itself a New York paper. We wouldn't be the first—plenty of beer calling itself New York beer gets brewed somewhere else.

"So, go forth, Grosbeck. I dub thee, Sir Harvey, and I hand you your Excalibur. Only remember—it's tin and bends easily. I hope I am not being cryptic."

Grosbeck rose and bowed elaborately. "No, Sir Martin, you sure are not. I'll see you at the Round Table. And my vanity thanks you for the accolade."

"*Pas du tout*," Greenspan assured him. "That's French, you know. And think nothing of it," he added. "In due time, you will also be stoned."

18

Closely adsorbed in Grosbeck to his Manichaeanism-turned-inside-out was an equally spurious tenet of behavior he was pleased to call *fruitful avoidance*. The very name he gave it—so hoity-toity, so gracefully antonymous—was the essence of what it was: circumlocution, evasion, the performance of so many irrelevances on the way to something else that they took on the quality of a compass gone mad at the bottom of an iron mine—all in the unswerving belief that these would lead him unerringly to his goal. That this had almost never been borne out had never deterred him. Nor did it now in the case of the mansions and Alice Forsythe. As he had so often in his life, he developed a thick coating of *appearance* without to cover the tangle of conflicting impulses within, impulses which, for the moment, reduced thought to tatters of memory and desire. He would not call Alice Forsythe at once, as he had been enjoined to. He did not inquire into the progress of the rape of the mansions, although he knew vaguely that it was well along.

No. Daily, he dressed with, if possible, greater care than usual to go to the office, even going so far as to wear a button chrysanthemum in his lapel. He locked the door of his office, hung his jacket in a closet, took off his tie, flexed his wrists, rolled up his sleeves (he had been unable to find a pair of sleeve garters), put on his cracked green eyeshade, shoved a sheet of paper into the typewriter with an unnecessarily jaunty twist of the roller, sat down, rubbed his hands (they were cold), and then took off his shoes, lay down on the couch provided each editor and pulled the eyeshade over his face. He did not sleep; he indulged his velleities, whatever they happened to be. At such times, he resembled nothing so much as an Egyptian beggar in the cast-off clothing of a minor British colonial official, deep in hashish, his face on the dirty stones of some ratty souk in Alexandria.

Five minutes later, exhausted, he was up to wash his face in the bathroom also provided by The Newspaper for each editor. Should he have had a fever of inspiration, The Newspaper had also provided a tiled shower and heavy bath towels discreetly embroidered with its logotype. Physically, Grosbeck had never been so clean in his life. He washed his face raw, took an inordinate number of showers, and caught cold in the air conditioning. He wrote his little *feuilletons* from time to time and avoided Greenspan's eyes at Editorial Meetings. He was constantly assailed by a vision of himself as Laocoon and the serpents as lengths of Varney, Kazanjian, Tracy, Denman, and Forsythe. They would crush his typewriter and eat it, eat him, his clothing, shoes, shirt, and underwear, no doubt in a dressing of the primordial ooze out of which they had been spawned. Outwardly, nothing showed. The middle-class mad carry their bombs in their heads; when they go off, they go off silently and the most that comes out of the victims is a neighing followed by collapse.

One day, Grosbeck left the office in midafternoon, telling Greenspan he had to think. He wandered downtown until he found himself on Delancey Street. There, opposite Ratner's dairy restaurant was something called a Mitzvahmobile, one of those large vans used by the ferocious Lubavitcher Jews to propagandize not the *goyim* but the fallen-away or faint-of-heart Jew. A powerful young man dressed all in black stopped him as he was about to enter Ratner's. "Are you a Jew?" he asked.

"What else?" Grosbeck asked back, falling into the historical mode of Jewish address. "Why else would I be going into Ratner's?"

Without his beard, earlocks, and severe black coat (with cloth buttons to match), the young man could have been any rising Mafioso operating out of a storefront. (The Lubavitchers are, if not as numerous, certainly as well organized as the Mafia, and, by comparison, harmless. They put out contracts for converts. The only time they use knives is to perform circumcisions.)

"Do you believe in God?" the young man asked. "Are you a Jew?"

"What else?" Grosbeck wondered where the Puerto Rican lady God was just then, but there were no manifestations from above. Instead, he asked the young man, "Haven't you noticed we answer every question with a question?"

The joke was as old as Deuteronomy, but the young man refused to respond to it. "Will you pray with us?" he asked.

"Why not?" Grosbeck answered.

"Will you follow me inside?"

Grosbeck found himself inside the Mitzvahmobile and the door was closed. There were three other Lubavitchers there, one sitting behind a desk, an open Bible before him; another holding a set of phylacteries at the ready; a third piling up heaps of colored booklets in Hebrew and English. The man at the desk (a golden oak discarded by a prosperous benefactor who had gone in for wood-grained plastic and steel tubing as he came up in the world; he had faithfully obeyed the ancient injunction, "Don't jump, Sam, cut velvet") was old, his beard a beautiful white, there was a red-green wart at the side of his beveled nose. The man with the phylacteries directed Grosbeck to take off his jacket and roll up his left sleeve. The leather phylacteries, the *t'fillin,* were applied to Grosbeck's forehead and arm and fingers and a prayer shawl was laid over his shoulders, a yarmulke on his head. He got the impression that should he not do what he was told, his body would be found in a day or two somewhere out in Queens. The *reb* at the desk asked him to repeat a prayer after him.

"Can I ask you a favor?" Grosbeck asked.

The *reb* closed his Bible on a finger. "What is it?"

Grosbeck longed for a statement rather than a question, but there was nothing for it. "Would you let me say the prayer for the dead? I've kind of neglected my mother and father. They're just over the river," he went on, pointing vaguely across the Williamsburgh Bridge, "and what with one thing and another, I don't get much chance to visit them." He added, in extenuation, "They *do* get perpetual care." The *reb* shrugged and opened to another page. "Not the whole thing," Grosbeck said, "just the beginning. I haven't got the time."

"You haven't got the time," the *reb* said. "A Jew hasn't got the time," he said to the ceiling of the Mitzvahmobile. He shrugged. "So, then, Mister-haven't-got-the-time, repeat after me,

> '*Yisgadal, v'yishkadash sh'me rabbo . . .*' "

Grosbeck did it haltingly.

> " '*b'olmo deevro chiruseh v'yamlich malchuseh,
> b'chayechon uvyomechon, uv'chayey d'chol beys Yisroel,
> baagolo uvizman korey 'imrue omen.*' "

"Do you know what it means?" the *reb* asked.

"I recognize 'Israel,'" Grosbeck said, "and 'amen.'"

The *reb* handed him a booklet with the translation of the Kaddish in it. "Here, take it home. Learn it. Find time to go over the bridge —did you know they once called it 'The Jews' Highway'?"

"Yes," said Grosbeck, "I know that. It was because the Jews on the Lower East Side used it to move to Brooklyn, to get out of the slums." He felt like a bright pupil.

"I am surprised you know even that," said the *reb*, in magisterial reproach.

The shawl was removed, the phylacteries unwound by two of the Lubavitchers. They made him feel like a boxer whose handlers were working him over in his corner after he had been knocked out. He put his jacket on again. The men in the Mitzvahmobile looked at him in silence. "What *should* I feel?" he asked. God, the Puerto Rican woman, held Its tongue. The look on the Lubavitchers' faces was one of sorrow, mingled with contempt and anger, but they still could not forebear from answering him with a question.

"What should you feel? What *should* a Jew feel? Go away and think long and hard about it."

Ah, at last, a declaration rather than a question. "Is it all right for me to go to Ratner's now?" Grosbeck asked. The four Lubavitchers grunted in unison. It was neither a yes nor a no. One of them opened the door of the van and permitted him to walk down the steps. He stuffed the prayer leaflet into a pocket, tried to remember what his parents' grave looked like, even tried to remember what *they* had looked like, changed his mind about Ratner's, and walked away. His father and mother had faced up to things, Grosbeck told himself. And, perversely, he also told himself, they were still facing up to things six feet under. Such perseverance. Had he not been able to say something so awful to himself, he should have cried aloud on Delancey Street.

Near the Bowery, he was solicited, obliquely and languidly, by a tall Caribbean whore—obliquely, because he might have been a cop and she was safe only if the cop asked first, and languidly, because that was her way. Delancey Street generously embraced everything now, including conveniently abandoned small buildings on streets like Eldridge, Attorney, and Sheriff where, amid the broken bricks, dust, shards of plaster and exposed lath, and filth, it was possible to buy and use drugs of many kinds, enough varieties to burst the head, melt the intestines and stop the heart.

The whore had a head covered with a huge hennaed wig. She wore blue shoes with exaggeratedly high heels, the bottom of a two-piece bikini with broad stripes of brown and blue (had she put on a rugby shirt upside down?) and a mauve blouse from which most of the sequins had been torn away; the threads looked like unconnected lines running from an old-fashioned telephone switchboard. She carried a blue shoulder bag, giving the odd impression that she had three breasts, all large. She walked along with him and circled him, passed him and gazed into store windows, rolled her eyes at him, bumped into him, and finally paused in front of him with her hands on her hips. How long her legs were! He was not without gallantry. "You're beautiful," he said, "but I have a previous engagement."

She wasn't sure what he had said; her English was brown and black, but he had talked *first* and so she felt safe. She preened. "Do it slow, do it fast, do it any way you like," she said. *That* came across. "I got a room on Allen Street. You be in and out in a hurry—that be twenny—or you stay the afternoon—fifty." She rolled her eyes and twined one leg around a fire hydrant. "You still big for a ole man," she said. "I bet," she added.

"It's nice of you to say so," Grosbeck said, "but I really must be getting on."

"You no fuzz, either," said the whore, looking off into some impenetrable distance. "You jus' an ole gent looking for his jollies."

"I assure you," Grosbeck said, "nothing of the sort." He was at a loss to explain just what it was he *was* doing.

"You wastin' time just jiving," she said. "You and me could . . . any way you like, long as you like . . . you don' know what you be missing . . . An', nobody gonna come in and steal you wallet out you pants." *That's* the clincher for her, Grosbeck realized. Integrity. She certainly was *built*, the romanticist in him thought. There arose in his mind memories of a Victorian wood engraving of a prostitute distracting a customer in bed while her pimp crawled through a sliding panel in the wall and emptied the man's pants as they lay on a chair.

He was thrilled, in a way, to feel that nothing had changed in a hundred years (give or take a few physical details) and he was touched by her crude reassurances. Would Alice Forsythe be as

kind? He was tempted to ask her into Ratner's for a plate of blintzes
and sour cream, but the chances were her palate required something
more fiery than that. Again, he shook his head.

"Ah, come on now," she appealed once more. "Get over here in
the doorway. It out of sight. You give me a feel an' you ain' gonna
have no previous engagements." She rolled her pelvis slightly.

Like everyone of his class, Grosbeck theoretically nourished a *nos-
talgie de la boue*, but only if the *boue* were hygienic beyond a doubt,
accompanied by antibiotics, clean sheets, painted walls; and only if
the subject were, say, a graduate of drama school out doing research
for a role in a play, in accordance with the dictates of Stanislavsky.
"Possibly," he said, "we shall meet again under more propitious circumstances."

The whore gave up. She was tired and she had caught a signal
from her pimp down the block. "You go shove your *pisshious*, ole
man," she said. "Who gonna put out for you, anyway, without you
pay? You wife? Some ole bag she be, I bet. Why you was' my time?"

"But, my dear," Grosbeck expostulated, "it was *you* accosted *me*."

"Bullshit," said the whore, "you and you 'costed. You talk first to
me. I know what goin' on. You jus' wanna *look*. Right? You coulda
done that, too. Now, you get you skinny ole ass outta here. I got
work to do."

"I'm terribly sorry," Grosbeck said, "for the misunderstanding,"
and started to walk on. But, she had to have the last word.

"You misunderstanding, mister, *that* between you legs. *It* don'
unerstan' no more, *it* don' raise it head fo' me'r anyone else. Right,
ole man?" Proudly, she turned her back on him and walked slowly
back down the street. Grosbeck watched her; when she reached her
pimp, he pushed her into a doorway. What happened then, if anything, he would never know.

Another day, he tried a Roman Catholic church in his neighborhood. He chose this one rather than three others nearby because
it had been put up in 1830, marble in the most harmonious neo-Clas-
sic Greek style; the others were bigger but later, and, by comparison,
ugly. He intended to light a votive candle. Halfway down the nave,
he saw a priest, a young man in a cassock of rough brown cloth tied
at the waist with a braided rope, exactly the sort of rough medie-
valism he liked. Perfect. Perfect, except for the fact that the cassock

had a long zipper down the back. Grosbeck hurried around the priest and remarked, "Is nothing sacred?"

The priest looked puzzled. "What can I do for you, sir?" he asked. "Confession? At once. Counseling? We make referrals." He took note of Grosbeck's clothes. "The charge, of course, would depend on . . ." His voice trailed off. Vulgate. Had Grosbeck expected Latin? The Second Vatican Council had done away with all that and probably decreed zippers as well.

"Tell me, Father," Grosbeck said, "where the votive candles are. I want to light one for two of the dear departed."

"Brother," said the priest, "not Father. But you can call me Jim. Everybody around here does. That is, except at confession."

"Well, then, Jim . . ." said Grosbeck.

"Over there," the priest told him. "Are you of our faith?" So they answered questions with questions, too.

"No," Grosbeck said, "but," and he could not resist the banality, "I like to touch all bases."

"Well, good," the priest said, at a loss. Mechanically, he added, "God bless you and I will pray for you."

"Thank you, Brother Jim," Grosbeck said. "My name is Harvey Grosbeck and that's more than Peter Stuyvesant would have done for a shipload of my ancestors when they landed here. I am a Sephardic Jew." It was an outrageous lie. Grosbeck's forebears had come to the United States in steerage out of a Russian *shtetl* a couple of hundred years later. But he could not stop himself now. "Many of my people," he said, "are buried in the cemetery of Shearith Israel downtown at St. James Place." He added smugly, "The ones in the cemetery near here, you know, Sixth Avenue at Eleventh Street, were, ha ha, Johnny-Come-Latelies." The priest laughed with him and passed on out a side door.

Grosbeck hurried over to the bank of votive lights. There, he searched for candles and the tapers to light them with but found neither. The little red cups were there, all right, and there were lights in some of them, but, curiously, no flickering. What he found were tiny, candle-shaped electric bulbs in the cups, and, before each cup, a coin slot. On the wall behind the votive lights was a discreet little hand-printed sign (Gothic lettering) informing him that he could light up for the dead by dropping a quarter into the slot for four hours, two quarters for eight. Exact change, please. Tully had been right. He turned away. Confession? He could imagine that: the peccant talked into a tape recorder fixed in a wall of the confession box; there was no priest beyond the screen; later, the cassette was removed, the priest recorded his answers and injunctions, spliced them into the tape at the appropriate places and handed it to the sinner (carefully labeled with name and date) at Sunday mass (sometimes performed on Saturdays); Communion, in all likelihood, consisted of identically molded potato chips out of a cylindrical can and paper cups of diet soda.

Grosbeck's peepshow *Wanderjahr* was over. It was only a short skip from the jukebox votive lights to the Video Display Terminals in his office, to the mansions, to the state of things as they were. The afflatus with which he had begun the day might not have been divine, but it had been begun on a note of uplift and now it was gone. The night before, he thought, he had quite redeemed himself with Madeline. Before his walk, he had seen Dr. Salomon, who had clapped him on the back after reading from end to end of eight feet of electrocardiogram and blowing a kiss to the ceiling with his thick fingers. Grosbeck had so far been elevated as to throw away a long cigarette stub he had picked out of a lobby ashtray in the doctor's building. Slowly, he told himself, he was acquiring character. The Mitzvahmobile, the whore, and the church had taught him otherwise. He felt for the nitroglycerine bottle in his pocket. An onset of angina? (He frequently confused disappointment with illness.)

He left the church for the office. From the maiden receptionist who could not have known his state of mind (nor cared about it even had it been more than a lump of self-pity), he elicited a stony "Good day, Mr. Grosbeck. It's nice to see you looking so well." How could she have said that? Was there no discernment there, no realization that beneath the ruddy cheeks there lay a pale heart and a tremulous spirit? Was this no more than perfunctory comment on a skillful embalming job? She did not see within. "There's an envelope on your desk," she said, touching her bun with the pencil through it. "Mr. Greenspan would like you to have a look at it as soon as you can."

"What's in it?" Grosbeck asked.

"I'm sure I don't know, Mr. Grosbeck," she said. "I'm not in the habit of opening editorial department mail unless specifically instructed to."

From the bottom of the well, Grosbeck whispered up a timid remonstrance. "How could I have instructed you to," he asked, "if I didn't know you had it?" He trod water, feeling about for the rungs on which to climb out.

"You couldn't have, could you, Mr. Grosbeck," she responded, removing the pencil from the bun, putting it between her teeth, and dismissing him.

"Landmarks Preservation Commission," it said on the envelope. It had been sent to Greenspan, and Greenspan had sent it to him, scrawling on it, "Well?" He sat down without removing his jacket. He pushed the envelope to one side. That pushed a pile of papers and clippings to the floor and scattered them. He got down on his hands and knees to sweep them together. Then, he started to read them, sitting where he was. In the still, carefully controlled air circulating through the room, he felt a chill. No, it was a wave of heat. Both at once? And, over what? An envelope, a woman, and his wavy notion of a crusade.

One of the clippings quoted, in another context, a city commissioner, "*A lot of old buildings stand up by memory. Once you start disturbing buildings you run into trouble.*" Not bad. But how did that come to be the first? The Puerto Rican in the Sky? Jahweh in the Mitzvahmobile? Blessed Brother Cash of the Coin Slots?

Another told him, "GOD, I AM TROUBLED. *Nervous—poor health—Debts and Money Problems. Family Troubles, Love Troubles, Loneliness. How can I overcome my troubles?* Come Closer to God, *enjoy Radiant Health, Success and Happiness?* Dear Friend, We Have Wonderful News for You—*News of a Remarkable* New Way of Prayer *that is helping thousands to* Conquer *and* Overcome *the dreadful obstacles in their way! . . .*" Who was the audience for this steaming hyperbole, this hysterical circus typography? "*. . . Mail this message NOW with your name and address and we will rush you this Wonderful New Message of Prayer by return mail. Absolutely* Free! *We will also send you FREE this beautiful GOLDEN CROSS for you to keep and treasure . . .*" He crumpled the clipping and picked up another piece of paper. Apparently, he had hit on his own form of Ouija.

"Rock music," it said, "is saturated with adultery, fornication, uncleanness, lasciviousness, heresy and revelry." Noted.

Still, he sat cross-legged on the floor, plucking and reading. "Men who like leggy women tend to have nicer personalities than those who like women with large breasts or buttocks . . . Men who like women with large breasts tend to be outgoing, showoffy, independent and don't care to help other people. Men who prefer women with large buttocks are orderly, socially dependent, guilty and self-abasing . . ." And, finally, "Fat women like fat men and swinger-type women tend to like skinny, wiry-type men." Noted. He recognized a dogmatism which, for all of its maquereauoniness, was not too distant from his own lofty Black and White. But, read on, Grosbeck. It will kill time.

From London: "Patrick Cullen, an Irish palmist who claimed he could predict the future by reading women's breasts and bottoms, is dead at 69." Whose ass had he pinched that told him he would be dead at 69? He could imagine Patrick Cullen's tapering thumb and forefinger closing down on a buttock (left or right?) hard and the subject, leaping up from the examining table, covering herself with a sheet and screaming at him in pain, "Patrick Cullen, you will be dead at 69." Whereupon Cullen, who had celebrated his birthday the day before, by pinching and predicting for no fewer than four-teen women whose bodies sought answers urgently, dropped dead in his atelier under the anguished eyes of his naked Cassandra who had had to call the police.

And a business story: "Three men were charged today with operating a 10-girl prostitution ring out of the New York City morgue at prices ranging up to $250." "Delicious," Grosbeck said aloud, having put genuine concerns at the back of his mind. "That is what made America great. Love amid the stiffs." But, he had been mistaken; there were no assignations on the slabs or in the iceboxes. "The services available began at $50 and covered a wide range of acts apparently limited only by the imagination of the client. Two of the three men arrested were employees at the morgue assigned to the evening shift. Investigators said the ring used the medical examiner's telephones to arrange dates for the girls. Other sources said the medical examiner's car was also used by the ring." Any fool could see this was quite normal—no necrophiles, no smell of formaldehyde, no purple faces or slashed throats, torn-up vaginas; the girls were all alive.

But could the clientele have told the difference? So many questions left unanswered. But what about that manila envelope on the desk?

Not yet. There was still intelligence from all over the world to be digested. From Davenport, England: "*A chief petty officer in the British Navy was demoted today and stripped of his Good Conduct medal for kissing another sailor in the Gunga Din Bar in New Orleans.*" You're a better girl than I am, Gunga Din. From Bonn: "*A 21-year-old man killed his wife in a fit of rage after their poodle urinated on him as he sat naked listening to records in their apartment.*" What kind of records? Sloppy reporting.

From Jerusalem: "*May an Orthodox Jew listen to a woman singing on the radio?*" Again, a question. This time, would it be followed by an answer, a straight answer. Yes: "*. . . only if he doesn't know her personally, says Israel's chief rabbi.*" Grosbeck knew he must eventually run out of distractions, but he would not forebear. The only concession he made to the envelope on the desk was a finer discrimination. From New York: "*The passengers in the subway car at the World Trade Center saw a woman wearing blue shorts get on. What attracted their attention was that she was wearing only blue shorts. She was in her 30s. 'Cover yourself up,' a male passenger hollered. She smiled. 'Where are we going?' she asked. 'Newark,' the man said.*" Served her right, Grosbeck said to the drapes.

And, further: "*Donald Wells says he's invented and hopes to market a talking tombstone that also shows movies of the deceased.*" And: "*A mortician who says he's been searching for 20 years to cut funeral costs has a new formula. Part of it is a $6 coffin made of cardboard.*" And, "*If you want a patriotic funeral, for a little extra money, you can be laid to rest in a coffin of red, white and blue adorned with two American flags.*"

Incredible riches. Oh, the world is so full of a number of things . . . and yet, Grosbeck told himself, really they were only synechdoche, there must be more, and he scrabbled around among his clippings to find it. Sure enough: "*The Bible has a word of advice for all who have become pessimistic or cynical about the state of the world. The word is: Rejoice!*" And now, eight more bars, ensemble, and out: "*The dollar is shrinking, unemployment is rising. Millions of people are threatened by starvation. What is there to be thankful for on this Thanksgiving? The answer? Peace! Health! Opportunity! Freedom!*"

Grosbeck rose to his feet and threw out his arms. "I thank whatever God there is," he said fervently, circling his desk and looking at the unopened envelope from The Landmarks Preservation Commission. What now of his petty concerns? For shame. Just then, the cosmos arranged for his telephone to ring. It was Greenspan. "Harvey, you looked at that material yet?"

"I was just about to open it, Marty."

"Sure you were. Come on now, no more dogging it."

"Fast as I can, Marty. What's in it?"

"You damn well know," Greenspan said, and hung up. The phone rang again. "If you don't, it'll be in the paper tomorrow anyway and sooner or later we're going to have to tell people where we stand editorially. You better get busy," and hung up again before Grosbeck could say, "Right, chief."

Grosbeck put on his jacket again, shot his cuffs, sat down at his desk and opened the envelope. He was wary of it but nevertheless reasonably confident that it would not go off in his face. It did not advocate independence for Puerto Rico at the end of a timer attached to a piece of plastic explosive. It did not ask for contributions to alleviate the sufferings of the innocent, hollow-cheeked Roman Catholic women and children of Northern Ireland who, curiously, seemed to feed on boxes of Uzi machine guns, clips of ammunition, ingenious land mines and yards and yards of electrical wire to set off bundles of dynamite to blow up British soldiers, Protestants and—often as not—themselves in the belief that this would settle their stomachs, empty and rumbling since the Potato Famine of 1845. It was not pushing Arab irredentism or the Polisario or Bonds for Israel to paper the West Bank of the Jordan River.

It had to do, when one came right down to it, only with a small group of adjoined old buildings, serene, handmade, in scale, easy on the eyes and soul, which some hustlers wanted to get rid of to put up one big badly constructed *thing*. But, in Grosbeck's case, his obsession with the mansions was no different from his hatred of the Video Display Terminal, the end of the Linotype machine and the composing room and all the rest of the casualties of exuberant, mindless technology, not excluding the bits and pieces of people scattered by the atomic bomb or sickened by chemicals and other products of up-to-date thinking.

Was the analogy far-fetched? Was he simply unable to grasp that it was all a *matter of degree,* that it was absurd to make such comparisons? Yes, he was unable to grasp it, and, yes, he refused to admit to himself that this time his obsession had been sauced up by yet another piece of irrelevance: a hankering after a woman he did not know beyond the exchange of a few words and who, moreover, must be his enemy since she was the ally of his enemies.

Nevertheless, the first document removed from the envelope was a cry of anguish, or so Grosbeck construed it to be. (Greenspan had not bothered to put everything in order.) It was a letter from someone obviously as unhinged as Grosbeck. It read, "According to The Landmarks Preservation Commission, among the purposes for designating a structure a landmark are 'to honor it, to reflect its historic place in our past,' (and) *'to protect it against the threat of destruction or defacement . . .'* Defacement of a building can take many forms. To impose a modern tower onto nineteenth-century townhouses certainly destroys the architectural continuity of the site. To remove a building from its context is to rob it of its history, and to do this is surely to deface the building."

Beneath that was a heap of legalese almost an inch thick which, when placed in order, detailed the remorseless advance of Varney and his army. The language, of course, made no mention of the subversion of politicians and other interested parties, the presence of banks, the nods and winks of understanding, the florid piety of the religious who made the deal for the mansions, the application of *force majeure* where necessary, the extortions, bribes, promises, lies, and cozenings, the forgiveness of taxes in return for the throwing-up of the *thing.* It was not simply banal, in its repetitiveness, it was legal. Nothing was to be found in these arid legal fictions, heaped up over a period of years (Grosbeck marveled at the persistence of entrepreneurs such as Varney, but they were all alike) other than the dry bones of the commission's remains.

Grosbeck bent down and extracted a whole cigarette from a cuff of his pants. He had swiped it out of a pack on McFarland's desk in the City Room some days before, transferring it from cuff to cuff as he changed his clothes, saving it for an emergency, like an Indian down to his last chew of pemmican in a blizzard. It was bent but, thank God, not broken. He kept matches beneath a pile of file folders in the bottom drawer of his desk. He lighted up, took a long puff, became dizzy, searched around in another drawer until he found the top of a tin snuff can which he used for an ashtray (he washed it scrupulously after every illicit smoke and flushed butts down the toilet), reached for the telephone and called Kazanjian's office. (The Newspaper had furnished its people with the new button phones. Dialing was no longer good enough, oh no, and while he did not talk about it, Grosbeck would gladly have gone back to the days when one lifted a receiver and got a live woman operator, instead of the maddening musical notes which now issued forth from a telephone. As it was, he dialed the wrong number first time out. Would he ever master Touch Tone?)

"Miss Forsythe, please," he said.

A woman at the other end asked, "May I ask who's calling, please?" He made book with himself on what would be said next.

"I'm afraid she's stepped away from her desk, Mr. Gasbeak," the voice said.

Stepped away. Stiff-legged, like a flamingo or a stork or an ostrich. People didn't walk any more. They stepped away, legs lifted high, heads jerking erratically from left to right and up and down. And *Gasbeak!*

"Grosbeck," he said. "Harvey *Grosbeck*. Not *Gasbeak*."

"Oh, I'm *sorry*, sir," the voice said. "Can I help you?"

"No," Grosbeck said, "that's why I'm calling *her*."

"Could you tell me what it's in reference to?"

Grosbeck carefully twisted the ember out of the cigarette and put the butt back in his cuff. "No," he said, "it'll carry more weight if she hears it from Grosbeck rather than Gasbeak."

"I *said* I was sorry, sir," said the voice. It was a little whiney-piney voice, the face behind it somewhere else, the pigeon brain dreaming, hoping to be discovered for television commercials.

"Never mind," Grosbeck said. "Can you give me any idea when she's apt to step back to her desk?"

"It couldn't be more than a moment, sir," said the voice.

"How long is a moment?" Grosbeck wanted to know. He realized he was being at least as big a pain in the ass as the defective at the other end of the phone.

"I'm sure I couldn't say, sir," said the voice.

"I was sure you couldn't," Grosbeck said. "But you *are* sure, aren't you, that it won't be for eternity?"

"May I have her return your call?" Grosbeck recognized finality when he heard it.

"Yes, you may. Are you prepared to take a number? I'll spell my name for you. Have you got pencil and paper? Ready?" Silence. "You still there?" Grosbeck asked.

"I'm waiting, sir," said the voice. What in hell did she have to get angry about? Grosbeck thought. *Gasbeak!* He spelled out his name for the woman and gave her his number at The Newspaper and made her read it back to him.

"I'll have her call the moment she returns," she said. "Thank you, sir," she added with a vicious trill, and hung up.

But, she had not been lying. Alice Forsythe did call back within five minutes. "What did you do to my secretary?" she asked Grosbeck.

"Do?" Grosbeck asked. "Nothing. Forgive me, but where she is they don't run trains any more."

"I got your message, didn't I?" Alice Forsythe pointed out. "And I did call back, didn't I? You had that poor girl almost in tears. I will not have my people treated like *that.*"

"Why don't you send her home on compassionate leave?" Grosbeck asked. He was about to launch into a disquisition that would have taken them ballooning far afield, when he remembered the purpose of his errand. "All right, just tell her Mr. Gasbeak is sorry and you did just step away and not fly away or just plain walk away and you did return my call."

"That's hardly an apology, Mr. Grosbeck."

"Let it do for now, *please,*" Grosbeck said in an access of irritation. "I'll send over a complete set of amendments, side clauses and a bottle of wine in the morning." Alice Forsythe was waiting and smiling a trace.

"What I'm calling about is the mansions. Mr. Greenspan asked me to." And Mr. Greenspan hadn't asked him to call Alice Forsythe about anything else, although he would not have been surprised at what was on Grosbeck's mind.

"Certainly. Would you like to have lunch? Shall I bring Mr. Kazanjian, Mr. Varney?" Howard Tracy's guess had been right. Something about the enraged little man did have an effect on her, she was not sure just what.

"Best not the first time," Grosbeck said. He was still fast on his feet.

"Where would you like to go?" she asked.

"Anywhere you say. I don't much care, just so long as it isn't anywhere around The Newspaper. I need a change of scene."

"Are you sure The Newspaper won't think I'm subverting you if I pick up the check?" she asked.

"How about tomorrow? Preferably over your way."

"Good," Alice Forsythe said. "One o'clock?" She named a restaurant in the East Fifties.

"That's fine," Grosbeck said. He despised the place. The waiters, busboys, maître d', captains, manager, and owner were servile only to certain of their clientele, merely frigidly polite to everyone else. Their arrogance was as misplaced as their food was inferior. They pretended to be French, but Grosbeck believed firmly that they were all illegal immigrants, having materialized first somewhere in Transylvania. (They smiled like basilisks.) The tables were too small. There were far too many knives, forks, spoons, serviettes, wilting flowers, glasses, and menus so large that, when flourished, they threatened to sweep everything onto the floor and they blocked off the faces of diners. There was no end to the finger-snapping, eye signals, and dance steps performed by the waiter-captains as people made their way to tables down aisles no more than two feet wide, and the place was so dimly lit that lawyers, say, wishing to exchange briefs had long since learned to eat somewhere else. The indifference of the food and the inferiority of the wine could not be disguised by sauce, price, label, arrangement on plate (a collage of one kind or another), or manner of serving, which was acrobatic, something like that of a modern dance company in flight amid a crash of cymbals, trombones, and French horns.

"Very well, then," said Alice Forsythe, "see you tomorrow, Mr. Gasbeak."

19

Tremulous, bristling, exhilarated, depressed, belligerent, craven, Grosbeck entered the restaurant ten minutes early—he had always been a master of anticlimax, too early for everything, too late for dénouements—and was seated at Miss Forsythe's table upon identifying himself to the satisfaction of the maître d', a polished thug with black hair and a hole in the heel of one of his socks, who managed a pinched smile from somewhere in the recesses of a narrow head, a disdainful nose, and a face pale as a sheet of cheap stationery. Would Monsieur Greusbeuk like a drink? Madame Forsythe most assuredly would be along in a moment, but you *are* a bit early, sir? A bloody mary with a double shot in a small glass? The thug looked away and blinked. Certainly, sir, at once. The man had an accent combining the less attractive elements of Swabian German and debased Greek. His shirt crackled as he put the drink before Grosbeck, put it before him as though it were an act of revenge. Where did they find so many of them, Grosbeck wondered as he drank, drank quickly.

Grosbeck was a bad drinker and he was elevated in no time. His head began to whirl with knowledge of an almost unbearable sweetness: the pursuit of a righteous cause, the pursuit of an ignoble woman. His lips began to move in song, his voice audible only to himself: "As I walked along the Bois de Boulogne/ With an independent air,/ You can hear the girls declare/ He must be a millionaire;/ You can hear them sigh,/ And wish to die/ You can see them wink the other eye/ At the man that broke the Bank at Monte Carlo." He was halfway into "Ace in The Hole" and his voice had risen just enough so that the diners nearby glanced up in surprise from the dreadful messes they were eating and then went blind out of the same kind of tact which made them drop a dollar in a derelict's dirty palm, averting their eyes, torn between the belief in an act of charity and the knowledge that they were probably feeding a ravening drug habit.

Their curiosity was quickly sated. Alice Forsythe appeared out of nowhere in the labyrinth of tables, a vision of lubricity, Grosbeck believed. The mansions sank into a pit as he rose, tilted his flat, black gaucho hat down over his nose, pulled the leather string tight under his chin, and advanced upon her. With a faint, arrogant smile, he ripped her clothes off slowly and then bent her back in a slow, languorous tango, "La Cumparcita." It was short of perfection only because she was a head taller than he. His thin, cruel lips rested on the nipple of her left breast, which had fallen out of her camisole, while the wide, round brim of his hat struck her chin and fell down over his eyes. Then, he tried to clap his hands in the sharp rhythms of a flamenco and stamp his feet, succeeding only in stepping on his own toes and banging his ankles together. His scarlet cummerbund fell down, bound his feet and brought him to a halt. "How do you do?" he inquired, half rising from his seat.

"Please," she said, "don't get up. Did I hear you singing, Mr. Grosbeck?"

"Call me Harvey, if you will."

"Only if you call me Alice."

"I can't think of anything I would rather do, but only if you call me Harvey."

"Well, then," she said, "that's settled, isn't it?"

"It does sound ridiculous, doesn't it?" he asked. "At this late date. I mean, who these days calls anyone Grosbeck or Forsythe. Right?" She waited patiently as, standing in a crouch, he took both her hands in his. "Do sit down."

"I can't," she said. "You've got my hands."

"Of course. How inconsistent of me." He pulled back her chair with a dangerous flourish. "There, now," he said, pushing her up to the table as though she were a drawer in a filing cabinet and, returning to his own imitation Thonet, flushed and breathing hard.

"You *were* singing, weren't you, Harvey?" she asked.

"It was nothing. I like gambler's songs, Alice." By now, he had his elbows on the table, which rocked slightly because one of its legs was shorter than the other three. Nothing uneven about *your* legs, he thought. He clasped his hands under his chin. (He had to feel about to find it.) "Sing them whenever . . . whenever . . . oh, I just sing them whenever I feel . . ."

"Feel what?" Alice Forsythe asked.

"Just feel," Grosbeck said. He got one hand away from his chin and slid it across the table, but missed hers. "I don't want you to think I'm an . . . eccentric."

"Not at all," she said. She made one hand available to his.

"May I join you?" she asked. "A dry rob roy on the rocks, please."

"Double?"

"No, I think not," she said, withdrawing his hand so that he could wave it at a waiter. "I've still got a day's work ahead of me."

"Isn't this work, too?" Grosbeck wondered.

"It is and it isn't," she said. Coyness? Archness? Me!

"What is and what isn't?" he asked profoundly.

"It's too complicated," she said.

"Good," Grosbeck said. What was good? What the hell were the two of them talking about? He tried to snap his fingers at a waiter, but the fingers seemed to be made of cornmeal and passed each other soundlessly. A waiter did come eventually and did bring her a drink.

She took out a pack of cigarettes. "Would you mind very much if I had one of yours?" Grosbeck asked after patting his pockets elaborately. "I seem to have forgotten mine."

"If you can stand these," she said, leaning forward and lighting both of their cigarettes with a near-gold lighter. As the smoke curled downward into his lungs, veins, arteries, belly, and toes, mingling with the fumes of the bloody mary, he pretended interest in the lighter, holding it up with one hand and slipping another cigarette out of her pack into a pocket of his jacket, a master of deception and legerdemain.

"It's not the real thing. Why did you take another cigarette?"

"It's a long story," he answered seriously. "It's for charity. I save them for athletes—squash players, joggers at the end of a run, that sort of thing. It's a kind of quiet public service. I don't like it to get around. There *are* people like that . . . go all their lives unnoticed and next thing you know they're dead and they've left the output of several cigarette factories to soup kitchens in perpetuity. First you hear about it is when their obituaries show up in the paper with a photograph taken thirty-five years before."

"Mr. Grosbeck," said Alice Forsythe. "Harvey. Do you know why we're here?" She focused the medical mirror on his face.

"Yes," he said, and the mansions rose out of the pit as though on a stage elevator. "We're here to talk about the mansions and . . . listen, you really want to know about the cigarettes? I had a heart attack some time ago and I'm not supposed to smoke. My wife . . . my wife would kill me if she found out. She has her own afflictions, one of them being a sterling determination to keep me alive. But, I'd rather kill myself on my own time and I'm not so sure, either, that I believe in all that scientific crap about nicotine. I think the surgeon-general is a knee-jerk liberal. Probably eats wheat germ and what they call those goddamned 'stress pills,' whatever they are. They make you pee green, did you know that?" She shook her head. "It's getting so, by the way," he went on, "that you go to someone's house and you can't find an ashtray any more. They give you a lump of fake crystal, a gutted mermaid you can't put a cigarette down in, and people move away from you. The men are as bad as the women. Middle-class virtue is the end of civilization as we know it." He pounded on the table. "Excuse me," he said. He took a small vial out of a pocket, extracted a pill from it with difficulty and swallowed it with the rest of his drink.

"What's that for?"

"Irregular heart beat, my *cri de coeur*. Nothing to do with smoking." He was lying with magnificent ineptitude.

"Give me back that cigarette, Harvey."

"You might as well let me have it. I'll only get another one somewhere else. Why are you so concerned, anyway? Isn't that an unusual, even presumptuous intimacy on such short acquaintance, which I hope it is, the intimacy, I mean, not the short acquaintance."

"I think I'll have another drink," Alice Forsythe said. "I don't need a weatherman to tell me which way the wind is blowing. Will you order one for me? And some food, too? Have you looked at the menu?"

"No, I haven't," Grosbeck said. "Anything will do in this kind of deadfall. I think I'll have another drink, too. Just a single this time," he added reassuringly. He took another cigarette out of her pack and lit up. She found herself drinking with less deliberation than usual.

They ordered omelettes. The omelettes were decorated with sprigs of parsley, and Grosbeck, as was customary with him, threw them into the bud vase, which blocked his view of her and which he pushed to one side, almost off the table. "I know I should at least put them in the ashtray," he said, "but, would you believe it, there is something sacred about an ashtray for me. It was made for ashes, not parsley or pins or pieces of torn-up paper. Some day, if time permits, I will give you my thoughts on the architecturally perfect ashtray. The closest I've come to one in my life are those plain, thick, square ones with a semicircular groove at each corner. I've had some serious talks with designers about that. They all agree with me." His upper lip was now red with a smear of bloody mary over the egg of the omelette. Alice Forsythe played field hockey with her fork on her omelette, paid closer attention to her drink and then had a third. She leaned across the table and wiped his lip with her napkin. "It's nothing," he said, "just a flesh wound. I've been lucky."

"We're drunk, aren't we?" she asked.

"You recognize the symptoms, don't you?" Grosbeck asked.

"I drink enough, I suppose, but not much over lunch."

"It *does* give you crowsfeet, doesn't it?" Grosbeck asked sympathetically.

"Crowsfeet!"

Harvey was quick to recoup. He swayed forward until his head was almost on the table and examined her face conscientiously. "Doesn't seem to have done much to you," he said.

"Yet," she said. "Not yet."

"You're getting sentimental," he said, judiciously, "with a trace of self-pity. You're ripe, Alice. I mean *ripe*. It'll be a while before you're over the hill."

"Thank you," she said, quietly. "Coming from an expert like you, to say nothing of being an utter stranger . . ."

"I hope," he said, in what he hoped sounded like the open diapason of an organ, thick with unplumbed depths of hint and meaning, "that we will come to know each other better." She laughed hard.

"You little weasel. I caught on to you the moment I met you in your boss's office. I liked you immediately. And I told Howard Tracy that the night before he got married, the last night we spent together. He didn't like hearing it, but he *was* getting married the next day, wasn't he, so he had no right . . ."

"The night before he got married to Marjorie Denman?" Grosbeck asked. "The night *before!*"

"Yes," she said, "I don't know how your name came up, but it did."

Grosbeck held up a hand. "Wait a minute. I know we've both had a few, Speedy Gonzalez, but that's a little too much for me to take in all at once."

"It's true, all true. Are you shocked? At *your* age? Haven't you ever . . . ?"

"Yes, but, as they say in Vermont, I've 'gone by.' Mostly these days I read books and take my simple pleasures at home. Straight uptown to work, straight downtown to home. My wife is a beautiful woman."

"I know, I met her at the wedding."

"You must have dinner with us sometime," Grosbeck said.

"I'm sure. Never?" she asked.

"Well, hardly ever," Grosbeck said and was moved once again to song. " 'Oh, tell me pretty maiden/ Are there any more at home like you?/ There are a few, kind sir . . .' Florodora. Did you know everybody spells it wrong?" Bloom, wasn't that what Duffy called him? Was there something in what that old Mick believed?

"Do you want to?" he asked. "Do you?"

"Don't doubt it for a minute," she said. "But not so fast. Haven't you forgotten what we're doing here?"

"My blood is boiling, my poor thinned-out blood full of several kinds of crap my very good friend, Dr. Salomon—by the way, if you need a very good doctor, I'd recommend Salomon unhesitatingly—is counting on to keep me alive, alive-oh. Are you willing to take a chance?" She thought she was. "I warn you," he went on, "I wouldn't be the first, but how would you like me to die in the saddle? How would you handle that?"

"Nonsense," Alice Forsythe said, "and first things first. You're not even there yet."

"True," he said, with melancholy.

"Your kind may have heart attacks and creep around expecting to die any minute, but I've looked you over pretty carefully and I wouldn't be the least bit surprised if you outlasted me."

"That's very flattering," Grosbeck said. He lifted one of her hands and kissed it on the palm.

"You're so old-fashioned, so childlike."

"Childlike?" He expanded like a pouter pigeon. "You think so!"

"Do you have any idea what you're doing?" she asked.

"Not much," he said. "Maybe I'll find out, though. Remember," he added, grinning, "I love my wife . . ." paused for the sake of timing and concluded, "but, oh, you kid."

Alice Forsythe ran her tongue over her lips. "Do you know who you are, Grosbeck, my Grosbeck? Once, before I decided to become an architect, I thought I would be an anthropologist. Africa."

"All that business with skinny cattle and goats and women hanging down to here and babies with bellies out to there and sand and mud and Land-Rovers and grinding corn mixed with blood and milk, or whatever it is, before they find some pieces of stone and a broken bone that make the race a million years older than the other anthropologists thought?" Grosbeck asked. "And elephants and elands . . ."

"You're talking about paleontologists, Harvey, I think."

"What difference does it make?" Grosbeck asked. "Don't interrupt me . . . and tigers and wandering tribes and wands and heat and dust and grunting and chanting and those dances where they all look as though they're going to the toilet in line, one hand on the next one's shoulder and Kick One, Kick Two, Kick Three. Rattle any good bones lately?"

"I realized it wasn't for me," Alice Forsythe continued patiently, "and I became an architect. But the little I picked up tells me who you are."

"Man I know thinks he knows who I am, too. Leopold Bloom. What do you think? Chinese Gordon. Kitchener at Khartoum. You know how Kitchener died? On a battleship . . . *a battleship* in the North Sea . . . not in the desert. Gordon died at Khartoum, where he should have. Who, then?" Grosbeck put down his drink, pushed away his plate and shook hands with Alice Forsythe. "Dr. Livingstone, I presume. I am Henry Stanley of the New York *Herald*. It's good, sir . . . ma'am . . . to see you looking so well . . . We had thought . . . I hope you're prepared for this, Doctor. Actually, I'm illegitimate . . . the by-blow of a Jewish textile manufacturer from the Midlands (his legitimate son helped Marx out a lot) and a barmaid of Welsh descent living in Manchester and with nothing better to do after closing time. You know, 'Time, gentlemen.' Some time. Some gentleman. I think you ought to know that before we keep on discovering darkest Africa. I am an exception. Anyone will tell you that Africa is for *goyim*. Like space . . ."

Tears of laughter rolled down Alice Forsythe's face. "Don't cry for me. Not for me, honey. I'm not worth it, can't you see? I'll just pack my things and go. Drown myself in Victoria Falls . . ."

"Stop it, Harvey." Alice dabbed at her eyes. "Let's talk about the mansions. That's why we're here. We can't just make a mess of this lunch. We're supposed to do business. I'm supposed to *influence* you in the nicest way possible."

"What is the nicest way possible?" Grosbeck leered. He was so excited, he forgot to take another cigarette.

"That's for another time," Alice Forsythe said.

"All right, then, who am I?"

"Not so different from Bloom. You are Eshu," she said.

"What shoe?" Grosbeck asked. "Left shoe, right shoe? One, two, three, four? Shoo-fly-don't-bother-me? Bother me, I beg of you."

"Eshu," she went on slurring her words, "a lesher deity of the Yoruba of Nigeria."

"Lesher?" he asked.

"Eshu," she went on, "is a trickshter, commitsh misshuf . . . Escuse me." She ran her napkin over her lips as though that would make her mouth behave. There was a smear on her chin.

"You got something on your chin," Grosbeck said. "Here, let me help." He leaned across the table with his own napkin and wiped her forehead.

"We must be a sight."

"Never saw one I liked better. But go on, go on, I'm interrupting you. Two-shoe, you said?"

"Eshu. Plain Eshu."

"Trickster, mischief-maker?"

"He is short, like you," Alice Forsythe said. "His torso is rather attractive—smooth, round; his legs are short . . ."

"He *has* got a pot belly," Grosbeck said. "Like me."

"Yes," she said. "He wears a long pigtail. Phallic in shape."

"Hell of a place to hang it," Grosbeck observed. "How is he hung otherwise?"

Alice Forsythe continued: "He holds little calabashes of medicine, one in each hand."

"What's in them?" Grosbeck asked.

She ignored him. "He is disruptive, defiant, erotic . . ."

"What'll I do for a phallic pigtail?" Grosbeck asked.

"He is the messenger of the gods who are greater than himself," Alice Forsythe said, "and he deposits his calabashes at shrines in marketplaces, crossroads, and doorways, all places of change and potential conflict . . ."

"No question of potential conflict between us," Grosbeck said.

"He smokes a pipe."

"Nasty, bad-smelling things," Grosbeck said.

"He is irreverent . . . he . . . that's enough, I think," Alice Forsythe said.

The restaurant now revolved rapidly about the two of them, spewing customers out the door into the late afternoon, whirling waiters, captains, and busboys out of sight into the kitchen. The cloakroom was a blizzard of coats and hats and briefcases flying off hooks onto the backs and into the hands of the departing to the chink of coins in a plate baited with a dollar bill. And still the two of them had not got down to the work at hand. Tablecloths, silverware, plates, condiments disappeared as the whirlwind reversed itself and a phalanx of indentured servants, ticket-of-leave men, blew forth from the kitchen. The maître d' was tapping one foot two tables away. It sounded like the ticking of an old Seth Thomas clock. He was ignored by the lovers, the antagonists. He looked conspicuously at his wristwatch, which he wore on an arm ten feet long so that it could be thrust between their noses. He retracted the arm, walking backward, biting his lips, lifting his eyes heavenward and hissing.

"Has anyone ever told you . . . ?" Grosbeck asked.

"A good many people," said Alice Forsythe. "Told me what?"

"That you . . ." Grosbeck said.

"Oh, that. How do *you* go about it? Let's see if you can ring up any changes."

"You chill my blood," Grosbeck began. "It's thin enough as it is. You dampen my ardor. You forget what we already mean to each other . . . dancing to 'La Cumparcita,' drinking, smoking . . ."

"Dancing? 'La Cumparcita?' What are you talking about?"

"Don't interrupt me," Grosbeck said. "You know very well." Grosbeck continued amid the soughing of strings and woodwinds. "Oh, stay me with flagons and comfort me with apples, for I am sick of love. You wiped my lips with your napkin. You looked deep into my eyes . . ."

The table had been cleared, magically, and all that remained on it was the cloth, soiled with cigarette ashes and food and a check placed face up (how dare they!) under Grosbeck's glazed eyes.

The maître d' hissed again, kicked one of the slaveys in the ankle, pointed to Grosbeck and Alice Forsythe, and whispered, "Get them out of here. And start setting up for dinner." But the conversation continued, as dirty villeins coughed, shuffled, knocked things to the floor, picked them up and threw them into a cart pulled by the smallest of them. Another broke two plates and a cup. A third gathered up silverware in bundles and clanged them together loudly six inches from their table. In the kitchen, a television set was turned on at full volume. It was playing an old, old horror movie and the screams of victims resounded through the restaurant. A fourth slavey bent over the table and swept the cloth off—presto!—and only the face-up check stayed in place, halfway between Grosbeck and Alice Forsythe. They were, for the moment, as oblivious to the rising storm as gulls off Cape Hatteras.

"Try again," Alice Forsythe said.

"I shall. We shall not be moved." The crew, expressionless but determined, mopped—great swinging slaps on the floor, over Grosbeck's freshly shined shoes, halfway up Alice Forsythe's legs. She made a brushing gesture with one arm, but gave no sign otherwise that she was aware of the presence of anyone but Grosbeck. "I think of you," he said, "as a nautilus . . . paper nautilus . . . Argonauta . . . silver nautilus . . . full fathom five my boss lies . . . and I have betrayed my trust for . . ."

"That's not too bad," Alice Forsythe said.

"What time is it?" Grosbeck motioned imperiously at the maître d', who moved near and put his face close to Grosbeck's.

A low noise surrounded him like the munching of a million termites on a piece of mahogany. He was grinding his teeth. "It is four fifteen, monsieur," he said, with a smile of the sort one bestows on a Jew in a prison hole in Buenos Aires who is about to have his testicles pinched for subversion. "It must be quite late for you. As you can see," he added, his voice strangled to a murderous squeak, "we are about to order the *établissement* for dinner." He picked up

the check, examined it as though it were a traffic summons, and
thrust it under Grosbeck's nose.

"Why, so it is. Alice, we do seem to have overstayed our leave.
There's such a thing as—what's the name for it now—oh, of course,
'accountability.' Letsh ush be fully accountable."

"Would you mind very much if I paid the check?" Alice Forsythe
asked. "Or would that be a body blow to your integrity and that of
The Newspaper?"

"Only objects valued at a hundred dollars or more," Grosbeck
said. "Much like the government of the United States. But, why
don't you let me buy lunch? It isn't going to cost either of us anything."

"Somehow," Alice Forsythe said, "I'd like to do it the first time. It
will leave me with an indelible memory; it is a ceremony . . ."

"Something you picked up among the Yoruba?" Grosbeck asked.
She did not answer. Instead, the two of them struggled genteelly for
the check until they had torn it in three or four pieces. The maître d'
closed his eyes and the grinding noise coming from his head could be
heard again.

"All right, it's on you. I don't much care. And besides," Grosbeck
said eagerly, "you did say something about the 'first time.' Did I hear
that right? I have a speech impediment in my ear; it comes and
goes."

"How can anyone have a speech impediment in an ear?"

"You can," Grosbeck said. "You know, there are a few things you
didn't pick up in Africa, let me tell you." Alice Forsythe plunged
into her handbag, an exercise in any woman that never failed to
arouse in Grosbeck something so far beyond impatience that there
was no name for it. "Fucking rat's nest," he shouted. She pulled out
a wallet and from it extracted a credit card. The maître d' handed
her the pieces of paper that had been the check. But, before signing
for the lunch, she asked Grosbeck, "Where are your glasses?"

He drew back and offered her a superior, drunken smile. "Here,
naturally," he said, patting his breast pocket. The pocket was empty.
Panic. Clumsily he went through all of his pockets. Nothing. He
demanded his topcoat from the checkroom, waving a dollar bill
above his head. The coat was brought to him with a look of immea-
surable relief on the face of both the checkroom girl and the maître
d', who, at that point, bowed, left for the cash register and per-

formed the occult rites prescribed for credit cards. Pretending a casualness he no longer felt, Grosbeck went through the pockets of the topcoat. Nothing. He might as well put it on while he was about it. It felt at least four sizes too large for him.

"Had enough?" Alice Forsythe asked. "Your glasses are on your nose."

"Do you suppose we could continue this conversation elsewhere?" Grosbeck asked. "Neither of us is so tied to the wheel that we cannot conclude our business in some place less urgent, more congenial . . . follow me?"

"I follow you," said Alice Forsythe. "I follow you to the ends of the earth," she said, struggling into her coat. "What were we doing here in the first place?" The afternoon had begun to wear itself thin. It needed something substantial if it were to be rescued. "It is my distinct recollection," Grosbeck said, "that we came here—at your instigation—to talk about the mansions." His speech appeared to have cleaned itself up. "We seem to have let it all run out. But," he went on, taking a deep breath, "nothing's been lost. Suppose we go over to a place I know near the paper."

"Your *querencia*, eh?" Alice Forsythe asked. "Not my stamping ground."

"Let me just call the office, will you? I'll have to miss the Editorial Meeting, but Greenspan will understand that our discussion is taking longer than either of us anticipated. So much material and so forth."

"I'll have to make a call, too," said Alice Forsythe. The maître d' returned with the credit card and the small piece of paper which was the admission of guilt—forty-eight dollars, on which Alice Forsythe entered a ten-dollar tip.

"I would have stiffed him," Grosbeck said. "The son of a bitch."

"I do business here often," Alice Forsythe said, "and he's among the lesser sons of bitches in my life."

The afternoon had turned cold and gray. The cheapjack sidewalk merchants with their tatty skirts, blouses, belts, jewelry, pots and pans, folk objects run off lathes in a Newark, New Jersey, factory, all laid out on dirty cotton sheets; the sellers of fresh orange juice, tacos, hot dogs, ropes of bad lamb and smelly beef on long splinters; the three-card monte hustlers with their cardboard boxes and shuffling shillabers; the chamber-music trios (two bearded men and a girl with hair so long that she bowed it as often as she did her viola); the emissaries of side-street whorehouses snapping their handbills at passersby (they always withdrew at Grosbeck's approach); the passersby themselves, all looked dispirited this afternoon. Attaché cases seemed to walk by themselves in midair. The traffic moved slowly, resignedly through the side streets and on the avenues, the buses ran in fat, resentful strings. The great department stores looked down disdainfully on all this. Even the half-built new skyscrapers couldn't draw crowds of gawkers this afternoon. The great cathedral had its eyes heavenward. There, there was no evil.

Grosbeck and Alice Forsythe passed the mansions on their way across town to the West Side. They bumped into each other frequently and begged each other's pardon elaborately. "Phone booths," Grosbeck said. "Two of them. Here. Here's a dime. There's no time for you to go through that handbag of yours. Pay me back some other time," he added. She missed the slot. He picked up the dime, put it in for her and pushed her into the booth. "What's your number?" he asked. "I'll dial it for you." Then, he took the adjacent booth. He had made a mistake. It smelled strongly of urine and it was out of order.

He waited until Alice Forsythe had called Kazanjian to tell him that this was taking longer than expected and that she probably wouldn't be back that afternoon. Was she getting anywhere? "That depends on what you mean," she told Kazanjian and hung up.

Grosbeck called Greenspan. "I probably won't be back this afternoon," he said. "This is taking longer than I expected, an awful lot to go over . . ."

"Certainly, Harvey," Greenspan said. "I fully understand. No small matter. Lots of ground to cover, particularly at the bottom of a glass. Primary research. Mustn't come back without all our ducks lined up in a row."

"You said that, Marty, not I." His dime started to run out and his conversation with Greenspan to be interrupted. It was making just as much sense that way as it would had Grosbeck dropped another dime in the slot. "I'll see you . . ." Grosbeck said into the mouthpiece. Interruption. "Tomorrow. Yes, and . . ." The phone went dead. "Fuck you, Martin Greenspan," Grosbeck said into the phone. "Five cents for the next three minutes," a tinny voice said into Grosbeck's ear. "And screw you, too," he said to the recording. He had a little difficulty extricating himself from the folding door of the telephone booth and it was only when he was halfway out that he realized that his topcoat was caught and that he was still holding the receiver. He dropped it. Alice Forsythe got his coat free. "Let's go," he said.

"Thish wash a mishtake," Grosbeck said. The liquor had returned. "We should have met at my office. Or yours. Fewer dishtrashuns." A breeze blew up dust. Alice Forsythe pulled her coat tightly about her and tried to hold her head high. "All bizhness from now on," Grosbeck said, patting her arm. "You'll sec. Itsh wearing off. We'll get right down to it." His mind wandered. "Why izh every woman in the world taller than I?" he asked.

"Don't feel bad about it. The world is full of great little men."

"You really feel that way?" Grosbeck asked. She nodded and squeezed his arm. They arrived at the bar across from The Newspaper. "Coffee," he said. "That'll do it. They've known me here for years and nobody'll mind if we just have coffee." The bar was brown and dark, served good plain food and was prosperous because the two smart homosexuals who ran it knew better than to bother people, in particular the newspapermen who worked across the street and spent both time and money there. It was an anachronism and would undoubtedly be torn down some day soon. The waiters wore long white aprons over black jackets. The bar and the tables were crowded from the moment the doors opened (printers) until the place had finished with the night shift (reporters and editors), at two in the morning. It had about it an air of comfortable shabbiness that had taken a lot of work to create.

Tully, McFarland, and Martha Sloane were there. They saw Grosbeck come in with Alice Forsythe and ignored them until Grosbeck walked Alice over to their table. "Like you to meet a few friends of mine," Grosbeck said. "Alice Forsythe, John Tully, Martha Sloane, Bob McFarland."

"You've been drinking," Martha Sloane said. "Pleased to meet you, Miss Forsythe."

"All part of the job," Grosbeck said. "Doctor *wants* me to." He thumped his heart. "Miss Forsythe and I have things to talk over. I hope you'll excuse us, we'll just drift over there . . ." He pointed vaguely toward the back of the room.

"Smoking, too?" Martha asked.

"Now, Martha," Grosbeck said, reproachfully. "You know me better than that."

"Indeed, I do," she said.

"Let him alone," Tully said.

"What's it like upstairs," McFarland asked, "among the gods? And what are you doing down here at this hour?"

"Little project I've got to talk about with Miss Forsythe," Grosbeck said. He took off his coat. "Lots to talk about. I'll tell you later." He tugged at Alice Forsythe's arm and led her to a booth. He aimed his coat at the corner, and watched it fall on the floor. He retrieved it with difficulty and sat down, puffing. Alice Forsythe hung up her own coat effortlessly. "Some of my best friends," he said. "They watch out for me. Do I need watching out for, you think?"

"I don't know," Alice Forsythe said, "but I'll find out, Harvey, won't I?"

"Keep an eye on him," McFarland called down the room. It was doubtful anyone heard him beyond his table. "He's small, but oh my . . ."

"What's that all about?" McFarland asked Tully and Martha Sloane.

"How would I know?" Martha Sloane asked. "Come to think of it, though," she added, "the only woman I ever saw him in here with was Madeline. What do you think, Tully? You've always kept a close eye on him."

"I don't want to sound portentous," Tully said. He put a hand on the arm of a passing waiter. "Same again. All around. Thank you." He finished his glass. "I haven't seen much of him since he went up to Olympus." The fresh drinks came. The place began to fill up. Duffy came in. Tully called him over, sat him down, and ordered up a drink for him, too. There was no need to ask Duffy what he was drinking, not after so many years. "Duffy, what is Grosbeck doing over there with a woman? Not a bad-looking one at that."

"I couldn't say, Mr. Tully. Never saw her before in my life. But, then, remember, I watch the third floor, not the twelfth."

"Come on now, Duffy," Martha Sloane said, "there's damned little goes on you don't know."

"Beggin' your pardon, Miss Martha, you exaggerate. Maybe it *is* just business. They do business differently upstairs."

"Not that differently," Tully said. "You're a lying old sod, Duffy."

"God's my judge," Duffy said. "You give me too much credit."

"Well, what do you *think?*" Martha Sloane asked. Not one of the four looked up. They might as well have been playing poker in a hotel room.

"I've known him to play a little in his time," Tully said, "but he never brought anyone here. That's like putting it on the front page or taking her home to Madeline. Unthinkable. No, this is probably legitimate. Some press agent, maybe, some contact he needed for something he's writing."

"Who gets smashed in the middle of the afternoon and then winds up the day in this place with a woman none of us ever saw before?" Martha Sloane asked. "I don't see any notebooks out, any pens, any material spread on the table. And why not in the office, even her office?"

"Because then," Tully said, "none of us would have anything to talk about. Still . . ." Gossip brightened the room for them. "Find out, will you, Duffy?" Tully asked.

"I'll do what I can," Duffy said, "although something tells me we're not going to find out from him."

"Is he still drinking?" asked Martha Sloane, who was sitting with her back to Grosbeck and Alice Forsythe.

"No, just coffee," McFarland said, "but he's taking an occasional puff on her cigarette."

"Hmmm," said Martha Sloane.

"The two of them look awfully serious," Tully noted.

"It's simple enough, darlings," McFarland said. "It ever occur to you that it's business *and* pleasure?"

"I don't think he's known her that long," Martha Sloane said.

"How long does it take Grosbeck?" Tully asked. "Or anyone else?" He made a kiss at Martha.

"I've got to go," McFarland said. "I wouldn't dream of interfering with the rest of you social scientists, so I won't ask any of you to leave with me. But why can't we leave them in decent solitude?"

"Solitude? In this place?" Martha Sloane asked.

The place was pleasantly noisy with drinkers now and the bartenders had their hands full. "Bob," Martha Sloane asked, "why don't you hang around."

"I shouldn't," he said. "But, hell, why not? Let me call home. I'd like to get a line on this just as much as the rest of you." He rose, went to the wall telephone at the back, careful not to look at Grosbeck or Alice Forsythe as he passed, and told his wife in New Jersey that he was going to be a little late, oh, maybe an hour, he'd just run into Tully, he didn't get to see him that often these days, he just wanted to have a few words with him. On his way back to the table, he nodded pleasantly at Alice Forsythe and Grosbeck. He believed fervently the devil was making work for idle hands.

Across the room, Grosbeck sat slumped in his chair, his coffee cold. "Let me get another pot," Grosbeck said. "Sure you don't want anything stronger?" She shook her head. "You're right," he said. He was so far down in his chair that the toe of his shoe was halfway up her leg. She did not withdraw it. "The mansions," Grosbeck said. "That's why we're here, isn't it?" He looked at her closely. "Didn't you even feel a twinge when we walked past them?" He straightened up and poured himself another cup of coffee, half of which went into his saucer, a third on the tablecloth and the remainder into the bottom of his cup. "May I help you?" he asked, lifting the pot.

"Better not," said Alice Forsythe. "Let me do it."

"Well, what about the mansions?" Grosbeck asked. "And why me?"

"There's no mystery about it," she said. "Mr. Varney would like very much to have the good opinion of The Newspaper for the Mansions Project. That's why I went to see Mr. Greenspan about it and he suggested that I see you, fill you in on what we propose to do. I'm aware of your special interest in New York and Mr. Greenspan thought . . ."

"I've already been filled in, as you put it," he said. "You've got the Landmarks people in your pocket already, haven't you? And the Planning Commission and the Board of Estimate and the banks and the contractors and all the rest of the boodlers. Why do you need The Newspaper, too? And what in hell did Greenspan have on his mind when he suggested I talk to you? You heard Greenspan tell you how I feel about these things . . ."

"We thought it possible," she said, "that we could make you understand more fully that we're not simply trying to tear down, but combine the best of the old and the new on one site, rather than tear down something old and replace it with just another tall building. If you will look at it reasonably, you can see that something is better than nothing at all."

"Do you really believe that?" Grosbeck asked.

"No," she said.

"You don't need anybody's good opinion. You've got all you need —tax abatement, shoddy construction, some horrible green-or-blue-or-brown-glass tower thrown up over the shell of a series of buildings that are not only beautiful and low and old but that leave something on the street that *belongs* there, has belonged there for a hundred years, that tells people where they are, and ought not to become the shrunken balls of a big cock at the back of a place of worship which, I might add, parenthetically, is no better than it ought to be. In my time, I've seen so much of it"—he leaned forward—"you make me despair. You say you don't believe in it, either. Or did you?" Somehow, meaning emerged from Grosbeck's senseless flow.

"Harvey. Mr. Grosbeck. I am only an errand boy, too. A very well-paid errand boy, but that's all. I fully share your sentiments—my, how flossy I sound—but I do."

"What sentiments?" he wanted to know. "What do you share with me other than a random tickle? But we're not talking about that at the moment."

"You're being difficult," she said. "You distress me. I wish you didn't, but you do."

"I know, but you have a job to do, too, don't you? A job to do," he said. "Do you know, I think Greenspan is the devil. Greenspan sent you to me. There are a dozen other people he might have picked, but he picked me."

"I have come very close to loving you for the way you think," Alice Forsythe said. "I don't use the word lightly. There is nothing you feel about New York City that I don't too."

"So I've noticed," Grosbeck said. "More coffee, please, I don't seem to be able to handle the pot myself." Alice Forsythe filled his cup. Grosbeck sipped loudly. "I don't even know, can't even guess, which way the paper will go on this. Wait a minute, yes I can. I think The Newspaper will back Varney. It will back him because it's got a lot of its own real estate on the West Side to think about, which it would like to get rid of, and it wouldn't mind unloading it on Varney. I do not exclude the building in which it is published. Then, we'll see a campaign on how it's time for the West Side to be built up, rehabilitated; relieve the overbuilding on the East Side; improve traffic flow; and so on and so forth. Greenspan *knows* how I feel about this and this is his idea of a good joke. He *knows* what I intend to write, if I ever get to it. And anything I have to say about it will never see print. I might as well frame anything I have to say and put it in a closet. I keep my defeats in a separate closet."

"I would like to think you're right," Alice Forsythe said, "much as I know it's wrong."

Grosbeck went off on a tangent. "*Would* like! *Would* like! You don't mean you 'would like to think.' You mean *think*. You *think* . . . I don't need any of your pissyass conditionals."

"I *think*, then, you're right," she said. "And I'm sorry."

"Sorry," Grosbeck went on in a fury. "I doubt you've ever been sorry about anything in your life." He put his fists on the table, rose, then sat down again abruptly. "I don't want to make a spectacle of myself," he said. "Particularly in here."

"But, I *am* sorry," Alice Forsythe said. "And I have no choice. I told you how I feel about this project . . ."

"And feelings aren't enough, are they?" Grosbeck asked. "They don't keep an East Side apartment, do they? And whatever else the money does for you."

"Is that so inhuman?" Alice Forsythe asked.

"I say it is," said Grosbeck. "And I say that everything is black and white, one or the other."

"And I stand for black and you stand for white, is that it?" Alice Forsythe asked. "I thought you were less of a stuffed shirt, less simple-minded. Ah, but you've got a lot to learn. You do want me, don't you? And you do hate what I stand for? And for reasons I don't fully understand, I seem to want you. Is that black and white? Tell me."

Grosbeck was baffled. "One thing's got nothing to do with the other," he said. Even to him, it sounded lame. "I'm not responsible for my lech and I am for the mansions and whatever else I think can be kept."

"Then, if that's so," Alice Forsythe said, "why don't you just get up and leave? I can find my way out. I'm beginning to be angry with you, not sorry for you."

"That isn't going to help either of us," Grosbeck said, for want of anything better to say.

"Here is my home telephone and address," Alice Forsythe said, writing on the back of a business card. She chucked him under the chin—derisively?—with a forefinger. "We'll be black at business and white at home." She smiled faintly. "I do believe my eyes are a little blurry. Walk me out, please. Walk me right past your friends and say good night pleasantly to them. I'm very good in bed, not just in business. You'll see. As for The Newspaper, we'll see about that, too."

"What is there you see in me?" the callow Grosbeck asked.

"Enough," she said. They were flushed and tired and out of sorts. Grosbeck felt a pain across his chest. He turned to one side, fumbled a tablet of nitroglycerine out of the small bottle in his pocket, swallowed it discreetly, helped Alice Forsythe on with her coat, paid the check, took her arm, and the two of them made their way past the table occupied by Martha Sloane, Tully, McFarland, and Duffy.

"Good night, all," Grosbeck said.

"It was nice to have met you," said Alice Forsythe. They said it was nice too.

"You coming back?" McFarland asked Grosbeck. Martha Sloane nudged McFarland sharply with an elbow.

"No," said Grosbeck, "I'm on my way home, put Miss Forsythe in a cab, she's going the other way, get another for myself." He was a compound of confusion, guilt, and angina pectoris. And, for the moment, the old and beautiful had receded deep into the recesses of his black-and-white mind.

20

Grosbeck dismissed the cab a block away from home, deciding he could use the air before seeing Madeline. He felt as though he had endured a particularly arduous ride on a half-broken camel. The driver was a Lebanese this time. He had a face gouged out of one of Max Beckmann's more excitable canvases—tangled beard, accusing eyes with lightning in them—and he disdained the protective shield between himself and his passengers, but he spared Grosbeck any conversation, instead humming snatches of The Internationale to himself, banging on the steering wheel for emphasis. "Why, I know that," Grosbeck said. "We used to sing it at meetings of the John Reed Club at college. 'There's a better world in birth . . .'"

"Pah," said the driver. He drew up where Grosbeck told him to with so little warning that Grosbeck was thrown forward and sideways into a corner, adding a headache to his receding drunkenness, to his guilt at having been with Alice Forsythe for reasons that would not have withstood the scrutiny of a cretin, and to the sure knowledge that something was about to happen to him which never before in his life had.

"You're here already." Grosbeck overtipped him. He bade farewell to Grosbeck by blowing his nose with thumb and forefinger on the sidewalk less than six inches from Grosbeck's shoes. Then he aimed his cab at the other side of the street, cutting off two trucks and another cab whose driver had thought to pick up a fare. Grosbeck watched the other driver get out of his cab to argue. The Lebanese came out from behind the wheel and stood before the other driver, hands on hips. The other driver had a fist upraised, but it suddenly fell to his side. God, the Puerto Rican lady, had seized it and pulled it down, saying, "Man, you crazy? Get you back in that hack and get youself gone fast as you can." The customer who had been waiting had long since fled.

Grosbeck sneaked into, rather than entered, the apartment. What he expected to gain by turning the key softly in the lock, hunching his shoulders and whistling, he did not know. Madeline was leaning against the bar with a wooden cooking spoon in one hand. "Ah, darling," he said, "there you are." He kissed her, a statue. "At last. Tough day, sweetie. One of those days when nothing seems to go right . . ." He thought and wrinkled his brow. "I called, didn't I, and told you I'd be late?"

"No, you didn't," Madeline said. "It must have been someone else."

"See what I mean?" Grosbeck asked. "Nothing went right. Nothing."

"I wouldn't say that," Madeline said, inspecting him critically. She drew near with the upraised spoon. He flinched. "Nobody's going to hit you, silly," she said. She touched his face and kissed him. "It seems to me," she went on, "you've begun to make your mark already."

"Mark? What mark?" Grosbeck asked.

"The way you smell. Whiskey, perfume. And you've got lipstick smeared halfway down your right cheek."

"I have?" he asked.

"It isn't blood, is it?" Madeline asked. "I wouldn't want to think of you hemorrhaging in a cab. It is lipstick, isn't it?"

"Come to think of it, you're right. It *is*, isn't it? What do you know," he added in wonder, wiping at it and further enlarging the smear.

"You and Greenspan been kissing each other," Madeline asked, "over a glass of sweet vermouth? I'm broadminded enough to know how that could happen. Everybody has to kiss the boss every now and then. Isn't that so?" She paused. "Usually, though, he gets kissed in the ass and the nose is brown instead of the cheek being red. I'm angry and you're late . . ."

"And dinner is ruined," Grosbeck said.

"No, I waited."

Grosbeck tried to engage her in a technical discussion of the cooking times involved. She would have none of that. He returned gloomily to the subject of the original conversation. "Madeline," he said, "I wish you wouldn't be so Pineroish about something perfectly innocent. What kind of farce are you making out of this?"

"Suppose you tell me," Madeline said. "I'm reasonable, I'm understanding. I can understand almost everything you do, in particular."

"It was business, Madeline. I was at lunch with Alice Forsythe talking about the mansions."

"And she kissed you right into her point of view?"

"Look," Grosbeck said, "you know me better than that."

"Much better," Madeline said. "You look as though you've got four or five drinks in you."

"How can you tell that?" Grosbeck asked.

"Harvey, you're not only the worst drinker in the world, you show it. One of your shoelaces is untied, your tie is a little cockeyed, and your coat is halfway down your arms to the ground. Other than that, you look as sedate as a broker."

"Madeline, listen to me, if you don't mind."

"You're going to deliver a monologue," Madeline said. "Before you start, though, do me a favor. Tell me about the lipstick."

"Easiest thing in the world," Grosbeck said. Fluency had returned to him. "You know what people are like these days. Kiss, kiss, kiss, on no provocation at all. Like shaking hands. She must have just stuck her face out as I was saying good night to her—I really don't remember at all, any more than a handshake—and slobbered all over my cheek." He tried an expression of distaste.

"And you didn't slobber back?" Madeline asked.

"I don't wear lipstick, Madeline," Grosbeck said in a splendid non sequitur. "Not yet."

"Very well," Madeline said. "Go on, then."

"There's no convincing her. Far as she's concerned—and Varney—that building's going up. I was a fool ever to see her, but Greenspan made me. I didn't get around to marshaling all of my arguments . . . I don't think it'll do any good, but I'm going to need more time."

"I'll bet you are," Madeline said.

"I'm afraid I was a little too general in my approach . . . I told her that there had to be an end to the remorseless grinding up of New York—just as there had to be an end to the remorseless grinding up of Vietnam . . ."

"My," said Madeline, "that must have made an impression."

"I'm afraid she didn't make the connection," Grosbeck said. "Do you want to hear me out, Madeline, or shall we just eat?"

"Eat?" Madeline asked. "I doubt butter would melt in your mouth."

Grosbeck made a noise of irritation and hopelessness with tongue and teeth. "I told her," he said, and went on for fifteen minutes. Nothing Madeline hadn't heard many times.

"You said all that? Did you actually?"

"Well, pretty much."

"So much eloquence," Madeline said, "on a few drinks. And to so little point. She must have thought you insane."

"Probably," Grosbeck said. "I suppose I did get carried away some." He had no recollection of having said any of these things.

"And you expect talk like that to have any influence on those sharpshooters? Harvey, you shouldn't drink and lecture at the same time. I would have walked out on you. Why didn't she?"

Grosbeck was not yet completely sober. "Pure force of personality," he said, "is all I can think of."

"Are you hungry?" she asked.

"I could eat," he said. "I've been looking forward to it all day. Lunch was awful."

"It was the bartender's fault, wasn't it?" Madeline asked. "I'll bet you just picked at what was on your plate and pushed it aside, didn't you?"

"Something smells awfully good," Grosbeck said. "What's for dinner?"

"What's for dinner, my poor over-the-road truck driver just in from Cleveland? Veal piccata, cavatelli . . ."

"*Very* nice," Grosbeck said. "You're the only superb cook I know . . ."

". . . and a salad and off to bed with you. I can understand how tough it must have been for you today."

"Ah, come on now, Madeline," Grosbeck said. "We all have things to do we don't like to do. Greenspan . . ."

"That slavedriver," Madeline said, "forcing you to have lunch with that woman."

"Would you mind if I had a small drink while we're waiting?" Grosbeck asked.

"Just to get the juices flowing again?" Madeline asked. "The juices are flowing down your chin. Go get your clothes off and get into the shower. And hang everything up and put on a robe."

"I like to eat dressed," Grosbeck said. "What if I just whip into a pair of pants and a pullover."

Madeline shut her eyes. "Do you think you can handle it? Get into the shower. I don't care if you come back in white tie and an opera hat. But, go. You feel you need a drink? Take it in the bathroom with you. Here . . ."

She put down the cooking spoon and made him a martini.

"Could I have *two* olives?" he asked, holding out the glass. "No, wait a minute. A couple of pearl onions?"

She dropped the onions into the glass with the olives. "Here, you greedy little man."

"Let me set the table first," Grosbeck said. "It's the least I can do. I can imagine you didn't have the easiest day of it, either." He tried for the same tone of voice he had used on Alice Forsythe. By this time, his coat was lying on the floor. He dropped his jacket on top of that, his pants on that and stood before Madeline in shirt, socks (held up by the garters his father had taught him to wear) and shoes, which were scuffed. Somewhere in the back of his head, he thought, damn, I had them shined only this morning.

"Madeline, where can I find a tablecloth? I don't seem to be able to find them."

"Look," Madeline said, "I think I'm going to have a drink too. I think I'm going to need one."

"May I make it?" Grosbeck asked. "What's your poison?"

"I'll make it myself. And forget about the table. Take your shower."

"Fast as I know how," Grosbeck said cheerfully. "I'll just pick up my clothes first." He scooped them up in an untidy bundle and shuffled, shoulders bent, into the bedroom, and threw everything onto the bed.

Madeline followed him in. "I thought so. Hang all that up. And don't forget to take off your shoes and shirt before you get into the shower."

"Socks too?" Grosbeck asked. "Hear from the kids?" he asked, standing naked before her.

"The kids?" Madeline asked. "You're a grandfather, remember?"

"They'll always be kids to me," Grosbeck said sententiously. He felt he was handling things well, all things considered. He sat down on the bed, martini in hand. "By God, Madeline, nobody in the world makes a better drink than you."

"I'm the best cook in the world, too, aren't I?" she asked. "The best everything."

"The best," he said. "Best pair of legs, best behind, best breasts, most languishing eyes—I see fire in them now—smoothest skin, most beautiful face—that ivory tint drives me out of my mind—the hair like a black cap, the slender, tapering fingers . . ."

He had finished his drink, put it down with reasonable care, and lay back on the bed, eyes closed. Madeline regarded him. She finished her own drink, put it down, and then pulled him up. "Up. Up and into the shower."

"But the table," he said. "I've got to set the table."

"Into the shower."

He turned the taps on. First, he burned himself, then froze himself. He found the bath sheet too big to handle; he had forgotten to put the bathmat in front of the tub; and he left puddles on the floor. The mirror on the medicine chest had fogged up and he rubbed at it to see what he looked like. He remembered saying to himself, Nothing I can't handle, looked at his face in the mirror, and changed his mind. He had trouble finding clothes, but finally came back inside and sat down heavily in his place. "Ready for anything," he called out to Madeline in the kitchen. "God, I feel good. Another drink, sweetheart?"

"No, thanks," Madeline said. "None for you, either. Everything's ready." She brought out the veal and the pasta and the salad, looking first at the table and then at Grosbeck. She took the food back into the kitchen for the moment, returned to the table, and lifted Grosbeck's head, which had sunk to his chest.

"You're behaving even more strangely than I thought you would. I'll set it." Nothing more.

The two ate in silence, for the most part. Once, she looked across at him and said, "You've got soap in your hair."

He felt his head. "Soap," he said. "That must . . . what happened was someone else upstairs must have turned on his shower and it got scalding hot and I ducked. I must have forgotten to duck back under. Also, I was having trouble adjusting the nozzle." He wiped his head with his napkin and then his lips, leaving a string of soap bubbles under his nose. "I simply can't tell you how good this is," he said. "May I trouble you for a glass of wine?"

"You may trouble me," Madeline said, "but you're not going to get it."

Grosbeck shrugged. He ate his veal with genuine appreciation, also the noodles; ate the salad for Madeline's sake and the sake of Dr. Salomon; praised the dressing; dropped things off the end of his fork and said, "Leave it for the cat. She's no mouser, but I've never known her not to finish anything we put before her. Better than a vacuum cleaner." He bent down to pet the cat—a precarious undertaking—but the animal had gone somewhere else, possibly sensing that something was in the air.

"I'll do the dishes," he said, rubbing his belly.

"No, you won't," Madeline said. "Go to bed."

"You're not angry at me, are you?" Grosbeck asked.

"Yes, I'm angry at you," Madeline said. "And, no, I'm not. I don't know what I am. Just don't ask me any more questions. Get into bed."

"Anything good on the box?" Grosbeck asked.

"I don't know," Madeline said. "You find something—without knocking it over, if you can. Whatever it is, it won't make much difference. You'll be out cold, anyway."

Grosbeck sat where he was. "You seem so distant toward me tonight, sweetheart. What have I done?"

Madeline, clearing away, said, "Nothing yet, Harvey."

"Darling," he said, groping, "have you ever known me in all the years of our marriage to . . . ?"

"No, I haven't," Madeline said, "but I can't be everywhere, can I? Yes, I think you have," she went on, "but it didn't mean anything. It only hurt when I laughed."

"As God is my judge . . ." Grosbeck began. God, the Puerto Rican lady, materialized through the ceiling, rapped Grosbeck smartly on the head, and evanesced. "Never," Grosbeck said. God's hand, at the end of a long arm, came through the ceiling again and shook a finger under Grosbeck's nose.

"Bite your tongue," said the Holy Ghostess. Madeline looked down at the table.

"Well, I have, too. You didn't know that, did you?"

"No, tell me," Grosbeck said. "I'm really interested." That was the wrong approach.

"Are you trying to make conversation, Harvey?"

Grosbeck looked contrite. Then, he tried to look angry. "And you never told me?" he asked.

"No, and you never guessed, and I will never tell you." A museum colleague, another curator, had once cornered her in his office toward the end of an afternoon, bringing coffee and little cakes with him. He was an expert in Greek art and, in his wispy fashion, was working his way around to the Greek way of life and this and that and so forth, and she had permitted him to go up and down her body, which he did as though he were cleaning off a plaster cast of Venus with a feather duster. When it was all over, she had smiled sympathetically at him, straightened her dress, and thrown him out of the office. That was all, except for the ardent looks he had given her for the next month or two.

"How could you?" Grosbeck asked reproachfully.

"I did, though," she said, "and so have you. Two or three little tootsies and popsies every now and then, Harvey? I knew. But, then, you always made it up to me so beautifully in your dumb, obvious way. I love you dearly, Harvey, but I don't know how much I'm going to love you after Alice Forsythe."

"Madeline, you're mad," Grosbeck said, without much conviction. "In my condition?" He saw himself once more lying in a hospital bed, his hands clutching at the coverlet, surrounded by his dear ones barely able to suppress tears, blowing their noses, looking away from him. "The thread of my life that thin? Not knowing from day to day?" He looked past Madeline. "I forgot to take my pills. I'll just go get them."

"Stay where you are, Harvey. Pills or no pills, Harvey, I've come to one conclusion—that you're going to live forever—and another conclusion I've come to is that I don't know whether I can go on living with your dumb adventures. The mansions, the mansions—it's the classiest excuse I've ever heard out of you. And the most serious. But, let's be sensible. Let's see what comes of it. Then, I'll make up your mind."

"No, you mean you'll make up yours," Grosbeck said.

"Whatever," Madeline said. "Now, let's get to bed."

"I swear to you, Madeline . . ."

"Don't swear," Madeline said. "There's only one thing remotely amusing about this—you've been caught before you even got started."

Once again, the imp took hold of Grosbeck. "Wait a minute," he said, "there's something I have to show you." He went into the bedroom and returned with a business card in his hand. "Here," he said, "maybe this will help." The card said on it: DR. ARTHUR B. DEUTSCH, M.D. GENERAL OFFICE PSYCHIATRY. SUBSPECIALTY: PEOPLE OVER 40 WHO WONDER WHAT ON EARTH HAPPENED." Madeline smiled unhappily. A tear rolled down the side of her classic Mediterranean nose. "It's the real thing," he said. "Someone gave it to me in the office the other day. See? There's an address on it—Park Avenue in the Seventies, I should say—and a phone number. And it's good paper . . ."

"Ah, Harvey, jokes, always jokes. Did you tell your popsies jokes, too?"

"No," Grosbeck said. "They were no laughing matter, or rather they were, so there was no need to tell jokes, if you follow my line of reasoning."

"Harvey, some day you'll make a joke and the roof will fall in. I love you so. I hope you love me as much."

"Forever," he said, gravely. "When I die, I will die knowing that no one on earth ever loved you as much as I did and you will, too." Already he had moved himself to a funeral parlor. "My ashes—I'm planning to be cremated—will whisper it to you from their place on your dresser. Some of them, anyway. The rest I want scattered on the highest hill in Green-Wood cemetery overlooking the bay . . ." He was in full flight, but she stopped him.

"That's enough for one night, Harvey," Madeline said. Whatever deep distress she might have felt she no longer showed. She got him up from his chair, put an arm around his waist and led him off slowly and gently to bed.

21

It is difficult to deal with an obsessed man, worse in the case of one who, like Grosbeck, insisted doggedly on learning from what he called "experience." The mere fact that he seldom did, did not deter him from snuffling after "experience," something that, older and still dumb, he was about to do with Alice Forsythe. God's Fool, embracing life until it bit him in the nose. Once, many years before, he had wandered disconsolately between marriages, smarting from failure, unattended, frenetic, in search of pleasures which vanished in mirage, upset his stomach, expanded his reading, shrank his field of vision, and froze his blood. The first marriage had been a scourge, but one to which he had clung until, surrounded in the bush by the Fuzzy-Wuzzies, he had fired the last round from his smoking Lee-Enfield, dropped it, and been run through by a spear. He had bound up the gaping wound and plunged into a second disaster out of which Madeline, for her sins, had plucked him without his even realizing that the "experience" had been hers, not his.

So scarifying had been the intervals that he had decided, but only grudgingly, to take the advice of a friend and see a psychiatrist. "It can't hurt, can it?" the friend argued reasonably.

"Anything can hurt," Grosbeck said. "I could be deflected from my course."

"What course?" the friend asked Grosbeck, looking around the furnished apartment on the West Side in which Grosbeck was then living, severely constrained by alimony payments and the support of three children whom he loved so that they returned it. Socks and shorts dripped from a rope strung over the sink. There were holes in at least half the socks. Grosbeck had sewed the other half, but he might as well not have made the effort. The toes resembled the window bars in a lazaretto. The wallpaper was covered with a strikingly inferior floral design intertwined with endless repetitions of an eighteenth-century lady and gentleman displaying some sort of courtesy to each other. There were water stains on the yellowing ceiling, and no food in the refrigerator save for cans of frozen orange juice, which he spooned up because he could never tell when the water in the sink would run hot or cold. There were piles of books and magazines on the floor and whorls of gray dust, too many articles of clothing packed into a closet that was too small, no rug (had he been so inclined, he could have boasted about the good hardwood floors), a bathtub and shower sized for dwarfs, a gas range on which Grosbeck never cooked because he could not. He slept on the couch, since it saved him the trouble of making the bed. And to reach this wretched eyrie he had to climb four flights of wooden stairs. They sagged and creaked whenever Grosbeck mounted them (always risking a bad fall because of the loosened banisters), which was as seldom as possible, since he had become ingenious enough to find the bed of one girl or another to sleep in a few nights a week and to leave changes of clothing in her apartment.

What finally sent Grosbeck to the psychiatrist was none of these things but a fantasy that entered his mind in the middle of the night after leaving one of the sad, hungry girls he had been seeing. In the elevator going down, there had entered his head the picture of one of those ancient Swiss mechanical clocks: the hour strikes, the cuckoo comes forth. Beneath the cuckoo, two tiny wooden figures emerge on tracks beneath arches. The tock and tick cause the two figures to nod at each other jerkily, left, right, and upward in anticipation of the cuckoo. But something has gone wrong with the clockwork. The figures bump into each other, back away, and bow. Then, the man figure advances, bows once more to the rigid woman figure, removes his head, lets the head fall to the floor, and then falls off the track after it.

The next day, Grosbeck telephoned the psychiatrist. He turned out to be another of Grosbeck's "experiences," a brief one. The man had broad shoulders, wore a tightly fitting double-breasted suit, smoked a fat cigar that suited his fat face, seemed to have difficulty keeping his eyes open (although he saw through Grosbeck with perfect clarity), kept his hands folded over his paunch and rocked back and forth in a wine-colored vinyl armchair. His desk was cleared of everything but a large round glass ashtray with a wooden base and a box of tissues on a desk pad of fake green leather with a fake border of gold-colored cartouches. He wore a pen-and-pencil set in his outside breast pocket, like a carpenter, and glasses thick as two jelly jars. "How do you do, Mr. Grosbeck," he said, putting out five thick fingers. Grosbeck shook the limp hand. "I'm Dr. Schwartz."

"I know," Grosbeck said. "Your name is on the door and you're in the telephone book. And I called you up and made an appointment and came here. Remember?"

Dr. Schwartz shrugged and closed his eyes. "Have a seat," he said, pointing across the desk.

"You *must* be a psychiatrist," Grosbeck said. "I know you've got a medical degree, but no couch. What happened? Never go the whole way to psychoanalyst? Lose your nerve? Give a patient an opinion? Offer advice? Couldn't afford the couch and the towel service?"

The psychiatrist opened his eyes—they were mild and amused—and looked at Grosbeck. "You're being gratuitously nasty, Mr. Grosbeck. And on such short acquaintance. But, after all, we're here to listen to your story, isn't that so? What seems to be bothering you?"

"None of your business," Grosbeck said.

"Then, why are you here?" the psychiatrist asked. "I charge fifty dollars for fifty minutes." He frowned, plucked a tissue out of the box on his desk, blew his nose and dropped the tissue into a fake-leather basket at the side of the desk. "Care for one?" he asked Grosbeck, pushing the box toward him.

"No, thank you," Grosbeck said. "I blew my nose before I came in." He looked belligerently at the psychiatrist. "Your doorman seemed to think I was some kind of nut," he said.

"I'm sure you're imagining that, Mr. Grosbeck," Dr. Schwartz said. "Are you a nut?" His cigar had gone out. He opened a drawer in the desk and removed a box of kitchen matches. "I find," he said, "lighters and book matches don't work very well with cigars. Feel free to smoke yourself, Mr. Grosbeck. Remember, you are free to do anything you wish here—except destroy the furniture or try to hit me. I'm bigger than you are. A little out of shape, but stronger, too. Suppose we get on with it, Mr. Grosbeck, shall we?" He added, "It's your life, isn't it, and there's obviously something disturbing you or you wouldn't be here, would you?" The tip of the cigar glowed ferociously.

"Let's get one thing straight," Grosbeck said, "I don't go around in the subway pushing up against little girls. Little boys, either. I did use to go to burlesque a lot when I was in high school." The psychiatrist nodded, blinked, was all attention.

"That enough for you?"

"I don't see how, Mr. Grosbeck. I don't even know what you do."

"I work for a newspaper," Grosbeck said. "Been married twice, live alone, hate it, sleep somewhere else whenever the opportunity arises. I see my children whenever I can. Their mothers don't give me much trouble about that, but just let me be late with a payment! I bet you hear a lot of that, eh?"

Smoke eddied in the gray room. "You used to play football?" Grosbeck asked.

"Soccer," said the doctor. "Weekend golf now."

"You could stand to take off a few pounds," Grosbeck said. "How come you don't wear a beard?"

"You're being childish, Mr. Grosbeck. I came in early to see you. You told me it was an emergency. I will have ten minutes to shave between you and my next patient."

"You're trying to make me feel even guiltier, aren't you? The load I'm carrying now isn't big enough to satisfy you?"

"Think of it any way you like, Mr. Grosbeck, but you haven't even begun to tell me what that load is." He placed the cigar carefully in the ashtray, and, putting the tips of his fingers together, began playing Here Is the Church, Here Is the Steeple, Open The Doors and Let in The People."

"I'm tired of your fucking patience, Doctor," Grosbeck said. "Why don't you just lose your temper? I have."

"Ah," said the doctor.

"Ah, my ass," Grosbeck replied. "We're not going to get anywhere this way."

"Which way do you want to get, Mr. Grosbeck?"

"Out of here," Grosbeck said. Dr. Schwartz said nothing. "I apologize," Grosbeck said, "but I haven't got three or four years to go through toilet training, masturbation, my mother and father, my insufferable family . . ."

"Insufferable?"

"I'm exaggerating."

"But, you did say insufferable," the doctor pointed out.

"Doctor," Grosbeck said, "you sure went after that like a dog after a bone. No, I'm sorry, this isn't for me."

"What is, then?" the doctor asked. "What happened to the emergency which brought me in here unshaved? And you in a panic. Yes, in a panic. Isn't there a great deal you have to tell me? Aren't there all sorts of possibilities?"

"Doctor," Grosbeck said, straightening his tie, "evangelism doesn't become you. Confession doesn't become me. I guess I'm just going to have to stumble along best as I can."

"You still have ten minutes, Mr. Grosbeck. Shall I make another appointment for you?"

"No," Grosbeck said, "but I would like a cigarette and you might as well finish that thing you're smoking. You know, it rather becomes you." He sat, sunk in himself.

"You got any coffee?" Grosbeck asked.

"Just instant," the doctor said. "And black. I don't have a refrigerator to keep milk in. There *is* a gas ring for hot water." Dr. Schwartz looked at him.

"Are you judging me?" Grosbeck asked.

The doctor shook his head. "Shall I put you down for next Tuesday at a somewhat later hour?"

"No," said Grosbeck in a low voice. "Best not. It's not for me. I didn't mean to insult you, believe me I didn't. But, I think if I kept coming here, I might learn a lot of things I'd just as soon not. Just as bad, I might not learn anything at all."

"That's the chance we all take, Mr. Grosbeck," the doctor said quietly.

"Not at fifty bucks a pop, Doctor. The prospect of learning too much or nothing at all is more than I can contemplate. I regret having disturbed you."

"Mr. Grosbeck," the doctor said, "I don't like making snap judgments, but since you won't be back, I will. In the short time you've been here, you have said 'sorry' and 'regret,' things like that . . . It is my belief—remember, I said it was a snap judgment—that you have done very little that most of us have not. I may be fat, I may smoke cigars, which you can't abide, but I am not stupid. You are Jewish, are you not?"

"Sort of."

"Then," said Dr. Schwartz, "you are at least as Calvinistic a Jew as any I have ever seen in my life. You may very well punish yourself into collapse. I would not say this ordinarily, certainly not on a first visit. But, I think you are, essentially, a kind man, full of *mishigas*, full of notions which have no more to do with the middle-class New York City life you lead than the man in the moon. I wish you well. I wish I could spare you pain, but you are as closed as a locked safe. Possibly, someone else could do better with you, but not I. Our time is up. I will send you a bill. I wish you well. I have probably said too much and I may be all wrong, but there *is* something about you which made me do it." He shook hands once more with Grosbeck, limply, and turned his back on him as Grosbeck put on his coat and left the office. Still another inconclusive departure, Grosbeck thought. Still no answers.

One day, following the afternoon Editorial Meeting, Greenspan asked Harvey whether he had come to any conclusions about the mansions, and Grosbeck told him, no, he hadn't, needed more time, intended to see Alice Forsythe again, had some more questions he wanted to put to her, might want to have a word with Varney, although he didn't know how much good that might do ("He wants to go over us like a steamroller") but remember we still stand for something in this city, there's a couple of other pieces I want to get out of the way meanwhile—wriggling like a grasshopper on a pin . . .

"You can't stall forever, Harvey. The paper hasn't got that long to make up its mind about that project. It hasn't, you know, and we have to hear what you think about it. Not that yours would be the last word on the subject, but there *is* more than one thing to be said about it. I grant you it's not Vietnam—we all understand that—but it is a matter of great civic interest—not least of all to The Publisher. It'll change the face of the avenue, and do we want to do that? He's of two minds about the thing, and we've got to help him make up his mind. Whither he goest, there go we." He paused. "You sure there isn't something else on your mind?"

"Marty, you know me better than that."

"Yes, I do, deedy I do. Let me give you two pieces of advice. Speed it up and be discreet." He came around from his side of the conference table and put an arm over Grosbeck's shoulders and said, only half joking, "I wouldn't want to see a good man go wrong. You think I'm kidding? A man with a bad heart, nice wife—the last, I hope—and a position of respect in the—ah—community. Gets invited to all sorts of cocktail parties now that he's a public figure. People hang on his every word, read back to him everything he's written, think he's somebody. But only as long as they can find his name on that page."

"Marty, I think this is an intrusion into my affairs." He didn't carry that off too well.

"It certainly is, Harvey. I'm trying to save you from yourself."

"Marty, I find you . . . I don't know what I find you . . ."

"No, but I've found *you*, Harvey, and I say this in all kindness. If you have to mix business with pleasure, you ought to show a profit. I didn't get to be managing editor jumping up and down on the bedsprings with some press agent trying to sneak a client into The Newspaper. It gets around. There's no use pretending it doesn't happen to a lot of us and where do they wind up? In the gutter. You're a talented man, Harvey. Conform, conform. Wear blinders. Keep your eyes straight ahead. I say all this out of who knows what misbegotten liking I have for you."

"Ah, you did take me out of the gutter, wiping windshields with a dirty rag on the Bowery, didn't you? Aren't we being preachy today, *mon vieux*, not to say fatherly? I know what bedsprings *you* bounced on, Marty."

"I don't deny it," Greenspan said, "but they *were* the right ones and with whatever else I had it got me where I am now. Also, remember, one false move that anybody else finds out about and it's your ass, not mine, and no worse for me than a reflection on my occasionally bad judgment."

"I'll be sure not to stain the good name of The Newspaper *or* my pants, Marty."

Grosbeck returned to his office, his skin crawling, locked the door and telephoned Alice Forsythe, all the while looking around the room as though he could be overheard. The first thing she said was, "Who? Oh, Harvey Grosbeck. Why're you whispering?"

"I'm not whispering."

"Then, you must have a cold?"

"No, damn it, I don't have a cold. I'd like to see you."

"You want to talk about the mansions again?" she asked. "I thought we had said just about everything there was to say about them."

"No," he said, "I just want to see you." At her end of the phone, she signed some papers and waited. "I thought," Grosbeck said, "we might have dinner." The tone of his voice was shy as he could make it, his meaning unmistakable. But he invested the word "dinner" with a blatancy so steamy that it fogged his glasses. It was part of his vestigial charm to some women that he could still appear to be offering a girl a hot dog on a Sunday afternoon in Central Park and proposing that the two of them wander over to watch the lawn bowlers when what he actually had in mind was a tumble in the underbrush of The Ramble.

In her own feral way, Alice Forsythe was tickled. "Dinner," she said. "That would be nice. What did you have in mind? And when?"

"I was thinking tonight," he said.

"Isn't that awfully short notice, Harvey? I'm teasing," she added.

"Maybe some little out-of-the-way place?" he asked.

This time she could not keep from laughing. "I haven't heard anyone say that for twenty years. There isn't any such thing anymore. Your newspaper took care of that." She went through a box of file cards on her desk and nodded her head. "I've got just the right out-of-the-way place for you, Harvey. My place. I'll cook, but you'll have to give me until about nine o'clock." She had no intention of cooking; the box of file cards had yielded up one of those private caterers she called in for just such evenings.

"You're sure you're free?" he asked.

"I'm free," she said, "but what about you? What about Madeline?"

"As a matter of fact," Grosbeck said, "she's out of town for the night, one of those seminars on the future of the past."

"Then, nobody will be inconvenienced, will they?" Alice Forsythe said.

"Not in the least," Grosbeck said. "See you at nine." He telephoned Madeline. "Sweetheart," he said, "it looks as though I'm going to be late tonight. You know what Greenspan can be like . . ." For an instant, Grosbeck felt as though he had plunged a knife into Madeline, then tied a noose suspended from a chandelier around his neck and jumped off a chair. "Don't wait up for me," he said to Madeline.

"You sound so strange," Madeline said.

"Just a cold, sweetheart," he said. "Greenspan's on everyone's back these days."

"I hate to think of you sitting all alone in that gloomy place. Call me from time to time if you can."

"I will," Grosbeck assured her, "even if it's two in the morning."

"That late, you think, Harvey? I hope you'll have a cab waiting for you downstairs."

"I've already arranged for one," Grosbeck lied. "I think of everything."

"Miss you," Madeline said.

"Miss *you*, darling," Grosbeck said automatically. "Sleep well. Come to think of it, maybe I better not call. No point getting you up at some ungodly hour."

Gehenna and Paradise. Grosbeck had about four hours to weigh up the consequences of what he was about to do. The bowels of his compassion for his wife, the cloaca of lust for a woman he barely knew ran free; he sank gratefully and guiltily into what he hoped would be a dangerous adventure. He felt constricted in the chest, weak at the knees; his forehead itched; he thought there might be a hole in one of his socks and took off his shoes to make certain there was not in either one. He had time to kill. He undressed and took a shower in the bathroom of his office. He looked at himself naked in the full-length mirror and saw, first, Jean Gabin, and then Lon Chaney as The Phantom of the Opera. Violins echoed in his ears; then the honking of tubas made fun of him. Whatever dignity might have attached itself to him through his crusade for the mansions had left his mind. A man in rut is a cartoon. He thought he was unique. He took himself seriously. He left the building and decided he would walk uptown and come to a slow boil. Was that advisable? Would it not be better to husband his strength? Or, if he breathed deeply and walked slowly, would that be to his advantage?

Alice Forsythe made her preparations to receive Grosbeck with rather more care than he had exercised, the extent of her experience being what it was. As an architect, she had not confined herself simply to renderings, elevations, trusses, cantilevers, vaults, and reinforced concrete. As a woman, she had run through several dozen men of varying ages, almost all of whom she had gauged accurately.

The one mistake she conceded herself was a marriage at a relatively tender age. This one had been to a muscular specimen with a straight nose and large biceps in an occupation so vague that he was unable or unwilling to explain it to her. They went out a lot and had no visitors. He was forever getting telephone calls in the middle of the night from people in California, Texas, Queens, and Hong Kong, and, since she had now and then answered the telephone, she had heard Italian accents, Greek accents, and once, in the purest and hoarsest New York, this: "Where is the son of a bitch?"

"Here," she had said, one third in fear, another in hope, a third in curiosity.

Her husband had taken the telephone from her and talked into it briefly. When he hung up, he had said to her, "From now on, I'm not home. You hear?"

"What *do* you do?" she had asked him, rubbing his biceps.

"I sell take-out oil from Libya," he had answered.

He had twice been indicted for interstate fraud and had bought his way out with ease. Then, pouf!, he vanished one day. He had reappeared later, when she was at work, with a moving van, bribed the doorman, and, with two bulky assistants, had emptied out the apartment.

She had obtained a divorce in the Dominican Republic. The last she had heard of him was a year or so later when his body had been found stuffed in the trunk of a late-model Lincoln (his own) near a sewage-disposal plant, his hands bound and the back of his head missing: two rounds of No. 8 buckshot. His killers had been considerate enough to leave the shotgun and several unused shells with the body. The police wrote him off. He had been as much a casualty of industry as any coal miner in Kentucky.

She had been rather more choosy after that. As for Grosbeck, she had decided that, while a rascal, he was also delicate, probably a little brittle with age and long use, not unlike a fourteenth-century Tingware *blanc de chîne* footed cup (Yung Cheng period), a subtle blend of pink and ivory, swallows on one side (for happiness), and, on the other, a stag amid pine trees, head upthrust, sniffing the wind (erect below, she hoped), a symbol of long life if not necessarily of great stamina.

With this in mind, she had instructed the caterers to bring a celery remoulade, a salad of chicory and arugula (skillfully dressed with French cold-pressed walnut oil and Italian balsamic vinegar. She had arranged for a *pâté de campagne* (not too large; his stomach was probably no longer the celebrator of gluttony it might once have been), a *boeuf en daube* (tiny morsels of good beef, tiny carrots glazed with sherry, tiny *pommes de terre* and the remotest suspicion of garlic—in short, meat and potatoes, but easy on the guts). And, if he could handle it, there was a kiwi tart and a *crème brulée*, espresso to bring him down, Armagnac or Courvoisier to round things off. Then, there was the matter of costume.

On the way uptown, Grosbeck simulated a casualness that would have attracted the attention of any cop, had there been any around. He looked into shop windows and whistled. He glanced over his shoulder frequently, waved off cab drivers, picked up a piece of paper and threw it into a wastebasket. He walked so slowly that more than one young woman was tempted to offer him help; if they did not, it was because they caught a glimpse of his fixed glare and absent smile and shied away uneasily from what could have been a mugger in a Burberry. He found himself humming, " 'We tried it on the sofa,/ We tried it on the chair,/ We tried it on the window sill,/ But we couldn't do it there./ We tried it on the back porch,/ We tried it in the hall./ We tried it in the living room, backed against the wall . . .' " He sounded like an Indian with a new set of mantras. He rose and fell inside his pants. He trod Madison Avenue, Sixtieth Street, Park Avenue and Seventieth Street, Lexington Avenue and Eighty-first, remarking to himself on this building and that. His fingers became chilled. He should have worn gloves. His head was so hot, by contrast, that he did not miss a hat.

Half an hour before he was due, he had run out of ways to make time pass more rapidly. He stopped in a bar, which he knew to be a mistake. The place was chic, fetid with loneliness amid the presence of dozens of men and women pretending to roister. He ordered a bloody mary with a double shot "in as small a glass as you have," he said, "and, please, no garbage, maybe just a twist of lemon." He was about to tell the bartender that lime would have been all wrong, but the drink appeared before him too fast. He drank reflectively (he thought)—finishing the drink in about two minutes—and strength (false) poured into his veins in an Atlantic tide. Hadn't Dr. Salomon adjured him to have a drink every evening? Shertainly he had. He left money on the bar, waved a good night at the bartender's back and went the rest of the way to Alice Forsythe's briskly. (He thought.) By God, by Zeus, it was good to be alive, Leopold Bloom.

The doorman, upon making a snotty examination of him, then made an inquiry upstairs and motioned Grosbeck through the door with the deference a foreman might have accorded a millhand about to punch in on the night shift. Grosbeck, of course, promptly forgot the number of her apartment (he got the floor right) and Alice Forsythe called to him from the other end of the hall in a voice that, to Grosbeck, was the tinkle of chimes, the parting of beaded curtains in a Bangkok whorehouse. He seemed also to hear the chunking of paddles below on the muddy waters of the Nam Chao Phraya, but it was only the banging of steam pipes.

"This way, Harvey."

"Where did I go wrong, Alice?" Grosbeck asked, taking both of her hands in the doorway and kissing them back and forth.

"You'd better come in," she said. "It's cold out there."

"It is, isn't it?" he asked. "The weather's been so changeable." So begins the *Kama Sutra*.

Alice Forsythe had taken pains with her appearance. She had put on an at-home gown of forest-green silk, floor length, gathered well above the waist and with a neckline that plunged recklessly. It was also slit up the thigh at the right, and she wore nothing beneath it. It set off her hair, which she kept a persistent dark blond. She wore gold mules with moderately high heels, keeping in mind that Grosbeck was no giant, and a minimum of jewelry, a cabochon emerald ring, a thin gold chain, thinking that a certain amount of roughhouse might ensue in the course of the evening. She had painted her fingernails and toenails a deep brownish-red, an appetizing crème caramel, matching that with her lipstick. She had combed her hair out. She was ready.

Grosbeck was not. He had committed a reckless oversight. Did history condemn Achilles for his naked heel? Dr. Salomon had prescribed an anticoagulant twice daily to thin Grosbeck's blood, so that clots would not block off the relevant arteries and veins, deprive his lion's heart of oxygen, and pinch off his life. While he had encouraged Grosbeck to drink in moderation, Dr. Salomon, knowing his customer to be both inattentive and a medical idiot, had also warned him of the abnormal speed with which alcohol would reach his brain. Grosbeck had noticed lately that it took relatively little to render him a bull in the head and a nullity in bed. He firmly believed that to be no more than coincidence, that Dr. Salomon must have been talking about other people. The stop at the bar could not have been more effective in achieving both ends. "Alice," he said fervently as he dropped his coat on the floor, "you look like a goddesh thish evening." He moved to kiss her on the lips, walked over his coat, and, as she bent down to pick it up, stumbled into pastel-colored air. "Where are you?" he asked.

"Just hanging up your coat, my dear," she said. "It needed a little brush, too," she added, getting his footprints out. "Here I am, over here, at the closet." He followed her there and stood on tiptoes to imprint a burning kiss on her neck. A drop of saliva fell to his chin and he wiped it away with the back of a hand before returning to her neck. She stiffened ever so slightly under his ministrations, turned, took his head in both hands, bent down and kissed him on the lips, embosomed him as she kissed, removed his jacket, opened the top button of his shirt, and loosened his tie. "There," she said, "that's better, isn't it?" Grosbeck stood swaying and pigeon-toed with pride. Jesus, thought Alice Forsythe, was I wrong? Will he make it through the night? She smiled at him and sat him down in a love seat so deep and soft that one of its cushions almost wrapped him around like a vest.

"Would you like a drink?" she asked. "Champagne? Something harder?"

Grosbeck extricated himself from the cushion and struggled forward. "Champagne, I think. Ish shelebratory, 'propriate. Shealing of the bonds between ush. I'll open it," he said, trying to get to his feet.

She pushed him back. "Let me do it. Total guesthood tonight."

There's no such thing as *partial* guesthood, Grosbeck thought. Forget it, he told himself. She returned with an open bottle and two glasses, which she put on a glass-topped coffee table with chrome-steel legs. It resembled a performing platform for a seal. "Now, would you give me one?" she asked.

"Darling," he said, managing to fill both glasses and leave the table dry, "bucket to put it in?"

"I didn't think it would be necessary, Harvey," she said. "It'll be gone soon, don't you think?"

"An' more where that came from?" Grosbeck asked with a wink that made it appear as though he were attempting to keep his eye from falling out. He wore the most curious expression on his face: its features had slid into a pile composed of equal parts of archness, adolescent anticipation, and saddest of all, misgiving. His eyes bulged with determination. Yet, however hard he tried to bring to mind the wonderfully sordid, riotous breakfast scene between The Late Mister Jonathan Wild the Great and his doxie of a wife, Laetitia, in eighteenth-century London, the best he could arrive at was the spectacle of a traveling salesman in the late twentieth century in a mirrored motel in Omaha with an off-duty barmaid, a bottle of scotch, his airline tickets on the dresser, and a television set with dirty movies. The life of the mind is a painful one.

Alice Forsythe urged the pâté on him. He took a small piece on a Bath biscuit and his stomach waved a monitory finger at him. He fumbled at her breasts as though he were weighing grapefruit in a supermarket. He nuzzled at her neck and bit it. His teeth closed on her chain. He drew back, alarmed, rolling his tongue over his upper denture, fearful he might have cracked the chancy mechanical marvel that had cost him twenty-five hundred dollars. It had slipped a little but his tongue told him, beyond that, it was intact.

"Anything wrong, Harvey?" Alice asked. "Nothing, nothing," he said, still preoccupied as his tongue slipped it back in place. The abyss between loose bridgework and lovemaking is beyond calculation. Nevertheless, he gathered himself. "Could I trouble you for the last of the champagne?" he asked. He gave up her neck and stuck with her breasts as she obliged him. Playing for time, he dredged up a classical architectural metaphor. "I see you," he said, running an exploratory hand up one thigh, just short of where it met the other, "in the words of Vitruvius"—that ought to get her attention—"'Firmitas, utilitas, venustas.' Commodity, firmness, and delight."

Now, there's a new one, thought Alice Forsythe. Perhaps he'll go the distance. "How charming," she said. "Are you sure you're all right?"

"Never better," Grosbeck said. She placed a hand between *his* legs and raised her eyebrows. Maybe, she told herself.

Grosbeck slid off the love seat, knelt before her and ran both hands up her legs. She moved enough to permit her gown to slide up and to give him the idea that he was having a profound effect on her. He kissed the place between her legs and sat back on his haunches, a tiny, curling hair between his lips, which he wiped away with his forearm. Ah love, could you and I conspire to change this sorry scheme of things entire . . .

"Shall we eat?" Alice asked. "You must be hungry." She was not entirely remorseless and perhaps things would get better. He had stopped slurring his words, she noted. Grosbeck ate without much interest, fire in his head, ice between his legs. He took strength from the meat and potatoes, picked at his salad, passed up the kiwi tart for the *crème brulée*, came back strongly with the espresso and poured a few drops of Armagnac into it. Confidence entered his veins again, but there must be no lingering. It was touch and go.

Grosbeck labored under certain other disadvantages about which Alice Forsythe knew nothing, nor did Grosbeck intend to regale her with the clinical details. (Madeline, his wife and confidante, knew all of them and adjusted her behavior accordingly.) In addition to the anticoagulant, Dr. Salomon had provided Grosbeck with a diuretic which, maddeningly, sent him tearing off to the toilet not only often but at the most inauspicious times. At the same time, the doctor had informed him (with a ruthless finger in a rubber glove) that, like most men of his age, he had developed an enlarged prostate. The net effect of this was an unending, irritable quarrel between prostate and bladder. The bladder commanded, "Pee!" while the prostate decreed, "Thou shalt not pass!" Dribble, dribble, dribble was the best Grosbeck could do, and it depressed him inordinately, since the combination of these things interfered dismally with the gratification of his sexual urgings. There was nothing for it but to improvise as one does with a pinball machine. There was, as well, the pill the doctor made him take to regulate the beat of the heart which is apt to become wildly irregular in the commission of coitus.

Steam hissed in the pipes. Grosbeck imitated it, in lieu of passion. He took Alice by the arms and sank to the bed at her side. He was about to take his shoes off, but good manners dictated that he undress her first. He hauled up her legs and removed the mules. He picked at the gown, and she took it off, letting him think he had. She got his tie off and his shirt and pants and shoes, socks and shorts, and tossed them over her shoulder to the floor anyhow. He made great sucking noises as he kissed her lips and breasts. He crawled down her torso and kissed her between the legs again, coming away red-faced and blowing hard. She applied herself to him. They murmured and mumbled and rolled about. She ran a finger down his spine and stuck it up his behind. He felt the sharp pain he had when Dr. Salomon played hob with his prostate. "Excuse me,

Alice," he said through clenched teeth. (Four of them, on the bottom, were his.) "Bathroom?" he asked.

"Over there," she said, and lighted a cigarette. "Hurry back." He kissed her palm.

"I'm not kidding, Harvey," she said. "Hurry back."

It took him three minutes. He shook it and squeezed it and pulled at it. He looked down at it. It was a poor thing; it needed a splint. Standing over the bowl, working like a hod carrier, he thought of Alice Forsythe's breasts, legs, backside, lips, and neck. He got it over with, for the time being.

Back in the bedroom, he told himself, Easy does it, you're not on deadline. Alice Forsythe took him in her hand. She pressed herself against him and writhed. She dropped cigarette ashes on his head before remembering she had a cigarette between two fingers. Another metaphor, Grosbeck thought, brushing the ashes (and a single vicious spark in his hair) from his head, taking the cigarette away from her and throwing it into a potted plant on the window sill. His heart beat as though it were punching him in the chest. He ached from pelvis to buttocks and all the while he wore on his face a look of absorption so intense that it might have been thought he had died lifting a carton of rare books. He, too, tried to make the right noises, but they died in his throat with a croak. He had, indeed, as they say in Vermont, gone by. Had he, though? He would have Alice Forsythe if it were the last thing he did. Once more, he excused himself, ghastlily jaunty. This time, he belched loudly, which relieved him, and, out of some kind of physiological kindness, the prostate relented long enough to get rid of a stream which, he was firmly convinced, would otherwise have forced its way through his navel.

By now, Alice Forsythe had a better idea of what was going on, if not why, but, for reasons she would never be able to explain to herself, she was aroused and at least as determined to get Grosbeck through as he was. Additionally, she was not a bad woman. "Here, Harvey," she said. "You sit on the bed. I'll be right back." In a few minutes, she stood before him, so naked, so toothsome, so . . . with a cup of tea in her hand. The Puerto Rican lady God didn't know whether to laugh or cry, but She was so interested that She dropped everything else She was doing and a dozen people were murdered from coast to coast, to say nothing of how many in the rest of the world. "Drink this . . . slowly, Harvey," Alice said. Grosbeck sat foolishly on the edge of the bed sipping the tea.

"Would you mind if I smoked?" asked the fool of the universe.

"Not at all," she said, lighted one for him and set an ashtray next to him on the coverlet. "Now, drink your tea." As he did so, and smoked, she knelt before him, parted his legs and went to work on his poor twig. She was expert, and, before too long, she had made it into a slender branch, to the annoyance of the bladder and the prostate.

"There, now," she said with satisfaction. "I think we're about ready. I know *I* am."

"Hurry, hurry," he said, abandoning all pretense at abandon.

She took the cigarette and the teacup from him, put the ashtray on the night table, sat carefully down on him and began to move like a child on a carousel. She was surprised to find how much pleasure she was getting. Grosbeck was surprised to find that he had not fallen out of her. The laws of physics and physiology were being denied. He was even beginning to get large ideas. She worked earnestly, as though she were at a drafting table. He ruminated. She tired with the effort. His insides began to argue again. His brain exulted. She brought him off in five minutes and then lay calmly down on him, her breasts in his face.

He had the bad grace to say, "I can't breathe." It was over.

"Ingrate," she said tolerantly. "Rotten little man. *You* can't breathe!"

"Forgive me," he said. "It was wonderful. You'll never know."

"It was, wasn't it?" she said soberly. Hers was an access of tact, which was also a dismissal. As usual, Grosbeck did not recognize it.

He lay on the bed like a flattened carrot. "It's late, Harvey."

"How late?"

"Three o'clock. How are you going to explain this one?"

"Does it matter?" he asked, in his best romantic manner.

"Yes, it does," she said, deciding to give him one more tidbit. "You're insatiable, simply insatiable!" she said. She had awarded him the Victoria Cross. "What are you going to tell Madeline?"

"Leave it to me," said the carrot on the bed. "Something. I told you she was away tonight."

So you did, Alice thought, only she isn't. She slipped into a nightgown. "Come on, Harvey, you're going to have to go."

"So soon?" he asked. She pulled him into a sitting position. "Finish your tea." (It was cold and bitter.) "Get your clothes on." She gathered them up. "Shorts first," she said. "We mustn't forget anything."

"Don't rush me," Grosbeck said. He was a man, wasn't he? "Give me a chance to clean up."

"All right, Harvey," she said, patiently, "but don't take forever. I've got things to do in the morning too." Grosbeck tidied himself up and dressed slowly. Alice Forsythe tied his tie and shoelaces. She helped him into his jacket and coat and told him to sit in an armchair while she had the doorman call a cab for him.

"Why not an ambulance?" he asked, annoyed. She kissed him out the door affectionately and bade him a farewell unmistakable to anyone but Grosbeck. "It was lovely, Harvey. Lovely."

"Shall we see each other soon?" She nodded and touched his face. It cost neither of them anything.

Grosbeck let himself in at home to find Madeline waiting up for him. There were tears in her eyes. "Don't tell me where you've been, Harvey. I know." He tried to lie, but, stupid, honorable, desiccated specimen that he was, he simply fell off his kiddy car. It all came out in a rush and a tumble. She slapped his face. Hard. The blow hurt her. She took one of his hands and slapped her own face with it. "It will be a long time," she said, "before I forgive you. A long time. And a long time before I ever let you touch me again. And I will never believe you, not even about the way you feel about the mansions." What was she saying? She wasn't certain. Who is at times like this? "I'm not going to leave you because I love you and because I know you love me—even though I don't believe you—and because . . . Harvey, Harvey, you never did know how to take care of yourself. Alice Forsythe. A buzz saw, a grindstone."

"I've heard better analogies," Grosbeck said.

"For that alone," Madeline said, "I should throw you out. Stop editing me! This instant!" She turned to another subject. "Did you take all of your pills . . . ?"

Grosbeck thought of what to say to that. "Pills, pills, those goddamned pills." His voice grew low and soft. "Is that all you can think of, Madeline?"

"Right now, Harvey," Madeline said, "it's all I'd *better* think of. Go to bed. Alice Forsythe. ALICE FORSYTHE . . ."

"I can understand," he said.

"*You* can understand," Madeline said. "How quick you are, how bright, how percipient! Go to bed. I can't stand the sight of you."

"You coming to bed, too?" he asked.

"What!" she said. She stood with her hands on her hips, looking at him for a long while. "Why not. I suppose I might as well." Later in the night, he began to snore, and Madeline had to roll him over several times to get him to stop. She did not sleep. He had a single dream: a neon sign, with a single word on it, came toward him in the black. When it got close enough to him—in his dream, he reached for his glasses—it said, "Louse." Over and over, for the rest of the night: "Louse, louse, louse."

The meeting in Greenspan's office had been requested by Corydon
Varney. Varney himself had put through the call; there had been no
swordplay between secretaries and Greenspan understood the impli-
cations of that, but he could as well have done without it today.
Marty Greenspan was not the man to indulge in fantasy, as was
Grosbeck, but he had imagination enough to see before him something more than just four people selling something that meant very
much to them to someone of whose response they were not yet certain. There they were: the distended Varney asking permission to
smoke a cigar; at Varney's left, the egregious Marjorie Denman,
whose button Varney would push to speak; at Varney's right, his architect, Aram Kazanjian, whose face this day had taken on the texture of contaminated concrete—too much sand in the mixture, too
liquid for the time put aside for it to set (it would set imperfectly
and crumble); next to Marjorie Denman, the lawyer, Howard Tracy,
her husband, a life-size reproduction of a man in black and white on
plasterboard, prepared—again on Varney's push—to sway backward
and forward and utter texts out of lawbooks in an even, matter-of-
fact voice recorded elsewhere.

In Greenspan's presence were four predator birds of dark hue, with
long, curved, sharp beaks sitting above his head on a thick wire, on
confident claws and pink, knotted legs. Their beaks opened to reveal
white tongues and gray-red mouths waiting to shriek, then fly at him,
pick him to death and drink his blood. Grosbeck was not there. Alice
Forsythe was not there. "Mr. Greenspan," Varney began, "I think
you know why we're here today." He imparted as much unction to
his voice as he could. "It is a matter," he continued, looking past
Greenspan out the window, which gave upon the façade of a de-
cayed hotel, "of importance to all of us." He gestured expansively to
take in the entire room, to imply, as well, that he was speaking of all

of New York. "Our City, its past, its present, its future, its . . . its dynamics, the vibrancies of it, the . . . forgive me, I am making a speech, I suppose, but there are times when, in contemplating it, I cannot help myself . . ."

"I share your concerns, Mr. Varney," Greenspan said. "The Newspaper, no less. Isn't it possible, though, that we're all being a bit too formal? May I send for coffee? A drink?"

"Coffee would be nice," Varney said.

"Would tea be possible?" Marjorie Denman asked.

"Mr. Tracy?" asked Greenspan.

"It's near enough to lunch as to make no matter," said the voice back of the plasterboard Tracy. "A little scotch, no ice, no water."

"Certainly, certainly," Greenspan said. "And you, Mr. Kazanjian?"

"A little wine please . . . for the sake, ha ha, of my stomach . . ." Greenspan spoke into some void and the refreshments were brought by the oldest executive servant on The Newspaper, a thin man in gray trousers and a shiny alpaca coat who appeared through a narrow door elsewhere in the room, set things out on a table near a couch and vanished. He was as much a part of The Newspaper as any of its Gothic affectations. Greenspan waved his visitors from their place in front of his desk to the couch.

"Our errand is a simple one, Mr. Greenspan," Varney said.

"You've come to talk about the mansions," Greenspan said.

"The mansions *and* our great city," Varney amended.

"You find the two inseparable, do you, Mr. Varney?" Greenspan asked.

"I could not have put it better," Varney said.

"If I may," Marjorie Denman said, "we have a dream."

"I take it then," Greenspan said, "you've all been to the top of the mountain." Polite titters all around.

"All this bullshit," God, the Puerto Rican lady, said to Itself from Her position on the molded ceiling. So interested was She in what was going on that She had taken Her eyes off the least sparrow, Grosbeck.

"Let me make myself plain," Varney said. "We have devoted two years to this endeavor. We have acquiesced in what, in other social and political circumstances, we should have thought unreasonable. I will not say outrageous. We have expended our best efforts and we have satisfied the Landmarks Preservation Commission of our good intentions. You are familiar with the details. The mansions will not be pulled down . . ."

"No, merely gutted," Greenspan interrupted.

Varney was unperturbed. "The tower will simply rise above them, and, in the place of a single jewel on the avenue, there will be two, each flawless in its own way. The tug of the past will have been met, the needs of the future will have been satisfied. Ideal, ideal."

"What you mean, Mr. Varney," Greenspan said, ". . . I think I have it right, is that you're putting up a skyscraper and pasting the walls of the mansions around its base as a sort of anachronistic decoration entirely out of keeping with what you had in mind originally, that you were forced into what I see not even as a compromise but a profanation. Mind you, now, I didn't say I was against it or for it, but that's what it is, isn't it?" Varney shifted his body in an indication of dissent so subtle that he might almost have been thought to be agreeing with Greenspan. "I'm not an expert in these matters— that's what we've got Mr. Grosbeck and our critics for—but you won't deny, will you, that the mansions are no more than an expensive annoyance for you, aren't they?" Flutters of indignation from the other three, incredulity. In polite society, one simply did not talk that way. Greenspan began to enjoy himself. Varney took his little company in hand by looking at each one, enjoining all but himself to silence.

"I think you do me an injustice, Mr. Greenspan," Varney said. Howard Tracy finished his drink and put his attaché case back under a wing. Marjorie Denman finished her tea. Kazanjian gestured for more wine, but it was not forthcoming.

"I don't think so," Greenspan said, "and you don't, either. I think I do you all the justice to which you are entitled. Sir, you've got your banks, the unions; you've got City Hall, the Landmarks Preservation Commission—which was the easiest of all, though time-consuming; they're a prissy lot. There is nothing, I gather, that has been overlooked, no hitch of any kind, nothing to prevent you from bringing in the cranes and the bulldozers tomorrow morning. Why, then, have you come to me? What is there that I can do that would polish up this crown jewel of yours any further? On the basis of what I know about you, I find myself puzzled to find you here. And, in force," he added, looking at the others. Greenspan was not at all puzzled, only curious to hear what would be said next.

"An intangible, Mr. Greenspan," Varney said. "A good name, a name I intend to endure when I am long gone. *My* name. Approval, approbation, call it anything you like."

"I would not have thought you would care that much," Greenspan said. "I would have thought, rather, since we are being quite open with one another, that that would be, ummm, secondary. Aren't you expending a good deal of effort, not to say emotion, on something which will mean nothing to you when you are under the ground? Isn't it the here and now which interests you most?"

"Mr. Greenspan," Varney said, "it may be that I haven't explained myself fully. It is now, too, of which I am thinking. My health is reasonably good; I expect to be alive for, oh, say another twenty years, and the approval I want now while I am fully able to enjoy it, while my wife, of whose civic activities you may be cognizant, can take pride in it and in me, and my family, of whose Boston background you must know. My father was an Episcopal priest of standing, in whom love of God and pride of family carried equal weight. I cannot do less for him than he did for me." The lie was breathtaking. "This is the first building I have put up—will put up—which I have decided to name after myself. If that is presumptuous, I am in a numerous company, not the first to presume. Many men before me have behaved similarly, many of my contemporaries, more to come. Do you find that strange?" Greenspan said nothing.

"I come before you—I do not exaggerate—naked, Mr. Greenspan. I want The Newspaper's endorsement of what we are doing. Physically, financially, I do not need it—but there is that deep inside me which does, which demands it, will *have* it. There, I have bared myself. Before you, before my colleagues." He had done a superb imitation of the father he hated. His cigar had gone out and he lighted it again.

Greenspan rubbed his chin. "Mr. Varney," he said, "you surprise me." He was no more surprised than Varney had been spontaneous. The yearnings of monsters were something with which his years on The Newspaper had made Greenspan familiar. In his own way, he was no less a scoundrel than Varney. As a young reporter, he had carried bags full of cash to pay off sergeants and captains at stationhouses at Christmastime; he had conspired to conceal the frauds and peculations of mayors and commissioners when they, not the federal government, had been powerful men, because The Publisher wanted them under his thumb; he had seen the most ardent of reformers tire and work the other side of the street. And, in particular, he knew a great deal about the rise of Varney. As George Washington Plunkitt of Tammany Hall had once said, "I seen me opportunities and I took 'em." Also, he knew that, between them, Varney and The Publisher owned a great deal of real estate in the very neighborhood of The Newspaper, which had become a howling desert, a battlefield full of cries, a battlefield on which the police held no power, on which murder and mayhem and the nihilism of the mindless—armed, drugs in their veins, menace on their faces—destroyed whatever stood in their way, indifferent to their own end. But, he would tease.

"Mr. Varney," Greenspan said softly, "if I remember correctly . . ."—he looked down at the two sheets of paper on his desk— "among the first of the dealings with which you reached the eminence you now enjoy, was the purchase of almost an entire block of two- and three-story tenements in the neighborhood of"—he looked down at the sheets—"Third Avenue in the Fifties. I won't mince words, Mr. Varney. You turned them into whorehouses for as long as it suited you. The girls were all over the streets and in your doorways. They were a disgrace to nice people like yourself who lived in somewhat better buildings a good many blocks away. The police were taken care of, whatever city departments had to be stricken blind were; the amount of grease spread on the number of palms is incalculable. And, there they stayed until the real-estate market changed and you tore them down, put up thoroughly respectable, expensive, poorly built office buildings—with the able assistance, of course, of your architect, Mr. Kazanjian"—he nodded at Kazanjian—"and, lo, there you were, a rising monument to civic good instead of a super-pimp." He glanced down at the sheets again. "Shall I go on?" Greenspan asked. "I am not being accusatory. Some of our finest people . . ."

"No offense taken, Mr. Greenspan," Varney said. "I am used, by now, to the rough and ready ways of journalists. Only a fool would not be, but, as you say, some of our finest people . . . I mean to be no less than some whose beginnings were, possibly, a little different, but not that much . . . a matter of degree . . . but who were no less urgent in seizing the main chance . . . Whitneys, Belmonts, Astors, Vanderbilts, Harrimans, Lehmans, Rockefellers, Roosevelts, Delanos

. . . pillars, every one of them, of the community that is New York City. I am not entirely unacquainted with its history. I seem to remember a man named Ned Stokes shot one such pillar, Jim Fisk, for the love of Josie Mansfield on the grand staircase of the Broadway Central Hotel . . . pity it fell down . . . the National Baseball League was founded there also . . . and that Harry Thaw shot Stanford White over a drab named Evelyn Nesbit . . . in one of White's superb buildings. I am no metaphysician, Mr. Greenspan, so I have never attempted to reconcile the contradictory things people do. I could go on and on about many other such worthies who, in the intervals of shooting down miners and steel workers, set up foundations and charities, but I will not. I remind you only that I have shot no one, had no one killed, have led a life of comparative rectitude. That is a slight exaggeration, I suppose; I don't doubt you have a file of some kind on that. You newspaper people are so damned inquisitive." He smiled. "But, you cannot touch me, and I am in a position to be of some help to your Publisher."

"In what way?" Greenspan asked; he knew very well.

"Why," Varney said, "in the very fact that the two of us have so much in common"—the smile grew broader—"very much apart from the fact that he entertains his mistress in an apartment in this very citadel of uprightness, your newspaper—only, of course, on those nights when his presence is required, when there are overriding editorial decisions to be made, when the future of The Republic is in the balance and a firm hand must be on the tiller. I know . . . I think his wife must know . . . where that hand is on such nights and what tiller guides him. If I sound a bit florid in my exposition, lay it to the example of the father from whose pulpit resounded so many rounded eloquences that I could scarcely avoid picking up some of them. They are often difficult to suppress."

Varney leaned forward. "But, more to the point, The Newspaper owns a good deal of property around it. So do I. I have noticed lately that The Newspaper has devoted a great deal of space to a proposed revision of the zoning laws, which would shift the emphasis of construction from the East to the West Side, which would, in the course of time, change the face of the West Side, eliminating the cesspool of degeneracy and danger which it is now to something more to the liking of your Publisher, certainly to his profit—the tax exemptions would be most agreeable—and to that of the people of the City of New York. There are good hotels and office buildings to be put up and infestations to be extirpated, the streets made safe, commerce expanded, a flowering of the West Side in a manner not seen since the creation of The Ladies Mile well over a hundred years ago. The world moves on, Mr. Greenspan, and your Publisher and I are in a position to give it a nudge. I will not go into tedious detail. All of it has been published in The Newspaper. I could add, without being harsh, *fulsomely*. What more fruitful alliance could there be than between my interests and those of your Publisher? I think I do not make the point too strongly when I say that, between us, and others, we might drive the devil out and replace him with a vision— if not of heaven—only my father would have expected that—but of a city in redemption. I make so bold as to say that I am what your Publisher has been seeking, probably without even knowing it."

Greenspan was deeply impressed with the performance. "What you are proposing," he said, "is *news* coverage *and* an editorial— perhaps more than one—favorable to *your* plans, in return for which . . ."

"You could not have put it more succinctly, Mr. Greenspan," Varney said. "Trust you newspaper fellows to do that." He stubbed out his cigar and looked from one to another of the birds of prey with him.

Greenspan was not yet ready to let go. "Let me ask you, in all candor, Mr. Varney, Miss Denman, Mr. Kazanjian, Mr. Tracy—you, especially, since you are a lawyer—isn't that a form of conspiracy, of bribery, of the suborning of the independence of thought of a great newspaper? I realize," Greenspan concluded, "it may not be prosecutable." Tracy shrugged. His wife—who had kept her maiden name —crossed her hands over her chest and goggled. Kazanjian giggled.

Varney answered. "It is all of those things, Mr. Greenspan," he said. "Has it ever been any other way? I think we understand each other. I doubt you think less of me for it or more of yourself. It is the way the world is. I have adduced examples enough. Cabals of men, out of view, more or less, out of the light. But, for the greater good, the greater good. It is what history and great cities are made of: deals. Let's make a deal, as they say on television."

"I take it," Greenspan said, "your Miss Forsythe was unable to make any headway with Mr. Grosbeck."

"I regret to say not," Varney said. "Persuasive as she is, she found him adamant—in that respect, at least."

"What do you mean, 'in that respect'?" Greenspan asked.

Varney permitted himself an indulgent smile. "I'm afraid," he said, "that she confined herself to the aesthetics rather than the practicalities of the thing. Mr. Grosbeck was not to be budged. She found him to be a . . . for lack of a better word, I say 'purist' . . . a purist much to be praised for his singlemindedness, but utterly intransigent. Impractical. A dreamer in that respect. But, not in all respects."

"What are the other respects?" Greenspan asked.

"I hesitate to say," Varney said.

"No, you don't. You haven't hesitated to say anything yet."

"Then, I shall come right out with it, Mr. Greenspan. I don't have to tell you that there is, in the most high-minded of us, a nagging of the flesh which will not be subdued. Mr. Grosbeck, I am afraid, is all too human for all of his principles."

"You mean," Greenspan said, "she took him to bed? To get his approval?"

"That is the first time you have misunderstood me, Mr. Greenspan," Varney said. "Rather, it was the other way 'round. He pursued her—diligently, may I add, and with whatever success I leave the two of them to judge."

Greenspan slapped his desk with the palm of a hand, half in annoyance, half in amusement. "I knew that was going to happen," he said. "My apologies to the lady."

"You need not bother yourself about that," Varney said. "As I have said—sorrowfully—we are all of us, are we not, flawed, frail, subject to the winds. But, I have reason to believe you will hear no more from that quarter."

"Why not?" Greenspan asked.

"I don't mean to be indiscreet, Mr. Greenspan, but the impression I received was that Mr. Grosbeck's reach exceeded his grasp. I am not sure he knows that. He returns to you relatively unsullied, and, as you must know, absolutely uncorrupted in his principles. Miss Forsythe proposed no deal; nothing was farther from Mr. Grosbeck's mind. Had it been otherwise, we should not be here today." He rose. "I fear we have taken up too much of your time. You've been very kind." As though at a signal, the other three rose, the flat lids of their glassy eyes opening and closing, their feathers smoothed and neat. "Good afternoon, good afternoon, good afternoon, good afternoon," they said one after the other, "Mr. Greenspan, Mr. Greenspan, Mr. Greenspan, Mr. Greenspan."

Greenspan showed them out under the arch commemorating The Founder, past Emily, upon whom it was not lost that great decisions had been made—she could tell that from the very posture of all of them—and to the elevator. Fingers were extended in handshakes, the elevator door was opened, and they disappeared—Varney, Mrs. Tracy-Denman, Kazanjian, Tracy. Greenspan said, "Emily, would you see if The Publisher is in and if he will see me? And would you tell him it won't wait. Is he alone?"

"I think he is," she said.

"Tell him I'd like about fifteen minutes with him," Greenspan said.

She bowed her head and telephoned The Publisher's secretary. "Yes," she said, "he'll see you."

"Thank you, Emily," Greenspan said and walked down the hall to The Publisher's office. He was slightly more formal with The Publisher than he had been with Varney and the others, but no less at ease. Recapitulation.

"That Varney is some piece of work," Greenspan said. The Publisher agreed.

"We've seen a good many of his kind, haven't we?" The Publisher sighed. "What's your opinion, Martin?"

"I think you know that already," Greenspan said. "And, if I may say so, I think I know yours. The greatest good for the greatest number, is that right?"

The Publisher nodded. "I do wish, though, he'd given us a little more time to think about it." He gestured diffidently. "I don't like it," he said, "I don't like him, but we don't always choose our bedfellows, do we?"

"Occasionally," Greenspan said. "Grosbeck, for example."

"What do you mean?" The Publisher asked. Greenspan explained. "The flesh, the flesh," mused The Publisher, who knew a thing or two about that. The Publisher was a disembodied figure in the end, one difficult to describe; the symbol of The Newspaper would have to do. Greenspan, for all of his years on The Newspaper, had always found it hard to say what The Publisher looked like. He looked like

The Newspaper, nothing less, and Greenspan had made himself content with that.

"I don't think there is anything else for it," The Publisher said. "We sacrifice nothing in what in essence is no more than a temporary alliance. The control is ours; the trumpet is ours. And, more to the point, the property is ours and he needs that as well as his own. Nothing but progress can come of it. We meliorate, we judge discreetly, we act—in moderation, we're not a tabloid, but The Newspaper of record—and we prevail. Not always, but often enough. We are a power—quiet, but a power. The world swirls about us in its disorderly, often dangerous, careerings, and yet we stand on it firm and unswayed." The Publisher tapped his nose. "I see I have made a speech," he said. "I am a good deal like my grandfather in that respect. But, like him, I pride myself on being a practical man." He said, "I find that here is about the only place I make speeches. The Newspaper does it for me in public. I think they are in keeping with what I am, what The Newspaper is. That is the end of the speech. Go ahead. I would like the campaign to begin in two to three weeks from today. First, a story, which will begin under the fold on the front page and run for about three columns inside. A searching analysis of the project by two of our critics—art and architecture—not omitting criticism of certain minor details, for balance, a pinch of regret for the preservationists, but, on the whole, something forward-looking and optimistic. I will give directions on that. And, then: an editorial, third from the top of the page, which is not too high; also, not too long, not too . . . what am I groping for? . . . not too . . . not so roseate as to make us seem overeager, but, unmistakably, an advocacy. Need I say more? You, of course, will write that editorial."

"Thank you, sir," Greenspan said, and left to deal with Grosbeck at the other end of the hall.

Greenspan sat down on a corner of Grosbeck's desk. "When are you going to give up that typewriter, Harvey, and use the VDT?"

"If possible, never, Marty."

"You might at least take the cover off it for the sake of the decor," Greenspan said. "It jars."

"I don't even know my code number," Grosbeck said, "much less even how to turn it on. There's no reason on earth why I should. I do my writing, you approve it, and someone else puts it on the goddamned thing. Does it bother you that much? You here to nag me

about that again, or is this just a social visit?" Grosbeck was appre-
hensive and depressed. Alice Forsythe had been forthright with him
since that night, and it had left him believing he was no more than a
bag of bones with an appetite. Madeline had displayed an upsetting
combination of pity, contempt, love, distance, and duty; had shrunk
from his touch; fed him well; and left him to his own devices, which
were few. "Marty, something tells me you have something to tell me.
You've got much more to do than pass the time of day. For a
change, I don't mean to be rude. I'm too distracted to be."

"You're right, Harvey. You might as well hear it quickly. The Publisher is going along with Varney, with the Mansions Project. You
must have sensed he would."

Grosbeck felt his face turn to stone, his legs to sponge rubber, his
stomach to the size of a pea, his heart deflate as the blood stopped,
his head, broken, to disengage itself from his neck. After a while, he
asked, "Did Alice Forsythe have anything to do with it?"

"Harvey, Harvey," Greenspan said. "No, Harvey, Alice Forsythe
had no more to do with it than The Publisher's mistress."

"Then, what?" Grosbeck asked. His eyes filled with tears. "I must
have done something wrong."

"Yes, you did, Harvey," Greenspan said. "You were born a hundred years too late, but, even so, your reading of history should have
let you know. Things were no different then." Grosbeck nodded
dumbly. "I sent you over to see Alice Forsythe for your sake, a matter of form." He put a hand on Grosbeck's arm. "At least," he said,
"you got something out of that." Grosbeck said nothing.

"The Newspaper is for it, Harvey. It has to be. You—and I—don't
count." He got up from the desk, meaning to get out of Grosbeck's
sight as quickly as he could. "There'll be stories in the paper in a few
weeks, Harvey, and I'm going to write the editorial to go with them.
It's done. The City needs it; The Newspaper needs it. You'll live.
Greater outrages—I'm not even sure that it *is* an outrage—have been
perpetrated on all of us and we've lived. It's not as though you'd
been knifed in the subway and pushed down to the tracks . . . and"
—he hesitated—"I'm sorry." He had hesitated only because he was
not sorry, only to display good manners, like handing a man a linen
handkerchief to stanch a hemorrhage of the ears and mouth and rec-

tum. "I'll see you later," Greenspan said. "Why don't you take the rest of the day off?"

"I think I will," Grosbeck said. Greenspan closed the door behind him, and Grosbeck put his head down on his arms on the desk. He did not move for about an hour.

23

Dr. Salomon was on the telephone when Grosbeck entered his office. "No, Minnie," he said into it, "there is nothing wrong with you that was not wrong the other day. Your health should be mine." Grosbeck detected a note in his voice that had not been there before. Dr. Salomon listened. "My sweetheart," he said, "take the pills I have prescribed for you. Take them at the times I told you to. Take one extra a day." He listened. "You'll run out?" He listened. "I will see to it that you have all you need. I will call the drugstore myself." He listened. "They cannot hurt you. I assure you." He listened. "The pain is somewhere else now? That is one of the symptoms. It has no significance." A squeak in the receiver. "It has so little significance that I refuse to pay any attention to it." Another squeak and several shrill squawks. "Minnie," Dr. Salomon said without the least trace of impatience, "*Ce n'est rien, de nada, garnichts. Pris ce que je t'ai dit. Souvent. Oui. Oui. Oui. Et aussi, promenez, promenez, promenez. Non. Pas aujourdhui. Attends. Jeudi. Huit heures demi. Oui. Ici. Non, pas l'hôpital. Ici! Tu es la jeune fille de ma vie. Quoi? Si tu veux. Alors, à jeudi.*" He hung up. To Grosbeck, he said, "They want my life so that they may live to be two hundred. Minnie is seventy-eight years old, twenty in the head. Demanding, demanding."

Grosbeck stripped down for his regular examination, keeping on only his shoes, socks, and garters. Once more, and with greater sorrow, he saw in the mirror the frame built in an earlier time and permitted to run down, a paradigm of neglect, a paradigm made the crueler because of what had happened with Alice Forsythe and with Marty Greenspan. The bright mirror compelled greater attention than before. The muscles in the neck and shoulders had melted and the collar bones stuck out like the spokes of a broken umbrella. The Adam's apple was a vulgar intrusion in the crepey guzzle. Why had he never looked more closely? The paps on the chest slept complacently on the ghastly ribs. The small pot belly flowed downward and smiled maliciously back at him out of the mirror, and the cockeyed belly button winked. The liver spots on the hands and temples condemned him. He shuffled two steps to the right, out of range of the mirror, so as to reduce despair, regret, loathing, but the image in the mirror was in his brain and his spirit old and fat and tired.

He shrank within himself, remembering that so short a time ago he had lain in bed with a woman, grunting theatrically, murmuring what he took to be depravities, but which would not have been out of place at a strawberry festival. He had crawled about the bed looking for, in the disgusting military phrase, "targets of opportunity," and found none new, none that had not been explored among the worms in the Garden. And the physical humiliations! Bed to toilet. Force, force, force. It *must* happen. But Alice Forsythe had had to make it happen, for all everything was tricked out with food and perfume and whiskey, lighted with arty irregularity, touched up with sound, ventilated with sharp cold. Alice Forsythe had been tempted to laugh at Grosbeck's comings and goings, but she had not, because she knew that there was more there than rolling eye, lip, tongue, throb, spurt; much more that he wanted.

How far short he had fallen of his ideal: something between the plaster cast of a Greek athlete with fig leaf barely covering an enormous apparatus, empty head, classic face with ardent eyes; a cigarette advertisement with a mustache and deep lines in the cheeks (all of Grosbeck's deep lines were in the cheeks of his behind now); and a gentleman by John Singer Sargent, in tails, flat-waisted, six feet tall or more, with a spade beard, three railroads in his pocket, a polo mallet in one hand, and May Irwin waiting for him at a table in Reisenweber's.

But, Alice Forsythe had not laughed (was not she, too, flawed?) even when Grosbeck's legs got caught in the tangled sheets. "God damn it," he had trumpeted, seized his puny lance and plunged. He had broken it, he well remembered, against La Belle Dame Sans Merci. More of that night returned to him. She had raised his right arm and proclaimed him the winner. He had been mistaken in his brief elation. Knew it at once. "Winner!" he had exclaimed half furious, half desolate. "Winner of what?"

"Just the winner," she had said. "We all want to win something."

"What did you win?" he had asked.

"I . . ." she had said. "Never mind. Nothing. Something."

"What are you saying?" he had asked. "Is this some sort of court tennis?" All the while dressing and being dismissed. "I just fell off the *dedans*, didn't I?" he had reminded her.

"I don't know what the *dedans* is," she had said. "I know I should, but I don't, and you *did* fall off it."

"And you picked me up." She nodded. He refused to talk about it anymore. And, just before she closed the door of her apartment on him, she had pulled up the zipper of his pants and he had rubbed at his eyes, like a child, and left. And then, Greenspan had done to him what he had done. Precious little left to dare all with, Grosbeck thought.

"You have been out on the tiles, *mon vieux?*" Dr. Salomon asked.

"Yes," Grosbeck said. "I didn't do very well." There was nothing, it seemed, that Dr. Salomon did not know. "Henry," Grosbeck said, "I've got no eyes for jokes this morning. Besides, I'm due at the office in an hour."

"How very important," Dr. Salomon said. "No, you have no eyes at all, professor. Interesting patches under the sockets, but no eyes, professor. That is my professional opinion. You have been drinking?"

"Not much."

"Smoking?"

"Some."

"Fooking? Forgive me. Fornicating? Carnal converse? See? My English is letter-perfect, too."

"Yes."

"Bravo, professor. Yes. And now you are afflicted with an acute case of conscience. You are coming down with terminal guilt. You are *desolé*. You have *le cafard*. You are no better than my tiny old Minnie with *her* complaints. And her varicose veins. Her *various* veins? You see the grasp I have on the language? She stood up to things much better in Bergen-Belsen. She should be an example to such as you."

"There's more to it than that," Grosbeck said. "I won't bother you with it."

"But . . . but," Dr. Salomon went on, "I suppose we all grow old, get slack, complain where once we would have endured in silence or ridden over everything. I have a dozen Minnies of both sexes who have followed me here from Europe. I have grown old with them. I put up with them. They pay me too little for too much and they try my patience and they take up my time and I am one with them. But you, what about you, professor? What is your complaint this morning? Have you not just fought the good fight? What ails you now?"

"Cramps in my feet," Grosbeck said. "Goes up to the shins."

"How often? Especially this morning?" Dr. Salomon pursed his lips.

"No, Henry, not especially this morning. But, maybe once a week, every two weeks."

"But, definitely not this morning?"

"No, damn it. I just made a note to tell you."

"Nothing," Dr. Salomon said. "Muscle fatigue."

"Not circulatory? How is that possible? You know I do very little exercise."

"Is that so, professor? Very little exercise. And the other night? Possibly at home now and then? Oh ho. Well, then, you strain a lot sitting down, don't you, writing all those fine opinions of yours?"

"Come on now, Henry, cut it out." What possessed Salomon today?

"I will think of it," Dr. Salomon said. "Take off your shoes." He sat Grosbeck on a stool, pulled up another for himself and squeezed Grosbeck's feet and ankles. "No, there is nothing wrong." Pause. "Not there, anyway."

Grosbeck looked more closely at Dr. Salomon, listened more closely. "There's something wrong with you, Henry," he said.

"You noticed."

"You've lost weight. You're green-looking."

Dr. Salomon took off his stethoscope. He patted the waist of his white coat. "Twenty pounds," he said. "Green? What else? Since the last time I saw you, two weeks in my own hospital. A bleeding ulcer I did not even know I had. *I* did not know."

"Had?"

"Have. Still. Until the day I die, professor."

"Henry, Henry, how bad is it?"

"They did not have to operate. It has subsided, but I will have to be careful. As careful as you. More. I have a good opinion of myself."

Grosbeck's heart beat harder than he wanted it to. Dr. Salomon put the stethoscope to it, nodded, turned him around, listened to his back, nodded again, turned him around once more. "*You* are fine, *mein kind*," he said. "Now, give me blood . . ." He inserted the needle in the crook of the elbow, withdrew it, swabbed, put more cotton on the pinhole, took it away, and put a plaster in its place.

Grosbeck was worried. Over someone else, for a wonder. Dr. Salomon had seen him through children, a heart attack, and a number of subsequent "episodes," as they were called, not to frighten the patient. He had come into possession of one of those episodes, having wormed it out of Dr. Salomon. It was rife with the poetry of indifference:

This 60-year-old male is referred for evaluation because of chest pain. There is a past history of heavy cigarette smoking and of borderline cholesterol elevation. He has not been hypertensive or diabetic.

(I should hope not. Hypertensive? What the hell do you know?)

In 1973, he was hospitalized with a myocardial infarction [there it is again] and has noted recurrent chest pain since that time, variably associated with exertion, more closely linked to emotional stress and job pressure.

(Why, in God's name, couldn't I have stayed downstairs instead of going up to editorial, stayed in the box?)

He has noted increasing fatigue during the past few years, but has correlated this with occupational changes.

(Varney, Greenspan, the mansions, Alice Forsythe, Madeline. How's that for occupational changes?)

On the day of admission, he had sequestered himself in the Municipal Archives, a closed and stuffy environment, quite dusty, almost airless, seeking out material for a project which appears to have given him considerable anxiety. He was preparing to leave for home when he noted the gradual onset of substernal dull pain, nonradiating, unassociated with dysphoria, nausea, or dyspnea. This Pain persisted for over an hour . . .

(More than, *more* than, not *over!*)

. . . and led to his presentation at the hospital.

(Presentation! Say *deposited* by himself on the doorstep, medical card in trembling fingers, fright dripping from the slack chin. Help me, help me! It is not yet time to go.) There were other entries in this dithyramb of the commonplace:

He is a well-developed, articulate and anxious middle-aged man in no physical distress.

(What could you possibly know of rage and disappointment and a chronic bad opinion of self and everything else? Of longing so inchoate that it had grown into incoherence?)

If negative, discharge in three days following ambulation within hospital. Exercise, stress testing and possibly coronary arteriography should be performed subsequently.

Dr. Salomon had ignored all of this. "An ambitious resident," he had said, "with pronounced proclivities for making two hundred thousand dollars a year." The only thing with which Dr. Salomon had agreed was the last line of the keen diagnosis:

Strong stress on discontinuance of cigarette smoking.

Dr. Salomon had wagged a finger at him. "I have told you repeatedly. How many?"
Grosbeck had lied. "Five a day," he had said.
"In that case," Dr. Salomon had concluded, "cut it to eight."

Grosbeck said, "Henry, you've never talked about yourself before, at least not like this."
"There was nothing wrong, professor, or I *thought* nothing was wrong. Or I preferred to think so. Now, there is."
"Why don't you take a vacation?"
"Thank you, Doctor Grosbeck. It was just what I had in mind."
"When? How long?"
"Soon. How long . . . ?" Dr. Salomon looked at Grosbeck and rubbed his chin. Then, he put an arm around Grosbeck's naked shoulders, and operated quickly. "Forever, Mr. Harvey Grosbeck," he said, "I am selling the practice . . ." He stood back and looked at the incision.
NO, Grosbeck shouted in his stomach. His ears were choked.
". . . I will take my savings. I have a house in New Jersey and I

am going there with my family. No one will call me anymore in the middle of the night. No one will pester me with nonexistent symptoms. No one will force me to say, 'What do you expect, you are seventy-five years old?' There will be no more fights with the board of trustees of the hospital which wants all those new machines and all that money and no more covering the bloody footprints of incompetents from South American medical schools . . ."

"But, Henry, you fought in the *maquis*," Grosbeck said foolishly. "You drove sports cars. You have been my doctor . . . our doctor . . . for twenty-five . . . no, twenty-seven years . . . you can't . . ."

"I will be sixty-nine years old in three months," Dr. Salomon said. "What more do you . . . they . . . want of me? I own an ordinary sedan. No more Grand Prix. I have not picked up a gun in many years."

Seated on the stool, naked to the waist, Grosbeck grew ill. (". . . gradual onset of substernal dull pain . . .") and then his natural pessimism rose from his stomach into his nose. (". . . anxious middle-aged man in no physical distress . . . emotional stress . . . and job pressure . . .")

"I can't *stand* it," Grosbeck said, in panic. "I *will* not."

"Now, you are Minnie, the way you are behaving. Look at yourself."

"But, warning, you gave me no warning . . ."

"Other than my wife, you are the first to know . . . besides the man who will take over the practice."

"What will I do?"

"Why do you find it so hard? Here, wipe your eyes. Blow your nose. Put on your clothes. And go to work. Eat and drink and be good to Madeline. Tell *her*, of course. It is not the end of the world."

"Henry, all these years I have been coming here . . . to this office . . . on this block . . . Mark Twain's house around the corner . . . the Episcopal church across from that . . . It was hard enough seeing the Brevoort come down . . . the Lafayette . . . the junkies move into Washington Square . . ." The idiocy of panic.

"Perhaps they have your Edith Wharton for a customer? I do not mean to rebuke you, *mein kind*, but had you lived in France during the war, you might have learned better what it meant to adjust yourself to things."

Grosbeck started to sniffle again. "That's no help, Henry."

Dr. Salomon handed him a box of wipes. "Here. You are taking up too much of my time, your time." He was much moved and added, crossly, "Do your mourning somewhere else." Then, kindly, "Why *is* everything the end of the world for you?"

"Because it is," Grosbeck said, blowing his nose, throwing the wipes into the basket next to him, scratching his head and chest (it was moist and the few white hairs on it had begun to glisten), turning from side to side on the revolving seat of the stool.

"First the heart," he continued. "Then, the prostate . . . Peeing is murder . . ." He hesitated. "Sex . . . not murder, but . . . I hate having to think of the prostate at the same time . . ."

"Someone very competent, whom I have chosen myself, shall pinch it out of you . . . the prostate . . . when the time comes. And, behold, you will pee free and clear from then on and sex will give you no afterthoughts. I promise you, the jackrabbit has not been born who will equal you in bed."

". . . then the teeth . . . one after another . . ."

"See your dentist twice a year," Dr. Salomon said. Patiently, he held up a hand mirror to Grosbeck's face. "Look," he said, "you have all your hair." He put a hand to his own head. "I do not. You are handsome, well thought of, a fine writer. You shall help me with my memoirs, come to New Jersey and sit with me. Everybody writes memoirs now. I do not have your grasp of the language. I will call it, 'Memoirs of a Family Physician Who Fought in the Resistance and Who Was At Last Vanquished by Medicare, Government Forms, The Income Tax, Nagging Patients, and Time.'"

"I cannot bear change, Henry."

"No?" Dr. Salomon asked. "I will get you a wet nurse before I leave, Harvey, and you may suck on her until you get bald like me and the rest of your teeth fall out and you return to your beginnings when everything was soft and warm and stayed the same."

"Please, Henry, it's not that simple. You don't understand."

"How complicated is it? Do you suppose you are different from the rest of the world?"

"Yes. No. I came to you as much because you were my friend as because of the medicine, the treatment." It was, for Grosbeck, as though he were addressing a body in a coffin. "How odd . . . We never saw each other outside of the office. Yet, you must know how much it meant to me."

"And to me, professor."

"So that . . . your leaving . . . going . . . I will be alone . . . I . . ."

"I have almost never found you tiresome, Grosbeck," said Dr. Salomon, looking at his watch, "but both of us have a long day before us. There are patients waiting outside whom I must tell also." He made a face. "You are not alone . . ."

"All right," Grosbeck said, getting up. "I'll go." He put on his things slowly, knotted his tie as though he were braiding love knots, patted his pockets and stood before Dr. Salomon, awaiting yet another dismissal. He was granted it, with a valedictory.

"You will not be alone," Dr. Salomon said briskly. "I have sold the practice to a good man. He is, it is true, an Indian, but not Mukerji or anyone like that. I sold it to him because he is a good doctor and does not dally in laundry closets with the help. He will pay particularly good attention to you because I have told him to. Already, he knows all about you . . . what is on your record . . . what is not. And, remember, he is of a civilization at least as old as ours, so that the two of you will have much in common. He will be able to discuss with you such recondite matters as British architecture in Peshawar and Calcutta in the nineteenth century, to say nothing of the thousands of years of indigenous building which preceded those arrogant Englishmen.

"For a doctor, he is a cultivated man. I am leaving you with more than you deserve . . ."

He walked Grosbeck to the door of the room and shook hands with him. "We still have two more visits, you and I. And, I have one more thing to say. I give you back the joke you have told me you tell people with whom you want to put an end to an argument. Do you remember what it is?"

"No," Grosbeck said, "how should I? There are so many and so many arguments."

Dr. Salomon said, "You tell people, 'The thing that tickles me is this: you are all going to die . . .' Such bad behavior. Possibly now you will listen to your own jokes and remember that and remember . . . in the *gederim* . . . your guts, Mr. Grosbeck . . . I don't know how much Yiddish you have . . . that it is true." He looked at Grosbeck in fond farewell. "Why," he asked, "do you have such trouble seeing things which are as plain as the nose on your face? Go out and live what is left, *mein kind*, and stop complaining." Tully had said much the same thing when he was in the hospital. "You have things to do before you twitch and stop altogether. And . . . write me a letter in New Jersey every now and then, if you can find the time. Even if the age of correspondence is over. I shall not write any memoirs. But, I will look forward to hearing from you, to be amused and startled by what you can tell me that is not in the newspapers. Only . . . one last thing . . . do not whine to me in your letters."

Grosbeck took Dr. Salomon's hand in both of his. "Goodbye, Henry," he said.

"Ridiculous," Dr. Salomon answered, withdrawing his hand. "After two more visits. I will be as corny . . . corny? . . . as you. It will not be Goodbye, Only Au Revoir." He danced a few steps of a waltz and made as though he were blowing out candles in a ballroom.

"I promise you," Grosbeck said to Dr. Salomon.

"I will hold you to it," Dr. Salomon said, and pushed him gently through the door, once more into the world of which he had always been so terribly afraid.

24

Thereafter, the days of Harvey Grosbeck were dictated. He would dare all as Tully had minded him that Trollope had advised: ". . . 'But if you have not sufficient command over yourself to enable you to sit in repose . . .'"—which he did not have any longer— "'. . . always quiet, never committing yourself to the chance of any danger . . .'"—he could not be quiet any longer—"'. . . then take a leap in the dark; or rather many leaps. A stumbling horse regains his footing by persevering in his onward course. As for moving cautiously, that I detest.'" How seriously he would dismiss the consequences of doing this: home, eating, amusement, the company of friends, the detestation of enemies, the ministrations of his wife (and others); the chance friendliness of children, the cut of clothes, theatre, motion pictures, good restaurants, books good and bad, walks on streets which gave him pleasure, those which gave him pain in their despoliation, the departure of Dr. Salomon, which had given him such a pang, the long, long contemplations in which the absence of motion was so notable as to mark Grosbeck a narcolept, a catalept.

He found in himself the beginnings of a cunning of such dimensions as to make nothing of the loving deceptions practiced on him by his wife; the offhand dismissal of his dreamy prurience by Alice Forsythe; the pitying brutality of Greenspan who really wished him no ill; the real or imagined blows and pricks of his life; not even the decencies performed on his behalf by Tully, by McFarland, by Martha Sloane, by Duffy, were excepted. They would be put to use by his new cunning.

On his way to work, Grosbeck made a detour to the mansions, before which he stopped and looked intently for about ten minutes. He said aloud, and the passersby, otherwise intent on themselves, heard him say, "If I cannot save you, I will do for you what I can. And, there is something I can do for you." The passersby knitted their brows, glanced at one another and passed on. He walked from the curb to the side of the mansions and ran a hand over their brown-stone skin—Triassic sandstone carved out of Connecticut quarries and moved down Long Island Sound on clumsy stone barges to be affixed to the brick walls which it concealed. For him, the mansions were the essence of New York and a demesne in Rome. He stood in the cobbled driveway, a revenant in revery. Then, he took a deep breath and left for The Newspaper.

Traffic bore down on him as he crossed the avenue, still transfixed. Brakes squealed, fenders were bent, a fiends' chorus of shouting arose about him: "You dumb son of a bitch." "Fucker." "Who let you out of the nuthouse?" "Get your ass back on the sidewalk before I break it." "You'll pay for this." Grosbeck came out of his abstraction long enough to ask, "How?" and "Who?" Two firetrucks appeared. They inched their way through the tangle of cars, denting more of them, oblivious. The screams of indignation rose even higher and this time they were directed at the civil servants. Grosbeck was ignored in the turmoil. A policeman arrived. He pushed a ham hand under Gros-beck's armpit, half lifting him off the ground. "Now, listen to me, you," he said. "I'm going to get you through this, off the avenue and down that street and I want you to disappear as fast as you can. I don't know who you are or what you did, but from the look of you you're more stupid than anyone has a right to be." The policeman was sweating, Grosbeck cold and remote.

He was pulled into the side street, well down the block, past where the curious were pushing the other way toward the avenue. A cart selling organic foods and fresh orange juice was overturned, but the cop had no time for that. He was a plain hot-dog man himself. "One last thing," he said to Grosbeck. "I got to know if you're as clean as you look. Get in this doorway. If I do what I'm going to do out in the street, it'll only bring another crowd."

"Anything you say, officer," Grosbeck said, as though he had a choice. With the officer's hand under his armpit, one shoulder was fully a foot higher than the other. The doorway was the entrance to one of the last few narrow buildings on the block and its lobby, lead-ing directly to a flight of wooden stairs, was no more than five feet wide. "Put your hands on the steps," the policeman commanded. "Back to me. Fast." Grosbeck complied. The policeman, grunting, ran his hands down Grosbeck's back, his behind, his sides, his legs, his crotch. He pulled up one trouser leg after the other. (Hidden small gun? Knife?) The shoulder holster from the cop's extra gun banged heavily into Grosbeck's lower back.

"Hey, that hurt."

"I'll hurt you," the policeman said. He stood up, pulled Grosbeck to his feet off the stairs and turned him around. "Nothing," he said. "God, are you lucky. They were ready to kill you out there and *I* sure would have given you a good going-over if there'd been anything on you." He stood behind Grosbeck and pushed him out into the street. "Now, get out of here and don't let me catch you around here again. I got one last thing to say to you. You know what my kids call someone like you? 'Doofus.' Dope. I got enough to do without handling doofuses." He started to shout in frustration. "Doofus, doofus, doofus . . ."

"Officer," Grosbeck said, "you're behaving like a child in a school-yard."

"What!" said the cop. "Get out of here. Please."

"Thank you," Grosbeck said, brushing his hands off. "I knew you'd see reason before this was all over." The cop turned, made his way back toward the maddened avenue as quickly as he could. Grosbeck watched him shake his head, take off his cap and scratch his bald spot, but he never looked back.

So held in thrall was Grosbeck by what he intended to do that when he arrived at the office and entered the conference room for the afternoon Editorial Meeting nobody could have guessed what he had been through. It was true that there was a stare of preoccupation in his eyes, but it was turned inward on a picture in his brain.

"Gentlemen," Greenspan said, "that does it for tomorrow's paper. There is one other matter I would like to let you in on. As you know, we have for some time debated whether to support the Mansions Project. There have been discussions pro and con among us—not least of all involving Mr. Grosbeck—whose stand on the mansions is, by now, well known to all of us. As I say, a decision has been reached. Before I tell you what it is, I would like to take an informal vote among you." His face was blank of hints. "Whatever you say will, I assure you, make no difference, but I would very much like to have your opinion. Here we are, eleven of us. How many of you would like to see the Mansions Project stopped? A show of hands will do very nicely. One thing more. No reprisals, either way. All those against . . . ?"

Grosbeck closed his eyes. When he opened them again, he saw six hands raised—timorously, but raised. His made the seventh. "So," Greenspan said. "I see there is no need to count the number in favor —five, including myself." He rubbed his chin and then spread his hands on the conference table. "Well, gentlemen," he said, "the die is, if I may be the least bit dramatic about it, cast."

"Yes?" asked one of the Editorial Board. "What is it?"

"The Newspaper is for it," Greenspan said. "Shall I tell you why? The Publisher has *twelve* votes. He has a thousand votes, he has a million votes. It is his newspaper. He wants the project built for reasons that do not concern you and he has entrusted to me the writing of an editorial favorable to it. Needless to say, I have been working over it. It is not quite finished. It will be tomorrow, at which time I shall have copies of it for all of you and it will run next Tuesday, exactly a week from today." He picked his hands up off the table and clasped them. "I think that's all for now. There's the usual tea, coffee, or a drink for anyone who wants it. If my announcement . . . or the circumstances of it . . . seem a little unusual to you, I can say only that The Publisher wanted it that way. It is neither a declaration of war nor even a national domestic crisis. On the contrary, it is, in my opinion, no more than a parochial issue, a narrow one . . ."

"You're wrong," Grosbeck said.

"That's a matter of opinion, isn't it, Harvey, as who should know better than an editorial writer." Greenspan adopted a deprecatory tone. "I am only carrying out The Publisher's wishes. I doubt it will affect any of us with the exception of Mr. Grosbeck. And here, I will, in keeping with my efforts to hold back as little as possible, tell you something. Mr. Grosbeck, in deference to his strong feelings about the mansions, was told about it some short time ago. I think that's all." He made his way toward the door first. "Tomorrow afternoon," he said over his shoulder as he left. "The usual time. Four o'clock."

Grosbeck returned to his office and locked the door. His hands were trembling slightly as he picked up the phone and dialed McFarland downstairs. "McFarland, what are you doing tomorrow night?"

"Nothing, except going home."

"Not tomorrow night, Bob," Grosbeck said. "I want you to do me a favor. I want you to have dinner with me. It's important."

"What is?" McFarland asked.

"I'll tell you then. And, oh, Martha around and Tully?"

"Right across the room," McFarland said.

"I almost forgot," Grosbeck said. "Duffy, too?"

"Out at reception far as I know. But why Duffy?"

"I'll tell you tomorrow night. And, I want to bring Madeline."

"Madeline!" said McFarland.

"Yes, I want her in on this."

"Well, I don't know, Harvey. You know they could all have other things to do . . ."

"Please, Bob, I said it was important. How often have I asked you to do anything like this?"

McFarland looked around the City Room. "All right, Harvey, I'll call you back in about five minutes. But why all the mystery? And who's buying?"

"I'll make the jokes, Bob. But please hurry and round up the honored company."

"That's all you've got to say to me?" McFarland asked.

"I'll tell you all you want to know tomorrow. I need your help. Badly. All of you."

"So, it's got to be tomorrow night, Harvey? And badly?"

"That's right," Grosbeck said. "I'll be waiting for your call."

McFarland walked over to Tully and told him. "You've known him longer than I have. What do you suppose is going on in that disjointed head of his?"

"I don't know," Tully said, "but he's never asked us for . . . I think it has to do with something I once told him and I think he wants to do something and I think we'd better humor him. There are enough of us to sit on him if he goes crazy. Let me talk to Martha. You go out and get Duffy. He can be elusive when he wants to."

Tully went over to Martha Sloane. She was not surprised. "I've seen this coming on," she said. "I don't know what I've seen coming on, but you know a woman's intuition."

"I don't," Tully said, "but I've heard of it. You'll come then?" She nodded.

Duffy was seated in his chair in the reception room, his eyes half closed. The day was coming to an end. McFarland told him what Grosbeck wanted.

He said something McFarland had not expected to hear. "Leopold Bloom."

"What did you say?" McFarland asked.

"I said Leopold Bloom," Duffy said.

"Spare me, Duffy. Will you be there?"

"Yes, my boy," Duffy said, "I'll be there. I don't know, any more than you do, what we're letting ourselves in for, but I'll be there. Someone's got to keep a close eye on him. I've seen enough of you sensitive newspapermen."

"He's bringing his wife," McFarland said.

"Ah," said Duffy, "that proves it."

McFarland called Grosbeck back. "They'll come," he said. "Where'll we eat, across the street?"

"No," Grosbeck said, "somewhere away from the paper. I'd just as soon we didn't run into anyone."

"It's that serious?" McFarland asked.

"*I* think it is," Grosbeck said. He named an Italian restaurant downtown. "Wednesday's a slow night and I think we can get the back room. Also, it might not be a bad idea if we all came separately."

"Separately!" McFarland said. He held the receiver against his chest for a moment. "Anything you say, Harvey. You sure you're all right?"

"Never better, Bob. Clear as a bell."

"I think I hear a crack in the bell," McFarland said, "but we're at your disposal."

"Thank you, Bob. You'll never regret it. About nine o'clock."

"Shall we come in mufti," McFarland asked, "just to throw people off?"

"Fuck off, McFarland," Grosbeck said and hung up.

"Madeline," Grosbeck said to his wife that night, "give me an extra kiss."

"I don't know why I should give you even one," she said.

"Please?" he begged. She bent down and took his face in both hands and kissed him on either cheek and then on the lips.

"Will that do?" she asked.

"Do you love me again?" he asked.

"I never didn't love you, but you and that Forsythe woman . . . that was a shock. No, a humiliation. I thought you had better taste."

"You've got even better taste than I have."

"That wasn't funny," Madeline said.

"We're going out to dinner tomorrow night," Grosbeck said.

"And seal our reconciliation?" Madeline asked.

"Not exactly. I've asked Tully and McFarland and Martha and Duffy along."

"A public celebration?" Madeline asked. "With all your buddies?"

"No, Madeline, I've reached a decision—on my own—and I don't like to do that unless you're around."

"I wasn't around the night you went off with Alice Forsythe."

"That was no decision. That was a . . . it was a foible."

"A foible," Madeline said. "What is it this time? An aberration which will leave me mopping up after you? I still can't put that out of my head."

"I can't tell you right this minute," Grosbeck said, "because there're a couple of details . . . Will you wait until tomorrow night?"

"I don't see any reason why I should," Madeline said, "but the heart has its reasons . . . you know the rest of it. All right, I'll come. It'll be a diversion. I like your friends—at least what you tell me about them. Do you realize I have never met them all together at the same time?"

"All the better," Grosbeck said. "I don't mean it that way," he added. "You won't regret it."

The Editorial Meeting on Wednesday afternoon found the Board in a state of anticipation to which it was not accustomed. It went over the business of the day almost by rote. The lead editorial (based on a poll) found that the President of the United States had betrayed a sacred trust and would do well to set a historical precedent and resign. That, the editorial said, would constitute an act of patriotism the like of which the Republic had never witnessed and might serve to help bind up the wounds of the nation, already so grievously torn asunder by the war in Vietnam. Once again, it could go forward into a future which, while ever uncertain, at least would not be shadowed by the stain of a crime so heinous as to be beyond imagining. It was the poesy of semiliteracy and it was approved.

Editorial No. 2 was a scolding of the Department of Sanitation which had been repeated so often, in one way or another, that the writer had simply switched paragraphs around, deleted one set of statistics for a later one, and concluded with the same sentence: "Whatever the financial strictures the City faces—and we know there are many—there is no substitute for good old-fashioned elbow grease. Clean streets are a desideratum, we think, far more easily achieved than putting a man on the moon, which, as all of us now know, is dusty not filthy, despite the moon's lack of a budget certain." Approved. With a touch of humor.

The third editorial was a short reflection on the migration of the birds southward. ("Wheeling in perfect formation," "nostalgia," "the inevitable march of the seasons," "so high that the thunderous clamor of wings is not to be heard here below," "darkening the skies as they hasten away," "leaving us, but only briefly, with intimations of mortality," "the sure knowledge that they will be back, that the promise of ever-burgeoning life renews itself, that buds will peep forth" . . . etc., etc. . . . . " 'if Winter comes, can Spring be far behind?' To that, we say, 'No! and again, no!' ") Approved.

For the editorials to have been anything other than models of dullness, to exhibit the least trace of flair, would have been unthinkable.

"All right, gentlemen," Greenspan said, "here's what you've been waiting for." There was some coughing, some straightening up in chairs, a few faint signs of unusual interest. "Let me pass out copies to each of you. I am going to do something which I have never done before." Greenspan straightened his tie. "I am going to read it aloud —neither for cadence nor fact nor opinion—but simply so that it will register better with you, so that should there be some tiny note you find jarring or inapropos, you will better be able to call it to my attention. I confess to being somewhat rusty; I do not often write editorials. More to the point, The Publisher does not often ask me to."

Grosbeck had prepared himself well. He had managed to make himself look as innocuous, as harmless as the rest of the Editorial Board.

Greenspan's voice had a peculiar quality to it, a sort of rasping reluctance, as though there were an obstruction in his throat:

"For as long as this newspaper has existed—give or take a year or two—the Delancey Warren Mansions have stood on that slight rise signaling the northern end of the valley of Murray Hill and beginning the valley which will rise to become Beekman Hill. We, our children and our children's children have paused before them in admiration, sometimes even in wonder at the dignity of their perfection. Once, in gentler times, they were flanked by, if not their peers, then certainly neighbors worthy of being built near them. Down the decades, we have seen these neighbors, inevitable victims of the advance of the City northward, fall to the wreckers, to the inevitable march of technology, to the demands of commerce which are not to be withstood however much we would like to say 'Stop!' Those are the demands which have made this city great—greatest in the world, for all of its decline at the moment— its willingness, nay eagerness, to take to its bosom the new and the needed and to turn them to its advantage. We remind you that, at one time, only a short way east of the mansions, steam trains ran in an open cut, between rows of miserable hovels, their coal smoke fouling the air, rendering black and unfit another great avenue. And we remind you again that not until adventurous minds covered the cut and substituted electricity for coal did that avenue achieve the splendor it knows today. There is an analogy here—a benign one—between the rise of that avenue and the Delancey Warren Mansions. There are many among you who may say, 'But if the mansions disappear, what sort of grotesquerie would replace them? Another tower of No Character?' The answer to that has been provided by Corydon Varney & Associates. And the answer to that is: 'They shall not disappear. They shall remain, pleasing to eye and spirit, solace to those who cherish the old and beautiful.' At the same time, the sort of vaulting imaginings which conceived of covering the tracks, have arrived at what we think is the very model of a solution. The mansions are not to be torn down. They are to provide, as some of you already know, the lower facade of, shall we say, one of 'the topless towers of Ilium' and thus assure us, at one and the same time, of a cherished continuity of our city's history and of its striving toward the skies, the stars, of history yet to be made. The Mansions Project, we believe, is of the very essence of New York City: its flesh, its bones, its vibrant aspirations. We wish its creators—for they are nothing less than that—every success in their endeavor."

Greenspan tossed the sheet down before him and looked around the conference table. "Any corrections, gentlemen?" he asked. "Any emendations? Any omissions?"

"Nothing."

"None."

"Can't think of anything for the life of me."

Grosbeck was the first to rise. He carefully folded his copy of the editorial, waved it at Greenspan, and said, "Claptrap, Marty."

"You've broken the rules, Harvey," Greenspan said, smiling. "But . . . no recriminations. Have a drink."

"No, thank you," Grosbeck said. He slipped the editorial into his breast pocket and shuffled out of the conference room with the rest of the chain gang as the sheriff broke his shotgun and called the dogs to heel.

"I suppose you're all wondering why I asked you here tonight," Grosbeck said. "That's a joke," he explained.

"Thank you for explaining, Harvey," McFarland said. Duffy sat at the round table with his arms crossed.

Martha Sloane said to Grosbeck, "Do you have any idea how peculiar you look?" She said to Madeline, seated across the table between McFarland and Tully, "Have you noticed anything lately?"

"He's no worse than usual," Madeline said, "but now that you mention it, I do detect a wild look in his eye. But that's not as unusual as you think, Martha. Remember, I live with him." Tully said nothing, but he caught Duffy's eye and the two stared at each other as Grosbeck picked up his drink, finished it, and put it down. Grosbeck had made a late reservation, specifying the round table near the back of the room. Since it was a Wednesday night, the place was almost empty, and the owner, whom Grosbeck had known a long time, was grateful for the business.

"Drink up, drink up. Could I bother you for a cigarette, McFarland?"

"Harvey!" Madeline said.

"Just this one, sweetheart. By the time we've ordered and the food gets here, you'll forget I ever had it."

"Don't make me make a scene, Harvey."

"Forget it, Madeline. Just this night, forget it." She sat back, angry and troubled. They ordered. Grosbeck took a long puff on the cigarette, stubbed it out, cleaned the burned end and put the stub in his lapel pocket. "Only one, as all of you can see. I get the rest of it later, with coffee. Remember what we used to call that, Tully? The 'dinch,' right?"

Tully removed his eyes from Duffy's and said, "Right, Harvey. Come on now, why *did* you ask us all here tonight?"

The waiter disappeared into the kitchen after pouring wine. "It's a sort of Last Supper." He removed an envelope from his pocket and passed around copies of the Greenspan editorial. "Read this." They drank wine and read. The pasta came, oil, fried garlic in a cap on top of it.

"Yes?" Tully asked. "You don't mind if I start while you're explaining, do you, Harvey?"

"Not at all. We might as well get to the point on a full stomach. May I recommend the chicken *paesana*? It's filling but delicious."

"Harvey, *will* you stop killing time," Madeline said. "These people haven't got all night. Neither have I. And, I'll say it right out—we're among friends—you *might* have told me first."

"No, Madeline, I gave it some thought and decided it would be best this way. This way, no one, including you, has any time for second thoughts. There'll be no mulling this one over." Silence fell over the table.

"That editorial," Grosbeck said, "will run next Tuesday. I am against what it says. So were most of the people on the Editorial Board. It wasn't even written by one of them. Greenspan did it himself. On The Publisher's orders. I tell you all this to prepare you."

"Prepare us for what?" McFarland said.

Grosbeck addressed himself to the waiter. "The chicken's unusually good tonight, Mario." He waved his wine glass around the table. "More wine, Mario, madder music." The waiter, an illegal immigrant from the north of Italy, was deficient in English, but he had served Grosbeck and Madeline before; he heard the word "wine," poured, stored the words "madder music" in his head, and retreated to the kitchen.

"Somewhere, it's all got to stop," Grosbeck said. "All of you are old enough to remember what this city looked like before they—I don't have to tell you who *they* are—got their hands on it. It's coming down, piece by piece, and what's taking its place makes those sets in *Metropolis*—the movie—look bucolic. So, it's got to stop."

"It can't stop, Harvey," Tully said. "No one's ever been able to stop it." He added, "And I'm just old enough now not to care that much anymore." He pointed a finger at Grosbeck. "And I've got an old joke for you, too: 'New York'll be a great place if they ever get it built.'"

"Tully, I know I can't stop it. None of us can. But there is something I . . . we . . . *can* do."

"Such as?" asked Martha Sloane.

"Outside of putting pieces of the old city in museums?" Madeline asked.

"You want the El back?" Duffy added.

Grosbeck continued, stubborn, lightheaded, his forehead wet. "I can't keep that editorial out of the paper, but I can . . . I think *we* can . . . replace it. Sometime during the night. With an editorial that will say the exact opposite. We all feel pretty much the same about the City, more or less. I suppose it . . ."

"What in God's name are you proposing?" McFarland asked. "I'm not a nervous man, but you're changing that tonight."

"Replace it," Grosbeck repeated.

"In the middle of the run?" Tully asked. "You're incredible."

"Mr. Grosbeck," Duffy said, "hadn't you better go home and lie down? Mrs. Grosbeck, we'll take care of the check . . ."

"Listen to me," Grosbeck said, his voice rising enough to bring the waiter from the kitchen. Grosbeck waved him away. "Got everything we need. I'll call you for coffee. What I want to do is get the last seventy-five to a hundred thousand copies . . . the copies that hit most of the City. I don't care if I go down in flames."

"You don't care if we go down in flames, either, do you, Harvey?" Tully asked.

"I can't do this alone," Grosbeck said, "and, yes, I do need your help."

"That's a lot you're asking, darlin'," McFarland said.

"I'm desperate," Grosbeck said, "or I wouldn't be asking you this."

"Well, just for argument's sake, Harvey, how are you planning to carry out this . . . this . . . I don't know what to call it?" Martha Sloane asked.

"All right," Grosbeck said, "I haven't got it all worked out—that's why this meeting—but what I want to do is get into Greenspan's office at about, oh, say one in the morning, about twenty minutes before the beginning of the last run, wipe out that editorial, and put mine in."

"But why do you need them, sweetheart?" Madeline asked. "Why can't you just do it yourself and not run the risk of getting anyone else in trouble."

"That's easy," Grosbeck said miserably. "I don't know how to use the goddamned Video Display Terminal."

"I told you a long while ago it was time you learned," McFarland said.

"My fingers get arthritic every time I look at one," Grosbeck said. "I can't and I won't. All of you except Duffy—begging your pardon, Duffy, you don't have to—can. I can't do it without all of you. Not you, Madeline, but you had to be here to hear about it."

"You know, don't you, Harvey, there's a security system for those VDTs?" McFarland told him.

"Security system? What security system?"

"Ah, what an infant it is," McFarland told him. "Down in the City Room anyone can use anyone else's, but not up in editorial. They want to know just who does what, what machine it came off, when it was approved, what time it went down to the white room to be pasted up, photographed, transmitted, put on one of those flimsy plastic plates, and sent to press. Every one of the VDTs up in editorial has a *code* for the man who writes on it. It's called 'identifying yourself to the system,' 'log-on,' 'sign-on,' 'registering.' Otherwise, it doesn't work."

"I thought you just flipped a switch," Grosbeck said, "and punched out what you wanted and it came up on the screen and you flipped another switch and it went downstairs and came out printed on a piece of paper."

"No, Harvey, it doesn't work that way. It works the way I told you. Do you even know Greenspan's code number?"

"Of course not," Grosbeck said. "How could I be expected to."

"We don't, either," Martha Sloane said, "and if *we* don't . . . besides, how many times have you ever heard of the editorial page being made over in the middle of the night?"

"I can't remember," Grosbeck said.

"Of course you can't," McFarland said. "It's happened exactly twice since they put in the VDTs. Each time a dropped line that wasn't caught in time." He went on. "Now, Harvey, not only don't you know how to run the damned thing, but you don't know Greenspan's code and neither do we." The waiter brought strong black coffee, not enough to dispel the fumes of alcohol and the somnolence brought on by food, but sufficient to keep the level of conversation remarkably close to rational. "How do you go about getting that? And . . . let's cut this short and get to another point. Darlin', you want to get us all fired? We're none of us young, Harvey. There aren't that many newspapers around anymore and television is out of the question for people like us. Why should we help you out? Tell me why?"

"Because I'm asking you to," Grosbeck said childishly.

"Don't stamp your foot, Harvey," Madeline said. "Answer McFarland."

"I'll try," Grosbeck said, putting a hand on Madeline's arm. "Martha," he said, "Duffy, Tully, you, Bob, we are all of a piece. Look at us. You, Duffy, you've sat in that chair outside the City Room, picked up your piece of change on the outside, had kids, own a home, know everything there is to know about everyone in the building, read some books, and let it go at that."

"Mr. Grosbeck, sir," Duffy said, in irritation, "it satisfies me. And I never thought to hear you run me down."

"I'm not, Duffy. Please. Let me get it all out." Duffy, hurt now, ordered another drink.

"You, Martha," Grosbeck said, "I don't mean to be rough, but what have you ever done except turn out things on order? Was that enough for you?"

"No, it wasn't," Martha Sloane said, "but it is now. We're not young anymore, you heard McFarland."

Grosbeck continued: "And you, Bob, and you, Tully? Bob, you going to doze away the rest of your life making something passable out of something incoherent at that desk of yours?"

"Of a certainty, darlin'," McFarland said. "I'm going the distance."

"How about you, Tully?" Grosbeck asked. "Bag man, City Hall reporter, carrier of secrets to The Publisher? Is that enough for *you*?"

"It seems to be, Harvey, doesn't it," Tully said. "Let me ask *you* something. What about you?"

"Me?" Grosbeck asked, as though the thought had occurred to him for the first time. "Nothing. But, for me, this would be something, even knowing just what would happen to me."

"Then, why should the rest of us go down with you?" Tully asked. "I don't see any of us rattling tin cups on street corners for the rest of our lives for the sake of a futile gesture by you." He looked around the table. Everybody nodded.

"You've forgotten, John, haven't you? The slap in the face with the roses in the hospital. The hortatory quotations."

The owner and the waiter came out from the kitchen and began elaborately stacking chairs on tables around them. It was getting late. "Five minutes more, Ennio," Grosbeck said to the owner. "No more. And please, maybe, another couple of bottles of wine to make the time go faster?" The owner looked at the waiter, the waiter at the owner.

"This one time," the owner said. "A lot of cleaning up to do, a lot of getting ready for tomorrow. For you, too."

"I know," Grosbeck said. "Here, let me pay the check now." He added tips—one for the waiter, one for the owner—more than double the amount of the check. "I won't abuse the privilege again, Ennio, I swear."

"Surely not," the owner said. "I can see this is rare, a *festa*. We thank you." He and the waiter went back to stacking chairs on tables. He returned to the table. "For you, Mr. Grosbeck," he said, "any time."

Grosbeck made an appropriate face of gratitude. He took up his theme again. "Did it ever occur to any of you that nobody has to get caught but me, that nobody will? Security in that building is a joke, has been forever. One guard—only one—ever goes up to the editorial floor after The Publisher and Greenspan go home and he shows up only once every two hours to punch in that time clock. The only modern things they've put into the building are the VDTs and automatic elevators. Mmmm. I forgot—electric typewriters, too. Everything else is the way it was thirty years ago. This Newspaper sits in a district worse than the Five Points could ever have tried to be, but everyone on the inside is still a gentleman."

"Come on now, Harvey," said Tully. "Give us the rest of it." The two extra bottles of wine were having the effect Grosbeck hoped for.

"Here's what I've worked out," Grosbeck said, improvising as he spoke. "First, you, Duffy, you get Greenspan's code."

"Me!" Duffy said. "Why me? What makes you think . . ."

Grosbeck interrupted him. "Duffy," he said, "the only one other than Greenspan and The Publisher apt to know that code is Emily

Braestrup, our receptionist. She's been after your body for thirty years. Everybody knows it—if not why. You can get it out of her."

"God save us all," Duffy said.

"Then, you give it to McFarland," Grosbeck continued.

"I think it's time for me to leave," McFarland said.

"No it isn't, Bob," Grosbeck said, pushing him down. "I'm depending on you to operate the VDT."

"Oh," said McFarland.

"Martha," Grosbeck went on, "it would be a good idea if you were with McFarland and me. We'll have to do this in the dark and two of us will have to carry flashlights. You hold one on the VDT so McFarland can work. I'll have the other so I can dictate the editorial to Bob."

"What about me?" Tully asked.

"You stay in the hallway, outside Greenspan's office and get Martha and McFarland down the freight elevator and out the back way. I'll either wait for the security guard to show up or I'll go down the front way so no one will miss seeing me. By the way, no one'll need keys. The editorial offices are never locked."

"Harvey, my boy," Duffy said, "one thing you've forgotten that Emily Braestrup won't—that she gave me the code, if she does."

"Duffy," Grosbeck said, "that woman has hankered after you so long that wild horses couldn't drag it out of her." He pleaded. "I mean that as a compliment. Wild horses."

Duffy was flattered. "Maybe," he said. "Maybe."

"Oh, yes," Grosbeck added, "bring gloves."

"Bring gloves!" they all said at once.

"What makes you think we're going to do this?" McFarland asked.

Tully said, "Aaagh, what the hell. Why not? I'm as responsible for this as anyone."

Grosbeck looked around the table. "You'll do it?" he asked. The wine and all that had gone before had taken good hold. The six people around the table bore an uncanny resemblance to roisterers in a drunken tavern scene from a Victor Herbert operetta.

"Why not," said Martha Sloane.

"You're asking an awful lot of me with that Braestrup woman," Duffy said.

"You'll never regret it," Grosbeck assured him.

"All right," McFarland said.

Madeline said, "I'm appalled." She was smiling.

"Then, you'll all do it," Grosbeck said.

The rest is anecdote (Grosbeck thought to himself later), but of proportions he had only dreamed of or shoveled into his head while eating or drinking or lying next to Madeline, half asleep, still half excited after they had done many things to each other when they were younger. Nothing was barred between them. Then, not even this engine of foolishness would have been thought too much. And now, nothing from that Wednesday night on seemed out of the ordinary or fortuitous—if it were not to be this event, it would have been another—as certain as the turning of the planets. Grosbeck did not know, nor did his friends, how he came to persuade them to do it, but it seemed to him that no matter what he proposed that night in the restaurant—short of murder—they would have done it. They had no guarantee of Grosbeck's visceral certainties; they were taking as much chance with their lives (neither more nor less commonplace than his) as he was. He could only speculate that within them was the same necessity to cheer something on, however footless, to a conclusion. There had been a conjunction of minds, minds brought together by the last source in the world from which they might have taken inspiration: Harvey Grosbeck.

But, back to Duffy. What had he told Duffy about Emily Braestrup? About that severe, graying, thin mountain peak (ever scaled, never scaled?) of suspicion and mistrust, that formidable barrier to the green vale of the Editorial Department? All, all of it came true as though Grosbeck had laid it out for him with calipers and drafting tools, beginning to end. Such a queer ambition for Grosbeck to have been driven to after so many years suspended between subservience and defiance and accomplishing neither; only a bad heart and a swollen prostate, the loss of teeth and weight on the shanks and thighs and behind as the belly grew until it resembled a cast-iron bean pot.

Duffy came up to the editorial floor just before Grosbeck was leaving on Friday night, with a sour expression on his red face and a small piece of paper in his right hand. "Here," he said. "If I were the kind went to confession, I would go. You owe me more than you will ever know. This is Greenspan's code. I will never rush the growler for you again and I hope I've heard the last of it."

Grosbeck put the piece of paper in his breast pocket. But he could not leave well enough alone. He put out a hand to shake Duffy's. Duffy ignored it. "You sure didn't waste any time, Duffy," he said. Grosbeck's delicacy was beyond compare.

"Would you have a drink with me, Michael?" he asked. "I would like to thank you."

"You could not enough, ever, Mr. Harvey Grosbeck. I don't know what possessed me. I am well out of it." But, Grosbeck prevailed, wriggling, backing and filling, pulling Duffy out to the elevator with him, leaving his coat behind.

The two men isolated themselves in a swirl of people from The Newspaper in the bar across the street, and the drink loosened Duffy's tongue if it did not lave his spirit. He had gone upstairs at a time when he knew Emily would be alone. She was always the last one to leave the floor. She was as surprised to see Duffy as he was to find himself there. She fussed with the gray bun of her hair. "What brings you here, Michael?" she asked.

"How's tricks, Emily?" Duffy responded.

"I was just going home," she said. "But, if there's something you need . . ." Duffy swallowed hard, leaned across her desk, seized her head and kissed her with a loathing that welled up like bile from the bottom of his soul. It was lost on her. She put her arms around Duffy's head and held him to her face. The desk was a wide one, and Duffy was afraid he would pull a muscle in his back if he stayed in that position much longer. He maneuvered his way around the desk, keeping his lips on hers until he stood over her.

"You and me, Emily," he said. It was all he could get out. He was filled with shame, Emily Braestrup with tongues of fire. Duffy's thick fingers pulled away the fake-lace bertha over her prim black dress. Emily's blunt-nailed fingers sought out his fly. They sank to the floor, she bleating in tongues, he panting in disgust. She pulled up the dress, to reveal underclothing of a kind now found only in museums. Duffy tore the various layered garments away from her. She found him. He had become erect. There are determined men who can do that in the face of odds even as great as Emily Braestrup. Her lips were as thin below as they were above. She smelled of lavender and repression. She died and went to heaven. Duffy died and went to hell.

"Michael, Michael," she murmured later. "Only twice before," she said. "And now, the third time . . ."

"Don't count, Emily," Duffy said. "We're not here to count." His throat constricted and his next words came out choked. "We waited too long is what I have to tell you." He had never been the man to scamp a job. Duffy looked at his watch. It would be less than half an hour before the house cop came around to punch the clock on the wall before Emily's desk.

"I've got to go now, Michael," Emily said. "It would seem strange if the two of us were seen together."

"Now, my girl," Duffy said, "don't you go about upsetting yourself. There's plenty of time. And, there's one other thing. I need a favor of you."

"Ask me, ask me," Emily Braestrup said. No one knew better than Duffy that he could say nothing plausible about his request.

"I would like Mr. Greenspan's VDT code number," he said, bold as brass, bold as he had been in taking Emily Braestrup.

"Whatever for?" she asked, the guardian in her taking shape once more.

"I can't . . . I'm not in a position to tell you, Emily," he said, "but I need it."

"And you won't tell me why? Not after what we've just been to each other?"

"No, Emily," he said, "you'll just have to either give it to me or refuse me. I'll say no more."

"Will we do this again?" she asked.

"As God is my judge, we will, my girl," Duffy said, closing his eyes. Had he sentenced himself to life at hard labor? No, because if she gave it to him there was no one on earth she could reveal it to. If she did not, there was still no one on earth she could tell the rest. Duffy was a good gambler. He knew when he had a live one.

Emily opened her desk drawer. A list of the Editorial Department codes was pasted on one side of the drawer. She handed him a sheet of paper and then snatched it back: it came from a memorandum pad and had her name on it. Duffy found an envelope from the telephone company in one of his pockets and handed it to her. She wrote: E-2-SOB-W. Time was beginning to run short, but Duffy's curiosity was aroused. "Why that?" he asked.

"It's simple," she said. "Or it is once someone's explained it to you. It could have been a million, a trillion combinations. But, I will tell you. 'E' stands for Editorial Department."

"That figures," Duffy said.

"And the '2' means that Mr. Greenspan is the Number Two man in the department."

"And the rest of it?" Duffy asked.

"I asked Mr. Greenspan that when he first took that code. He's really more of a boy than you know. 'A long time ago, Emily,' he told me, 'I believed newspapers to be something other than what they are. I saw a play called *The Front Page* and I have never forgotten the last line of the play. We all remember things like that.' 'What was the line, Mr. Greenspan?' I asked him. 'I haven't got time to tell you the whole story, Emily,' he said, 'but that last line was "The son of a bitch stole my watch," and so I decided to use that in my code. We've all got something personal in our code numbers, if I'm not mistaken. It's one of the few things we do have like that in this . . . this . . . postindustrial age. So, now you know: SOB for son of a bitch, W for watch. It just tickled me, that's all. You likely are the only one who knows it. Nobody's ever bothered to ask me.' "

Yet again, Grosbeck's genius for saying the wrong thing manifested itself. "Michael," he said, "that's more than I ever wanted to find out about Greenspan's code." He tried to recover. "But, Michael, I owe you a debt for life. I don't know how to thank you."

Duffy looked down at the bottom half of his drink, thought about something for a moment, then threw the drink in Grosbeck's face. "You don't, indeed, know how to thank me, Mr. Harvey Grosbeck, and I bid you good night and goodbye. And, thank *you* for letting me buy you a drink or two. I trust you will enjoy that last one." He walked out of the bar. Nobody paid any attention to what had happened.

Grosbeck sat dripping. He wiped himself off with a napkin. He cursed himself out. Then, he examined the code number to be sure it hadn't got wet inside his jacket. He left the bar and went damply home. "I've got it," he crowed to Madeline. "I've got it."

"How'd you get so wet?" she asked.

"Spilled a drink in the excitement," he said.

On Saturday, Grosbeck wrote his editorial, wrote it in longhand, realized he could barely read his own handwriting and transferred it to hand printing. He fretted. That won't do it, either, he said to himself. I'll have to type it up. The typewriter he had at home had not been cleaned in years and it took him better than an hour to transcribe, pulling stuck keys back, turning the ribbon around until his hands were black, drinking more coffee than he should have, excluding Madeline from everything he was doing. He knew that the editorial would have to be almost exactly the same length as the one it would replace.

On Sunday, he took a long walk with Madeline. "Are you going to show it to me?" she asked.

"I'd rather not, sweetheart," he said.

"Why not?" she asked.

"I don't know why not," Grosbeck said, "but I'm not." She was not offended, only filled with a pity that would have stopped Grosbeck altogether had she let him see it. On Monday, he went about his work at the office in a condition which defied any attempt to define it.

Any misgivings he might have had were as absent as reason in a madman. He called Tully, McFarland, Martha Sloane. He steered clear of Duffy, even on the telephone. The first edition for Tuesday started up at eight o'clock in the evening. They were to go to the Editorial Department, one by one, slipping through the trucks, over the loading docks, into the back door, up the back elevator, and meet at one A.M. in Greenspan's office. Was he sure the door wouldn't be locked? No, he had checked again. At nine o'clock, five blocks away from the office, Grosbeck bought a copy of The Newspaper. There was the editorial, the imprimatur for Corydon Varney: Nihil Obstat. He took an extra heart pill, tried to drink a cup of coffee at a hot-dog stand while looking at the editorial, found he had an overwhelming need to pee, and had to buy a drink at the bar next door in order to use the toilet. He paid for the drink before peeing, tore the newspaper in shreds in the toilet, and left the bar without touching the drink. The night was mild for the time of the year, but he found himself shivering. He walked through the awful streets near The Newspaper but was neither accosted nor attacked. (The Puerto Rican Lady God.)

At a quarter to one, he went up. The hallways were black, except for the red light over the fire stairs. First, Martha Sloane. Grosbeck turned on his flashlight as she came down the hall. She turned her flashlight on him. They covered their mouths to suppress laughs. Then, Tully. Then, McFarland. Then, into Greenspan's office, the door of which they closed and locked. They felt the rumble of the presses subside. There were some ordinary changes to be made on the news pages. In twenty, twenty-five minutes, Grosbeck's precious edition would begin to roll. McFarland sat down before Greenspan's VDT, with Martha Sloane's flashlight on it and him. Tully stood facing the locked door. Grosbeck pulled out his editorial and looked at it a last time. It satisfied him. He whispered to McFarland, "Now."

McFarland turned on the machine. Grosbeck handed him Greenspan's code. "Read it to me," McFarland whispered. "There isn't enough light from the flash for both of us."

Grosbeck read, "E-2-SOB-W." The letters came up green-white and flickering. Then, the machine spelled out, "Function?" McFarland typed, "Rewrite." The impassive machine came back with, "Title?" McFarland told it, "The Mansions." The VDT asked another question, "File?" McFarland wrote, "Last Late City." The machine displayed the brainless caution that had been built into it: * * * Warning * * * You are requesting to rewrite a first edition Editorial. Enter End of Transmission character to halt process." McFarland did so. "Enter carriage return," the machine ordered. McFarland punched the carriage-return button. The damned machine's curiosity was endless. "New Title?" Martha Sloane's flashlight shook in her hand.

"For Christ's sake," whispered McFarland, "hold it steady." "The Mansions, second version," McFarland wrote. An arrowhead showed up at the left side of the screen. "That's a glitch," McFarland whispered. "It means 'Go ahead.' Now, Harvey, go ahead."

Grosbeck cleared his throat, took the editorial out of his pocket, smoothed its folds open, and started to read.

McFarland followed him to the letter:

THE MANSIONS

"For as long as this newspaper has existed—give or take a year or two—the Delancey Warren Mansions have stood on that slight rise signaling the northern end of the valley of Murray Hill and the slope to its north which, as all of us know, becomes

Beekman Hill. We, our children and our children's children have paused before them in admiration, sometimes even in wonder. Once, in gentler times, they were flanked by, if not their peers, then certainly neighbors hardly less classic in their beauty. Down the decades, we have seen these neighbors, inevitable victims of the advance of the City northward, fall to the wreckers, to the inevitable march of technology, to the demands of commerce which were not to be withstood. What has made this city great—greatest in all the world, for all of its decline at the moment—is its willingness, nay eagerness, to take to its bosom the new and needed and to turn them to its advantage. We remind you that, at one time, not far from the mansions, the railroad trains ran in an open cut, between rows of hovels, fouling the air, rendering black and unfit another great avenue. And we remind you again that not until adventurous minds covered it over and substituted electricity for coal did that avenue achieve the splendor it knows today. Now, an attempt is being made to draw an analogy between the rise of that avenue and the future of the Delancey Warren Mansions. There are many among you who say, 'But if the mansions were to disappear what sort of grotesquerie would there be to replace them? Another tower of No Character?' One answer to that has been provided by Corydon Varney & Associates. Their answer is: 'They shall not disappear. They shall remain, pleasing to eye and spirit, solace to those who cherish the old and beautiful.' They say to us they have arrived at what they believe to be the very model of a solution. The mansions, they say, are not to be torn down. They are to be, as many of you already know, the lower facade of, shall we say, one of 'the topless towers of Ilium,' and thus assure us at one and the same time, of a cherished continuity of our city's history and of its striving toward the skies, the stars, of history yet to be made."

Grosbeck had delivered this in a whisper, but whisper or not, the histrionics of what he was saying could not be overlooked. He paused for breath and then trained his flashlight on the paper again.

"Harvey," McFarland said, "don't stop now. Get it over with. We've got to get out of here."

"Right, right," Grosbeck said. "There isn't much more. Here's the finish":

"We do not agree. We could not disagree more strenuously. The mansions, we feel, are of the very essence of New York City, so much of which has been lost in dust and rubble. Something must remain as it was. Otherwise, how would we know where we are? There is precious little left to tell us. We may not be able to dissuade Corydon Varney & Associates from their course, but we can—and do—register our strongest objections, however small our voice may be."

"That's it, Bob," Grosbeck whispered. His voice sounded as hoarse as though he had been shouting for an hour. McFarland shut off Greenspan's VDT. Martha Sloane aimed her flashlight at Tully standing at the locked door with his back to them. He heard the whisper, half turned, and then unlocked the door. "Out you go, Bob," Grosbeck whispered. "You, too, Martha. You, Tully. One at a time. Down the back elevator if you like, down the back fire stairs if you want to walk twelve floors. Security doesn't watch them, either, I found out."

"What about you?" Tully asked. Grosbeck waved his flashlight bashfully about.

"I'm going down the front elevator," he said. "I've got to be *seen.* You mustn't be." There was a premonitory rumble from the basement of the building. "They're turning over for the new plates," Grosbeck said. "They should be running in just about five or six minutes." The four of them were in the dark hallway. Grosbeck trained his flashlight on them. Martha Sloane went last, since she had the only other light. Grosbeck saw McFarland leave first. The elevator came back up and took Tully. Minutes later, it accepted Martha Sloane, and Grosbeck's was now the only light on the floor. He waggled it at the buttons on the front elevator. When the doors opened, the light hurt his eyes.

In the lobby, he made an elaborate show of saying good night to the two guards on duty. "Late night," he said. Sweat was pouring out of his eyes. "Don't like this place that much," he said.

"Hardly blame you, Mr. Grosbeck. It isn't that often we see you here this late."

Grosbeck agreed. "No more than two or three times, if I remember right."

"You do," said one of the guards. "It must have been something important."

"It was," Grosbeck said. "Something I might have forgotten if I hadn't stayed late. I don't envy you guys your hours."

The presses started up. By the time he got through the lobby door onto the street, they were running at full speed. Grosbeck crossed the street, out of the tangle of trucks, and stood on the sidewalk to listen and feel. The mighty rhythms shook his body. The knowledge of what the presses were printing shook his soul. He had done, for once, what he set out to do. His future was painfully clear to him. He would not again stand before The Newspaper and listen to its voice, that voice he loved so much, stood in so much awe of. He did not know what he would do. "Seventy-five to a hundred thousand copies," he murmured aloud. "No hard feelings, Marty. Everybody has to do something."

He couldn't wait until morning—what was there to wait for, anyway?—crossed the street again, squeezed through the trucks, and edged his way into the mail room, to the place where The Newspaper came off the press and was shoved mechanically into the automatic bundlers. "Mind if I steal one?" he asked one of the mailers.

"It'll louse up the count," the man said, "but I guess it's all right. You work here, don't you? I've seen you around." He handed Harvey a newspaper.

Grosbeck walked off with it, opening to the editorial page, and fell on his hands and knees from a loading dock and regained his balance on the sidewalk. His hands were not even bruised. He had been holding The Newspaper in both of them, enchanted, no longer hearing the presses. Harvey read the editorial and swelled, put The Newspaper under his arm and found a cab. Madeline was waiting up for him. Grosbeck put The Newspaper, folded to the editorial page, in front of her. "There. What do you think of that?"

"What are we going to do now?" she asked him.

"Love will find a way," he said. "Suddenly, I'm hungry." It was two o'clock in the morning. Madeline made him a small steak and a salad and put a beer before him. Then, they got into bed. Neither of them slept.

Grosbeck got to the office early next morning and began to clean out his desk. On the leather-bound blotter, he found one of those notices sent to all employees from time to time. It said, "I am pleased to announce that the very popular workshop, 'Managing Personal Growth,' will be offered again at the beginning of January. This workshop, as many of you know, deals with the following topics:

Personal Values. Skills Inventory. Improvement Planning. Development Discussion. Process Skills and Attitude. Format of the Workshop: an intensive, stimulating, highly participative learning experience. There is very little lecture by the workshop leader." Grosbeck was tearing up the notice when Greenspan entered his office.

"You did it, didn't you, Harvey?" Greenspan said. "Threw it all away. You're the dumbest thing I ever did in my life. I've never trusted anyone. What made me think I could trust you?"

"You'll have to answer that one for yourself, Marty. I'm in no position to answer for you."

"All right, Harvey. Beat it. I did like you. A lot. I don't hate you now. Answer just one question for me, though, will you? How did you find out my code?"

"Pure guesswork," Grosbeck said. "Marty, you really don't expect me to tell you that."

"You couldn't have done this thing all alone, Harvey," Greenspan said. "There had to be others involved."

"I don't think you'll ever know, will you, Marty?"

Greenspan sighed. "This could be my job too. Did you ever think of that?"

"No, Marty," Grosbeck said, "I didn't. Goodbye." Greenspan didn't answer.

The Newspaper published a front-page apology for what had happened. It said that the anonymous writer (its odd sense of honor forbade it to name editorial writers since, historically, they were anonymous) had been discharged, that The Newspaper deeply regretted what had taken place, and, in particular, offered its deepest regrets to Corydon Varney & Associates. It would republish the original editorial in all editions of Thursday's paper.

Grosbeck stayed at home. He heard nothing from Tully, from McFarland, from Martha Sloane. He did not wonder why. For all he knew, his telephone was being tapped by now. On the third day, at about noon, it rang. A gruff voice asked, "That you, Grosbeck?" Grosbeck acknowledged as much. "Who is this?" he asked.

"You don't know me," the voice said. "You wouldn't. I'm in television. News. My name is Brad Northfield and I put on an hour-and-a-half news show—half hard news, half soft, on Sunday mornings."

"I'm afraid I don't get the connection," Harvey said. "Are you sure you've got the right Grosbeck?"

"Yes, I'm sure," Northfield said. "Can I get you to listen for a minute?"

"I'm listening. I've got plenty of time for that now."

"Have you ever thought of going into television?" There was silence at Grosbeck's end of the line. "You still there?" Northfield asked.

"I'm here," Grosbeck said.

"I'm asking you, have you ever thought of going into television?"

"No," said Grosbeck. "I despise television, television news in particular."

"No surprise," Northfield said. "That's why I'm calling you. How would you like me to take you out of the abyss whence you have been cast?"

"What do you mean?" Grosbeck asked.

"Now, listen carefully, Harvey. I may call you Harvey, may I not?"

"Yes, you may," Grosbeck said.

"Well, Harvey, how would you like to do television commentary for three to four minutes every Sunday? Anything you like. Within reason."

"You're obviously lacking some nuts and bolts, Mr. Northfield."

"Just call me Brad," Northfield said. "This is no joke," he added.

"I'm too old," Grosbeck said, ". . . Brad."

"You're a celebrity, Grosbeck. And you wouldn't believe what makeup could do for you. We can scale you down to merely mature."

"Do you have any idea what I look like?" Grosbeck asked.

"No, Harvey, I don't, and I don't much care. I told you about makeup. All we ask is that you don't say 'fuck' or 'shit' on the air. You'd be pretty much on your own. Will you come in for an audition? Tomorrow?"

"Just a moment. I've got to consult with someone." There was no one to consult with. Madeline was at work. Grosbeck picked up the receiver again. "Yes," he said. "I'd be glad to. What time?"

Gilbert Millstein has written extensively for the New York *Times*, *The New Yorker*, *Life* and *Time* magazines, and other publications. His previous books are *The Late Harvey Grosbeck*; *New York: True North*; *New York*, a text accompanying photographs; and, as editor, *Short Stories, Short Plays and Songs by Nöel Coward*. Mr. Millstein, News Editor for NBC Nightly News, and his wife live in Greenwich Village, New York City.